A GATHERING OF FOOLS

JAMES EVANS

Visit the author's website:
http://jamesevansbooks.co.uk

PROLOGUE

Seen from afar, a corpse in the surf tells few tales worth hearing. A dozen corpses strewn along a beach littered with nautical wreckage might suggest a story of storm and wind, of rolling sea and breaking rope, of timber and terror and death.

But what if one of those corpses should cough and retch and roll onto its back as the crabs scurried and the seagulls cried in alarm? If that happened then, surely, there might be a story worth telling, a story worth hearing. More importantly, there might be a story that some people might want to bury alongside its incompletely deceased owner.

As awakenings go, the almost-corpse in the surf could see no merit in splashes of cold seawater. He hacked and coughed and scraped sand from his face as he tried to work out where he was and why he was on his back, staring at the sky.

He remembered the storm, the creaking of ill-maintained woodwork and the shouts of the deckhands as they struggled with the sails. He remembered the crack as the mast snapped and the awful sound of men screaming as they were swept overboard. He remembered the crash of the wave that capsized the ship, the horror as he realised what was happening and the fear that there might be no escape from the cell in which he had been locked. To wake on a beach, wet and desolate though it might have been, was a considerable surprise.

He levered himself upright and looked around, shading his eyes against the early morning sun. His fellow travellers seemed to have been short of luck and some at least were now feeding the local wildlife. Still, on the bright side, maybe he could find some proper clothes to replace the rags he was wearing.

A search of the nearby corpses yielded a serviceable coat, a reasonable shirt and a pair of trousers that would just about fit. Stripping corpses was a grim task but he worked quickly, discarding his rags with a quick prayer of thanks to whichever deity might currently be watching over him. He had searched most of the corpses before he found one, a guard, with boots. The fit was far from perfect but he pulled them on anyway and cursed all barefoot sailors as he stuffed torn lengths of shirt into the boots to pad them out.

The booted guard also had a dagger, which the man wedged into the pocket of his newly stolen coat, but he found no swords or money and precious little else of value. Some of the guards had carried charmed weapons and other tools but they hadn't made it to shore. As the sun rose and the new day began he stood, clothed and booted, on an unknown shore without food or water, money, friends or charms. Revenge, long dreamt of, was as far away as ever. But at least he was free.

And now he could run.

1

P rison; small rooms, bad food, beatings and curses. Confinement had given Marrinek long months to think but no opportunity to act.

Now he was free.

He shook his head, unsure about what to do next. He thought he remembered a shipwreck but it wasn't clear. The beach was strewn with wreckage and corpses but his memories were jumbled and confused.

He wasn't sure how long he had been at sea. He didn't know when they had moved him from the cell on the mainland to the windowless wooden cage on the ship. He could still feel the effects of the stupefying drugs they had fed him but he had no memory of the voyage except for the hour of mind-numbing terror as the ship had broken apart around him.

He shook his head again, trying to focus. He was free, at least for now, and beyond the reach of his enemies. He had schemed and planned in his prison cell in the rare moments of lucidity between meals but none of his schemes or plans had started with shipwreck.

He thought the ship had been heading for the prison island of Ankeron West but he couldn't be sure. Prisoners had no rights and his questions had brought only discouraging beatings. He had stopped asking, after a while, and focussed on staying alive.

He looked around, searching for landmarks. There was a beach, a wide sweeping bay, the sea to the south, low cliffs to the north. The Tardean Sea, he thought, maybe at the south-western edge of the Empire, near the border, if he was lucky.

Dying on a windswept beach, as he surely would if his enemies caught him, was not what Marrinek had planned. Leaving the Empire would be his best option for survival, which meant heading west.

First, though, he had to get off this beach and find food and shelter.

He stood for a few more minutes, shaking his head to try to clear the effects of whatever drug his jailers had fed him but that only brought him a twinge of nausea and pain. Then he turned and stumbled away from the surf, abandoning the ship's crew to dry in the morning sun as the waves lapped ever lower down the beach.

He had a twinge of guilt as he left the bodies unattended. Imperial servants, even the sailors and guards who had imprisoned him, deserved better. Then he looked at the rising sun and the ebbing tide and felt the exhaustion in his limbs, the growing ache in his head. There was nothing he could do for these men. He had no tools and burying their bodies would take time he didn't have and energy he couldn't spare.

He nodded once, a silent tribute to the men who had died. Then he turned his back to the shore and began to trudge towards the cliffs that rose behind the beach.

A short walk took him beyond the high tide line and into the lightly grassed dunes. The cliffs weren't high but he was out of shape and he didn't fancy his chances, even on a short climb. Instead he turned west and walked along the dunes until he found a ravine that cut upwards, away from the beach.

He sweated his way through the ravine, scrambling through the brush to emerge at the top of the cliffs. From up here, the narrow path, hidden from below and easily missed, was clear to see. It wound up from the beach like rope draped over rough stone and he cursed his luck at missing it.

He stood near the cliff edge for some minutes, looking south and east toward the wreckage of the prison ship. Only a few broken timbers had reached the beach. A mast lay tangled with a large rock further out to sea but there was nothing else to be seen, no fishing boats, no smoke, no people. He was alone, except for the corpses.

Then, as he turned to head inland, something moved.

He hesitated, searching for the thing that had caught his eye. A rider. No, four riders! Local watchmen, maybe, from the uniforms and the glint of armour, coming along the beach from the east. They hadn't reached the corpses, might not even have seen them amongst the rocks, but they surely would if they stuck to their current path.

Cursing his luck, Marrinek ducked down into the vegetation and hurried away from the beach, heading for the forest. The shrubbery, wind-blown and salt-laden, tore at his feet and grasped at his stolen trousers as he pushed desperately through it.

The indignity of headlong flight from a group of provincial heavies was merely the latest in a long list of humiliations he had suffered since his fall from grace. That he, a man once known and respected across the Empire, should be forced to run for his life, was extremely annoying.

But run he did, straightening now as the edge of the cliff fell away behind him. He risked a glance over his shoulder and caught his toe on a tree root. He fell heavily into the bushes and gasped with new pain as he pulled himself upright, cursing again. Anyone following would see the damage to the bush and the marks on the ground and would know which path he had taken.

He hobbled on, ignoring the pain from the ill-fitting boots and the tears in his hands from the thistles that had broken his fall. He ached all over and he was tired, so tired. All he wanted to do was sit in the shade and rest until his headache had passed but instead he pressed on. He had to put as many miles as possible between himself and the corpses of eleven men and a ship. It wouldn't do to be caught near the wreck by the local Watch. There was no telling what they might do to him if they thought he had robbed the dead, even if they didn't recognise him.

So, on he stumbled, wearing the clothes and boots of dead men, carrying the seawater that had killed them and the lice - now dead, drowned like their former hosts - that had ridden on them. He pushed through bracken and ducked around holly trees as the forest thickened and darkened.

A mile from the cliff's edge he stopped to check for sounds of pursuit. The forest was quiet and still; even the birds were silent. If there was anyone nearby or following his trail then they were better woodsmen than he.

He pushed himself on, moving as quickly as he could but as the undergrowth thickened and the trees grew taller, he was forced to slow to a walk. He was soon sweating inside his rescued coat, damp though it was, and his breathing was laboured as he struggled through the undergrowth.

Another hour brought him to a clearing through which a chalk stream babbled. He stopped, slumping down on the bank and cupping his hands to drink. The water was warm and tasted of muddy forest but it washed the salt from his mouth. He ducked his head to clean his hair then pulled off his boots to look at his feet.

Sore, blistered and unused to so much walking, his feet were suffering in the uncomfortable boots. He washed them in the stream as best he could, cleaning away the dirt from months of imprisonment before resting them up on a stone to dry. Then he pulled on his boots and sat looking at them. They were not the most stylish footwear he had ever owned and they certainly weren't appropriate for a ball at the royal court. Today, though, they were the finest shoes he possessed.

Marrinek considered his position. He would have plenty of water if he stayed near the stream and his clothes were drying as the air warmed. He was free and he had a pair of boots and a knife but that was the end of the good news. He had no money, no weapons and no charms. He had no food and to find anything more exciting than berries he was going to need tools for cutting, scraping and bludgeoning. Not good. He had to get out of the forest and back to a city, or at least a large town, where he might find people and resources and tools.

Then he found himself thinking about weapons. He turned the knife in his hands. A workman's blade, sharp and rust-free, it would be useful for dressing meat but it wasn't going to help in a fight. His preferred weapon would be a well-seasoned staff, a solid length of oak or ash, shod in iron and shaped for his hands. A peasant's weapon, ignored by nobles and disdained by the gentry but one with which he had always excelled.

Out here in the forest, though, the wood was still green and growing. Imperfect, maybe, but still useful if he could find something of about the right size and length. Given time, and assuming the bloody drugs ever wore off, he could fashion a staff from almost any piece of wood. Here, with the continuing fear of recapture, he resolved to take the first piece of wood that was about the right thickness and length.

It was ash, as it turned out, from a grove a short walk west of his spot by the stream. A sapling, decently long and straight, just waiting to be harvested.

As Marrinek focussed power to slice free the wood he needed, he was wracked by a tremendous wave of nausea. He sat down quickly, hands shaking like a teenager suffering his first hangover, and waited for the spots to disappear from his vision.

"Fuck," he said quietly as the trees swam slowly back into focus.

The drugs, clearly. Some sort of side effect that brought on nausea while still blocking his talent.

He pulled out the knife again and crouched down at the base of the sapling. Hacking through the wood, removing the branches and trimming the top of the stave took a good deal of effort. The knife was sharp but not at all suited to hewing trees. It took thirty minutes of hard work to produce a usable and almost straight staff about six feet long. He made an effort to tidy the ends of the staff before realising he was just wasting time. It was better to get moving and craft the staff once he had eaten something.

He grabbed a bunch of the thinner branches with the idea he might strip the bark to make snares to catch rabbits. Twisting rope would take time and he might need to leave the snares out overnight but by tomorrow, if he could find a likely run, he might have fresh meat. Branches under his right arm, staff in his left hand, he continued along the bank of the stream. He walked north west and paid little attention to his surroundings, planning the details of tomorrow's breakfast as he went.

Suddenly he froze, hardly breathing, abruptly aware that he wasn't alone in the forest. From downstream, back the way he had come, a horse whinnied.

Horses didn't wander forests alone, they would have riders. That was bad news for Marrinek and he cursed with frustration. They might be local farmers walking the path-less forest for their own amusement but he didn't believe that. It was far more likely that someone - the Watchmen he had seen on the beach, probably - had found the bodies and followed his path across the beach and into the forest, wanting to know why he had left in such a hurry.

He crept up the bank until he had a clump of low bushes between him and the stream. Setting his branches down on the forest floor, he took a firm grip on his staff and peered through the leaves. It sounded like two men were leading horses along the stream itself.

He shook his head at his own lack of care but what else could he have done? They must have tracked him across the dunes and into the forest, found the butchered sapling, followed the footprints he hadn't bothered to hide. They might want only to talk about his time on the high seas but Marrinek had learned to expect the worst of people.

Could he run? He shook his head again, discarding the idea almost immediately. Running wouldn't have been an option even if his boots had fitted, he had been well rested and he had known where he was going. As it was, he'd be lucky to stay ahead of them in the forest once they realised how close they were. There would be no way to hide from them once he made it beyond the woods. Horse against human over unknown ground in broad daylight? No contest; running wouldn't help.

And so he squatted down behind his bushes and waited for them to come into view along the stream. Maybe they would talk, maybe they would offer him food, maybe they would have tools or weapons he could use. Whoever they were, and whatever they wanted, he wouldn't let them take him back to prison.

He sat, quiet and still, barely breathing, and waited.

2

Sergeant Snare was a 20-year veteran of the Imperial army. Upon retiring from the ranks, he had found service in the Watch of a small harbour town at the western edge of the Empire. It was an easy life, safer and far more comfortable than military service but also somewhat dull. His duties mostly consisted of keeping the peace in the dockside taverns or patrolling the market square, dealing with petty disputes or crimes. After a big storm, though, like the one that had come down from the west last night, he would ride the beach and the cliffs checking for debris that might indicate that a ship had been lost.

This morning the sea was calm and the clouds were clearing as Snare rode along the beach with the three near-useless constables from today's roster. He sighed as he guided his horse toward the wet sand where the going was easier. His three constables weren't just young and ignorant, having strayed no more than a day's ride from Heberon their entire lives, they were also crushingly keen and eager to impress. After three weeks of haphazard training they knew which end of a sword to hold and roughly how to use it but their general lack of life experience made them unreliable and unpredictable.

Better avoid stressful or dangerous situations, Snare thought, as if that was likely in the Watch, and so they made their way along the beach looking for shipwrecks. The sight of the first corpse counted, in Snare's opinion, as a stressful situation. He reined in his horse and paused to think, allowing the constables to catch up.

"Is that a body?" asked Jared, staring with his mouth open and eyes wide as if this was the first time he had seen a corpse.

"Hmm," said Snare, "could be. We'd better take a look."

They rode closer and quickly saw that, no, it wasn't a corpse, it was just the first of many bodies. They were laid out along the beach where the surf had left them, like dolls discarded by a careless child.

He signalled a stop but something further down the beach caught his eye - movement of some sort at the top of the low cliffs. A person, turning away after watching their approach, maybe? He stared but there was no further movement and his attention shifted back to the beach and the sea and the bodies.

"Awedom," said Snare to the second of his three constables, "ride back to Heberon, find the Captain and tell him there is a wrecked ship in Grace Bay. Go."

"Find the Captain, tell him about the shipwreck. Got it, Sarge. And then what should I do?"

Snare, still looking out over the beach, rolled his eyes in light despair.

"Bring the Captain back here, if he wants to come. If he isn't interested then just come back here with the cart and find me," said Snare, "and don't dawdle - go straight to the Captain."

Awedom turned his horse and trotted off back along the sands towards Heberon.

Snare sat and thought. Six miles to Heberon and another six back. Allow an hour for Awedom to find the Captain, for a patrol to be gathered, for cart and horses to be prepared. It would be at least two hours, possibly three or four, before anyone else arrived on the scene; plenty of time to have a sniff around.

Snare dismounted, handed the reins to Jared and walked to the first corpse. Bending down, he ran his hands through the pockets of the corpse's coat and searched him for weapons or coins. Nothing. There were footprints - bare feet - alongside the corpse and each of the next four that he inspected, as if someone had knelt by each body in turn.

The fifth corpse had been stripped of its trousers. Beside it Snare found, with some distaste, a discarded piece of torn and ragged cloth that might once have been a pair of trousers.

Corpses six and seven told no tales but eight was missing its shirt and coat, unless it was the fashion now for some sailors to work the decks half naked. There were other rags on the beach and to Snare it looked like someone had stolen clothes from the corpse to replace their own tattered garments.

The ninth corpse had bare feet and the footprints suddenly became boot prints. Snare was now sure that someone had been robbing the corpses. The boots had left a trail that led westward, up the beach and toward the low cliffs.

The bay was sheltered and the waves were small by the time they reached the beach but the sand around the corpses was nevertheless scoured smooth, except for the boot prints left by a single man.

"The man on the cliff," Snare muttered to himself.

The state of the corpses was unusual and Snare was uneasy.

"Jared, get over here," called Snare, waving at the trooper, who was still staring distractedly at the corpses as if worried they might lurch to their feet. Jared kicked his horse forward and came along the beach, stopping as he drew level with the sergeant. He held the reins as Snare mounted.

"What now Sarge?"

Snare thought for a moment, looking out to sea. There was no sign of the ship that had foundered and very little wreckage, if you didn't count the corpses. Most of the ships travelling these waters were traders carrying grain, iron, food, wine, wool, rope, coal or any one of a thousand other things that the coastal towns might need or want. Often there were barrels, cases, casks, chests or crates washed up on the beach or floating in the bay after a merchant ship had foundered but today there were none of those things.

Not a merchantman, then, thought Snare.

It hadn't been carrying troops either, if he was any judge. The corpses all looked like sailors rather than soldiers and if a troop transport had been lost there would be far more bodies. A small crew, then, but not a merchant. Pirate, perhaps?

Snare dragged his thoughts back to the present. Footprints suggested someone else had been on the beach and, more than likely, had rifled the corpses to steal valuables and clothes. That was annoying, since picking valuables from corpses was generally seen as a perk of the Watch and Snare didn't like the thought of sharing his prize. He jerked his horse around to point towards the low cliffs. Time to move.

"Spint," said Snare, "stay here, get the bodies up into the

dunes where the tide can't wash 'em back out to sea then have a look round for anything else that might have been on that ship. Jared, you follow me. We're gonna find the bastard that robbed these sailors and teach him a lesson about stealing from the dead."

Snare flicked the reins and moved off along the beach, following the footprints towards the cliff. Over the dunes they went until they reached the ravine in the cliff that the corpse-robber had used to escape from the beach.

Snare looked at the sides of the ravine, steep and covered in thick, thorny undergrowth. He swore under his breath and turned to Jared.

"Our man went this way but we won't get the horses up that path. Get down, give me your reins and climb to the top of the cliffs. I'll take the horses back down the beach and meet you up there. Don't wander off."

Jared dismounted, handed over the reins of his horse and started to push his way through the brush, grumbling under his breath. Snare watched until Jared disappeared into the ravine, then he turned his horse again and trotted back east along the line of the cliffs towards the path that led to the top.

From the cliff top path Snare could see further out to sea but there was still no sign of a ship. He was beginning to think that it was probably quite a small vessel with a small crew and that it had broken up in the bay itself. That would explain the bodies on the beach and the lack of debris, but he still had no idea what sort of ship it was or why it had been there in the first place.

Snare rode along the clifftop path until Jared eventually came into view, lying on the grass in the sun, dozing. He woke quickly enough when Snare's horse snorted and stamped its foot next to Jared's head, though.

"Get up, get mounted and let's find this bastard quickly," snarled Snare, "if he gets away 'cos of you sleepin' I'll have your fuckin' guts. Move!"

Jared pulled himself to his feet and climbed, chastened, into his saddle. Snare kicked his horse and together they trotted north from the cliffs.

The trail was obvious, even to Snare's city-born eyes. The long grass had been pushed aside and trampled down by someone heading towards the forest. As the grass gave way to shrubs, there were more signs. The heavy footprints in the lingering mud, crushed leaves and twisted grasses spoke volumes. A man, from the size of the boots, had run this way and taken little care about the trail he was leaving. Snare wasn't much of a tracker but he'd chased enough men to be able to follow this trail in his sleep.

As the shrubs became forest and the trees closed in around them, the low-hanging branches forced Snare and Jared to dismount and continue on foot in file, leading their horses. The trail was still leading them almost due north and their quarry was making things easy for them, sticking to the faint path and not trying to hide where he had been.

A little further on, they reached a small clearing with a stream and Snare stopped to examine the ground. It looked like their quarry may have paused to rest before continuing along the banks of the stream. That meant they were probably closing the gap. Snare signalled Jared and they pressed on along the bank of the stream, pushing forward as quickly as they could. The trail led them past a fresh tree stump surrounded by wood shavings and then on, deeper into the forest.

They hadn't gone much further when Snare caught a hint of something human in the air - the smell of unwashed tramp - rising above even the stink of sweating horse.

"Hold up," said Snare "we're getting close. Smell that? Dirty wool and six-week-old sweat, if I'm any judge."

Snare let go of his reins and loosened his sword in its scabbard as Jared pushed forward, moving up to stand beside him. Then the bushes shuddered and a man carrying an improvised staff - probably newly cut, reasoned Snare, thinking back to the stump they had passed - stepped into view. After an hour's pursuit across sand and through forest, Snare's temper had frayed and he had hoped to catch more than a beggar with wild eyes, filthy beard and ripped, ill-fitting clothes.

Snare eyed the beggar's staff warily and moved his hand to the hilt of his sword. The beggar watched closely and raised his staff, bringing it round so that it was gripped in both hands, one end pointing toward the watchmen.

"Now, don't do nothing rash," said Snare, hoping to calm things down, "just put the staff down and come along quietly with us." Five years in the Watch had honed his instincts and he could almost taste the approaching violence.

The beggar's eyes were wild and he suddenly swayed, almost fell, then shuffled himself upright.

"Give me your boots and your horse," said the beggar, in an unexpectedly commanding voice. The courtly accent was almost as weird as the instruction.

"Fuck off," said Snare, snarling, then he saw that Jared had dropped his reins and stooped as if to remove his boots, "what the..." he muttered, staring in surprise, then suddenly he understood and his eyes snapped back to the beggar.

"He's a fucking Caster," shouted Snare, yanking out his sword and keeping his eyes on the beggar, "draw your bloody sword!"

Compelling a watchman was a desperate act, a serious

offence across the Empire, and Snare was suddenly cold despite the warmth of the day.

He dropped into a fighting stance and raised his sword. He tried to step away from his horse but the bloody thing came with him, nudging at his back, crowding him and forcing him to step again. Snare risked a glance across to Jared's horse where an unloaded crossbow hung from a strap on the saddle, neglected and out of reach.

The beggar took half a step forward, cool as anything, and gazed down at him. The wildness in his eyes had gone, replaced by a steady determination, and his staff bobbed gently as the beggar weighed it loosely in his hands.

The pause was just long enough for Snare to believe the beggar might back down but then he moved, shifting his grip on the staff and surging forward with dreadful speed. Snare blocked the sudden downward strike then stumbled back to avoid a short thrust, colliding with his horse and falling as his back foot slid out from under him. His sword vanished into the bush as he scrambled to get out of range and back on his feet.

Then Jared hurled himself forward, swinging wildly at the beggar with a sword he hardly knew how to use.

The beggar barely moved. Feet still, he swayed out of the path of Jared's sword then thrust hard with the staff, striking the constable square in the ribs.

Bone snapped and Jared's mouth opened in shock, his face suddenly white. Then the beggar struck again, a short, vicious swing that caught the watchman on the side of his head and knocked him to the ground, unconscious.

Snare's fingers closed on the hilt of the sword and he rolled clear of his horse. He had time to see a wild flash of movement and then his leg exploded in pain and he lost hold of the sword again.

Snare tried to stand but collapsed back to the ground, agony shooting up his leg. The beggar just stood and watched, staff held ready. Then he relaxed and lowered the staff.

"It's broken," he said, nodding at the leg, "so just lie still while I rob you."

"Fuck you!" was about all Snare could manage, and that through gritted teeth. He snarled at the beggar as he calmly tied Jared's horse to a tree.

The beggar just grinned and all Snare could do was watch as his saddlebags were emptied in front of him. They didn't have much - a day's rations, a couple of water skins - but the beggar took everything, loading it onto Jared's horse. Then he scooped up both the swords, inspected them, and slid Snare's blade into Jared's scabbard before strapping it to his waist.

Snare stopped rolling around and tried to ease his leg into a more comfortable position. Sweat beaded on his face and he ground his teeth against the pain.

"It won't help, you know," said the beggar, as if making light conversation in a tavern, "you'll need to get it strapped. I'll leave you the other horse but I still want your colleague's boots." The beggar bent over the unconscious Jared and removed his boots.

"Cheap and poorly made," he said, examining the boots as he pulled them on, "you should be ashamed, issuing kit like this to a public servant."

"Fuck you. Who the fuck are you and what the hell are you doing here?"

The beggar paused as he pulled on the second boot and looked at Snare. He grinned, and Snare felt suddenly uncomfortable, as if he were the butt of a joke he hadn't known was being played.

"I don't mind telling you that my fortunes are looking up," said the beggar, stamping his feet in his new boots. He grinned again.

"Yesterday, things looked very grim and by last night they looked downright deadly. Today I have new boots, sort of, a horse, a grimy coat and food to spare."

He slid the stolen sword a few inches from the scabbard.

"I have a sword as well as a staff. I'm a veritable one man fucking army!"

He plucked the crossbows from the saddles of each horse and tossed them into the stream.

"Can't have you getting any ideas when I turn my back, can I?"

The beggar leant over Jared a second time and searched him quickly, taking a dagger and a small purse, both of which he stuffed into the pockets of his coat. Snare just watched, unable to do more.

"I could tell you my name but you'd never believe me and it would rather spoil the chase, don't you think? Give my compliments to your commander. And don't feel too bad; you're probably the luckiest men alive, today."

Then he untied Jared's horse, crossed the stream and walked away into the forest, heading north.

3

"I don't like storms, Cranden, not one little bit. They're bad for my schedule and bad for my town." Administrator Nison was, by his own admission, a professional worrier. It was part of what made him so good at his job, he believed, but it also gave him sleepless nights, bad digestion and early morning bouts of extreme grumpiness.

"Yes, sir," said Cranden, aware that his master sometimes needed to rant at the rising sun.

They were standing on the rooftop balcony of the town hall, looking out across the coastal town of Heberon towards the sea. Nison often stood here to survey his little realm and today he turned full circle, checking every part of the town.

As far as Nison could tell, the town had escaped the worst of the wind and rain but still he worried. Its position between hills and at the back of a cove that formed a natural harbour seemed to have protected both the town and the few vessels that had spent the night behind the harbour walls. That spoke to the skill of the imperial surveyors and confirmed their choice of site but Nison was still uneasy.

Trading towns were always difficult and ports were the

most difficult of all. Heberon, with its trading connections via port, river and roads, was the most complex project he had worked on and he worried that parts of the plan were being pulled out of shape.

"Damned tricky," muttered Nison under his breath as he watched materials being prepared for the day's work on the shipping warehouse behind the eastern wharf. Eventually, that warehouse would store the iron ingots and coal that would come down the river from the northern hills for shipment across the rest of the Empire. A decade ago, this whole area had been beyond the borders of the Empire and home only to a few farmers. The discovery of readily accessible iron ore had changed all that and now Imperial money and resources flowed into the area, transforming a tiny fishing village into a large frontier town of about a thousand residents.

At the moment, there were maybe twice that number of transient residents and soldiers. The port and its small infantry garrison were all that upheld the Emperor's territorial claim.

Nison looked at the wooden palisade that surrounded the town on the landward side and then he looked west, where a stone gatehouse marked the first of the permanent defences. These defences hadn't been tested but to Nison's eyes they looked weak, pathetic. The troops stationed here were at the forefront of the Empire's westward expansion but for now their job was to support the survey teams building new infrastructure and taming the local wilderness.

Much of the effort within the town was focussed on the harbour and the river mouth where the port was being built. Government House was newly finished - a relatively modest, three-storey fortified manor house from which the town and surroundings would be ruled - as was the somewhat larger garrison complex next door. The harbour itself was being upgraded, the original wooden wharves replaced with new stone structures.

The palisade, its watchtowers and its gatehouses were all due for replacement once the harbour was finished. If thing went well, work would begin in the next few months.

Stone, that was the problem. And masons. Nison hadn't enough of either and he was juggling resources to keep everything moving. So far, that had worked well, but he knew, sooner or later, something would come unstuck.

He grimaced and turned to look east and north, where two more teams of engineers and labourers were cutting new roads through the forests and across the hills. In a few weeks, their work would be complete and they would link the town to the rest of the Empire. Goods, people and, most importantly, soldiers, would then flow swiftly and quickly between towns and Nison would sleep more easily at night. At the moment, though, and until the roads were finished and the surrounding regions occupied, most traffic arrived by sea, carried by licensed merchant ships and protected by a squadron of the Imperial Navy, which patrolled the sea for many leagues around.

"Do we have enough stone to complete the watchtower?"

Cranden checked his clipboard, flicking through pages of notes.

"No, sir, not until the next shipment arrives. That should be here next week. The masons have work to occupy them till then."

"Ha. And if we need to divert stocks to repair storm damage? That'll put us further behind, I'll wager."

"The Chief Surveyor is examining the works at the moment, sir. We should know more by lunchtime."

Nison grimaced at this, fearing the worst. To distract himself, he turned to look west where the first of the stone gatehouses had recently been completed. It stood maybe thirty yards beyond the wooden palisade, utterly useless without its adjoining walls, but a clear statement of Imperial intent. A good, stone road went straight under the gate and out to the west, ending after only a few hundred yards at the site of the half-finished watch tower, which was rising slowly on the headland. Beyond, there was only farmland and forest until you reached the villages and towns that clustered around the city of Vensille, far beyond the reach of the Emperor.

Nison sighed and thought over the work still to be done. The town was being built to the specification and design dictated by the Empire's central planners. They had given him a complete plan showing how the town was to be laid out, where the walls were to be built and the preferred routes for the roads that would link Heberon to the rest of the Empire. They had assigned teams of engineers and labourers, guards, administrators, cooks, quartermasters and various other personnel so that he could construct a standard Imperial town as quickly and efficiently as possible.

So far it was going well, although Nison had his doubts about some elements of the layout of the town. There had been a few problems - there always were with this sort of project - but the plan seemed to be basically sound. Nison reserved his ire, such as it was, for the surveyors who had chosen the site but failed to notice the extensive areas of marshy land along the river, right where the city walls and various other stone buildings had been planned. Draining the marshes and sinking deep foundations had taken time and had required some agile rearrangement of the planned buildings but the project was still largely on schedule and most of the major problems were now in the past.

Nison turned to look south across the port to the sea. Today had dawned bright and clear after the storm of the previous night. There seemed to be some disarray amongst the temporary buildings by the docks, possibly caused by last night's high winds, but the breaking waves had pounded the new stone jetties and those, he could see, were still standing, a testament to Imperial engineering ability. The harbour was still the main route into and out of the town, although that was starting to change now the roads had reached the nearby villages. Another month and the stone road would run all the way to Heberon's nearest neighbour, Asteron, 30 miles to the east.

But even on an otherwise perfect day the gods could always, in Nison's experience, be relied upon to introduce a little random suffering, a little pain and indignity to test their subjects. Today's suffering appeared, as Nison turned to look west again. From the direction of the border and the untamed forest there came a single rider, moving quickly toward the town. The method by which this person might cause the distress that Nison now fully expected was unclear, but the sense of foreboding as the rider passed the new gatehouse was strong.

Nison sighed again and leant on the parapet to watch the rider approach. It was a watchman, probably one of the squad sent to search the beaches for signs of shipwreck. The fact that he was on his own suggested they had found a shipwreck. Nison shook his head and stood up straight, hoping that the lost ship hadn't been carrying anything he cared about.

"Right, let's get to it, Cranden."

Nison opened the door and descended the spiral stairs

to the hallway below then followed the corridor to his suite of offices. Cranden came behind, following the Administrator through the outer office where the desks stood empty, waiting for the clerks to arrive.

Nison settled into his chair.

"Tell the Surveyor that I will inspect his progress later today. I want to see the jetties for myself."

"Certainly sir," said Cranden, heading for the door.

A little while later, as Nison contemplated an excruciatingly dull report, there was a knock on the door and Cranden returned.

"Excuse me sir, but there's a message from the Watch. Captain Tredgar is taking a squad to Grace Bay; they've found the wreckage of a ship and eleven bodies."

Nison steepled his fingers beneath his chin as he considered the news.

"One of ours?"

"No news on that yet, sir."

"Fine. Draft a report for the Governor's office and send it to Esterengel with the next mail package."

"Yes sir, straight away," said the clerk. He bowed and backed out of the office, closing the door behind him. Nison went back to his report, the wrecked ship already forgotten.

Watch Captain Tredgar led his squad through the gatehouse and out along the western road towards Grace Bay to inspect the wrecked ship. He rode with the frown he always wore when heading into the wilderness, not that the coast between Heberon and Grace Bay was really that wild any more. There were now so many farms and homesteads dotted across the landscape between the still-shrinking stretches of forest that even the most reluctant trekker could hardly call the land wild.

Still, wilderness it had been when Tredgar had first arrived in Heberon and, to his mind, wilderness it would remain until the roads were finished and there were villages, or at least inns, every few miles.

Heberon was the western-most coastal town of the Empire and beyond its walls there was nothing of any real interest until you reached Vensille, the first of the independent city states that controlled the region beyond the Empire's borders. There were a good thirty leagues between Vensille and the border of the Empire but just ten years ago that gap had been forty leagues and twenty years before that it had been sixty leagues.

Relations between the Empire and the Dukedom of Vensille were therefore somewhat strained and there had been a steady ratcheting of tensions as the Empire's seemingly inexorable expansion had continued.

As he rode beyond the border and down towards Grace Bay Tredgar was conscious of the need to avoid any entanglements with Vensille, although everyone could see that, sooner or later, violence was inevitable. For the moment relations were peaceful but Vensille's trade routes, tax revenue and navy made it a tempting target for anyone able to break through the formidable defensive walls around the city. If it came to a fight there could be no real doubt about the eventual winner but, so far, the Empire seemed to have slowed its westward expansion and was looking eastward instead.

Tredegar led his squad - two experienced constables on horses and another riding in the cart with Awedom - past the as-yet unfinished and unmanned watch tower and off the end of the road. Things were changing as new villages were founded and the local homesteads became farms but trade along the coast mostly travelled by sea rather than by land so the local roads were mostly used by farmers taking goods to and from the town.

Tredegar signalled a pause as they reached the headland overlooking Grace Bay. From here he could see the sweep of the bay and the pile of bodies and other wreckage that Spint had gathered in the dunes. Leaving the cart at the edge of the dunes, Tredgar and his two mounted constables made their way towards Spint and his fire.

Spint saluted as the riders approached.

"Good morning sir, welcome to Grace Bay."

Tredgar snorted and dismounted to inspect the bodies, poking at the nearest with the toe of his boot as if to check that it really was dead.

"Is this all of them? Eleven?"

"Yes sir, that's all so far, and I've been up and down the beach looking for more."

Tredgar nudged a piece of wreckage with his boot, turning over a large plank of wood; it was exactly the same on the other side.

"Anything to indicate the name of the ship or what it was carrying?"

"No sir, not that I can see, but I haven't found anything that looks like cargo yet. Maybe it sank?"

"Hmm, maybe. And where is Sergeant Snare?"

"He went into the forest with Jared, following someone who robbed the bodies before we arrived. That was a couple of hours ago, though, and they haven't been back yet."

That didn't sound good. Snare was a bit unimaginative but he was an experienced man; he should have been back by now.

"Constable Spint, isn't it? Take your horse along the

beach and find Bakker. Then you and Awedom load the bodies onto the cart and get them back to Heberon. They'll begin to stink if we keep them out here in the sun much longer."

"Yes sir".

"Prant, Binder. We're going to find Sergeant Snare and see what's keeping him from the beach this fine and sunny day."

Tredgar led the way back along the beach, following Spint, until they reached the cart. Then, with Bakker on Spint's horse, they made their way out of the bay and along the cliff top, following the trail Snare had taken earlier in the day. Spint and Awedom watched till they were out of sight then began loading the bodies into the cart.

Snare was not having a pleasant time, despite the sun. His leg was definitely broken and the pain was terrible; there was no way he'd be able to stand or ride. At least Jared was coming around, finally.

"Wake up. Jared! Wake up!"

Jared groaned and rolled over, pushing himself to his knees. He sat back on his heels and tried to stand, clutching at his head, then threw up noisily and sat back down again. There was blood on his shirt, he had an awful headache and breathing was horribly painful. Jared finally staggered to his feet and leant against a tree for support.

"Come on lad," said Snare, "are you alright?"

"Yes Sarge, I think so, but I feel awful. And that bastard took me boots!"

Boot-stealing, in Jared's opinion, was amongst the lowest form of crime, particularly as that had been his only pair and he was miles from home.

"What do we do now?"

Snare grimaced and bit back a sarcastic response. Now was not the time and this was definitely not the place.

"We head back to the beach and hope Awedom and Spint are there. I can't ride - you'll have to help me stand. And fish the crossbows out of the stream, will you? Don't want to leave those behind."

Jared retrieved the two sodden crossbows and shook them to get the water out. The weapons weren't going to be any use till they dried but he didn't want to have their cost docked from his pay just to keep his feet from getting wet. He loaded them onto the horse then looked around for a branch to splint Snare's leg with.

That simple task took far longer than it should have done. Snare screamed and cursed Jared's non-existent medical skills but, eventually, the leg was splinted.

They struggled upright and then, like two drunks leaning on each other for support, the two watchmen began to stumble slowly back the way they'd come, heading for the beach. Snare's horse followed behind, reins held loosely in Jared's free hand, while Snare concentrated on keeping his leg clear of the ground.

By the time they had reached the spot where their beggar friend had sat to rest by the stream, they were sweating heavily and suffering badly.

"Let's just take a few minutes, lad. Set me down here."

Jared lowered Snare onto a rock by the stream, tied the horse to a sapling then slumped down on the bank.

"He's taken all the food, my dagger, my scabbard, my purse, my arsing boots and my horse. He broke your leg, half my ribs and gave me a god-awful headache. This isn't what I signed up for," Jared whined.

He leaned over to wash his bare feet in the stream.

"And where did a beggar learn to use a staff like that anyway? Must have been in the army."

"I don't think so," said Snare, gritting his teeth against the pain, "it's not a good weapon for massed infantry. Pikes, yes, or swords or spears, but not short staffs."

Snare paused his lecture as a wave of pain rolled up his leg. He twisted slightly and held his breath till it passed.

"Staffs are more of a peasant weapon; cheap, easy to make, effective. But he wasn't a peasant either, you could tell from his voice. And he tried to coerce you so he must have been talented. I think we might have got off lightly. He could have killed us and taken everything we had."

While Jared was thinking about this the sound of voices reached them from the south. He reached for his sword before remembering where it was. Did waterlogged crossbows work? Jared didn't know but he grabbed one all the same and worked the lever to pull back the string. He fitted a bolt and pointed the bow in the general direction of the voices.

"Who's there? This is the Watch. What's your business?"

Captain Tredgar pushed through the bushes and stepped into the clearing, leading his horse. Jared, surprised to see his commander rather than a local peasant, quickly pointed the crossbow at the ground.

"Sorry sir, wasn't expecting you."

Tredgar just looked at him, seeing the blood and the dirt, his torn clothes and bare feet, then passed him the reins of his horse.

"Hold this. What happened, Snare?"

Snare grimaced and Tredgar's face darkened as the sergeant described the events of the day. By the time he had finished, Tredgar was exceptionally cross and determined to bring the beggar to justice.

"We'll need to strap your leg properly before we can take you back to Heberon. Prant, cut branches to make more splints and bind the Sergeant's leg."

"Yes sir," said Prant, drawing his sword and advancing on the nearest tree.

"As soon as you can move, Sergeant, I want you, Prant and Jared to head back to the beach. Awedom is there with Spint and a cart full of corpses. Get yourself back to Heberon and tell Administrator Nison that I'm pursuing the fugitive."

"He's armed sir, and dangerous. Might be best to shoot first and bring him back as baggage, if you get my meaning."

"I do," said Tredgar with a disapproving frown, "but he'll face the local Justice before we hang him."

Tredgar took his horse from Jared as Prant began strapping Snare's leg. The sergeant gritted his teeth and hissed as Prant fiddled with the bindings but it was soon done.

"Right, let's go. I'll see you in Heberon, Sergeant."

"Good luck, sir. And thanks for coming to look for us. You need to follow the trail along the bank of the stream then turn north. Didn't see where he went after that."

"Thank you, Sergeant. Bakker, scout ahead. Let's go, Binder."

Prant helped Snare onto his good leg and they set off for the beach with Jared and the horses following behind. Within moments the clearing was empty and peace had once more settled across the forest.

4

It took Marrinek an hour and a half of struggle and effort to wind his way through the forest towing the recalcitrant horse behind him. He had thought of taking both horses from the watchmen but leading one through the undergrowth was bad enough. He was glad he'd left the other one behind.

His route led him steadily higher as he pushed inland through the undergrowth. When he finally escaped the oppressive atmosphere of the trees and broke out onto the rolling hills of grass, the moment caught him quite by surprise and he stumbled, blinking, into the sunshine.

He stopped for a few minutes to drink and eat, luxuriating in his first meal as a free man. Warm, stale water and hard bread were not his favourite foods but at least they weren't laced with drugs.

Still, beggars can't be choosers. He sniggered at the thought; his clothes made him look like a vagabond and - he sniffed - an unhygienic vagabond at that. He looked like a tramp, a perpetual wanderer of the Empire's roads, surviving on the largesse of other travellers.

It was almost a good disguise. There was certainly no chance that acquaintances from his previous life of elegant comfort and semi-ritualised violence would recognise him but begging bowls and rags were not normally accessorised by horses and swords. Either one marked him as more than a simple beggar and although he could hide the sword under his coat, there was precious little he could do about the horse without just getting rid of it.

But beggars on horses travel faster and further than beggars on foot and right now he needed speed more than he needed a convincing disguise. He clambered into the saddle, relieved to take the weight off his feet, and looked around. From his high vantage point the hills stretched out before him for as far as he could see, their gentle slopes grazed by sheep and cattle and broken by homesteads and small villages.

To his right, in the east, lay the Empire and the shattered remnants of his old life. He thought, briefly, of riding back to seek revenge, of throwing himself on the mercy of the Gods and demanding justice for the crimes committed against him. But the gods smiled only on the rich and powerful; they granted precious few miracles to even the most deserving of beggars. No, he had long ago decided, there was nothing for him in the east but pain, humiliation, imprisonment and death. And so he turned westward and, with the sun on his left, rode out into the green.

His plan was very vague. Brief periods of lucidity amongst the drug-induced confusion and paranoia during his months of captivity had given him time to think. He had any number of ideas and schemes from which he could now pick but his sudden release had left him unable to prepare specific plans for his immediate survival. He was, to a large degree, making it up as he went along.

Whatever else he might want to do in the long-term, right now he needed to find a city outside the Empire where he could lay low, regroup, recover and prepare. It was only a matter of time before they came for him; it might be weeks, or even months if he'd shaken his pursuers in the forest, but they'd find him sooner or later. It was too much to hope that they would declare him dead after the loss of the ship; nobody would believe it if they didn't have a body and he wasn't prepared to go that far to maintain the illusion of his death.

Retaining his life and his freedom were the priorities. He hadn't travelled this part of the world but he had suffered interminable planning meetings during which the area was discussed in detail. It had been twenty years since westward expansion of the Empire had been a hot topic but, if memory served, and if he really was beyond the western borders of the Empire, there should be a town to the north and west. With luck, and if he had accurately recalled the map, he might reach it before nightfall; if not, he might miss the town by miles and only realise his mistake when he fell victim to some horrible accident.

He thought a lot about this possibility as he rode across the hills, skirting small villages and farms. If he was being pursued then staying out in the open was probably a quick way to be recaptured. The river town of Catshed for which he was aiming was outside the Empire and probably too small to conceal him for long but even the most reckless Imperial agent would think twice about entering a foreign town or city without direct orders.

But that wouldn't stop them for long, especially if real money was involved. There would be plenty of locals who might take the Emperor's money to put a knife in his back. He needed a larger city where he would be just one amongst

the teeming hordes. In a small town, the provincial authorities themselves might be tempted to hand him over, just to
curry favour with the neighbouring Imperial governor.
Catshed would offer, at best, a temporary refuge.

He looked back over his shoulder, spooked by a sudden
fear of recapture. The sharp movement brought on a fresh
wave of nausea and a stab of pain behind his eyes. For a few
minutes he did nothing but cling to the horse as it wandered
westward. His vision eventually cleared but the headache
seemed to be settling in for good. He kicked the horse to a
gallop for a few minutes before slowing to a rapid trot. The
nausea wasn't going away either and the ride got steadily
more uncomfortable as he bounced up and down.

After several hours he had covered many miles but
found no sign of the town and he was starting to worry. His
headache was steadily worsening and it was only a matter of
time before riding a horse became impossible. He kept
going - what else could he do? - pushing the horse on as fast
as it would go as his spirits fell and his earlier optimism
drained slowly away.

And then, as he stretched his back at the crest of a hill,
he saw to his enormous relief that the valley below held a
dirt track running broadly east-west and that, to the north
west and not too far away, there were the faint smudges of
smoke that signalled a town.

Following the road, uneven and dusty as it was, allowed
Marrinek to make good time. He kept the horse at a trot for
a while but eventually the nausea returned and he had to
stop to throw up at the side of the road. He struggled to get
back onto the horse, much to the amusement of the small
children watching from the side of the grass bank.

Even so, he managed to reach the walls of the town in
the early evening. The sun was dipping but the gates were

still open and the guards merely glared suspiciously as he passed under the arch of the gatehouse.

They might have stopped him, if he had been on foot, and refused him entry. He could see them twitching, torn between letting in a potential troublemaker and upsetting a noble; in this part of the world only the rich rode horses and no good ever came from upsetting the rich, however badly they dressed. Self-interest won and the guards just stared as they waved him through into the relative safety of the town. He had hoped to enter the town unnoticed but at least he was inside; things were looking up.

Captain Tredgar's day was going from bad to worse. Assaults on his men were not unusual but they were normally sparked by drunken brawls or minor villains evading arrest. A stand-up fight in the middle of a forest that resulted in two of his men being injured was a new and unwelcome occurrence. That he had then stolen their equipment and a horse before simply walking away just made everything that much more embarrassing.

Following the trail left by the beggar and his stolen horse was not difficult and they made good progress through the forest. Broken branches, footprints and disturbed leaves made it clear that the man was making no real effort to obscure his trail so maybe he hadn't anticipated a pursuit. Tredgar was determined to use that fact to his advantage and when they finally emerged onto the plains he wasted no time in mounting up and leading Bakker and Binder across the grasslands at a gentle trot.

Here also the trail was easy to follow. The man was walking his horse and only occasionally trotting, taking his time as if he had no real care in the world, and the earth was soft enough after the long damp spring to leave an easy trail of hoof prints. Tredgar spurred his horse to a fast trot and led his squad west and north, following the beggar's trail for several hours across the hills until it joined a dirt road. Here amongst the regular traffic and broken, well-travelled road surface, it was impossible to say for sure which way the beggar had gone and Tredgar was forced to make a decision.

He sat for a few minutes watching as walkers and carts made their way along the road. Would the beggar have turned east and headed back toward the Empire, or continued west, toward the city states? West seemed more likely; it was the prevailing direction of the tracks they'd been following so far and Tredgar didn't think the beggar would want to head toward the Empire so soon, even if he hadn't realised that he was being pursued. He made his decision and they kicked their horses to a gallop, following the road westward.

Tredgar's galloping pursuit carried them quickly along the road but they saw no sign of the beggar and eventually they were forced to slow their horses to avoid exhausting them completely.

It was mid-evening by the time they climbed a small hill overlooking the town of Catshed and Tredgar was forced to admit that his quarry was, for now at least, behind his reach. Either he had turned east and was lost somewhere in the Empire or he had reached the relative safety of Catshed. Hot pursuit through the wilds was one thing but continuing the chase within the walls of an independent town while dressed in the uniform of an Imperial watchman would cause all sorts problems, even if the guards allowed him into the town, which he doubted.

Tredgar sat his horse at the side of the road and gazed down at the town for a few minutes considering his next move. It was galling to have come so far for so little achievement but further pursuit just wasn't going to be possible. He cursed under his breath.

"You two wait here," said Tredgar, "I'm going to talk to the gate guards, see if they know anything."

He rode on down the road, dismounting to walk the last hundred yards, stopping just short of the gatehouse where several of the town's watchmen were waiting for him.

"You're a long way from home," said one, an officer maybe, although Tredgar couldn't work out his rank from the insignia on his shoulder.

"I am," he admitted, tying his horse to a hitching post, "and I'm tired and hungry to boot. It's been a long day and it's going to be a long night as well."

"Yeah, well," said the officer, smiling in grim sympathy, "we know how those go. How can we help, friend?"

"I'm Captain Tredgar, Heberon Watch, and I'm looking for a man who may have come this way, dressed as a beggar, riding a stolen horse with one of our saddles and carrying a long staff. Have you seen him?"

The officer shrugged and looked at his men.

"Anyone?"

"Yeah, I saw him," said one man, "long hair, big beard, right? He had a crappy old coat that had seen better days and he looked half dead and he didn't smell too good neither, but he were here."

Tredgar nodded along grimly. His hunch and been right; the beggar didn't want to return to the Empire. He turned back to the officer.

"He assaulted two of my men this morning and I've pursued him all the way from Heberon," said Tredgar, exaggerating slightly so that he didn't have to mention the shipwreck, "he's dangerous and I want him."

"I'd love to help, I really would, but I'll never get permission to hand him over to you, even if we knew where he was. Sorry, you know how it is," said the officer, a sympathetic look on his face as he held up his hands to show there was nothing he could do.

"Now, listen," said Tredgar, taking a step forward.

"No, you listen, mate. This isn't part of the Empire," said the officer forcefully, "and your uniform means nothing here. If you want to talk to his lordship about it then by all means, but you'll have to leave your sword, armour and horse here and I'll tell you now his lordship won't give you any better news than I did."

Tredgar hesitated, then held up his hands.

"Your town, your rules," he said, backing away towards his horse, "and he's your problem, now."

He untied his horse and climbed into the saddle.

"I tried to help," he said, "remember that, if he makes trouble for you, I tried to help."

And he turned the horse and kicked it into a canter back down the road to where he'd left his squad.

An hour after riding into Catshed, Marrinek lowered himself into a hot tub in the bath house of the Noble God, an inn near the town walls. The innkeeper had tried to turn him away, at first, but the man's concerns had disappeared under the weight of Marrinek's silver.

Now he had a clean room and his horse was safely stabled in the inn's yard, cared for by a groom who seemed to think the animal had been ridden half to death. A few days' rest would do the creature a power of good.

New clothes, acquired from a merchant only too happy to accept Imperial coins, were laid out by the tub to replace the worn, ill-fitting clothes he had stripped from the corpses. The travel-worn coat he had taken from the sailor was old but still serviceable and hung from a hook on the back of the door.

He played with the soap, luxuriating in the experience as two years of grime was slowly eased from his skin. The trimming of his beard and hair would have to wait but at least now they were clean. Long hair was rare in the Empire but here, where fashions often ran counter to those across the border, his look was only a little unusual rather than totally outrageous. He ran his fingers through his hair and tied it back with a strip of cloth.

Aching muscles were soothed by the warm water but the headache, brought on he knew, by withdrawal from the drug fed to him by his jailers, was getting worse.

He lay with his head resting against the edge of the tub, breathing deeply to hold back the pain and nausea.

He dozed gently then jerked awake, head spinning at the sudden movement. The thought he might drown in a bath after surviving prison, shipwreck and pursuit forced a sudden bark of laughter and then an immediate groan of pain as his head pounded.

Overall, though, his position today was rather better than it had been yesterday, when his only prospect was a long life of confinement in the prison at Ankeron West. Now, beyond the borders of the Empire and, he hoped, the reach of his enemies, he could begin to rebuild his life and plan his revenge.

When the cooling water dropped below a comfortable temperature he heaved himself carefully from the tub and dressed in his new clothes. Back in his room, he lay down on the bed with a damp cloth on his forehead and reviewed his situation. The clothes, food and room had almost exhausted his meagre supply of stolen coin but at least he had a bed to sleep in and warm food to eat. He had left enough money with the landlord to cover several nights, time he knew he would need to recover from the effects of the drugs.

With nothing more to be done and his head feeling like it was about to split, Marrinek closed his eyes and tried to rest.

He woke the next morning having slept fitfully throughout the night. His headache raged and when he pushed himself off the bed he stumbled immediately, only arresting his fall by snatching at the frame of the door.

He stood for a few moments then fell back toward the bed, stomach heaving violently as he spewed the remains of last night's meal into the chamber pot. He sat there for maybe an hour cuddling the pot, vomiting repeatedly until, finally, the sickness subsided and he was able to stand. He stretched his cramped muscles but his body wasn't ready for such a movement and he stumbled back against the door, catching the handle in the small of his back and only just remaining upright.

He wrenched the door open and stood for a moment in the doorway, leaning heavily on the doorframe for support. Then he grabbed the tray of food left for him by the landlord on the shelf outside his room and staggered back to his bed, kicking the door closed behind him as he went.

Exhausted by these efforts, he collapsed back down on the bed and wrapped himself tightly in the thin blankets, food forgotten and abandoned on the floor. He was shivering now despite the warmth of the day, and the chill was deepening quickly. As the shivers worsened he closed his eyes, covered his head with the blanket and curled into a stinking, sweating ball to try to keep warm.

He must have slept again, and slept soundly, because

night had fallen when he next woke. Someone must have been in to check on him, though, because a candle had been lit and his pot replaced. A jug of water now stood on the small table alongside a fresh plate of food and Marrinek gave silent thanks to the landlord. His headache was down to a dull nagging pain and the shivering and nausea seemed to have passed.

He dragged himself upright and managed to walk across the room to the plate of food. He picked at the bread and cheese but his appetite had left him and all he really wanted to do was sleep. He stood there for a few minutes, staring out the window, then he went back to bed and slept till morning.

The next day he woke weak and hungry. The small mirror on the wall told him all he needed to know; he was alive, just about, but he had lost weight and his eyes had a haunted, sunken look that seemed new. He turned his head this way and that, taking in the prominent cheek bones and grey-tinged skin. He looked like a three-day dead corpse but at least he was free.

He ate every scrap of food in the room and washed in the basin then turned his attention to his goods and chattels. For a man who had spent almost two years in prison, he wasn't doing too badly but he could hardly have been said to be doing well.

He set out his possessions on the bed and took stock. The corpse-clothes were gone, so his wardrobe was limited to the clothes he was wearing, a pair of worn boots, a spare shirt and the sailor's coat. He had a few coins left but not enough to be of any real use. The standard issue Imperial sword and matching dagger, both made to the latest pattern issued to the army and watch, were in good condition, new and barely used. Finally, he had a fresh-cut staff that was little more than raw wood.

It was the staff to which he paid most attention. Given the right tools and a selection of materials he could transform the plain staff into a formidable weapon but at the moment his options were limited. That said, there were useful things he could do with only the staff, the knife and a little time.

The first step was to tidy the rough edges left when he hacked the staff from the tree. The knife wasn't quite the right tool for this - it would have been much easier with charming tools, or even a set of rasps - but he whittled and carved and sliced until eventually had a finish that was, if not good, then at least reasonable. He stripped the bark away to expose the green wood then shaved away the stubs of the branches to produce a smooth, rounded shape along which he could slide his hands easily as he changed grip.

That left him with a damp, green stick better suited to ornament than to fighting. It wasn't possible to charm living things and green wood of the staff was too close to alive for Marrinek's purposes. Seasoned wood was far more straightforward and could, to some degree, be worked without charming tools.

Most people would have seasoned the staff by simply leaving it in a loft or storeroom for a year to dry out, or maybe, if they were impatient, baking it in a bread oven. Marrinek couldn't wait for the staff to dry naturally and he didn't have an oven so that left only one option.

He paused briefly, wondering if this was really a wise thing to be doing, then he threw caution to the wind, held the staff in front of him and concentrated.

Focussing power into green wood was risky. There was a

chance that the wood would simply react badly to the power. Even for a man of his talents, such work would be difficult but today, somehow, it wasn't working at all. The effects of the drug, maybe, still blocking his power.

He tried again and again but each time, although he could feel the power, he couldn't quite grasp it. At every attempt the power slipped from his grasp like water running through his fingers leaving him with nothing more useful than a cold wet sensation.

After an hour's effort he gave up, exhausted, frustrated, angry and hungry. He threw the staff down on the bed and went in search of food.

The rest of the day he spent tidying himself up, eating and exercising. He cleaned his boots then worked through the staff fighting forms he had learned years before. He paused for something to eat then exercised again, his withered muscles aching with the effort, his breathing laboured. He kept going, practising and eating, eating and practicing, until, by late afternoon, exhaustion forced him to stop.

Eventually, Marrinek sank back onto the bed. Pain came from every muscle but it didn't matter; he was free. Within seconds, he was asleep.

5

It had been a long and ultimately profitless day for Tredgar and his dispirited squad of watchmen. Trekking home across the western hills on tired horses was hard going. The heat of the day had faded quickly after sunset and they were soon shivering. Camping without tents or even warm clothes held little appeal but their progress, without lamps or starlight, was so slow there was no point continuing. Tredgar called a halt as they entered a sheltered hollow at the foot of one of the hills.

"We'll camp here for the night and continue on to Heberon at first light." He slid from his horse and tied her reins to a nearby bush then removed the saddle, slinging it to the ground a short distance away.

"Let's get a fire going for a little warmth then turn in."

Bakker and Binder settled their horses for the night then gathered firewood, building a pile where Tredgar had cleared a patch of earth. He stacked the wood in a pyramid, stuffing the gaps between the larger branches with twigs, then pulled a charm about six inches long from his inside coat pocket.

He stuck the end of the charm into the kindling and a small hot flame appeared, spreading swiftly to the twigs and branches. He blew gently to fan the flames then returned the charm to his pocket as the smaller branches began to burn.

It was a cloudy night and cool but even lying on the grass with saddles as pillows, warmed only by the flames of the fire and far from their loved ones, sleep came quickly.

Dawn found Tredgar and Bakker still sleeping, snoring noisily. Binder woke as the sun rose above the horizon, stoked the fire and refilled their water bottles from a nearby stream. She sat on her heels warming her hands over the fire and thinking about the route back to Heberon and what she might tell her husband when she eventually made it home.

She sighed, prodding at the fire until the rising sun finally woke her companions. None of them, it turned out, had slept well enough to be truly refreshed and as they broke camp they all found pains and aches they hadn't noticed the previous day. A night under the stars after a day of hard riding had served as a solid reminder of why they lived in a town. Another few hours in the saddle would see them safely home but the prospect of more riding was not comforting.

But ride they did. They had eaten all their food the previous day so they were all hungry and keen to return home. Their spirits rose as the rising sun warmed their faces and they made good time, reaching the walls of Heberon after only three hours in the saddle. They rode quickly under the arch of the gatehouse and more slowly through the town, where traders were already opening the shops and stalls that lined the main streets. The smell of new bread dragged at their heads but Tredgar kept them going until they reached the watch house.

A night of al fresco camping in the hills was, to Tredgar's way of thinking, more than he could rightly ask of his constables so he sent them home with instructions to report for duty the following morning. They stabled their horses then left and Trdegar grabbed bread and cheese from the kitchen on the way to his office before finally sinking gratefully into his chair.

His office on the first floor overlooked the courtyard and his desk was positioned so that he could look out across the stables and over the town. After five years, he had settled into his position and formed a strong attachment to the town, which had grown rapidly during his tenure.

His feeling of responsibility for the well-being of the town and its people was both an advantage, since he believed it helped him to do his job well, and a disadvantage, since it meant he took personal offence from unsolved crimes. The unpunished assault on his men was also an assault on his pride, on his ability to do his job and on his town; he did not intend to forget or forgive.

For now, he contented himself with writing a simple report for Administrator Nison. The practical difficulties of law enforcement were of no interest to the Administrator but he would support Tredgar's efforts to apprehend the alleged attacker. Or, rather, Nison would support his efforts if they could be quickly and cost-effectively concluded. Unplanned spending was, in the Administrator's eyes, a most severe crime against the state and Tredgar was sure it would far outweigh any though of justice for a mere assault.

Tredgar wrote swiftly, pausing only to take bites of food. Once he had finished he made two further copies, folding and sealing the original with wax and an impression of his ring of office. He kept one copy for his own records and put the other in the basket for filing then he stood and walked down to the common room.

Constables Awedom and Jared were finishing their breakfast as Tredgar entered the room. They stood and saluted before continuing their meal when he waved them on, taking a seat at their table.

"You're looking rather better today, Jared. How do you feel?"

"Fine, sir, thanks. My head still aches but Healer Ernst set my ribs. You want to see my bruises?" Jared leant over and before Tredgar could stop him, pulled up his shirt to expose an impressive collection of vivid blue and purple bruises.

Tredgar raised his eyebrows in mock appreciation.

"Yes, well. I'm glad to hear you're feeling better. And how is Sergeant Snare? You got him home without further fuss?"

"We did, sir," said Awedom, "we took him to the infirmary and they strapped his leg good 'n proper, trussed him like a chicken for market and stuck him in a bed. When we left, they were ready to begin the healing but they didn't want us to hang around. He should be walking again later today, if he's lucky."

"Good news, thank you. I will visit later, if time allows. Today, though, I want you two to make enquiries about the man who assaulted Jared and Snare. Find out if he came through the docks and who he was. Someone must know him - ask around. Report to me this evening or as soon as you get news." Tredgar stood to leave, then said, "And find out if anyone's heard of a practitioner who fights with a quarterstaff. That's bound to be rare, so someone must know something."

He left the room and walked through the public reception area and out of the front door into the town square. As always on a weekday the square was busy but today was market day so there were even more people than normal. Tredgar made his way across the square and climbed the steps to Government House.

He went straight to Administrator Nison's office, only to find that Nison was busy and could not be disturbed. He took a seat in the anteroom and settled down to wait. The noise of the clerks was strangely calming as they wrote, processed and filed their paperwork in near silence. The Watch house was always busy, always noisy, and this quiet sanctuary of paper and industry made a pleasant change.

While he waited, he couldn't help dwelling on his actions of the previous day. It was his failed pursuit of the beggar that was making him anxious, and not just because of the escape. Should he have pushed harder and caught the beggar before he reached Catshed? Could he have been more persuasive when talking to the gate guards? Would it have been sensible to enter the town in some sort of disguise to look around? It was all speculation; there was nothing more he could do so he shook his head to clear his mind and settled down to watch the clerks.

Nison sat behind his desk after Tredgar had gone and replayed the events of the previous day. Assault on a watchman was a serious matter but you had to be realistic about these things. The two watchmen were recovering, the perpetrator had made it beyond their immediate reach and there was no threat to the town or Empire. In practical terms, there wasn't much more to be done.

The loss of the horse was annoying but the Watch would just have to make do with one fewer beast. Tredgar was embarrassed at his failure to make an arrest but there was nothing more he could have done. At least he had brought his squad home without further injury.

Nison sighed and made a decision. The incident was unfortunate but it wouldn't be allowed to affect the wider project. Tredgar's report went into the filing tray, the assault was forgotten and Nison turned back to important matters, like the routing of the northward road and the slow rate of progress as the engineers cut their way through forest and across hills to reach the mines.

6

M arrinek slept late and woke, famished but refreshed, around mid-morning. He dressed quickly then stood glaring at the staff. He decided to eat before doing anything else so he made his way downstairs. A little while later, back in his room, he picked up the staff from its resting place against the wall and held it gingerly, weighing it in his hands. Then he reached out for power and this time, unlike yesterday, he grasped it immediately. He smiled to himself and sat down on the bed; time for the next phase of work.

He placed one end of the staff on the floor and held the other, focussing on the core of the staff and gently pushing power into the wood. The trick was to warm the wood and force its moisture toward the surface, where it would bead like condensation on a cold window and eventually run to the floor.

It was slow work and not without risk. It took a lot of concentration to deliver enough power to achieve the effect without pushing so much that the staff caught fire or exploded. Using power without a charm required a delicate touch; too little power and he would still be sitting here at New Year. Too much power applied too quickly would superheat both the moisture and the wood, causing an explosive release of scalding steam and a shower of fast-moving burning splinters. Not ideal.

After several hours of exhausting effort, the staff was seasoned and the room was full of warm, damp air. Marrinek relaxed his grip and stretched his fingers, then his arms and shoulders. It had been a good morning's work but all he really had was a plain stave; transforming it into a proper weapon required tools he didn't have and energy he couldn't spend.

He stood, hungry again, and gathered his possessions. His head was clear for the first time in months and now the folly of staying so long in Catshead was obvious. It was time to move on.

Marrinek wrapped the sword in a bundle with his spare clothes and tied it with a makeshift cloth strap. He hadn't seen anyone but the guards carrying weapons on his way to the inn and he wasn't yet sure how people might react to a man wearing a sword. Best to play it safe. Then he grabbed the staff, knife and the last of his money and left the room, throwing his bundle over his shoulder as he went.

Downstairs in the common room the crowd was already gathering for a light lunchtime drink. Marrinek found a quiet table and, after a little confusion over the serving girl's accent, ordered bread, meat and beer.

He watched the room as he ate and decided that he might have been right to hide the sword. Nobody else in the room was armed and even his hair and beard were already drawing more attention than he was comfortable with.

He ate quickly and ordered more food once the first portion was gone. As he sat he listened, soaking up the accents of the people around him. They were speaking Gheel, the language used along the river and throughout the city states, but the accent was strange, or maybe it had just drifted since he was last here.

He sat for a while longer, finishing his beer, then he tossed coins on the table and strode out into inn's courtyard, eating the last of the bread as he went. He stood blinking, enjoying the feel of sunlight and a full belly, as the stable boy bustled around preparing his horse.

From the back of the horse, Marrinek could see over the heads of the people on the streets and, almost at random, he rode slowly through the town, looking for a livery stable. After twenty minutes he found one, a rough-looking place where, he hoped, they would ask few questions about either him or the horse.

He rode into the main yard and a boy rushed forward to take the reins as he dismounted.

"Who's in charge?" Marrinek asked the boy.

"That would be Mr Jenkins, sir, he'll be in the tack room." The boy pointed at a door on the other side of the yard. Marrinek nodded his thanks, retrieved his staff from the saddle and strolled across the yard.

"Mr Jenkins?" he called.

A man looked up from a bench where he was working at a saddle with a brush.

"I have a horse to sell, in your yard. Are you interested?"

Jenkins sucked air through his teeth.

"Maybe, depends on the horse. Why do you want to sell it?"

"I have no need of a horse and I can't keep feeding the damn thing. It's yours for a fair price, if you want it. Or I'll take it elsewhere if you're too busy...?"

"I don't buy horses from strangers, as a rule, but if you're set on selling I'll take a look." He put down the brush and stepped out from behind the table, gesturing for Marrinek to lead the way back out into the yard where the horse was tied to a railing.

Jenkins ran his eye over the mare and his hands over her legs. He lifted her feet and checked her shoes and pulled back her lips to see her teeth then stepped back, left hand cupping right elbow, chin in his right hand. He sucked more air through his teeth, whistling quietly, and looked sideways at Marrinek.

"She's not a young horse. Done some hard years, I'd say. And she needs re-shoeing. And feeding up. Might be kinder to just send her to the knackers but I'll give you twelve shillings for her."

Marrinek snorted.

"There's nothing wrong with her shoes and she did fifty miles or more yesterday without any trouble. Twenty-five shillings and you're still getting a damn good deal."

"I'll give you eighteen but that's my limit. Take it or leave it."

"Done. Plus five for the saddle and tack." Now it was Jenkins who snorted.

"Five shillings for a used Imperial saddle? Don't make me laugh. I can't use it or sell it. I don't even want it on the premises in case it makes people ask where it came from, if you get my meaning." He looked at Marrinek with raised eyebrows and it was clear that Jenkins had his suspicions about how he had come by the horse.

"I'll give you a shilling for the saddle 'cos you seem like a decent bloke. I can always cut it up for parts." Jenkins stuck out his hand and they shook.

"Run to my box," Jenkins said to the stable boy, "and bring me the purse." He turned to Marrinek.

"I don't know who you are mister, and I don't want to know where you're going, but," he lowered his voice and leant closer, "Imperials aren't all that welcome in these parts. Best watch your back." He stood straight as the stable boy came running back with the purse.

Jenkins counted out nineteen shillings and dropped them into Marrinek's upturned palm.

"If that's all, I've got people to see. Get the horse into a box, lad," said Jenkins, heading back to his tack room.

Marrinek pocketed the coins and walked out of the yard. He stood for a moment in the street with the satisfied air of a man newly come into money, then strolled off into the crowd. He bought a meat pie at the mouth of an alley and asked the vendor for directions to a craft supply shop.

"Down the street a way, on the left. I reckon you'll find what you need down there, near the town walls. Here's your change."

Threading his way through amongst the shoppers and stallholders Marrinek made his way toward the town wall and a little way down the street he found the promised craft supply shop, Smyth's. Inside, the shop was small and close with walls lined with drawers, shelves, display cases and boxes, all holding materials or tools that a craftsman might use to construct or augment a charm.

Marrinek was looking at a display of small cut glass tiles when a man appeared behind a counter at the end of the room and cleared his throat.

"Good afternoon sir, my name is Smyth. Is sir looking for something in particular? Perhaps sir would like to describe his requirements so that I might serve him."

Marrinek walked over to the counter and leant his staff against the wood, calling to mind the list he'd been preparing.

"Sixty feet of fine copper wire and whatever copper netting you might have, six feet of iron rod, a couple of small copper ingots, a small fire charm, a dozen of the best brass and porcelain switch units and a set of simple charming tools, including the finest tool you have."

"Certainly sir," said Smyth, "just give me a moment."

He hummed to himself as he bustled around the shop retrieving the requested items. Smyth placed a coil of copper wire on the counter and set beside it six foot-long rods of iron rod and a set of tools in a rolled leather bag. He untied the straps that closed the bag and unrolled it to display the tools.

"We have two types of switch unit, sir," he said, produced a display case from beneath the counter, "but it seems to me that you might be looking for higher power, more reliable units that won't fail under stress." Smyth raised an eyebrow and looked meaningfully, if briefly, at the materials Marrinek had ordered. It wasn't that the making of power weapons was illegal, as such, but it was frowned upon by most charm-makers.

Marrinek grinned.

"Very high power, very reliable. Are these the best you have?" He picked up one of the switches and played with it, testing the spring and the action, checking the movement and the conductors.

"Yes, sir. Properly wired, those should be sufficient for any normal requirements. A dozen, was it?" Smyth counted them out and added them to the growing pile. Then he brought from under the counter another tray, this time with a selection fire charms.

Marrinek inspected the five tools carefully, handling each until he was satisfied with its quality. All passed his scrutiny except for the most slender of the tools, the one with the finest tip.

"These four are fine for my purposes but this one," he held up the fine-tipped tool, "is too large. Do you have anything finer?"

Smyth disappeared briefly into a back room and came back a few moments later with several more tools. He laid them out on the counter next to the fire charms.

"These are the smallest I have, sir. Might I ask what you are trying to make? I may be able to help."

Marrinek examined the tools closely, ignoring Smyth's question.

"I'll take that one," he said, placing one of the tools down on the leather.

"Very good, sir. It's a little costlier than the others but undoubtedly an excellent tool and a fine charm in its own right."

Smyth rolled up the bag of tools while Marrinek ran his eye quickly over the fire charms. He took the smallest and thinnest from the tray and set it beside the roll of tools.

"And I need some slide bars, good quality steel, if you have them."

Smyth nodded and hummed to himself, disappearing again into the back room. This time he returned with a box which he offered to Marrinek.

"Yeah," he said, rummaging through the modest selection of dials before picking out two of the larger pieces, "I'll take these as well. And do you have platinum or iridium?"

Smyth, who had picked up the tray of fire charms to replace it under the counter, paused to look straight at Marrinek. Then he finished replacing the tray and straightened.

"Difficult, sir, very difficult. I can get hold of a little platinum wire but I haven't seen iridium or had cause to handle it in years. I don't think I'll be able to get hold of any for many a week, sir, unless one of the river traders has some he might be persuaded to sell. These materials sell well in the cities and we see very little of them out here, I'm afraid." He paused slightly, then added, "I have a little gold in wire or bullion, a quantity silver and as much iron, copper, zinc and nickel as you might need for any personal matter, but if sir is asking for iridium I suspect sir has a particular use in mind that won't be satisfied by baser metals."

"Hmm," said Marrinek, "I might make do with gold for the time being. Silver I already have." He patted his purse.

"Ah. Sir might find, if sir is counting on using the local shillings for his supply of silver, that the quality is rather low. The mint has cut the silver content in our coins to reduce the cost and the material is hardly better than copper for most purposes."

"In which case I'll take a pound of lead for the moment. I'll be heading north tomorrow and I don't want to be carrying gold with me. Wrap those things for me, if you would, and I will be on my way."

Marrinek paid, gathered his purchases, nodded his thanks to Smyth and stepped out of the shop.

A little further down the street Marrinek found a stall selling leather goods. Almost on impulse he bought a wide belt, a large canvas backpack with tough leather fittings and straps, a wide-brimmed hat and a pair of gloves. He stuffed his new possessions, his purchases from Smyth and his bundled sword into the new backpack and slung the whole lot over his shoulder.

At the corner of the street he ducked into a bakery and bought a couple of loaves of bread and some fruit buns. From the shop opposite he bought a large piece of cheese, a brace of long spicy sausages, a bag of apples and some sort of meat wrapped in a heavy pastry. The food went into the bag alongside his other kit.

He paused to get his bearings then headed down an alley that should take him toward river. A twist took him on a narrower, darker path between overhanging buildings and he realised he may have taken a wrong turn.

There were fewer people here and more shadows and Marrinek wasn't entirely surprised when someone stepped out in front of him and waved a knife in his face.

"Your money and your bag. Don't make a fuss," said the shadow, "there's a good boy."

Marrinek could feel the few people who had been visible in doorways or at the ends of the alley melting into buildings or back to the streets. He risked a glance over his shoulder - there were two more figures behind him, figures that were now looming, rather than melting.

"Right, right, but I don't have much." Marrinek held up his left hand then hooked the strap of the bag from his shoulder and threw it down on the ground between them. Then he shuffled the staff around till it rested on his shoulder before fishing in his pocket with his free hand.

"Please, just take it," he said, pulling his purse from inside his shirt and tossing it toward the man in front of him, who moved quickly to snatch it from the air.

But not as quickly as Marrinek, who swung his staff over-arm and brought the end down hard on the mugger's shoulder. There was a loud snap of breaking bone and the would-be mugger was driven to his knees, his knife forgotten, his face turning white with shock.

Marrinek stepped smartly forward and kneed his would-be assailant in the face, snapping his head back and knocking him to the ground. Turning, Marrinek got his right hand on the staff then thrust wildly at the nearer of the two figures who had come up behind him. The end of the staff caught him full in the face and blood splashed across the man's face. The man dropped his knife and staggered backward, clutching at his broken nose as blood streamed down his chin and between his fingers.

The third man was big, well over six feet tall, and came forward hefting a long knife and trying to get close enough to use it. Marrinek stepped back then set his feet and moved the staff to mid guard to catch blade of the giant's knife as it swung down. The staff flashed back to catch the giant's jaw, snapping his head round, then Marrinek stepped back and swung the staff in a great arc, bringing it down hard on the giant's head.

Marrinek stepped past the falling giant and struck the second man again, snapping ribs and driving him to the floor. He turned quickly back to the first mugger, who was struggling to his knees, and pointed the staff at him.

"I think I'll take your purse. Pass it over."

The mugger struggled to find his purse then threw it toward Marrinek, all thoughts of resistance washed away by the pain in his shoulder. Marrinek retrieved his backpack then took the mugger's knife and purse from the dirt and found his own purse in the gutter, then looked down at the mugger still trying to get to his feet.

"Broken collarbone, possibly a broken shoulder blade. You should get that looked at. Now fuck off."

He gestured at the man with his staff and waited till he was standing, then jerked forward as if he was going to strike again.

"Aargh," said the mugger, as he fell back against the wall of the house behind him. He staggered back upright and stumbled off down the alley, glancing anxiously over his shoulder as Marrinek watched him go.

Marrinek turned back to the other two. The big man was obviously dead, head caved in and twisted to an unnatural angle. Marrinek ran his hands over the big man's coat and relieved him of his purse and a thin knife, stuffing both into his bag. The other man was sitting against the alley wall, bleeding heavily from his broken nose and taking shallow breaths. He'd never win prizes for beauty again but Marrinek couldn't bring himself to care.

As he turned to go, someone moved back along the alley where he'd entered from the street and Marrinek looked up sharply. Jenkins' stable boy was standing there, watching with his mouth open. Marrinek snarled at him and the boy ran off between the buildings, ducking quickly around the corner. Marrinek let him go, checked he had all his things then walked off in the other direction.

He moved quickly now despite the burning in his arms and the terrible exhaustion, sticking to the main streets and heading back toward the town walls. Drawing attention by killing muggers had not been part of the plan and it wasn't going to be long before someone came looking for him. He headed for the river; it was time to leave town.

Marrinek wandered the bank of the river looking for a barge to take him downstream to Vensille. Following the meandering river would be slow but it would give him time to plan and to think and in any case without a horse he had no real alternatives.

The river Guiln was already wide and slow by the time it reached Catshed. The wharves and docks, which all lay on the eastern bank of the river, were busy with barges unloading their cargoes and taking on new goods to be carried. Most would go downstream to Vensille, some would head upstream toward Riverbridge and the wild northern lands beyond.

Marrinek bought beer and roast meat from a stall overlooking the river and stood there for a few minutes watching the traffic and the trading. In an Imperial town, the trade would be regulated and controlled by the local customs officials but here everything happened informally at the wharf. Local merchants bought, sold and negotiated without a care for tax or tariffs and money changed hands quickly. It was busy and hot and noisy; Marrinek loved it.

He finished the heavily spiced roast meat - goat maybe, but it was difficult to tell - and threw the bone into the gutter. The wharves were busy with barges large and small, some carrying passengers, most taking only cargo. Marrinek pushed himself away from the wall and walked down to a barge that was just preparing to cast off from the wharf, having loaded cargos of seasoned hardwood and dried meat.

Marrinek hailed the man at the rudder.

"You heading to Vensille? Got room for a passenger?"

The man gave him a long look then nodded.

"Come aboard. Stand over there while we cast-off. There'll be a price and we've no cabins for passengers so you'll have to sleep on the roof."

"That suits me fine."

Marrinek threw his pack onto the roof of the barge and stepped across the narrow gap from the wharf. He stood there as the small crew cast-off the mooring lines, raised the sail and made ready to depart. With long poles, they slowly pushed the barge away from the wharf and out into the river then the wind filled the sail and they slid gracefully downstream.

"I'm Trant," said the barge master once they had passed beyond the walls of Catshed, "and that's my mate, Shaff." He pointed at the woman working the tiller at the end of the barge.

"Much obliged," said Marrinek, "is there anything you need me to do?"

Trant looked at him, eyes narrowed against the sun.

"You know boats any?" he asked. Marrinek shook his head.

"Not really, no. I've been to sea but only as a, ah, passenger."

"Then just keep out the way o' the crew and mind what they tell you," said Trant before he stalked off along the barge.

Marrinek spent most of the day sitting on the roof watching the countryside as they floated serenely along the river. Once underway the crew busied themselves with minor tasks but by early evening the Master was happy and the crew made themselves comfortable on the foredeck. Marrinek ate alone on the roof, ignored by everyone else on the vessel, listening to the crew laughing and joking as they took turns to pilot the barge.

Around mid-afternoon, with Catshed firmly behind them and no visible signs of pursuit, Marrinek took up his staff and opened the roll of charming tools. Traditional charm-maker's tools were named after their shapes and sizes and these were no different. The five tools had their names inscribed along their lengths; Needle, Quill, Twig, Chisel and Blunt.

Now that he had time, tools and resources he could work on the staff. He turned it around, examining the wood. The ash was plain, a bit mucky from walking through the town, scarred and marked from the tools and weapons it had encountered.

He took the staff in one hand and picked up the largest tool, Blunt, in the other. Then he closed his eyes and concentrated on the wood until he could see the grain and feel and understand its underlying biological structure. He focussed power through Blunt - and the feeling of charmed power flowing freely and uninhibited after so many months of imprisonment and restriction was intoxicating - and with deft touches he began to alter the very fabric of the wood itself, giving it the strength and resilience of high-grade steel and subtly altering its shape to better fit his hands and purpose.

As the power flowed and Blunt roved over its surface, the wood shifted and twisted as Marrinek played with its basic physical properties, thinning here, thickening there, lengthening a little, hardening everywhere. The bottom end he drew into a short, cone and hardened even further, pouring in power until the tip was tough enough to dent stone.

He fixed the imperfections in the wood's structure, addressed the weaknesses that might have caused the staff to break or fracture, straightened the slight kink two-thirds of the way along its length, smoothed the tool marks left by knife and the impact damage done by fighting. He tuned the wood to his touch, irrevocably linking the weapon to his hand; for him, and for him alone, it would feel barely half its true weight, allowing him to spin, strike and block, faster and harder than anyone would expect. For other talented practitioners, the staff would feel unnaturally heavy and would be impossible to wield effectively; the untalented would feel nauseous if they got too close to the staff and most would not even be able to touch it.

The final touch, as dusk darkened towards evening, was to change the staff's colour to a deep, dark green and to give the surface a gentle shine. Eventually he surfaced from his work, releasing Blunt from its labours and stretching his cramped fingers and arms. The staff lay in the last of the evening sun, a different shape and colour, tougher and harder than any natural wood, stronger and more robust than any steel.

As evening became night the master emerged from his cabin and lamps were lit fore and aft and amidships. In their pale glow the barge continued slowly down the wide river, following the light from another barge some way ahead. Marrinek shifted toward the front of the boat so that he sat in the light of one of the lamps. There he ate a second lonely meal before working again through the staff-fighting forms.

Sometime around midnight the barge finally drew up at a small quay alongside other river boats. The crew tied up, dropped the sail and, in minutes, everything was calm. All the lamps were extinguished except the one under which Marrinek, alone again now that the crew had retired, still sat at the front of the barge, cross-legged with his staff before him.

He stretched his neck and unpacked his tools again to begin the next stage of work on the staff. First, he took four of the foot-long rods of iron and used Blunt to join them into a single, continuous length. Then he picked up Twig and began to work his way along the rod, chipping away imperfections just as he had done with the wood of the staff until he had a perfectly straight, clean, smooth piece of featureless iron.

He switched back to Blunt and focussed more power

into the rod, changing its shape to elongate it into a thin wand almost as long as the staff. He checked the length against the wood then switched to Needle, the smallest of the five tools. Starting at one end of the iron he began to focus power through the tool, directing it to alter the structure of the iron in a particular way. After an hour's work, he was happy with the structure of the metal at one end of the wand; in ways he couldn't quite explain the new metal just felt right and he knew that it would work the way he needed it to work.

He picked up Blunt again and paused, preparing himself to channel the prodigious quantities of power that were necessary for the next stage of the job. He placed Blunt against the patterned end of the wand and balanced the far end on the railing of the barge, pointing out across the river towards the trees on the far bank. Then he took a deep breath and began to push huge quantities of power into the tool. Nothing happened for several seconds except that the tool grew rapidly hotter but as the power built the iron started to hum and then, suddenly, there was a whoosh and a boom burst across the river, shattering the peace of the night.

Marrinek dropped the now hot charm and splashed water on the singed skin of his hand; his hands were tough, calloused from long work with sword, staff and charm, but any longer and he'd have suffered a serious burn. He smiled to himself, inspecting the wand under the light of the lamp as the crew and master boiled up onto the deck, shouting to each other and trying to work out what was going on.

The crews of the other barges were also awake and lamps were being lit across the vessels tied up at the small wharf. Eventually, with no sign of death or danger, the crews went back to bed and quiet descended again on the river.

The master gave Marrinek a filthy look before descending the stairs to the lower deck having clearly decided that his passenger was at the heart of whatever was going on.

Marrinek waited until all was quiet and then ran his hand over the wand, inspecting his work. The iron, still smooth to the touch, now had an intricate pattern spiralling along its surface; it was no longer recognisable as the raw iron he had bought in Catshed and in the pale light from the lamps it almost seemed more liquid than metal. Satisfied, he set it down on the floor, trapping it under his leg so that it couldn't roll away.

He turned back to the staff itself, holding it in both hands and focussing his will upon it, concentrating until he could see the grain and understand the very nature of the wood. He used Quill to open the staff, working the wood to create a channel along the length of the staff. Into this he placed the iron so that one end was flush with the top of the staff and the other finished maybe eight inches from the pointed end. Then he worked Quill again to bind the iron to the wood, leaving the channel open to the night air.

At the bottom of the staff he fashioned another chamber into which he fitted the lead, stretching and sculpting it so distribute its weight as evenly as possible in the lower portion of the staff. Then he sliced the lead into a dozen pieces, flowing the wood between them so that each was separated from its neighbours.

He paused and stretched his neck and back to relieve some of the aches he had accrued from too long sitting on the deck of the barge. It had been a long time since he had worked like this and the effort was taking its toll. He shook his head and picked up the copper wire and the switch units, turning them over in his hands as he stared at the iron wand now embedded in the ash.

It took Marrinek another hour to build the switch circuit that linked the lead that would form the power reservoir to the iron wand. The copper wire was fiddly to work in the dim light of the lamp and Marrinek struggled to hold his temper as he worked the soft metals. Eventually, he managed to get everything connected so that both the switch units and the slide panels were mounted almost flush to the surface of the wood where they would fall easily under his fingers as he held the staff.

Satisfied that the circuit was good, he used Twig to close the channel, burying the copper wires, the wand and the reservoir within the wood, forcing the wood to flow seamlessly so that its natural grain was restored and only a small amount of the lead was still visible.

Then he used Twig to shape the copper ingots, pulling them into two long thin plates, each a foot long and half an inch wide. He laid these carefully on the floor then used Quill to open two narrow channels in the surface of the staff, one near the lower end, just above the point where the iron rod ended, and a second two-thirds of the way up the staff.

He laid each of the copper plates into a channel, one after another, using more copper wire to link the plates back to the reservoir, then he used Quill to bring the wood back, closing the gaps and securing the plates. More power flowed and the copper changed, just a little, to protect it from the effects of water and sweat and dirt. Then he changed focus to toughen the metal, working until it was more like hard steel than soft copper. He rapped the transformed copper with Quill and nodded to himself, grinning quietly in the dark. Then Quill closed the gaps in the wood and sealed the plates in the surface.

He stretched again and ate some more bread. The night

was quickly passing and if he didn't finish soon he would still be working when dawn arrived. He sighed and picked up the length of fine copper netting, wrapping it gently over the surface of the staff and joining the ends so that it formed a continuous sleeve stretching from one end to the other and broken only by the plates, the switch units and the slide panels.

Tired now, and with the start of a headache forming behind his eyes, Marrinek stretched his fingers and picked up Needle, focussing small amounts of power into the tool to open the wood beneath the wire of the copper net. He worked his way steadily along the staff from top to bottom, opening tiny channels in the wood, pushing in the copper net, checking that it was surrounded fully by wood, then closing the channels to seal the staff.

At the bottom end of the staff he used more of the copper wire to link the net to the reservoir and, as he did so, the weapon finally began to come alive. With no further effort, the copper net began to drag power from the atmosphere and dump it into the reservoir.

"Excellent," murmured Marrinek, grinning to himself despite his fatigue. He picked up Quill again and closed the last of the channels and the gap above the reservoir, sealing the staff completely.

He paused again, running his hands along the length of the staff, feeling the transformed ash and copper, learning the shape of the wood and the position of the plates and switches. He played with the slide panels, checking that they worked smoothly and that he could find them quickly and without looking. Then he took up Quill and focussed more power into the tool, running it along the length of the staff again and again, making ever smaller tweaks and changes until he was satisfied with the finish.

Finally, with everything now enclosed and working and solid, he worked Twig the length of the staff once more to check the hardening and to make sure there were no flaws in the tuning. Then he put down the tools and again ran his fingers over the surface of the staff, checking that the wood was completely sealed and thoroughly hardened.

At last happy with the staff, at least for the moment, he packed away the tools and stretched again. Then he kicked off his boots and removed his shirt and stood on the roof of the barge with his eyes closed. He hefted the staff in his hands, checking the way that it sat and the feel of the switches and the copper plates beneath his fingers, then silently he worked the staff-fighting forms he had learnt as a child.

For two hours, he moved smoothly from low-guard to mid-guard to high-guard, flowing through the strikes, thrusts and lunges that made the short staff such a dangerous weapon. His months of captivity had slowed and weakened his body and by the end of his practise he was sweating heavily, wearier by far than he had expected but also happier and more content than he had been for months.

Sitting once more on the roof, Marrinek laid the staff across his knees. It wasn't yet finished but even now he could feel the potential beneath its skin as the lead power reservoir absorbed the energy that the copper net was pulling from the atmosphere. Lead was a reasonable material for a reservoir and could absorb a lot of power but gold or iridium would hold vastly more.

For now, though, there was nothing more he could do. He ran his fingers over the surface one last time, then repacked his bag and lay down to sleep.

By the time he woke, the sun was up and the barge was

already making good progress down the river. The overnight rest stop was out of sight and the master was at the wheel, guiding the barge to one side of the river to allow a faster vessel to pass.

"Even a blind man could see you're not a regular traveller. What brings you out this way?" asked the master.

Marrinek stood and stretched as he considered his answer.

"I'm looking for my brother. Last anyone heard, he was heading for Vensille, so that's where I'm going."

"Big place, Vensille. Hard to find someone amongst all those people, 'less you know where to look, of course. He from the Empire, like you?"

"Was it the accent?" asked Marrinek.

"Aye. Had you pegged as soon as you opened your mouth. Might be easier to find a foreigner but a lot of folk in Vensille got no love for your Emperor. They might spill blood, given the chance. You any good with that staff you carry?"

"I can swing it around a bit, if I have to."

"Well, keep it handy, that'd be my advice. Might be you never have any trouble, if you stay in the decent parts of town, but unless you've got a load of silver you ain't showing my guess is you'll be sleeping in less friendly quarters."

"How long till we reach Vensille?"

The master look at the sun, gauging the time.

"Tomorrow, around dusk, all being well. We should get to the locks tomorrow afternoon and as long as there aren't too many boats going through we should be tied up and enjoying the pleasures of the city before sunset."

Marrinek nodded.

"Good. Wake me if anything interesting happens." And

he laid back on the roof of the barge, folded the hood of his coat over his eyes and went to sleep.

Marrinek woke around midday and ate a little more food. Then he spent most of the afternoon exercising, desperately chasing away the demons of captivity by working the forms with his staff.

He slept again in the late afternoon then woke, hungry, as the sun sank toward the horizon, and pulled the rest of his food from his bag. He finished the bread then nibbled the cheese down to the hard rind before tossing the last of it over the boat's low rail into the river and watching it slip below the surface. Then he pulled out a length of sausage he'd picked up on the quayside in Catshed and began to munch, staring out at the farmland laid out across land beyond the riverbank.

"I know that look, son," said Trant, sitting down beside him, "you're running away from something and you're not sure if you're doing the right thing."

Marrinek glanced at the old man, surprised that he should demonstrate such perception and suddenly worried about what else he might have seen.

"Aye, don't you worry, 'tis no business of mine. Sometimes a man just needs someone to talk to, someone who can hear his tale without judging."

Marrinek took another bite of sausage then offered it to Trant.

"No, thanks. That stuff they make in Catshed don't agree with my belly. I prefer proper Vensille sausages. They make sausages in that city like you've never seen before. I swear, the gods themselves would beg for the merest morsel, if they ever tasted a real Vensille sausage."

"I didn't always live like this," said Marrinek quietly, staring forlornly at the sausage, "I had the best food, fine wines, people to fetch and carry for me, beautiful homes to live in and a wife to love."

"Sure. And you gave it all away? Chose to walk the highways earning money as, well, as whatever you are?"

Marrinek sighed and tossed the sausage down on his bag, no longer hungry.

"No, I didn't give it away. It was taken, stolen, by a man I called friend. He destroyed me. Took my liberty, my reputation, my property and my wife. Everything except my life and even that he reduced to a pale shadow of its former self." Trant heard the bitterness and coughed.

"You're not joshing? You had all that and lost it? How?"

"I don't rightly know. I got fucked, that's about all I know for sure, royally fucked."

"Aye, well. I know how that feels, right enough," said Trant, nodding sympathetically.

Marrinek looked sideways at him then shook his head.

"Not like this you don't, not like this."

"Don't you believe it," said Trant with some passion, "I wasn't always a broken down old man with nothing but a ragged old boat and a crew of three. I was a ship's captain. The Undaunted Ardour, she was called. Beautiful ship. Sleek and fast. Gorgeous. I used to trade along the coast and across the sea. Spice, alcohol, silks. You name it, I carried it. And I was good at it, too. Never once did we get caught by the Excise men or by pirates. Too fast, too careful." Trant sighed and took a slug from his hip flask then passed it to Marrinek.

"That's good stuff," said Marrinek through gritted teeth as he handed the flask back. He wiped his hand across his mouth.

"So what went wrong? Gambling? Alcohol? A woman?"

Trant took another pull on the flask and grimaced.

"Nothing like that. Could have understood all that, enjoyed it as it was happening, even. But no, weren't like that at all. I had a partner. Known him all my life, best friend a man could ever want. He handled all the dockside stuff in Vensille, managed the warehouse, the deals, everything. Then one day he just ups and leaves, disappears into the wilderness, doesn't even tell his wife where he's going. Turns out the company had some pretty big debts by then, debts he hadn't told me about. God knows how, but all the money went with him, every last penny. I docked in Vensille, hold full of scented oils, wine, spices and liquor, and these people just storm up the gangplank with the Watch and throw me off the ship. Tell me they've got a court order to seize everything on board for payment of debts."

"And that was it? that was the end?"

"Like fuck it was. Fought 'em, I did. Spent two years arguing and fighting and arguing again. Took it right to the Duke, in the end, argued my case. Lawyers' fees took everything I'd saved. My wife left, took the kids with her, said I was obsessed. And she was right. I couldn't let it go, had to get my ship back. Didn't, of course, and by the time I realised it weren't going to happen I'd spent almost everything I had and borrowed more than was sensible. By the time I stopped, it was all I could do to get a place as crew on a river boat."

Marrinek shook his head and took another swallow from the flask.

"Very sad. Nothing like as bad as my tale but still sad."

Trant wasn't listening. He took the flask back, drained it and stuffed it into his shirt.

"Twenty-five years I spent hating my former partner.

Looking for him, never forgetting what he'd done and how he'd destroyed my life. Twenty-five wasted, stupid years."

"Did you ever find him?"

"Well, yes, as it happens. Ran into him in a bar in some godforsaken town up near the mountains, miles from the sea and from this fucking river."

He paused to spit over the side of the boat.

"He was drinking. Almost didn't recognise him without his hair and with his beard so grey it was almost white. But those eyes. I'd have known them anywhere and he recognised me just as quick as I recognised him. And he knew he'd done me wrong but there was no escape. I went straight over and smacked him between the eyes, knocked him right back off his seat. Made a real noise, stopped everything in the place. I'd have killed him there and then, had my knife out ready to do it, but somehow he managed to get back to his feet and he hit me right back. Never knew he had it in him."

Marrinek picked up the sausage again and took another bite. It looked like Trant was settling in for a long tale.

"That surprised me so much I dropped the knife and fell back onto a table, knocked everything flying. That was about the end of it, far as I remember. I woke up later that day in the town gaol, just me and my partner in the cell. Seems the watch arrested us for brawling, so we got a good opportunity to talk."

"Awkward," said Marrinek, "but still not really like my situation."

"No, well, maybe not. Still, we got to talking. Nothing else to do and twenty-five years of living to catch up on. I shouted a good deal at first, ranted even, and he just let me get it out of my system. Then, when I subsided, he just told me what really happened."

"What really happened? You mean he hadn't stolen the money?"

"Oh yes, he'd stolen the money all right, every last penny. Then he'd mortgaged his house, the warehouse, the ship, everything. Borrowed everything he could, liquidated all our assets, and given it all to some fucker called Tlome."

Marrinek blinked, surprised.

"He gave it away? Why?"

"Turns out I'd made an enemy, somewhere. Hadn't even realised it at the time but this mad bastard took offence at something."

Trant waved his hand and scowled.

"Don't matter now, not important even if I could remember. The point is that he came looking for me, in Vensille, him and his people. They couldn't find me 'cos I was at sea but they found my partner, found him and squeezed, squeezed so hard he had no choice. Tlome took the money, left behind a promise to kill me if he ever caught up with me, then left.

"And then when the banks came looking for payment my partner had nothing to give them. His only hope was that I would turn up before the debts came due but I'd found myself a woman, down the coast, and was enjoying some personal time."

Trant paused and shook his head.

"Not proud of that, gorgeous though she was, not proud at all. But for that, I would've been back in time to make the first payment. We might have worked something out, found a solution, turned things around. But no, I was thinking with my cock again and this time I'd fucked us all."

"So your partner wasn't to blame?"

"Nope. Completely innocent, fucked over by my offence and then screwed again by my fucking around. He couldn't pay the debts and only just managed to get out of Vensille ahead of his creditors. They had him formally exiled so he couldn't ever go back. By the time I arrived home, the story was that he'd taken the loans and done a runner with the cash. Nobody ever knew about Tlome."

Marrinek whistled and shook his head again.

"That's a sad, sad tale."

"It is what it is. No use dwelling on the past, however bad it was. Better to forgive and forget, although if I ever meet Tlome I'll gut him and feed him to the fish. Even got a description - tall, dark-skinned, tattoos - just in case."

Trant stood up and looked out over the river.

"You've gotta be grateful for what you've got. You're alive, safe and fed. What more could you ask for?" Then he ambled off down the deck to check on the crew.

Marrinek sat there thinking and chewing on the remains of the sausage. His situation was different, of course. Arrested, imprisoned, tortured, drugged. Of course it was different.

Only he couldn't help but think about Trant's partner, a man manoeuvred into ill deeds and misfortune by a malevolent third party. Could he have been the victim of something similar? No, it was ridiculous.

But then he'd known Tentalus all his life; was it really possible that his friend could have betrayed him? Marrinek shook his head. If not Tentalus then who? No, it must have been him. Nothing else made sense, nothing else explained what had happened.

Except. Marrinek couldn't shake the feelings of doubt that now assailed him. He'd never really thought about it in this way before. What if his position was more like Trant's than he knew? What if Tentalus had been tricked or deceived? It was impossible, surely?

But the more he thought about it, the less impossible it seemed. The evening was warm but Marrinek sat and shivered at the implications. His arrest had always felt strange, rushed, desperate even, especially as he knew he'd done nothing wrong. He just couldn't believe that Tentalus would have moved against him without strong evidence but that meant...

Marrinek swallowed nervously as he ground his way down this new path of thought. Could he have been wrong? Two years locked in a cell with little to no contact with anyone except his gaolers had given him a somewhat warped perspective; what if that perspective was wrong? What if Tentalus hadn't moved against him, at least not in the way it had seemed? What if there was someone else pulling the strings and Tentalus was just the tool to remove Marrinek?

He turned that thought over and over, unable to think of anything else. The only thing that explained all the facts, such as they were, was a conspiracy against both him and Tentalus, playing one against the other in a game that neither of them had spotted.

Marrinek sat there a long time, thinking it through, until, finally, he decided that Trant was right. Their stories were similar. He had been fucked over by person or persons unknown. He'd lost everything as a result, he was now convinced, of someone's scheming.

He was properly angry now, angry like he hadn't been in years, angry enough to burn down the world to find the truth.

And scared. The fear came suddenly, a familiar feeling of cold dread and worry. Where was Adrava? What had happened to her when he had been arrested? Was she alive, imprisoned, on the run? He didn't know, couldn't know, and there was no way to find out, not without contacting someone inside the Empire.

Contact meant danger but Marrinek had faced death before. He stood up and paced the deck, full of outraged, indignant energy.

For the first time in months he thought of something beyond his own revenge, someone other than himself. Tentalus was in danger, it was the only possible explanation, and out here, poor and ill-equipped, far from home and branded a traitorous criminal, there was nothing Marrinek could do.

Adrava too was out there somewhere and his soul yearned to be with her again.

He bit down hard on those thoughts, drove them away with his new-found anger, forced himself to focus on the present.

His wife was lost, beyond help for the time-being and he could only hope that she had survived. She was tough, far tougher than he was. Yes, he decided, Adrava would be out there somewhere, waiting for him.

He might not be able to help Tentalus either, not right now, but he could consider, he could plan, he could scheme and build.

And then, when he was ready, he would return to the Empire, find his wife, help his friend and bring down upon his enemies the most complete revenge he could conjure.

He stood there, alone on the deck as the crew settled down for the night, and swore a silent oath of vengeance, swore it in the most terrible terms he could imagine, swore it to every god and spirit that might be listening. And now that sense of purpose burned within him and he could barely sit for the need to be doing something.

Finally, it was time to go to work.

7

M arrinek sat on the roof of the barge as Vensille came into view. He whistled quietly, impressed despite himself, and stared around, taking in the view.

Where Catshed had been a town - small and provincial - Vensille was a city, proud and mighty. Over the last couple of miles, the banks of the river had grown steadily busier with jetties, wharfs, houses and other small buildings. A huge slum of rough wooden shacks filled the banks, right up to the walls of the city.

Tall towers sat on either bank, topped with crenellations and flying pennants and flags proclaiming the city's independence and heritage. The walls curved out from the towers to sweep along the bank to where a second pair of towers, even larger and taller than the first, looked down at the river and out towards the northern hills.

Sloped stone jetties stuck out from the base of the bank-side towers towards a third tower, broader than both its neighbours, that stood in the middle of the river itself. Ships and barges were slowly funnelled along the river through these artificially narrowed and regularly dredged channels.

Every vessel that entered or left the city at the River Gate could be stopped, boarded and inspected by the city authorities.

Marrinek scanned the towers, looking for weaknesses that might be exploited by an invading force. Then he shook his head to remind himself that this city wasn't a target, that his former life was over, that he had to find a new way to live.

It was clear that this was no provincial town but instead a major city with the wealth, determination and ability to defend itself. The city's fortifications were formidable and Marrinek could see no obvious points of attack for a conventional force. Even Imperial Shock Troops armed with powered weapons and charmed armour would find it difficult to assault and breach the walls, especially if the towers were manned by experienced troops.

And it wasn't just the size of the walls and the placement of the towers that gave the fortifications their strength - the stone itself had been dressed and worked so that the structures were as strong as possible. The stones weren't simply mortared together as they would have been in a normal wall. Instead they flowed seamlessly from base to turret, as if the towers had simply grown from the bedrock, pushing their way through clay and soil to form a continuous chain of defence around the city.

The technique, stone-flowing, was easy enough if you had the right tools, enough power, plenty of time and an affinity with stone. The stone masons would build the walls as normal - large outer blocks with a core of rubble and muck and timber - but they would use no mortar between the stones.

The outer face of each block might only be roughly shaped but the touching faces would have been cut to fit as closely as possible with their neighbours. Once in position, a Stone Mage would use a broad crafting tool to focus power on the stone, causing the surfaces to shift and flow and melt before settling into the required shape. Stone, with its relatively simple crystalline structure, was much easier to shape than wood but work like this still took a great deal of time and power.

Marrinek shook his head in wonder at the amount of effort that had gone into the construction of these towers and walls. It truly was an exceptional piece of work.

And they hadn't stopped at the surface joins. Running his hands over the stone of the jetty as the barge waited in line for inspection, he could tell that each stone had been completely joined to its neighbours. There was no mortar anywhere in the structure and there were no gaps between the blocks. In a very real sense, the jetties, towers and walls were a single piece of stone.

Marrinek whistled under his breath as he calculated the time that might be required to encircle the city with even a simple wall - a decade at least, even with several teams of masons and mages working flat out - and this was far from a simple design.

The walls were twenty yards high if they were an inch and topped with hoardings to shelter fighting men from a besieging force. Tall towers sprang from the wall every hundred paces or so and the gatehouses were taller still, with overhanging parapets and murder holes.

Low walls ran along the jetties and the stone mages had taken the simple structures and enhanced them, opening windows and gates, hardening the surfaces of the stone against frost and roots and attack. They had created gutters and gargoyles and shaped elegant windows. Even the platforms that supported the roofs and hoardings were made from shaped stone, called forth from the walls and finished with a beautiful attention to detail.

The tower in the centre of the river had been made the same way with great buttresses to withstand the flow of the river. It was a reminder, if one was needed, that the skills to shape rock and stone existed outside the Empire, as well as within. Marrinek had heard descriptions of the walls of Vensille but he'd never believed them. Now, he stared in awed wonder at the scale of the works.

As the barge drew level with the customs post Marrinek slid his staff behind the rail at the edge of the roof where he was sitting; he didn't want to attract too much attention and a power-formed staff could easily invite unwelcome questions. A bored customs official in a shiny breastplate and carrying the embossed warrant baton of his office came aboard as the crew tied up at the inspection jetty.

"Good afternoon, Master Trant," said the official, shaking hands with the master as he stepped onto the deck, "what are you carrying today?"

"Sergeant Durk, as I live and breathe. How are you?"

The two men shook hands as the sergeant stepped onto the barge.

"What is it today, Trant? Weevil-infested flour again?"

Trant looked insulted.

"Sergeant, that was just the once and you know it was good when I loaded it. No, today I have dried meat from Catshed - their speciality spiced goat sausages - and planks of cedar for the Duke's new ballroom; would you like to see?"

Durk seemed dubious but he dutifully looked at the stack of wood to which the master pointed.

"For the Duke, you say? Got any paperwork?"

"Certainly," said the master, producing a leather folio

from a cupboard in the wheelhouse and fishing out an order, "six hundred planks, twelve foot by one, to be delivered in four batches, first batch of one hundred and fifty due tomorrow. I'm to deliver them to Hopkins, who'll take them to the Palace."

The official inspected then handed back the paper.

"Fine, you know the way," said Durk, waving him through, "usual charge."

The master paid from his belt purse.

"Thanks, we'll be on our way," he said, turning to the crew, "cast off, head for Hopkins' Wharf."

As the barge nudged along the inspection channel and back onto the river Marrinek stared again at the towers. The island in the middle of the river supported a second tower a hundred yards downstream, beyond which the real city began. There were matching towers on either bank and high walls linked these towers and their upstream neighbours.

Together, these six towers controlled access to the city and saw everything that came down the river. Someone had gone to a lot of trouble to devise a system of defences that might withstand a river-borne attack. To Marrinek, that suggested a certain paranoia on the part of the Duke and his advisors.

The city itself slid into view as the barge moved past the second set of towers and the walls themselves. Both banks were lined with wharves and jetties and Marrinek looked around with sudden interest. Tall warehouses flanked the river on both sides, fighting for space with pubs and manufactories. Between the buildings were the dry docks and slipways of boat builders and the poles and walks of rope makers.

Dozens of river barges were docked or manoeuvring around the wharves. Scores of smaller boats traversed the river carrying passengers and goods across the slow-moving waters or from shore to vessel. Ahead, leaping over the wide river in long, elegant arches, was a tall bridge that separated the seaport from the river wharves.

Where the buildings of Catshed had squatted low and wooden, Vensille was stretched tall and much of it was built from brick and stone with slate or tile roofs. All the buildings along the eastern bank, where the barge finally tied up at a jetty between a pair of short-masted northern trading ships, stood five or more stories tall, great towers of timber and brick.

The embanked wharves swarmed with people and animals. The noise and smell, after a peaceful river voyage and months of solitary confinement, were overwhelming. Marrinek stood watching the bustle from the roof of the barge, taking it all in. Then he grinned. This was definitely the city for him. He collected his staff and pack and walked over to the master.

"Four shillings we said," said Marrinek, handing over the money, "and can you recommend an inn? I need to sleep in a bed again and eat hot food."

"Try The Jewel of Vensille - it's just behind this warehouse," said Trant, pointing at a large building of dark stone, "and has a naked woman on a sign over the door. Ask for Phyllis - she'll look after you."

"Thanks, I'll do that. Any idea where I might get some work? Life's going to be tough if I can't find my brother."

Trant narrowed his eyes and looked thoughtful for a moment.

"I've got some ideas, a few contacts I can try, if you don't mind using that staff of yours. I'll talk to people, see what's around, send a message to you at The Jewel."

"Thanks, appreciate it. Good luck, Trant."

Marrinek nodded to the master then stepped up onto the rail of the barge, jumped down onto the wharf and threaded his way through the crowds, heading for The Jewel.

Marrinek found The Jewel of Vensille just as Trant had said he would but, to his mind, it was a jewel that had seen better days. Or possibly better decades. He stood for a moment on the street, watching the front of the building. There were a few patrons sitting on benches outside the pub and a couple of toughs lounging next to the door and looking over everyone who went in or out. Marrinek strolled up, nodded at the thugs and pushed open the door. It opened straight into the main lounge, a large, noisy, smoke-filled room of rough furniture and rougher patrons, where serving girls scuttled quickly between the hatchway and the tables.

Marrinek stood in the doorway for a few seconds, taking in the scene, then walked over to the counter and smiled at the woman standing behind it.

"Are you Phyllis? Master Trant suggested I try The Jewel for a room."

The woman looked him up and down.

"That old rogue Trant sent you, did he? Yes, I'm Phyllis. I have a room on the top floor under the eaves. You might need to watch your head on the rafters but it ought to do. How long will you stay?"

"Not sure. A few days, a week maybe. We'll see how things go. Which way?"

"Hold on. You'll need to pay in advance - it's sixpence a day plus tuppence for food, if you want it."

Marrinek flipped some coins onto the counter.

"That ought to cover it. I'll take whatever you've got in

the pot if you send up a plate to the room, plus a loaf of bread."

Phyllis scooped up the coins and pointed across the bar.

"Stairs are over there, just keep climbing till they run out Mr...?" She left the question dangling until Marrinek caught the hint.

"Bay. Call me Bay."

"Right. Well, there's only one door at the top and that's your room, Mr Bay. I'll send up some food. Let me know if there's anything else you need." Marrinek shifted his pack on his shoulder and nodded his thanks.

The room, when he reached it after climbing five flights of stairs, was large but, as Phyllis had said, low. It was also dark and it had an unpleasant organic smell that grew stronger towards the rafters; pigeons, Marrinek hoped.

A single bed took up most of one wall opposite a locked door. A bench and table were the only other furnishings. A shuttered window let in a little light but opening the shutters didn't improve the look of the room. It would do for a few days but nobody would want to live here for long, if they could avoid it.

Marrinek sighed and put his pack on the table, ruing his lost fortune. There had been a time, not that long ago, when he wouldn't have dreamed of staying in a place like this. For a moment he lost focus, dreaming of times gone by, then he clamped down on the thought and pushed it away, snarling. Those days were gone and he had work to do.

He sat down on the bed and eased off his boots so he could massage his feet while he planned his next steps. Money, that was key. He had enough for a couple more days of frugal living but nowhere near enough to get him home.

And once he'd thought about home he realised he was going to have to go back to Khemucasterill, sooner or later. He had no idea how that might be done but it was going to take plenty of money and a host of friends or allies. Would anyone be prepared to admit friendship with him before he had squared things with Tentalus? Would they even talk to him?

His thoughts were interrupted by a knock at the door, which opened to admit a grubby street boy.

"Phyllis sent me up. Old Ned wants to see you. You're to follow me."

Marrinek stared at him in surprise.

"Who the hell is Old Ned and why would I want to see him?"

The boy blinked at him.

"Old Ned at the Crown," he said, as if that explained anything, "by the river. It's a pub."

"Right. Thanks. Great." Marrinek sighed and rubbed his temples. This must be one of Trant's contacts so maybe it's an opportunity. He had hoped to eat and sleep before doing anything else but an early start might be better.

He pulled his boots back on and stamped them down, then he picked up staff and checked his knife. He looked at the sword then decided against taking it. Without knowing the local rules, carrying a long weapon was just too risky. He left it on the table with his pack.

"Right, let's go." As they tramped back down the stairs, they met a girl coming up with a tray of food.

"Is that for me?" asked Marrinek, "Leave it in my room but give me that loaf of bread - I'll eat as I walk."

Outside, the boy wove between the buildings and around stalls, heading back toward the wharves and then along the riverfront. Marrinek strode along behind, his staff rapping on the cobbles as he chewed his way through the loaf.

When they reached The Crown, the boy pointed to a table in the far corner.

"Ned's over there," he said, before disappearing into the crowd.

Marrinek made his way through the crowds of drinkers and when he reached the table there was a man sitting alone, a strange sight in the otherwise crowded room. It looked like he'd been there a long time.

"Old Ned, I presume?" said Marrinek, "My name is Bay. What can you do for me?"

"Well ain't you the voice of authority?" said Old Ned, looking him up and down, "Just you sit yourself down there, lad, and we'll see what's to be done." Marrinek took the seat opposite Old Ned, turning slightly so that his back was to the wall and he could see the whole of the common room. He rested his staff against the edge of the table.

"I hear from Trant that you might know how to use that stick. True?"

Marrinek gave him a sideways look, face blank.

"What of it? You looking for muscle?"

"Maybe, maybe. Or maybe I know a man who appreciates fighting skills, if you get my meaning. Someone who might be able to make use of a man of your talents. Interested?"

Marrinek sat back to buy himself time to think. His plans, always fluid, had not included falling in with a gang of thugs but, given his current status as an outlaw, maybe he should have thought of it sooner. And here was this old man just offering to introduce him to the sorts of low people he might be able to use. How useful. Marrinek gave a slight smile and nodded.

"I'm interested, if the offer's right. I'm between work at the moment, new to the town and I could use the money. But you already knew that. What did you have in mind?"

"I'll talk to a friend. You're staying at the Jewel?" Marrinek nodded again.

"I'll send word tomorrow," said Old Ned.

8

L ord Rudston Sterik, Governor of the prison island of Ankeron West, liked to believe that escape was impossible. He prided himself on the brilliance of the design, on the training of his staff and on the procedures he had implemented. Above all, he had faith in his own ability to manage and control the Empire's most dangerous prisoners within the Empire's most sophisticated prison.

Built to hold people that were too dangerous to be allowed to roam free but too talented simply to kill outright, the prison island of Ankeron West was the final resting place for those that the Empire wanted to forget. It was to this high, rocky island that the Empire sent noble traitors, those men and women who, from their high offices in Imperial society, had sought to climb still further and in so doing had become a threat to the Emperor himself.

Political manoeuvring and plotting were rife amongst the Empire's noble houses and they competed fiercely, but discretely, for rank and favour. This competition was actively encouraged by the Emperor because it occupied those involved and dissuaded them from pursuing more radical objectives, like a change of government.

Indeed, the Emperor himself was an avid player of the game, dispensing or revoking privileges to stifle an aggressive House, raise a new favourite or cool the ardour of others. By these methods, the nobles were prevented from growing too strong and the ambitions of their Houses were checked before they became dangerous. In this the Emperor was supported by various branches of Government, principally the Order of Kareeth, who answered only to him and were rumoured to go to great lengths to protect his interests.

Ankeron West, thirty miles off shore at the western edge of the Empire, was where the strongly talented ended up if they plotted against the Emperor or his Governors and lost. A forlorn island far from the capital, the chances of escape, rescue or reprieve were slim to non-existent. The grim and dusty road from the port to the prison was likely to be the last glimpse of the outside world that prisoners of Ankeron West would ever get.

The island itself had been chosen as the site for a prison precisely because the cliffs, currents and lack of beaches or bays made it difficult and dangerous to land anywhere other than the heavily fortified harbour. The Imperial engineers, skilled at working stone, had turned the single natural bay on the northern coast of the island from a modest seaside village into a monstrous temple to stone and suffering. They had added a working port to the modest harbour, constructing elegant stone jetties and encircling seawalls with space for six medium-sized transport or cargo vessels and a variety of smaller boats.

The naturally tight entrance to the bay had been enhanced with towers and a long narrow channel through which ships had to pass to reach the harbour or the open seas. The view from the sea was one of high walls and towers, watchful guards and forbidding cliffs.

No lights shone in the watch towers or on the seawall; ships arrived by day or they did not arrive at all. More than one had been lost on the rocks at the base of the cliffs or in the mouth of the harbour while trying to make port at night, sometimes running ahead of a storm and deciding that the risk was worth paying. Others had been sunk or dissuaded from running the channel by missiles hurled from engines mounted in the guard towers or on platforms high on the walls. Ships arriving at the mouth of the channel and wishing to gain peaceful entrance would drop anchor, raise flags indicating the purpose of their visit and await the arrival of a pilot to guide them to safety.

Surrounding the harbour was a fortress-like structure of walls and towers that controlled access from the town and the rest of the island. All traffic to the harbour went through a single gatehouse, allowing the prison Governor to close the port if he feared attack or, in the nightmare scenario, the escape of a prisoner. The small town that rose behind the harbour was itself surrounded by a second ring of walls and towers, manned to watch both the town and the surrounding countryside.

Not that there was much to see outside the walls. The sandy ground was broken by occasional low trees or shrubs and grazed by scrawny goats but it was mostly empty, a desolate wasteland in which few people lived. Only one road led out of the town, running first to the quarry that provided the island with its stone and then to the prison itself. This was the road along which convicts would make their last journey under open skies; it was rare, very rare, for a convict to leave the prison except to take the short ride to an unmarked grave just beyond the walls.

From the top of the gatehouse in the wall between harbour and town, Lord Sterik could see out over the seawalls to the open ocean. Today the sea was calm, a brilliant blue in the shallows around the island. The mainland was no more than a grey smear on the horizon. Sterik shifted his gaze from the sea - he found the ever-changing colours of the seascape enchanting - and looked again at the ships in the harbour; there was no doubt that the Gilded Branch was both absent and overdue.

The Gilded Branch was one of a pair of ships that transported prisoners from the mainland to Ankeron West. The cells on the transport ships, like those in the prison, were designed to hold talented convicts without allowing them to reach the underlying wood of the ship. Even that wasn't enough for the most powerful or ingenious convicts and often the guards resorted to drugs or violence to control their charges.

Could the ship have been hijacked by a prisoner? It had happened before, several times, when careless guards had failed to manage the convicts correctly. In one notable case, the crew had been paid by a prisoner's family to take their charge to safety along the coast. Sterik shuddered. It had been years since a transport ship had been lost that way and he didn't want to imagine the consequences of losing this one, given the passenger it had been carrying.

Abaythian Marrinek, former Lord Commander of the Imperial Shock Troop. Nobody knew much about his childhood except that he had lived on the streets of Esterengel, running with gangs until he and some friends had fallen into the hands of the city Watch at the age of about fourteen years. Imperial records of the time, subsequently sealed but released to Sterik when sentence had been pronounced, showed that Marrinek and one other

boy had avoided summary execution only by the intervention of a talented Watch captain called Leonard
Kyngeston.

Noticing that both the as-yet unnamed Marrinek and his
friend exhibited characteristics suggesting a strong latent
talent, Kyngeston had suggested to the magistrate that the
two boys be sent to the Imperial military college for testing
and training instead of to the execution yard behind the
court. The magistrate, himself somewhat talented and a
former soldier, had been sceptical but had agreed on condition that Kyngeston remain involved in their education for
at least the next three years.

Marrinek's admission to and progression through the
ranks of the Imperial Army was a matter of public record, a
grim story of talent, prejudice, success against stupendous
odds, hard work and leadership. His achievements while
serving in the army, particularly the capture of the fortress
city of Ironbarrow, had made him famous and rich and
given him influence far beyond what might normally be
expected of a former street urchin. His subsequent betrayal,
disgrace, capture and exile had shocked the Imperial Court.

Sterik shook his head and dragged his thoughts back to
the present. The Gilded Branch had left port a week ago and
should have docked three days ago, two at the latest. The
Captain and first mate were both talented men, formidable
individuals in their own right. If they hadn't been able to
guide the ship to port it was almost certainly because something had gone wrong and that raised the dreadful possibility that Marrinek might again be free.

If they were lucky - and Sterik snorted to himself about
the things he was now happy to call 'luck' - if they were
lucky Marrinek was dead and the ship was gone, lost in a
summer storm or sunk by pirates. The alternative was not

something Sterik wished to contemplate but that didn't mean he wasn't going to do something about it, just in case.

Sterik motioned to his deputy, Yiliwyn Curteys, who had been waiting patiently while the Governor watched the ocean.

"Take the Lady Jessica to the mainland and inform Administrator Nison that the Gilded Branch is overdue. Gather whatever news there might be and then return as soon as you can."

Curteys raised her eyebrow.

"You want me to go in person, my lord? My duties here..."

Sterik interrupted her with a wave of his hand.

"Can wait. Go in person, and go now. Nison is an administrator; speak to him in person, make him understand the severity of the situation. Make sure he sends a messenger to Esterengel immediately. I don't care if he sends an aug-bird or a courier or a cat in a basket as long as the news is sent on. And when you get back, if Marrinek is really free, we must look again at our security arrangements."

Curteys paused.

"Are you worried that Marrinek might attack the prison?" said Curteys, frowning at the thought.

Sterik smiled grimly and turned to face Curteys for the first time.

"I worry all the time. Paranoia is what keeps our 'guests' in their quarters and would-be rescuers on the mainland. Can you imagine the alternative?" Sterik shuddered, "Time enough for that when you return."

Curteys nodded.

"My lord." She turned to leave the roof of the gatehouse.

"One more thing," said Sterik, "if they tell you that Marrinek is dead then for pity's sake check the body. You met him, didn't you? If there's any doubt at all that the body is his then I want to know about it."

Curteys nodded again and closed the door behind her. Sterik waited until he saw Curteys appear on the street below, heading for the harbour with two guards in tow, then went downstairs himself. In the small office behind the guardroom on the first floor Sterik found his aide, Captain Armstrong Heneghan, reviewing permit requests for transit between the town and the island. Heneghan stood as Sterik entered the room.

"Good morning, my lord."

Sterik grimaced. He had always found Heneghan's perpetual good humour somewhat grating and today was worse than usual.

"Nothing good about this morning so far," mumbled Sterik. He dropped into the chair in the corner of the office and pinched the bridge of his nose. With his eyes still closed he said, "The Gilded Branch still hasn't arrived. Curteys is on her way to the mainland to share the good news and no ships are to enter the harbour until she returns. Talk to the harbour master, make sure he understands; if he admits any ship that isn't carrying Curteys I'll have him flensed."

"Yes, my lord, right away." Heneghan shuffled his papers nervously and paused, not moving from behind the desk, "What reason should I give the harbour master? I don't like to think what he might say if we disrupt the smooth operation of the harbour."

Sterik opened his eyes and looked up at Heneghan.

"Reason?" said Sterik, rather louder than he'd intended, "We're running a prison, not a free trade port. Get down there and close the harbour; no ships in or out until Curteys returns or I say otherwise. Is that clear?"

"Yes, my lord, perfectly clear. I'll make sure it happens."

Heneghan shuffled his papers again then dropped them on the desk, saluted quickly and hurried toward the door.

Sterik ran his fingers through his hair and thought about the island's security. Surely Marrinek, if he was still alive, wouldn't come here? Sterik wasn't sure but he hadn't become Governor of the Empire's most infamous prison by making unwarranted assumptions or by taking risks.

He stood and quickly checked his personal weapons. He was only lightly armed at the moment, carrying sword, knife and a few minor charms. If it came to a fight there was very little that Sterik would be able to do to hinder Marrinek but that would probably be true however he was armed. Sterik grinned to himself; he'd better make sure he was never in a position where he had to fight fair.

Sterik left the room and stalked down the corridors until he found the Captain of the Guard. Time to shake things up a little and make life difficult for unexpected visitors.

"Close the town gates, sound the general alarm." Captain Stillman Ayers, a seasoned veteran of the southern wars, looked up at Lord Sterik in surprise, then gestured to his lieutenant, who hurried from the room to issue the orders.

"I also want you to double the guard on the watch towers," Sterik continued, warming to the task, "and make sure that the wall-mounted weapons are tested, in good order and well supplied with ammunition."

"My lord," nodded Ayers, "you expect an attack?"

"The Gilded Branch is late. Until we know otherwise we will assume that Marrinek is free, armed and intent on coming here to exact revenge."

Ayers blanched.

"Surely he wouldn't dare, my lord?"

"Probably not." Sterik paused, considering how much to

say before deciding to err on the side of caution, "but it won't hurt to exercise the troops, shake them out of their complacency a little." Sterik paused again as the alarm rang in the gatehouse bell tower.

"We'll review in twelve hours or as soon as Curteys returns from the mainland, whichever is sooner. I want everyone sharp and alert for danger, not exhausted from constant strain, so we'll stand down again as soon as it's safe."

"Yes, my lord, I'll make the arrangements."

"Good. And while we're at it lets drill the weapons teams and the fire control teams, then practise the prisoner escape procedures. Let's make sure everyone really does know what to do if things go very wrong indeed."

Curteys had almost reached the harbour, heading for the jetty where the prison's other transport ship, a supply cog called the Lady Jessica, was docked, when the alarm bell sounded in the gatehouse. She had gathered two guardsmen, Hurlee and Mauch, on her way through the gatehouse and together they walked quickly along the harbour walls. Curteys left her escort on the harbour side and strode up the gangplank, boots sounding loudly on the wood. She stepped onto the deck and stopped, looking around the deserted ship for the crew. She turned back to her escort.

"Hurlee," she called, "get yourself to the Love of Liberty and find Captain Warde. She'll be playing cards, if there's anyone left in town stupid enough still to play with her. Mauch, go to the harbourmaster and find us a pilot. I mean to be underway within the hour." The guardsmen saluted and hurried off, leaving Curteys alone on the Lady Jessica.

She had been leaning on the ship's railing for only

fifteen minutes when Hurlee returned, accompanied by a tough-looking woman in her mid-forties. Captain Warde was clearly not pleased to have been dragged from her game.

"Deputy Governor," she said through a grimace, "to what do I owe the pleasure?"

"Hurlee didn't say? We need passage to Heberon." Curteys explained the situation.

"You think the Gilded Branch has foundered? That's bad news. Bad luck to set sail this afternoon, so soon after getting news like that. And we're not due to leave till the day after tomorrow in any case - we need time to load our cargo."

"Forget all that, there'll be time for cargo later. And the luck might get a damn sight worse if the Traitor is free again. Find your crew, Captain, we need to be in Heberon this afternoon."

Warde looked sceptical as she boarded her ship, moving to sit on the hatchway opposite Curteys.

"Really? Well, if you insist, but we'll need a pilot and I can't be sure my crew are still sober - we've been docked for several hours already," she said, turning to Hurlee, "you know my mate, Barney Mutschler, yes?" Hurlee nodded.

"Find him - he'll be in the Green Flagon trying to chat up the serving girls. Tell him I want the crew back at the ship before noon."

Hurlee looked at Curteys, who nodded, then strode off towards the town's other inn.

"It might take a while to round up the rest of the crew. Do you fancy a friendly game of cards to pass the time while we wait?"

9

F loost and her twin brother, Darek, had been sleeping on the warehouse roof for a few days now, sheltering from sun, rain and prying eyes under the overhangs. The warehouses in this part of Vensille were tall so it was easy to move around their roofs without being seen from the street. Staying out of view from other buildings meant moving mostly at night or crawling behind the low parapets, so during the day she mostly slept or watched the crowds, peering through a gap in the parapet to see the streets below and the river beyond.

It was the wide, easily navigable river Vensi that made Vensille a natural conduit between the interior of the continent and the islands and coastal cities of the Tardean sea, into which the river flowed. The city's location attracted merchants and traders from hundreds of miles inland, from around the circle of the Tardean sea and from across the civilised world.

The Duke had done much to encourage this trade and even more to prevent it from slipping away. First had come new docks on the river banks and a harbour in the estuary.

Then he had replaced the old walls, building new ones in a great circle around the heart of the ancient city, expanding into the neighbouring plains. New towers had been added to defend the city and allow the Duke to control the ships that entered or left his realm.

The army had been expanded from a knockabout group of thugs into a modest but professional force, able both to guard the city and conduct operations across the Dukedom. Amongst the coastal cities, the army of Vensille had built an impressive reputation.

And then the Duke had turned his attention to the sea, creating a modest navy to protect the shipping routes upon which the city now depended. His decision to award letters of marque to some of the more successful pirates operating in the Tardean Sea had stirred anger across the region but by then it was too late. Rhenveldt's former pirates, now flying Vensille's flag, enforced a kind of rough peace and gave the Duke control of the sea. Vensille had arrived; the Duke's position was, largely, secure.

Since then, he had not hesitated to use his military power to disrupt the establishment of similar trading strongholds along the coast. He had aggressively defended his monopoly by intimidating or raiding his neighbours, expanding his territory as opportunities arose.

All this he had done to draw trade to and through the city, where his customs officials could tax the merchants. So successful was this strategy that Vensille was now the major gateway for merchants trading between the northern kingdoms and the coastal cities of the Tardean sea; any trader, company or guild that wished to avoid Imperial ports or tariffs moved their goods through Vensille and paid Duke Rhenveldt instead.

The arrangement worked well and Vensille had flourished in recent decades. It had grown swiftly in both population and wealth so that it was now the largest and most important independent city on the northern coast of the Tardean sea, rivalling its Imperial neighbours to the east.

The streets of Vensille were crowded with people, animals, market stalls and caravans. Almost any item that was made, grown or captured could be found in the markets or on the docks of Vensille making it a rich place for both thieves and merchants. From her perch on the roof of a warehouse behind the western river docks Floost could watch travellers arriving by boat, tradesmen selling their goods from market stalls, sailors working the ships that traded on the river and farmers bringing stock to market. The crowds were varied, the opportunities endless.

She was still watching the streets when her brother returned, slipping over the wall from the neighbouring building with a small sack of hard bread and stale fruit. Darek divided the food between them and they ate in silence for a few minutes.

"We're out of money," Darek said between mouthfuls, "we have enough for tomorrow but after that..." he trailed off into silence.

"Already? I thought we had enough for at least another week."

"We did but I got snagged by one of Lorn's new thugs and they took everything I had in my belt. They didn't find the coin in my pants but I've spent half of that on today's food. Sorry."

"We should leave this city while we still can. Please, Darek, let's just go. We could go along the coast, maybe be in the next town by tomorrow evening."

"But what's the point? It'd be even harder to find marks in a smaller town and there would be less places to hide.

We'd get pinched and hanged for sure, if we didn't starve first."

They'd had this argument a dozen times or more and it always ended the same way. Floost gave up and went back to watching the streets.

"We'll need to find some money, then. And maybe we should move on again, try to get further from the Flank Siders' territory so we don't keep runnin' into their enforcers."

"Yeah, ok. Maybe we could try the other side of the river. Might be better to pay the North End gang than risk the Flank Siders getting us again." They both stared across the river at the buildings lining the eastern bank. They were pretty much the same as the buildings on this side of the river.

"Pack up now or wait for dusk?" asked Darek.

There was less chance of being seen if they waited till dusk but moving at night had its own risks, especially near the docks. The city might be safe for traders and merchants with their bodyguards and tame watchmen but for homeless youths it was another story.

"Let's go now - less chance of being stopped on the bridge if we cross during the day amongst the crowds, and it'll be easier to find a safe place to sleep." She pulled herself away from the parapet and gathered her meagre possessions, wrapping them in a small blanket that she bound with string and slung around her shoulders. Darek was doing the same, pulling his spare shirt from under the edge of the roof and wrapping it in his own threadbare blanket.

Darek climbed back over the wall and disappeared. Floost knelt for a few seconds, looking around the rooftop, checking that they had left behind nothing of value, then she too pulled herself over the bricks and dropped down onto the next roof.

They crept around the edge of the roof, just inside the low parapet, to the next building, an inn with a poorly maintained thatch roof. They wriggled through the gap in the thatch into the roof space of the inn and slid quietly downstairs until they emerged into the hayloft above the inn's stables.

"Hold on," whispered Darek as Floost stepped out from the gloom, "let's have a look at the bags on that saddle."

"What? No! Please Darek, let it go." But Darek was already lowering himself to the ground next to the stall. Floost shuffled around in the loft until she was near the door to the stable but she couldn't see out.

"Darek, come on. There are people around."

Darek shushed her and flapped his free hand in her direction, still rummaging through the bags.

"Empty, empty, empty." He unbuckled the last pocket and stuck in his hand.

"Aha, what's this?" He pulled out a wooden box about six inches long.

"Come on," said Floost, lowering herself from the loft and peering through a gap in the stable door. She looked at Darek, who was stuffing the box into his blanket, then back through the crack in the door just as someone flipped the catch and pushed it open.

Floost yelped in surprise and stumbled backward into the stable as a youth, no older than her or Darek, came in carrying a bucket. They stared at each other for a moment, confusion showing on the stable boy's face, then Darek pushed him hard from behind and Floost jumped to her feet. The boy stumbled forward and sprawled in the straw, dropping his bucket with a clatter, and Darek grabbed Floost's hand, pulling her through the doorway. Floost jerked her hand free as soon as they were outside and latched the door closed behind them then followed Darek as he ran across the deserted yard.

They were almost at the gate when the door burst open and the stable boy yelled, "Hey!".

Floost paused at the inn's gate and looked at the boy in the doorway, covered in straw and dirt. She smiled sweetly at him then ran down the street after Darek, dodging between carts and horses as she made her way towards to the river. She caught up with Darek as he turned the corner of the street and they leant against the wall, breathing heavily. Then Darek sniggered.

"You should have seen your face when he opened that door!" Floost punched his arm.

"It wasn't funny, you idiot!" she hissed, punching Darek's arm again, "We almost got caught and then where would we have been, eh?"

"You worry too much. Come on, let's get over the bridge and have some fun."

Darek jumped back to avoid a third punch and then together they walked along the embankment toward the river's main crossing point.

The bridge was a wonder of stone and iron, built by the Duke as a gift to his people and, famously, the only free crossing on the river. It spanned the river in five graceful arcs, carried by great islands of power-wrought stone and pillars of black iron.

Not that the Duke's motives were entirely altruistic. High as it was, the bridge marked the furthest point that seagoing merchant vessels could travel up the Vensi. The banks of the river to the south of the bridge were covered in wharves where large merchant ships docked to unload. Their goods were taxed by the Duke's customs officials before being carted into the city or loaded onto smaller river boats to continue their voyage north.

Floost and Darek stopped at the highest point of the central span and leant out to look down at the river itself. The surface teemed with boats of all shapes and sizes but the most numerous by far were the water taxis that carried the city's wealthier denizens across the river. Only the poor, or those moving goods, crossed the bridge on foot.

A continuous stream of barges and cogs passed into the city from the north or headed out carrying goods and passengers upstream. To the south, the harbour was busy with seagoing ships.

Darek pointed out a large, squat vessel with four masts flying an unusual flag.

"Where do you think that one's from? Never seen that flag before."

"Dunno. It's not Imperial, is it?"

"Nah, that's an Imperial ship," said Darek, pointing at a sleek three-masted ship, "maybe it's from across the sea, or maybe it's from the northern kingdoms, full of furs and iron and, and, er, other stuff they make in the north."

"Yeah, or maybe it's one of the Duke's new warships, just waiting to defend us all from pirates and invaders." They sniggered; stories of pirates and barbarian invaders were still told in the inns but there hadn't been an attack on the city for as long as anyone could remember.

They stood a little longer, watching the ships, until someone cuffed Darek around the ear.

"What are you two doing here, eh? Go on, get moving," said the watchman, giving Floost a shove. Darek stumbled backward away from the watchman and made an obscene gesture, then they both darted into the crowd as the watchman raised his fist.

They pushed through the crowds until they reached the other side of the bridge then made their way to the riverside and strode along the paved streets of the embankment away from the centre of town. This part of the city was unfamiliar to them and they spent a good couple of hours just wandering the streets, working out where the alleyways went and which buildings backed onto streets or warehouses or squares.

By mid-afternoon they were tired and hungry and ready to find somewhere to spend the night. Darek's stolen box had turned out to be an empty pen case, good for scribes but worthless to street urchins.

As the sunlight disappeared from the narrow streets and the better inns began to light lamps at their doors to welcome visitors from the shadowed streets, even the alleys were starting to look tempting. Floost much preferred sleeping off the ground and out of sight but a narrow passageway or a sheltered door away from the main footpaths would do, at a pinch.

They doubled back down the street to an alley between a pair of warehouses, looking for a way up onto the roof. There was a lean-to halfway down the alley and a low building that might have somewhere they could hide for the night.

"This'll do. We can find something better tomorrow."

Darek nodded and Floost jumped up onto a barrel to get a better look.

Then someone grabbed Floost's belt and pulled her back down. She lost her grip on the roof and fell backwards to the floor. She stumbled onto the ground and cried out. A big red face with an ugly grin peered down at her.

"And where are you going, missy? Need somewhere to sleep?"

"Let her go!" shouted Darek, charging at the man holding Floost. It was a brave effort but slim fourteen-year-old boys weren't much of a threat and the man just back-handed Darek across the face, sending him tumbling back to the alley floor.

"Get off me or I'll scream!" said Floost, beating at the arm that held her.

"You'll do what you're told is what you'll do, missy. No husband, no guardian? We can soon sort that out for you," said the arm's owner, "we'll take you to Madame Duval, see what sort of price we can get, but maybe we'll 'ave a bit of fun first."

Floost felt another hand grabbing at her waist then her chest. She kicked out and drew breath to scream but the man twisted her around and slapped her hard enough to make her ears ring.

"Grab that one, Pratek, we'll take 'em both to Madame Duval," said the man who still held Floost. He looked from one to the other and laughed.

"Ha, twins! A nice bonus."

Pratek grabbed Darek by the shirt and heaved him upright then pushed him forward to his mate, who slapped Darek across the face, knocking him back to the floor.

"I'm givin' the orders now, and if you don't want a good slapping you'll do what I say. Stand up!"

Darek pushed himself unsteadily to his feet, blood running from his nose and lip. Floost kicked out again, beating at her captor with her fists and trying to bite his arm. He slapped her face, then again, and Floost subsided, all the fight knocked out of her. Then he took hold of Darek's shirt and pulled him close.

"No more trouble," he hissed, "or it'll be your sister who gets slapped, understand?"

Darek nodded, trying to think through the fog in his head for a way out. They knew Madame Duval by reputation and hers were some of the hands into which he and Floost had very much wished to avoid falling. Darek struggled feebly but the man just shook him then turned toward the alley entrance, dragging the twins along with him.

Marrinek left The Crown after his meeting with Old Ned and wandered along the riverfront, heading back to The Jewel. He bought a meat pie from a stall next to a small shop selling minor charms and tools and stood for a couple of minutes looking at the displays. Then, still working his way through the pie, he continued on his way.

As he passed the entrance to an alleyway he was distracted by the sounds of an argument and he turned to see two men grappling with a couple of youths about half their size. One of the youths was bleeding - it looked like he'd been punched in the face - and the other was kicking and biting against her captor. Marrinek stopped walking and took another bite of his pie as he watched the struggle.

Maybe he should just walk away. Maybe he should let them learn from their mistakes. Maybe it would be better to pretend he hadn't noticed, to walk on along the street, to concentrate on his own problems.

Then he sighed and cursed himself. Where would he have been, all those years ago, without a little help when he had needed it? He sighed and rolled his head from side to side, loosening the muscles in his neck, then strolled into the alleyway.

"Do you need a hand?" he asked in Gheel, flicking away the last of the pie crust and licking his fingers.

The nearer man, the one not holding either of the two

youths - although now Marrinek looked more closely he was sure that they couldn't have been more than fourteen or fifteen - seemed to notice him for the first time.

"Nah mate, just a couple of runaways. We've got this under control."

Marrinek took another step into the alley and moved his staff so that he held it in both hands. He tried to keep things casual, non-threatening.

"Yeah, well, I wasn't really talking to you."

He looked past the man at the two youths - children really.

"They don't look like runaways to me, except maybe from you and your idiot partner."

He looked straight at the first man.

"Why don't we keep this friendly. Let them go, leave now, and we'll say no more about it."

The man just gaped at him but his partner spoke past him.

"Fuck off, friend, or we'll gut you 'n leave you for the rats."

The first man smiled and reached into the small of his back, pulling out a long knife and waving it toward Marrinek.

"Or maybe we'll gut you anyway, just for the fun of it." He leapt forward, swinging wildly, but Marrinek had half expected some sort of attack and was already moving, knocking the knife away with his staff.

The would-be kidnapper's momentum carried him forward, off balance, and Marrinek stepped around him and struck him on the back of the knee. The man cried out as his leg gave way and he fell to his hands and knees, dropping the knife. Marrinek planted a boot on the man's upturned backside and shoved him down into the mud of the alley, then kicked him in the face as he struggled to get up. The man collapsed and lay still.

His partner backed down the alleyway dragging Floost and Darek with him as Marrinek turned to face him.

"Let them go," Marrinek said quietly. The man backed away, still clutching Floost and Darek by their collars, then he pushed them toward Marrinek and ran off down the alley.

"Are you hurt?" Darek asked Floost, holding her shoulders. She was shaking and sobbing as Darek hugged her.

"We're fine," he whispered, "don't worry."

Marrinek relaxed, grounding his staff.

"We should probably leave. He might have more friends, somewhere."

Darek looked at Marrinek over Floost's shoulder.

"Thank you, sir. Spare some coin for a hot meal?"

Marrinek raised an eyebrow then looked down at the man on the ground, still prone on the alley floor.

"I'm sure this fellow would be happy to make a contribution. See if he has a purse."

Darek let go of Floost and bent over the unconscious man. He patted the man's belt then, with Floost's help, rolled him onto his back. From the pockets inside the unconscious man's coat he pulled a small purse and two more knives.

"You want these?" he said, offering the knives to Marrinek.

"No, I have enough knives."

Darek threw the blades into the alley and pocketed the purse.

"Time to go," said Marrinek, "good luck."

He held out his hand and Darek shook it, nervously. Floost just backed away a little, still shaking. Marrinek stood for a few more seconds, uncertain, then he made a decision. Friends and allies, eh? Well, maybe he could start small.

"I have a room at The Jewel. Do you need somewhere to sleep?"

Darek cocked his head to one side then shook it.

"Thanks, but we'll be fine on our own. We just need to..." he shut up as Floost spoke over him.

"Thank you, sir, any night we don't have to sleep on the streets is a gift we can't refuse," she said, smiling at Marrinek. Then she hissed at Darek when he tried to object.

"They'll be looking for us, won't they. At least with him we'll be off the street."

Darek shook his head but the look on Floost's face told him he'd already lost the argument.

"Right, but don't you try anything, mister. I don't trust you and I'll be watching," warned Darek, puffing himself up to seem as tall as possible.

Marrinek held up his free hand and smiled.

"It's a deal. Food, shelter and a floor to sleep on. That's all. It's this way."

He turned and walked out of the alley back onto the street, waiting to see if they would follow him, then he led them around the corner to The Jewel.

10

Deputy Governor Curteys stood at the prow of the Lady Jessica watching Heberon harbour as the ship drew steadily nearer. She loved to travel by sea, to feel the roll of the deck, the wind in her hair and the sun on her face as the ship cut through the waves and an unexpected trip to the mainland, however unpleasant the task, was an opportunity to be savoured.

"We've been lucky with the wind and the tide," said Captain Warde, moving to stand beside her at the rail, "we'll be in the harbour quite soon - well before dusk."

Curteys nodded her understanding but didn't take her eyes from the harbour walls and the sight of manoeuvring vessels. There was an Imperial merchant ship leaving the harbour, sitting low in the water and raising sail as she pulled away from the walls, turning east to head toward the heart of the Empire. A second merchantman was heading into the harbour, dropping sails as she turned to dock, her crew moving quickly across the decks and through the rigging.

"Looks busy," said Warde, as the Lady Jessica

approached the harbour mouth, "so we may not be able to tie-up at the wharf. We'll lower the dinghy so that you don't have to wait."

She looked at Curteys and nodded her head.

"Yes, the dingy. You don't seem to be in a waiting kind of mood."

Curteys glanced over at Warde before looking back at the merchant ship that had slipped into the harbour ahead of them.

"No, I'm not. The dinghy it will have to be, as soon as you're ready."

Much as she loved the sea, Curteys also loved towns and the feeling of life that came from being around hundreds or thousands of people. Heberon was small with only a thousand or so permanent residents but the docks and harbour were buzzing as ships came and went and the continuous bustle gave the town a huge sense of life. After four months at Ankeron West even a small town like Heberon felt like a metropolis and Curteys leapt eagerly from the dinghy of the Lady Jessica onto the steps at the side of the harbour, closely followed by her escorts.

They made their way quickly through the town toward Government House. The streets were busy and the two soldiers had to push their way through the crowds, navigating around stalls, pack animals, people and carts and occasionally shoving their way through when there was no other option. By the time they reached the steps of Government House, the early evening sun was falling on crowds that were turning their thoughts from struggle and work to leisure and pleasure and the taverns were beginning to fill.

Hurlee climbed the steps ahead of Curteys and opened

the door, holding it for her to pass through into the hallway. The entrance hall was tall and bright, a statement of political intent wrought in stone and glass. That the Imperial architects should deem it appropriate to build a two-storey entrance hall of such elegant proportions in the government building of a remote border town was a bold statement of the Empire's resurgent power, wealth and confidence.

While Hurlee and Mauch gaped at the architecture like farm boys on their first visit to a city, a butler appeared through a door at the end of the hall and approached.

"Good evening, my lady. My name is Flattock. How may I be of service?"

"Good evening, Flattock. I am Deputy Governor Curteys from Ankeron West. I need to see Administrator Nison immediately on a matter of some urgency. Is he here?"

"Yes, my lady, although he is dressing for dinner. Should I interrupt him?"

"Yes. In fact, take me to him now and I'll interrupt him myself. He's an old friend and this issue can't wait while he chooses shirts."

Flattock looked sceptical but acquiesced and gave her a slight bow.

"Very well, my lady. If you would please follow me. I will arrange for refreshments to be sent for your men." Flattock turned and walked back toward the door through which he had appeared and Curteys followed, interested to see what Nison's private apartments were like.

Flattock led the way along a passage and into an inner hallway where a wide stair led up to the first floor. At the top of the stair Flattock turned left and paused at a door in the lobby.

"If you would please wait here, my lady, I will confirm that Administrator Nison is able to see you." He turned and disappeared through the door only to return a few moments later. He opened the door fully and stood to one side to let Curteys enter.

"Please make yourself at home, my lady, and Administrator Nison will join you shortly." Flattock closed the door behind her and she listened to his footsteps as he made his back to the stairs and down to the ground floor.

Curteys looked around the room as a servant discretely delivered wine and goblets. The short wall at the end of the room was lined with bookcases and Curteys ran her eye along the titles. She had known Nison for many years but never before realised he had a taste for early dynasty romantic poetry. She flicked carefully through a few volumes while she waited but she could summon no enthusiasm for the genre.

She replaced the book and turned away as the door at the end of the room opened and Nison walked in. He was dressed in a suit of black silk with a white shirt, evidently preparing to entertain as Flattock had said. Nison walked quickly toward her, smiling.

"My dear Yiliwyn, it's so very good to see you."

He grasped her hands in his and kissed her on both cheeks, then stepped back a pace and gestured to a pair of seats at a small side table.

"Please, take a seat. Let me pour you a little wine." He paused and smiled again, then a frown crossed his face as he poured the wine.

"I am always glad to see you, of course, but what brings you here? Flattock indicated an errand of some urgency."

"Thank you, Kaspar." Curteys sat and took a sip of her wine to wash away the taste of the salt air from the crossing.

"I'll come straight to the point. The transport ship The Gilded Branch is overdue. If it was running to schedule it would have docked sometime between the morning four days ago, and yesterday afternoon. By this morning there was still no sign of it and the prisoner transports always run on time. Frankly, we're worried."

Nison furrowed his brow and tasted his wine.

"A serious matter, especially for those on the vessel, but surely not a catastrophic loss. Was the vessel carrying anything of real value?" He paused, considering the likely cargoes, then asked with a rising sense of dread, "Why are you here? Who was being transported?"

"Abaythian Marrinek."

Nisons's hand shook and wine sloshed onto his robes.

"Marrinek? Are you sure?"

"Absolutely. He was the only prisoner on board."

"And you fear he has escaped? That he might have overcome his guards and fled to resume his previous... activities?"

"Maybe. We don't know. Transportees have escaped before but..."

"Really?" interrupted Nison, "That's something I didn't know. I assume it happens infrequently?"

"Very, and please don't publicise the fact."

Nison raised his hands and nodded his head.

"That secret is safe, worrying though it may be," he said.

"We took extra precautions, dammit. He was to be drugged for the entire voyage and unconscious upon arrival at Ankeron. There were extra guards on the ship - strongly talented individuals, I might add, not just the usual warders - in case of attack or mistake or escape. The dates of his transportation were known only to Governor Sterik and his counterpart at the jail in Malteron where Marrinek was held after his arrest. Even I didn't know he was arriving until Sterik told me earlier today."

Nison gulped at his wine while Curteys spoke and noticed the earlier spillage, mopping at it ineffectually with a handkerchief he found in a pocket.

"There was a shipwreck, four, no five nights ago..." Nison tailed off, thinking, then, "we found bodies, sailors I think, and wreckage in Grace Cove, a few miles down the coast."

"Oh, dear god. Where are the bodies now?"

"Buried. They were all sailors, according to the report, but nobody knew... there was no reason to think it was anything out of the ordinary, just another ship lost in a storm, nothing left to identify it. You know how violent the summer seas can be, how unpredictable they are."

Curteys sat back in her chair and put down her goblet on the table, her face now ashen.

"If the ship foundered in a storm he's probably dead. It would be nice to have a body but I think we might settle for 'almost certainly dead'. You are sure he wasn't amongst the dead?"

"Yes, definitely. The eleven bodies we recovered all had Imperial naval tattoos, including their names. We didn't recognise the ship so we took notes - height, weight, hair colour, that sort of thing - and prepared a report to be sent to Esterengel with the next slow despatch."

"So there's absolutely no doubt that Marrinek's body wasn't found?"

"No, not unless he'd taken another name and tattooed it on his arm twenty years ago in case he needed a disguise."

She picked up her wine again and took another sip.

"So where is he? He might have drowned and washed out to sea but what if he didn't? What if he didn't die at all?"

But Nison was staring into the middle distance and didn't seem to have heard. Curteys paused a few seconds, then said, "This wine is very good; is it local?" Nison looked round, seeming a little surprised to find her still there.

"Er, yes, I believe it comes down from the hills. Some forward-thinking businessman started planting vines around the time the town was being planned and he's been shipping in some reasonable wines in the last few years." He stopped again, distracted by something Curteys couldn't see.

"Sorry, I think we may have missed something, some detail in the report of the shipwreck." Nison finished his wine and put the goblet back on the table then walked over to the fireplace and pulled on the bell cord.

"It might be nothing but I would feel happier if we checked." The door opened and Flattock glided in.

"Ah, Flattock. Could you please find Cranden and ask him to come to my office immediately." Flattock bowed and disappeared back through the door.

"If you'll come this way," Nison opened a door, "I will try to find the report that describes the shipwreck." Nison led the way to his office, passing through the empty clerk's room, the desks now clear and tidy. He sat down behind the desk and began to search through the reports and folders in his filing trays as Curteys looked out of the tall window onto the main square, still thronged with people and stalls. Finally, Nison sat back, throwing his hands up in frustration.

"It's not here, I must have sent it for filing."

At that moment, a knock on the door preceded Cranden's entrance.

"Good evening, sir."

"Ah, Cranden, at last. I need Tredgar's report on the shipwreck at Grace Cove. Where is it?"

"It's been filed, sir. It contained nothing of obvious importance..."

"Well maybe it did and we just didn't spot it. Dig it out, man dig it out. And find Tredgar."

Cranden hurried out, returning a few minutes later with a thin folder. Nison snatched it from him and flicked it open, scanning quickly through Tredgar's notes as Cranden retreated back the way he had come.

"That's it. That's the thing we missed." He passed the report to Curteys.

"The Watch chased someone off the beach in Grace Cove where the bodies were found. They thought he was robbing the corpses but they lost him in the forest after he assaulted two of Tredgar's men and stole a horse."

Curteys read the report quickly, her face growing rapidly more ashen as she worked her way down the page.

"Dear fucking gods above. They followed his trail from the beach into the forest where he attacked them with a staff, one he might have cut himself just before they caught up with him."

She looked up at Nison.

"Marrinek was a great swordsman and familiar with any number of weapons but the quarterstaff was his favourite. He was famous for it. What if he survived the shipwreck and escaped through the forest after attacking your men?" She flicked through the rest of the report.

"There isn't a description. Maybe it wasn't him, maybe he really did drown, maybe we're worrying about nothing..." but she couldn't shake the feeling, the fear and doubt and a chilling realisation that the Empire's most feared traitor might be free and, worse, nearby.

"We could exhume the bodies, they've only been in the ground a few days; did Marrinek have any distinguishing marks?"

"He might have had an apprentice's mark but that would

have faded at death. I don't know of any other marks but why would I? And who would know, except maybe his wife, and she's beyond reach; we certainly couldn't persuade her to travel here and look at week-old corpses that might or might not be her former husband. But we know the identities of the corpses - we can definitely rule them out so there's no need to exhume them, no way that we might have missed him."

"But you found only eleven bodies and there were at least twenty people on the ship when it went down, assuming it really was the Gilded Branch."

Curteys went back to the report, re-reading it in the hope of finding some other clue, some scrap of comfort, some suggestion that Marrinek had just drowned. But there was no comfort in the short report and she threw it down on Nison's desk in disgust.

As she did there was a knock at the door and Tredgar came in.

"I got your message," he said to Nison, "and came as quickly as I could." He bowed to Curteys, "Captain Tredgar, my lady, Heberon Watch, at your service."

Nison completed the introductions then turned to Tredgar.

"The beggar your men encountered on the beach at Grace Cove and in the forest. Could you describe him?"

"The beggar? No, I'm sorry, I never saw him. We tracked him cross country but we didn't catch up with him before he reached the town of Catshed."

Curteys swore under her breath.

"We have to identify this man, Captain. Is your sergeant reliable, the one who had the run-in with the beggar? Could he give us a description?"

"Snare? Yes, I would say he's reliable. I couldn't say the

same for the constables who accompanied him - they were all new recruits - but Snare should be able to give us a description."

Tredgar looked from Curteys, who had clearly arrived recently and was still dressed for travelling, to Nison, whose normally impeccable clothes were disarrayed and showing signs of a spilt drink.

"I'll find Snare and bring him here as soon as I can. Should we close the town gates?"

"Close the gates? No, I don't think that will be necessary, just find Snare."

Tredgar nodded and hurried out, closing the door softly behind him.

Nison sat back in his chair and opened one of the drawers in his desk. He pulled out a small flask and nodded toward a dresser beside the door.

"I have a little brandy, if you wouldn't mind fetching the glasses."

Curteys obliged, taking two of the tall curved glasses from the dresser. They sat, waiting for Tredgar's return, sipping their drinks.

"If the ship was The Gilded Branch," said Curteys, gesturing with her glass, "then the man may have been Marrinek. Are any other ships late or missing?"

"No," said Nison, draining his brandy and pouring a second measure. Curteys held out her own glass and Nison splashed in a generous serving. They sat sipping their drinks for ten minutes, then another ten. Curteys was starting to wonder if Tredgar had got lost when here was a knock at the door and he came in, leading Sergeant Snare, who stood to attention in front of Nison's desk and stared straight ahead.

"Sergeant," said Nison, "we need you to tell us about the

beggar that attacked you in the forest. Can you describe him?"

Snare had obviously been briefed by Tredgar to expect this question and he quickly rattled off a description of the beggar's physical appearance.

"Was there anything else that struck you about him? Anything unusual?"

Snare considered this, frowning as he thought back over the fight in the forest.

"Well, my lord, I think he tried to compel Jared to give over his boots, and the lad has halfway to handing them over before I snapped at him."

Tredgar shuffled uneasily and Nison looked at him in annoyance.

"That wasn't in your report, Captain," said Nison, glaring at Tredgar and clearly unimpressed by the omission. He turned back to Snare.

"Go on, Sergeant, what else can you tell us?"

Snare paused again.

"Now I think on it, my lord, he didn't really sound like a regular beggar. It was his accent. He sounded rather like you, sir, begging your pardon. And he knew how to use his staff, proper quick he was, dangerous. I wouldn't want to face him again."

Nison looked at Curteys, who nodded.

"Thank you, Sergeant, that will be all."

Snare nodded and saluted, clearly relieved, and left quickly. Nison rang the bell to summon Cranden.

"Captain," said Nison, hardly able to believe what he was about to say, "we believe the wrecked ship in Grace Bay was the prison transport, the Gilded Branch, and beggar described in your report was Abaythian Marrinek. If that's the case then you and your men probably had a lucky escape, although I'm not sure the same can be said for the rest of us."

"Marrinek, my lord?" said Tredgar, frowning, "The Traitor? I thought he had been condemned to death months ago?"

"No, Captain, life imprisonment," said Curteys, "which for someone like Marrinek might have been a very long time indeed."

"We need to notify the Governor in Esterengel, although I haven't the faintest idea what she'll be able to do."

The door opened and Cranden floated quietly into the room.

"Ah, Cranden. I need to send an urgent message to Esterengel. Have an aug-bird prepared for immediate despatch."

"I'm sorry sir, we used the last one a few weeks ago and we are still waiting for replacements."

"Dammit," thundered Nison, his worn veneer of civil-service respectability failing completely under the stress, "we're a bloody front-line garrison town not a third-rate farming village on the plains of Khemucasterill!" he pointed at Cranden, "How have we managed to run out of Esterengel birds?"

"It seems the Master of Couriers made a mistake and sent us a crate of birds for Ironbarrow instead of Esterengel."

Nison shook his head.

"Well what the fuck are we supposed to do with them?"

The homing birds, augmented for speed and stamina, were the fastest way to send messages across the Empire. Unfortunately, they would only fly to their home roost, so to send a message to Esterengel you needed an aug-bird that had been created in Esterengel.

"Find a courier and impress upon him the importance of the message. I don't care how many horses are spent getting it to Esterengel."

Cranden bowed and slipped from the room.

Nison stared at the door for a more moments to calm himself. Then he wrote a short description of the situation in an elegant flowing hand and folded the paper. From his drawer, he took a shaft of black wax in a charmed handle, sculpted to resemble a snake coiled around the wax. He held the device over the letter and concentrated briefly, focussing his will on the charm so that hot wax dripped onto the paper, then he pressed his ring into it to form a seal. He slipped the letter into a message tube and then sealed that as well.

"I want the courier to leave within the hour and this message," he said, passing the tube to Tredgar, "must be delivered into the hands of the Governor herself. Understood? Nobody else, only the Governor."

"Yes, my lord," Tredgar gave a little bow and left quickly, following Cranden down the passage.

Curteys threw back the rest of her brandy and stood up.

"Well, this turned out to be a much worse day than I had expected," she looked out of the window as the sun finally slipped beneath the horizon, "I'll need somewhere to stay tonight and then in the morning I had best get back to Ankeron with the news. I don't think Lord Sterik will be amused."

11

The summons had arrived first thing in the morning and was delivered to his room when the maid brought up a tray of breakfast. Marrinek took the note and ordered two more trays of food from the maid then broke the seal on the paper and glanced at the message.

The Snarling Goat, noon

Succinct and potentially interesting. He stuffed the note into a pocket.

For the moment, though, he had more pressing questions, like what to do with Floost and Darek. He sat on this bed watching them devouring a tray of food.

"The problem," he said, "is what to do with the two of you."

He paused at a knock on the door. The maid came in with another tray piled with bread, cheese, dried fish, pickled onions and a jug of coffee. As she turned to leave

Marrinek said, "Can you pass me my staff please, miss? There, by the door."

"Yes sir, if you wish," she said, curtseying. She reached out her hand to grasp it but stopped with her fingers at least six inches from the green wood.

"I... I can't, sir, it's not right." There was a look of horror and disgust on her face as she bobbed another curtsey at Marrinek and fled from the room.

"Interesting, don't you think, that she couldn't pick it up?"

Floost shrugged, clearly not at all interested. Darek ignored the question and started eating a small loaf from the second tray. Life on the streets had made them suspicious of promises and they had quickly learnt to eat whenever food was available.

Marrinek opened his mouth to tell them why it was interesting then thought better of it. Not all questions had to be answered as soon as they had been asked. Instead he focussed on the food, conscious that he had lost a lot of weight over the last couple of years.

"You should really be in school, both of you, preparing to go to an Imperial military college, or something similar, but that's not an option at the moment, especially as the nearest suitable institution is hundreds of miles away. Maybe we could find you a local version but without the funds and a sponsor of good name the chances that they would accept you are slim. I think the only thing to do is for you to stick with me and I'll train you myself, at least for a short while." Marrinek stopped, as if only now realising that he had been speaking aloud.

"School?" said Darek through a mouthful of bread, "What for?"

"Yeah. What for? Anyway, we can read and write." said

Floost, defiantly. She smeared runny cheese across a chunk of bread and kept eating. Marrinek stared at them in open surprise.

"You can read and write? Good, that will make things easier. Tell me, Darek, can you pick up my staff?"

The twins looked at him as if he were an idiot, then Darek reached for the staff. He stopped, hand just short of the surface, frowning at something sensed but not understood, then stretched out and closed his hand around the staff and pulled it toward him. He held it out toward Floost, who grabbed the other end, quickly pulling the staff away from Darek before putting it down on the floor.

"It's strange," said Floost, "it feels like there's something wrong with it. As if it doesn't want to be touched."

"Like it's cursed," said Darek looking at Marrinek, suddenly worried, "it's not is it? Cursed, I mean? Is it safe to touch it? Why didn't the maid want to touch it?"

"Good questions. Safe? That rather depends on who you are and what you're trying to do. Safe? Yes, but only in the way a blade is safe while sheathed. It won't hurt you, if that's what you mean, and it definitely isn't cursed, but it has been made to feel, well, 'unclean' or 'wrong' to anyone other than me who tries to hold it. You felt it too, just as the maid did, but for her the feeling was so strong she couldn't even touch it, let alone pick it up. How do you think it works?"

"Is it like magic?" said Darek with a nervous laugh. Their father had told them tales of the great magicians of legend and their works, of how they had shaped the world and its cities, cast out demons and dragons, built towering castles and thrown down evil kings. Magic was the stuff of fairy tales and myth, used to entertain children and in the telling of tall tales around a low fire late at night. Few city dwellers really believed it existed. They believed in the application of scientific power, of course, because they could see it every day when they looked at the city walls or the lamps on the docks or the work of a craftsman-practitioner but that was just part of everyday life.

Marrinek smiled.

"Well, that rather depends. No, it's not magic, at least not in the way that most people use the word. There are no spells or incantations or potions that can produce the effect you are feeling but if you don't know how it has been done it can look very much like magic." He picked up the staff and rested it on the floor, point down.

"What I did was alter the fine structure of the wood, twisting it to change its properties. Exactly what I have changed and how I did it are things we might discuss in the future. For now, you need only know that this is an object whose form I have chosen and crafted, altering the raw wood to suit my purposes." He fell silent, thinking.

"It needs a name, really," he said quietly, half to himself, "one that reflects its character, its potential. At the moment it's just a tool, a shaped thing, like a shovel or a brush."

They ate silently for a few minutes, although the trays were now almost empty. Then Floost, pushing away her empty plate, spoke.

"It's dangerous but it moves with grace, like the tumblers you see in the market on holy days. Bone Dancer, because it breaks bones when it tumbles, a dangerous dancer."

"Bone Dancer," echoed Marrinek, tasting the words as they rolled across his tongue, "yes, that will do very well indeed. Bone Dancer it will be. Pass me that roll of tools," he pointed at the crafting tools in their leather roll, "and we'll make it permanent."

He unrolled the leather and laid it on the bed. Then he

placed the staff across his knees and picked up Needle, the smallest of the five tools.

"Move closer and pay attention. Empty your minds and concentrate on what I'm doing."

He shuffled the staff around so that the lower end was resting on his right knee then, wielding the crafting tool like a fine brush, he focussed his power and touched it to the surface of the wood. He worked quickly, drawing the tool over the surface while delivering a fine stream of power, tracing the staff's new name across the wood. Bone Dancer glowed brightly, pale yellow against the dark green of the shaft, then faded away until the letters were barely discernible. Marrinek returned the tool to the roll and fastened the tie.

"Did you see what I did, or feel it?"

"I, I think so," said Floost, "it was like you'd pulled something from the air and it was flowing into the staff, but I couldn't see how you did it."

She was leaning forward now, eager to understand, her earlier reticence and suspicion driven away by a sudden need to learn more.

"Can you teach us?"

"I can teach, yes, but can you learn? Do you have the strength, the will, the determination to succeed, or will you give up as soon as things get difficult or frightening or dangerous? Those may be the bigger questions and I don't have the answers," said Marrinek, looking from one to the other, "do you have the answers?"

Floost opened her mouth to answer but Darek go there first.

"How do we know we can trust you? We don't even know your name. What's to stop you leading us on and selling us to Madame Duval when you get bored?"

Marrinek raised his eyebrows, surprised. He scratched at his beard with long fingers.

"You're right, of course. I could sell you to Madame Duval. Or to anyone else, for that matter - there's nothing you would be able to do to stop me!" and he stood, suddenly, twirling Bone Dancer. He seemed to grow before their eyes, to become menacing and threatening and dangerous. Where before he had seemed like a kindly teacher, now he appeared as a malevolent spirit, a powerful evil bent on havoc and mayhem and death.

Floost and Darek, still sitting on the floor, scooted backwards as fast as they could until their backs were against the wall. They clutched each other and looked on fearfully but, the transformation was reversed as quickly as it had happened and suddenly the man before them was again the teacher of a few minutes earlier. Marrinek sat back down on the edge of the bed and propped Bone Dancer against the wall.

"But you have my word that I will not and that, instead, I will do whatever I can to keep you safe from harm while you are in my care. You will be my apprentices and I will expect you to study, work hard and follow my instructions, even when they seem strange or unpleasant. The work will be long and difficult but in return I will feed, clothe and house you and teach you the rudiments and details of my art."

"Why," said Floost, "why would you want to do that?"

Marrinek smiled sadly as he pulled the words together.

"Do you know how long talented people can live?" asked Marrinek. Floost and Darek shook their heads. "How old do you think I am?"

"About forty?" said Floost as Darek said "Fifty?" Marrinek snorted.

"Bloody hell. I'd forgotten how bad children were at

guessing the age of adults. No, I'm not forty or fifty. I look about twenty-five, which you'll appreciate when you've seen a bit more of the world, but I've looked this way for over a century, now. I'm a hundred and twenty-seven years old."

Floost and Darek goggled at him, stunned, then they giggled.

"No way," said Darek, "nobody lives that long, not even the priests, and all they do is sing and lecture and wave incense around all day!"

"One of the things you're going to have to understand very quickly is that I don't lie, as a general rule. I was born a hundred and twenty-seven years ago in Esterengel and I lived my first twelve years on the street, just like you." Marrinek paused to let that sink in. He could see the twins struggling to accept it and decided now was the time to share the full secret.

"As you learn to use your talents, which I believe are going to be strong in both of you, you too will find that the years stretch and that you age far, far more slowly than other people. It can be lonely but I'll teach you to deal with that as well."

"We might live to be a hundred?" said Floost, eyes radiating disbelief, her expressions comically identical to Darek's.

"Easily. Nobody really knows how long we might live. The advantages are obvious, the disadvantages, less so," he tutted and shook his head, "age is a distraction for now. Forget about it, just know that if you accept my teaching and learn to use your talents, you're going to have more years to fill than most people. That in itself is reason enough for tutoring apprentices; it gives us someone to talk to in the long, long future we have before us, someone with whom we have shared life experiences."

He paused, noting that the twins were looking at him strangely. Too much information, too quickly. And too weird. He sighed.

"So there it is. My offer is training and tutelage, apprenticeship, food and lodging, protection, loyalty and friendship. In return, you do what I say, when I say, for as long as your apprenticeship lasts. Do you accept my offer?"

The twins looked at each other, then Floost gave a little nod and they turned back to face Marrinek.

"Yes, we accept."

"Good, then you must commit, now, wholeheartedly, and we will begin immediately. Give me your right hands." He held out his hands.

Floost and Darek looked at each other again then back at Marrinek. Tentatively, they each held out their right hands, placing them in Marrinek's. He folded his hands gently around theirs and focussed.

"This may sting a little."

He pressed, just so, wielding a little power, and twisted a shape in his mind. Floost and Darek flinched but didn't cry out. Marrinek held them a moment longer then opened his eyes and released them.

"Now you are marked as apprentices. My apprentices. Anyone of talent will be able to sense the mark if they hold your hand and focus in the right way and they will know that you have been apprenticed."

The twins looked down at their wrists where they now each had a red dot the size of a penny, raised slightly above the surface of the skin.

"That will fade over the next few days but the effect will last forever. I'll show you later how to shield the mark, should you need to, or to disguise it so that your enemies can't see it." He paused a moment, then added, "Or my enemies, for that matter."

Marrinek sat back on the bed and looked at his new apprentices.

"So, Apprentices. You can call me Bay in private or Master in public, since that's what I will be. Appearances, especially in this city, are important, so you will learn to be good apprentices, to bow and to scrape when necessary, to lie and to cheat if appropriate, to work power and people and tools as circumstances dictate.

"I'll teach you about your power, how to wield it, how to control and how to hide it. I'll teach you the mysteries and the techniques, the methods of charm-making and the ways of their use, I'll show you Flow and teach you to use it for defence and attack. I'll train you in weapons and healing, philosophy and politics, history and languages and every other thing I can think of until you're sick of knowledge and thirst for a time of peace and quiet.

"But the very first thing you need to learn is trust. Or, rather, trust in me. This works in both directions, so I'm going to set you tasks and you'll return here this afternoon once you have completed them."

He pulled out his purse and removed six shillings, giving three to each of the twins.

"First, find yourselves some new clothes. Two sets each, plain, with travelling capes and hats, a pair of boots and packs to carry your belongings. We will stay here for a while but if we need to move I will want to move quickly. Then find a smith and buy two plain iron rods about eight inches long."

He looked at them both.

"Do you understand?" They nodded and he said, "Good,

then get going. I'll be out most of the day but I will return later this afternoon and we will begin your instruction."

Floost and Darek scrambled up and headed for the door.

"And be careful," said Marrinek, "I don't want to have to rescue you again."

When they had gone Marrinek finished the food and coffee then pulled on his boots, checked that his knife and purse were secure, slipped his almost empty pack over his shoulder and picked up his staff. He left his tools and the sword on the bed and followed the twins downstairs, pausing at the bottom to talk to the innkeeper, who was polishing the bar in the taproom and keeping an eye on her staff as they prepared for the day's trade.

"I'll need another room, something grander, with a sitting room, and second a room with two beds for my apprentices. Do you have something?"

The innkeeper stroked her chin thoughtfully and said, "I have a small suite of rooms on the second floor that's just come free today 'cos Master Warnt has left to return to his home upriver. It's small but it has two modest bed chambers and a shared sitting area, if that would do?"

"That sounds fine. You can move my things from my room as soon as you are ready, and make sure everything is properly aired and cleaned. That should cover board for a while," he said, placing three shillings on the counter, "and I'll want breakfast for three each morning when the first bell sounds."

The innkeeper nodded and the coins disappeared into a pocket in her skirts.

"Right you are, sir, I'll sort it out for you. Is there anything else you need?"

"I have business at The Snarling Goat. Where will I find it?"

"Ooh, that's a rough place, sir, and no mistake. But, if you're set on visiting, you'll find it in the Narrows, up towards the docks where the sailors drink. You watch your purse up there, sir." Her face showed genuine concern, maybe because she feared his purse wouldn't return to extend the rent on the suite.

"Many thanks, mistress, I will take care. Until this afternoon." He nodded to her and walked across the taproom to the door, his staff rapping on the boards as he went.

Outside the inn, the day was busy and the street full of people. Marrinek made his way toward the docks but stopped at a barber's shop, stroking his beard with his left hand. Then he made a decision and pushed open the door to the tiny shop. Inside he found a single chair for clients and a second for those waiting, both currently vacant. A tall thin man with no hair of his own was sweeping the floor and he looked up as Marrinek closed the door behind him.

"Good morning to you, sir. How may I be of service?" asked the barber, taking in Marrinek's dishevelled beard and unruly mop of hair.

"Tidy and trim the beard to match the current fashion, tidy the hair but leave it long."

"Sir is from out of town, I gather. In Vensille, sir, gentlemen wear their beards half an inch long and neatly cropped. Many of my clients have their beard trimmed every week. Hair is also worn short. If sir wishes to blend with the crowd then sir might like to consider shortening his hair as well as his beard."

Marrinek looked at himself in the small hand glass held

by the barber, turning this way and that as he pretended to consider the advice.

"As you see fit for the beard," he said finally, "but I rather like the hair; just trim the ends and, oh, I don't know, make it work in a tail of some sort."

"Very well, sir. If sir would sit back and relax," said the barber, preparing his instruments, "this will take a few minutes."

Half an hour later Marrinek again checked his appearance in the hand glass. He had to admit that the trimmed beard was a definite improvement over the chaotic thatch he had sported until recently but sartorial elegance had been a long way down his list of priorities for a very long time. He ran his fingers along his jaw line, enjoying the feel. Such a look would have been impossible inside the Imperial court, where beards were still considered a sign of foreign barbarism, but here they seemed to convey a certain power to the wearer.

"Many thanks," said Marrinek, paying from his dwindling purse, "and can you direct me to decent a bath house?"

"Well, sir, it depends what sir wants. If sir is looking merely to wash and change his clothes then sir might be best served by searching out Eastside Bath, an avenue that runs parallel to the river but several streets to the east of here. If sir is looking for a more complete service, shall we say, then there are specialist houses on the alleys off Eastside Bath that cater for every taste."

"And if I wanted a reputable bath house, one where a tailor might also be engaged, what would you recommend?"

"I would go to The House of Seven, sir, which is at the near end of Eastside Bath, on the left-hand side, under the sign of the clasped hands."

Marrinek thanked him, shook the linen from around his neck and headed for the door.

"If I might say, sir, The House of Seven has a certain reputation for measuring potential clients by appearance. Sir may find that they require additional financial persuasion before sir will be welcomed."

Marrinek turned back to face him, holding the door open with one hand, and said, "Thanks, I'll bear that in mind." He closed the door behind and stepped out into the street. He looked at the sun, orienting himself, then strode off through the crowds, heading roughly east.

Half an hour's wandering found him outside The House of Seven. It was indeed a superior establishment, although far from the most expensive on the street, and the discreet door wardens looked at him with obvious distaste as he lingered on the street. He smiled to himself and went back the way he had come before turning north towards the Narrows.

He soon found the area. As the name suggested the streets and alleys were noticeably narrower than those in the more popular or expensive areas of the city. Where Eastside Bath had been a broad avenue, widening as it approached the market square, the streets in the Narrows were no more than eight to ten feet across. In some streets, a tall man could touch the buildings on both sides with his outstretched arms. The side roads were even less spacious and the overhanging first and second stories of the houses and tenements lining the cramped streets made the whole area feel dark and oppressive, even on a bright summer day.

Marrinek stuck to the wider streets, working his way north and east through the area until he came to a small square at what must have been, he reckoned, the centre of the district. Even this public space, small and crowded, over-looked by buildings that reached three or four stories, was thronged with people, animals and small market stalls from which vendors called their wares. Marrinek threaded his way through the throng until he stood outside a large tavern with a poorly painted sign that appeared to be some sort of grimacing animal; The Snarling Goat.

12

Pushing his way through the main door of the Snarling Goat, Marrinek found himself in a large taproom. A smattering of people were drinking away the day, lounging at tables or dicing against the walls. In one of the darker corners, where secluded booths afforded a modest amount of privacy, several people were putting a lot of effort into getting to know one another a lot better.

Marrinek found a table in a booth in a corner away from the amorous couples and signalled a passing servant to bring him beer and food. It wasn't yet noon and breakfast was only a couple of hours past but the stew was hot and filling and he had learned not to miss opportunities to eat.

While he ate, he watched the other patrons as they drank and gambled and laughed. In years past he might have joined one of the games or told tall tales with a group of friends and acquaintances. Not today, though. This wasn't the time or the place and these people weren't like him. At least, he hoped they weren't like him. His plans were dead in the water if these people were all like him.

He was finishing his plate of stew, chasing the gravy

around the plate with a lump of bread, when one of the hard-faced, heavy-set men from the door wandered over to his table. The man leant his fists on the table.

"Are you the one Old Ned sent? The job-seeker?"

Marrinek chewed his bread, leaning back to get a little further from the man's rancid breath.

"Probably," he said, still chewing, "someone sent me a note." He produced the note and passed it across the table but the man barely glanced at it.

"Good. I'll take you up to see Hitton," the man snorted, "if you're sure you want to see him?"

"Sure, what's the worst that could happen?" said Marrinek, grinning.

The other man straightened up, shaking his head.

"This way," he said, heading for the stairs at the back of the tavern. He led Marrinek onto the gallery that ran around the first floor then pointed at a curtained booth.

"At the end." Marrinek looked along the line of the pointing finger then pushed past its owner and walked to the last booth on the gallery.

He pulled open the curtain and peered into the gloom. A couple of candles lit the booth, showing a tall thin man sitting in the far corner and a second, more powerfully built man sitting opposite him. A jug of beer and several mugs sat on the table. The thin man looked up as Marrinek twitched the curtain aside.

"Ah, you'd be Old Ned's man, right? Come in, have a seat. I'm Hitton, this is Tam." The thug ducked his head towards Marrinek but said nothing.

Hitton poured a mug of beer and pushed it across the table toward Marrinek as he took a seat.

"Thanks, you can call me Bay," said Marrinek, taking a

cautious sip, "I understand you might have work for someone with my... talents?"

"Well, that depends, don't it, on what those talents are and what you're prepared to do with them," said Hitton, sipping at his own beer. Tam was watching him closely, picking at his teeth with a long needle.

"You're not from round here. Imperial?"

Marrinek nodded.

"Yes, but I'll be staying here for a while. I don't plan to head back east anytime soon."

"Problems with the law?" asked Hitton.

"You could say that. Believe me when I say you don't want to know," said Marrinek, "I'll be in Vensille for some months at least and I need work, something to keep me busy and cover rent and food."

"You're a big lad, intimidating. Can you handle yourself in a fight?"

Marrinek looked at Hitton, face blank.

"I'm the most dangerous person you'll ever meet."

He said it flat and cold, no hint of a joke. Hitton just looked at him for a few seconds, unsure, then Marrinek cracked a grin and the tension broke.

"Sure," he said, "I can handle myself."

"Right, well," said Hitton, laughing in a high, unconvincing way, as if he knew a joke had been made but couldn't work out what it was, "I think we might be able to help each other, although we're gonna make you work damn hard for your money. How would you feel about dealing with a problem we've got with our, ah, competition?"

"Sure," Marrinek said again, shrugging, "what's the deal?"

"There's a stable over on the west side, run by a man

named Narrint. He owes money and he's been slow to pay. We can't have that, it's bad for business, so we need to teach him a lesson. Not kill him, just scare him a bit, encourage him to honour his debts, shall we say, maybe take a chunk of silver from him."

"Sounds simple enough. Why don't you send one of your people," he nodded at Tam, "to handle it?"

"Ah, well. The west side's not really our territory, see? And my boys, like Tam here, are all known men," said Hitton pausing to sip his beer, "but you, now, you're new in town, or so Old Ned tells me. Nobody knows you, so you can just saunter on over the bridge like you was buying apples or something, find our guy, beat the crap out of him and help him work out who his friends are. Easy."

Marrinek sipped at his beer, pretending to consider the request before nodding.

"I'll speak to him for you. Where do I find him and what does he look like?"

Tam gave him directions and a description while Hitton sat back in the gloom, filling a long clay pipe from a pouch he produced from inside his shirt. When the bowl was filled to his satisfaction he brought out a small charm and, with one eye on Marrinek, produced a flame with which he lit the pipe.

Marrinek raised his eyebrows in genuine surprise. Producing a flame from a charm was a cheap trick but not one he'd expected to see in a dive like this.

"Just so you know what you're dealing with, friend, in case you get any ideas about taking the money and leaving town. We're not without resources, and our reach is long." The flame flickered out as quickly as it had appeared and Hitton tilted his head back, puffing smoke toward the ceiling.

"I'll be sure to remember that," said Marrinek. He stood up and drew back the curtain.

"When do you want the job done?"

"Today, this afternoon. And then we can discuss another job this evening, if it goes well," said Hitton.

"Good. Till this evening, then."

Marrinek nodded at Tam and stepped out of the booth back onto the gallery. The taproom was a little busier now and as Marrinek walked down the stairs, Bone Dancer sitting casually on his shoulder like a hawk preparing to hunt, someone raised their voice.

"What do you know, if it isn't our do-gooder friend from the alley."

Marrinek looked up to see Pratek leaning against the counter with a mug of beer in one hand and a pipe in the other. As Marrinek walked toward the door Pratek called out to him.

"What, no word of thanks to your old mates Pratek and Gander? That's rude. Real rude, 'specially after the thumpin' you gave me," he paused and Marrinek felt the atmosphere in the bar turn suddenly hostile, "but at least we took care of those kids for you, so that's something."

Pratek laughed and turned to his companion.

"Real bit of luck, that was. Found 'em again this morning after this fucker stole 'em from us. Just walking around, they were, like they owned the place. No fucking clue. Had to slap 'em around a bit to teach 'em some manners."

He paused to allow his audience to appreciate his brilliance.

"Sold 'em to Madame Duval over on Eastside Bath, didn't we? A matched pair - got a really good price," he boasted, slapping at a purse inside his shirt.

Marrinek turned to look at him, eyes cold, face like iron.

"You did what?" he said, quietly, and nobody missed the menace in his voice.

"You heard," said Gander from behind Marrinek, "and there ain't nothing you can do about it, so you just run along before we gives you a beating."

Marrinek glanced over his shoulder. Gander was standing there, hand on the hilt of a long knife in his belt.

"This ain't a friendly place for you, so maybe you should just leave, now, before something nasty happens."

Around him Marrinek could feel the atmosphere changing further as the threat of violence grew around the three men. The quiet was spreading across the tap room as the patrons turned to watch the encounter, interested to see what would happen next. A man at the bar took his drink and carefully made his way to a table on the other side of the room.

Marrinek looked back at Pratek, who was grinning smugly and sipping his beer.

"Fetch them now and," he started to say but then Gander was right up behind him, hissing in his ear.

"You deaf or what? They're gone, sold, and you'd better be gone soon too if you want to live!"

Gander barged past him and Marrinek nodded slowly and took a step toward the door. Then he turned back, staff held in both hands, and said in a low, calm, slow voice.

"Last chance, fetch them now. Don't make me do something you'll regret."

Behind Gander, on the stairs, Tam was watching the confrontation, one hand resting on the hilt of a long-blade. Across the room several other men were easing forward, just in case the promise of violence was fulfilled. And the quiet now filled the room; even the barmaids had stopped their progress between the tables, turning to watch. Hitton had emerged from his booth and was leaning on the railing at the edge of the gallery to watch.

Then Gander laughed, a raucous noise in the quite room, making the most of situation and playing up to a friendly crowd.

"Ha. You're new in town, anyone can tell. The deal's done, you'll have to buy 'em back if you want 'em and Madame Duval'll make you pay richly, more than you can afford, country-boy."

Marrinek looked up at Hitton, shook his head sadly.

"Sometimes there's no other way," he said in a low voice.

"What was that, country-boy?" said Gander, cupping his hand to his ear theatrically, "I didn't..." but Marrinek was already moving, thrusting Bone Dancer hard into Gander's face. The big man fell over backwards, his head banging noisily on the floorboards.

Marrinek stepped quickly forward, raising Bone Dancer in both hands. As the fallen man focussed on him, he brought the pointed end of the staff down on Gander's forehead, shattering bone and caving in the skull.

Marrinek stepped quickly back and grounded Bone Dancer. He stood calmly but his heart was hammering and he desperately needed to breathe deeply. Instead he stood, silent and still, feet apart and one arm hanging at his side, just as if nothing unusual had happened.

Nobody moved. The room was silent, the air still, and even the bustle from the street seemed distant and dull. For a few long seconds, nothing happened and Marrinek sucked in air and waited for his limbs to stop shaking.

He looked slowly around the room but still nobody moved. Marrinek sneered then turned and headed for the door.

"Can't just let you leave, boy, not after killin' one of my

men," said Tam. He came down the stairs, the long-blade clenched in his hand. He signalled with his other hand and several of the men who had been watching from their seats, stood up, each drawing a long knife or a short sword. That was the cue for the other patrons, already shuffling nervously toward the doors. In moments the room had cleared, leaving Marrinek alone with Tam, Hitton, Pratek, four thugs and Gander's cooling corpse.

"Your men?" snarled Marrinek, now properly angry, and the sudden change in his face was somehow worse than the violence. One of the thugs dropped his sword and backed away; everyone else froze.

"They worked for you, Hitton, so you owe me," said Marrinek, pointing Bone Dancer at the thin man on the gallery, "for what your men have done today, you owe me. I'll be back later to collect on the debt."

Marrinek turned to go but one of the doormen blocked his way, sword drawn and raised. Marrinek hefted Bone Dancer.

"Really?" he said, eyebrows raised, "Why don't you just fuck off, save us both the trouble."

He could feel the men behind preparing to move, gathering their courage. Six was too many to fight, even if he'd been at his peak. He needed to end this, quickly, and get out of the inn.

He focussed and pulled power, preparing a surprise to even the game. The power came easily at first then stopped suddenly, as if someone had turned off a tap. A wave of nausea hit him hard and it was all he could do to stay on his feet as the lights danced in front of his eyes.

Marrinek half saw the doorman take half a step forward, maybe sensing that he wasn't entirely well. He stabbed out with Bone Dancer, hoping to knock the big man backwards.

The doorman was fast, though, and the thrust was crude and easily parried. Marrinek stepped forward quickly, pushing back against the sword. He brought the butt of the staff around to strike the doorman on the side of the head. As the doorman staggered back, Marrinek pushed forward again. He slammed the shaft into the doorman's forehead and the man fell heavily to the floor and lay still.

Marrinek spun back to face the men behind him. They'd barely moved and now they stood as still as statues, no longer keen to test their skill against him.

"Stay out of my fucking way, all of you" he snarled, looking around the room, teeth bared. Then he looked at Hitton.

"I'll be back to collect later."

Then he turned and stepped over the stunned doorman toward the door. He kicked it open and stepped out into the market square, letting the door closed behind him.

Almost as soon as the door had closed, Marrinek heard angry shouts from within the inn. He lurched across the small yard outside the inn as quickly as he could, heading for an alleyway. Behind him the door of the inn was yanked open and he heard more shouts as Hitton's thugs boiled out, weapons drawn.

Marrinek risked a glance over his shoulder. There were at least three of them and they were close behind. He ran as fast as he could, bouncing off stalls and pushing past people until he hit a dead end, an alleyway with brick walls on three sides.

He cursed and raised Bone Dancer as he thudded down the alleyway. Fingers fumbling for the controls, he kept running towards the end wall as he searched for the right control. The sudden booming noise as he released all the energy in Bone Dancer's reservoir echoed along the alleyway and drowned out the sounds of pursuit. The huge release of power blew apart the wall, smashing bricks and causing part of the wall collapsed. A huge cloud of choking dust rose from the collapsed masonry and filled the end of the alley.

Marrinek leapt forward through the cloud and scrambled over the shattered brickwork, almost braining himself as he ducked through the hole in the wall.

The floor on the other side of the wall was lower than the alley and he tumbled forward, carried on by his momentum until he fell to his hands and knees. Bone Dancer slipped from his grasp and skittered across the floor. He heaved himself back to his feet and charged on, bending to scoop up the staff as he went.

Something tall and soft - a bale of wool, maybe - reared suddenly up in front of him and Marrinek bounced off it in the gloom. Then he turned and staggered along a narrow corridor between piles of similar packages, dimly lit by sky lights in the roof. Behind him Tam shouted at his reluctant men to follow him through the gaping hole in the wall. Marrinek grinned at their superstitious hesitation then his face fell as a pair of burly men in aprons came around a corner, drawn by the noise.

He barrelled through them, flailing wildly with Bone Dancer as he went and knocking one to the ground. He almost fell, arms windmilling as he tried to say on his feet, then he righted himself and found his rhythm, pounding through the warehouse as fast as he could go.

He turned left at the end of the huge room and sprinted for a door, hoping it would take him outside. He hurtled through the doorway into some sort of office full of clerks and filing cabinets. The clerks stared in astonishment as he ran between their desks, pulled open the door to the street and charged out onto the street.

Marrinek slowed quickly in the crowds, sucking in air and desperately looking around for signs of pursuit. He ducked his head and pulled up his hood, hunching over and leaning heavily on his staff. Brick dust flapped from the cloak and for several long minutes he tapped and weaved through the streets until his heart slowed and his breathing returned to normal.

Eventually he paused, stopping to rest in the shade of a tall building whose upper floor overhung the ground. He stood there for several minutes, leaning back with his head against the wall, and waited for his hands to stop shaking and the strength to return to his legs.

What had gone wrong in the inn? He didn't know but he feared the worst. Tentatively, he focussed a little power, pulling just enough to prove that he could do it. That was fine, so he widened the draw to pull more. Almost immediately he was hit by another wave of nausea and he barely managed to hold down his lunch.

When the feelings had subsided and he could see clearly again, Marrinek pushed himself off the wall and staggered off down the street to find the twins. It took no effort at all to give every appearance of being mortally tired.

Eastside Bath, when he reached it, looked much as it had done a few hours earlier. Marrinek stopped at the first bath house he came to and went inside. A small hallway led to an archway but as the front door closed a voice from Marrinek's right said, "Good afternoon, sir. How can we be of service?"

Marrinek turned to see an elderly lady sitting behind a

counter in a small room just off the hallway. She looked at him with bright blue eyes.

"Are you looking for something particular?"

"As a matter of fact, yes, I am. I need directions to the house of a Madame Duval."

"Madame Duval, eh? You have expensive tastes, sir, but I'm sure we could find something to suit, if you'd prefer?"

Marrinek shook his head gently then rubbed at his cheek, which he seemed to have bruised, somehow.

"Just directions. I'm meeting some friends."

"I'll just bet you are, sir. Well, if I can't persuade you otherwise, you'll find Madam Duval's on the right-hand side of the street as you head away from the river, about a hundred yards along. Look for the green door, sir, under a golden 'D'."

"Thank you," said Marrinek.

"Good day to you, sir."

Back on the street, Marrinek pondered his next move. He knew little of the city and nothing at all about Madame Duval and her associates. Scouting the building, planning entry and exit routes and gathering equipment would all take time, during which the twins would be at risk. Things would get worse if Hitton sent people to find him. No, the situation called for prompt and decisive action.

He rolled his head from side-to-side to loosen his neck muscles. This would all have been so much easier a couple of years ago when he had more to work with than a flaky set of talents and a staff. He sighed and strode up the street looking for the green door of Madame Duval's.

He found it, as the old woman had said, on the right-hand side of the street under a discreet golden D. The large door was painted a bright green and fronted a tall, comfortable looking house. The ground floor windows were shuttered but the windows of the upper stories were open and he could hear music coming from one of the first-floor windows. On one side the house was bordered by a second, similar looking, establishment. On the other, a narrow alley lined on one side with small shops led between two buildings to connect to another street running parallel with Eastside Bath. A second door led into Madame Duval's from the alley but when Marrinek pushed on it he found it to be firmly closed.

He walked back round to the front of the building and reached for the knob only to encounter an unexpected charm. His fingers just above the surface, he trickled a little power into the knob and gently probed the nature of the charms built into the door and the lock; nothing dangerous, it turned out, just a lock with a link to a bell to announce new arrivals. He pushed a little more power into the charm and temporarily smothered the link to the bell, then he grasped the knob and opened the door.

He stepped quickly inside and closed the door behind him. The entrance hall was long, lined with polished oak panels and richly carpeted. A wide sweeping stairway curved toward the first floor, where a galleried landing overlooked the hallway from beneath an intricately carved ceiling decorated with erotic scenes of classical abandon. To the left and right through arched openings were comfortable sitting rooms lit by elegant charmed lamps that gave out a gentle, reassuring light. The whole atmosphere was soothing, friendly, welcoming. Marrinek, his clothes stained with travel and sweat and violence, felt somewhat out of place.

From upstairs came the sounds of laughter, mingled with music and conversation and beyond them the more muted sounds of passion. Marrinek ignored them and concentrated on the marks he had placed on the twins. Searching for someone using their apprentice marks was a technique born of desperation; easily hidden or obscured, the marks were difficult to sense and impossible to find at anything more than a very short range. He focussed his thoughts first on Floost, who was upstairs, possibly in the attic, and then on Darek, who was toward the rear of the building, maybe in the basement. Both close, both alive, neither currently in a state of pain but both in some degree of distress.

"Oh, hello," said a voice, "I didn't hear you come in."

Marrinek opened his eyes. A young lady dressed in a low-cut dress of red velvet had emerged from the room at the end of the hallway and stopped, clearly surprised to see someone standing unannounced at the bottom of the stairs. She smiled at him.

"Welcome to the house of Madame Duval," she said, recovering her poise as she reached the foot of the stairs and moving smoothly into her greeting, "where you can find all the delights that tempt or titillate. What are you looking for today?"

"Twins," said Marrinek bluntly, "one of each, about fourteen years old."

The hostess paused, thrown off-balance by the unusual nature of the request. She glanced back down the hall and her manner became cold.

"I don't think we can help. Maybe you should try another establishment."

She clapped her hands and a large man in leather jerkin and trousers emerged from the door at the end of the hall, moving to stand behind the hostess, arms folded, frowning down at Marrinek.

"It's very simple," said Marrinek, his voice calm and

unthreatening, "you have my apprentices, twins, a girl and a boy. They were sold to you earlier today, I'm here to take them away."

The hostess backed away leaving room for the thug to step forward.

"I think there's been a misunderstanding. Shad will escort you to the street," she said, backing further down the hallway.

The thug, Shad, moved forward, reaching out to grasp Marrinek's upper arm.

"This way," he said unnecessarily, pushing Marrinek gently but firmly toward the door.

Marrinek allowed himself to be shown back through the door, which was closed and then locked behind him. He stood for a moment, breathing, gathering, thinking. For the briefest moment, he considered knocking down the door and beating his way to the twins but he simply couldn't face the effort. The fight at the Snarling Goat and the subsequent pursuit had tired him more than he would have believed possible and he just wasn't fit enough to take on Shad.

He needed another way in. Cursing his prison-induced physical frailty, he walked around the corner of the building and along the alley toward the rear of the house.

The side door was still locked but the charm was unsophisticated and cheap, meant only to prevent the untalented from opening the door. Marrinek placed a hand over the lock and focussed, directing power into the metal. He closed his eyes, concentrating on the shape of the charm, feeling his way along the contours of the metal. After a few seconds, he had it worked out and a sharp twist of power was all it took to break the charm. There was a crack as the charm failed and a few wisps of smoke rose from the lock where the wood of the door had been singed.

The nausea was powerful, this time, and Marrinek stood there for several seconds, fighting the urge to puke. Then he took a deep breath and pushed open the door. He stepped into the back corridor, an area for the servants to use when this had been the home of a rich merchant, and moved quickly toward the front of the house. He paused to listen at each door and at the second heard the hostess explaining what had happened with their recent visitor; a second voice answered but Marrinek couldn't quite catch the softly spoken words. Time to act.

Marrinek pushed open the door and stepped swiftly into the room, a large study where a lady in her mid-thirties - Madame Duval, maybe? - sat at a desk with the hostess on the other side. Shad was not present, presumably not having been hired for his cognitive processes. Both women turned to look at him as he entered, the hostess showing shock and confusion on her face.

"How did you get in?" she said.

"I think we need to talk," said Marrinek, addressing the woman behind desk, "Madame Duval, I presume?"

The woman stood, waving the hostess to step aside so that she could inspect the intruder. She was, in Marrinek's estimation, a good-looking woman, dressed with style and care to make the most of her considerable assets, although not talented, as far as he could tell. Her dark grey silk gown was conservatively cut and she was wearing a modest silver net sewn with pearls to contrast her black hair.

"I am Duval. Elaine has told me of your request and you are mistaken if you believe I will give up my legally acquired servants. Twins are valuable, especially good-looking specimens like the ones Gander brought me this morning."

Madame Duval reached behind her and pulled a discreet black knob on the wall.

"I don't know who you are or how you got in but this interview is over."

As she finished speaking Shad came in through the side door, long knife in his fist. He moved quickly to stand between Marrinek and Elaine.

Marrinek held up his free hand.

"Peace, friend," he said wearily to Shad, "there's no need for violence here and frankly I'm too tired to make the effort. You are the innocent party, Madame Duval, deceived and defrauded by Gander, so let's drop the pretence. Hitton will be compensating me for the injury he has done by abducting my apprentices and if I ask nicely he'll find something for you too." He spoke calmly, lightly, as if discussing the weather.

Then his voice turned hard and cold.

"But your opportunities to surrender the twins peacefully are now exhausted. Bring them to me, now, then I will talk to Hitton."

Madame Duval held up her hand as Shad started to lumber forward and then sat back in her chair, thinking hard, weighing the situation. She looked at Marrinek, eyes narrowed to suspicious slits.

"Why should I believe you or trust you? How do I know they're your apprentices or that you can persuade Hitton, or even Gander for that matter, to give you, let alone me, a penny?"

Marrinek looked around to find a chair. He pulled the chair round to face Madame Duval, and sat down.

"Good, we're negotiating like civilised people; it's been a busy week for fighting and a few hours of peace would be nice." He gave her a lopsided grin before continuing, calm but firm.

"They're my apprentices and I know they're in the building. You certainly can't keep me from them," he said it with a confidence he didn't really feel at the moment and paused to let it sink in, "and Gander is beyond persuasion, unless you have necromantic powers. Hitton will do as I tell him, if he wishes to preserve his worthless hide, and that will mean money or some equally valuable favours. He doesn't yet know it but his luck has most definitely run out."

Madame Duval raised an eyebrow, and snorted doubtfully. She had long dealt with Hitton and knew from experience that he wasn't easily frightened. Then she waved at Shad and the hostess.

"Leave us. Put the twins in the sitting room next door, make sure they don't leave and don't let anyone bother them. Give them some food."

When the door had closed behind Shad's retreating bulk Madame Duval turned back to Marrinek.

"I'm not a monster, Mr Whoever-you-are, despite the stories people tell. Gander, though, was properly evil, a real shit of a man, and he deserved to die. Did you kill him?"

Marrinek nodded.

"Well I can't say I'm upset," said Madame Duval, "he came here once, before we knew him, and messed up one of my girls. Since then, he gets his perks elsewhere but he won't be missed, not by me or anyone else."

She paused, looking closely at Marrinek as he lounged; he seemed to be completely at ease in her favourite reading chair. She was used to dealing with thugs and brutes but this one was different, exuding an air of confident menace that spoke of long years of violence despite his apparent youth. Finally, she reached out and pulled a blue knob behind her desk.

"I don't know who you are but you must have damn great balls if you're prepared to threaten Hitton. He's a dangerous man, even in this city of violent killers. I dread to think what he might do to you if he catches you," but she smiled as she said it, as if 'dread' wasn't quite the right word. The side door opened and a servant came in.

"Tea please, Nandy, and some of those almond cakes that cook was making this morning."

Nandy curtsied and left by the same door, skirts rustling, and Madame Duval continued.

"This city is run by talented men and women but you knew that already; all cities are run by the same groups, the same types of people. Even some of the thugs and gang-masters have the power and they're not afraid to use it," she held up her hand as Marrinek opened his mouth, "please, hear me out. Those of us without talent have to take our friends where we can find them and we survive by treading a fine line between the blocs that control the streets and rule the city. You, Mr Unnamed Warrior, don't seem the type to follow the rules. Which bloc do you fall into, I wonder?"

Marrinek shrugged.

"Call me Bay. I don't really have a bloc, yet. I'm waiting to see how things go."

He fiddled briefly with the cuff of his shirt, then dropped it when he realised what he was doing.

"I wonder if we might grow to trust each other, Madame Duval, if we might form a bloc of our own?"

Madame Duval looked briefly down at her knuckles, then said, "Well, Bay, my brothers, my father, his brothers and their father all made a living with their fists, either as soldiers, watchmen or thugs. I have as well, in some ways, although these days I prefer to hire other people's fists rather than use my own."

She paused, looking up at Marrinek and wondering how much to say.

"I pay the Flank Siders for protection but all that really means is that the North Enders leave me alone. I can't be seen to take sides against Hitton and his crew, it would be the end of me and my House, regardless of what I pay, and I'm not ready for that yet. I would give much to get out from under the Flanks Siders' thumb but if you want my trust you'll have to do a damn sight more than just talk about threats and revenge and 'compensation'."

"Well, why don't I trust you a little and maybe we can see how things develop. I'm short of friends, you need some effective muscle. Maybe we can help each other."

He paused as the door opened to admit Nandy with a tray of tea and cakes. Madame Duval and Marrinek sat quietly as Nandy poured the tea and handed out plates of almond cakes. After she had left Marrinek continued.

"So how about this. You're out of pocket at Gander's hand; I'll make that up to you. You're paying the Flank Siders; I'll deal with them and their protection racket. In return you'll help me understand the city, get to know its people and work out where the power lies. I have plans and you'll help me flesh them out and then maybe, together, we'll both get what we want."

"How do I know you'll deliver and that you won't just bleed me dry? What's to stop you from taking everything I earn?"

"Ah, well. That's the thing about trust; it has to start somewhere."

Marrinek leaned forward and held out his hand.

"Do we have a deal?" he asked.

Madame Duval looked at him and his hand for ten seconds and Marrinek was beginning to think that she would refuse. Then she nodded firmly and grasped his hand.

"Yes, we have a deal, but you'll have to prove yourself before I even take my place at the table. If anyone asks, I'll deny knowledge of any arrangement and say you threatened to kill me to get what you wanted."

"Agreed. You have more to lose, after all," he said, standing up and walking to the door, "I have some things to do and I need to settle the twins. I'll need information from you later, before I speak to Hitton; till this evening?" He bowed shallowly then slipped through the doorway into the hall without waiting for her to reply.

Madame Duval waited, barely breathing, until she heard Bay walking along the hall with the twins. Once the front door had closed she let out a great breath and collapsed back into her chair, relief and fear rolling off her in waves. She pulled the blue knob again then walked over to the cabinet on the wall opposite the fireplace and poured herself a large measure of lakh, a northern spirit for which she had acquired a taste. She sipped it as she walked back to her desk.

Nandy came in through the rear door.

"Yes, my lady?"

"Fetch Elaine. And bring a pot of coffee." Nandy nodded and ducked out of the room. Elaine came in a few moments later and Madame Duval waved at her to sit in the chair that Marrinek had recently vacated.

"That man, Bay or whatever he's called, is going to cause trouble for us or for the North End gang or for the Flanks Siders or for the Watch, until someone hangs him. He has some big ideas but I don't trust him, not yet. Maybe never," she sipped at her coffee, "so we're going to be cautious. Close the door to all but our most important clients. Don't let anyone in today who you don't already know and get the other two bouncers in from wherever they're skulking; I want lots of hands around in case something happens. Make sure they're fed and comfortable but keep them sober, and don't let them bother the girls or the clients."

Elaine nodded.

"And find out how that bastard got in without coming through the front door. Get a locksmith in, if we have to."

"I'll have someone look at the front door as well, I think," said Elaine, a degree of concern on her face, "he was at the bottom of the stairs and I'm sure the bell didn't ring. Maybe he did something to the lock."

"Yes, have the front door checked as well. And strengthened, if that's possible. For the moment, get Shad to bar the side door." Elaine started to object but Madame Duval was firm.

"Bar the door. They will have to use the rear door for today at least, possibly tomorrow."

Elaine stood up and opened the door, then, turned back to Madame Duval, frowning.

"Was I wrong to buy the twins?"

"No," said Madame Duval, sighing, "we couldn't have left them with Gander, the man was a vicious, unreliable, ignorant, untrustworthy beast. Let's just try to make sure today doesn't get any worse."

13

The city of Esterengel sprawled across the floor of a wide, shallow valley, flooding across the plains on either side of the river Kacoost and flowing over the low hills to smother the countryside in a thick layer of palaces, temples, warehouses, shops, houses and slums. The earliest settlement - a small fortified outpost - had long disappeared under the Imperial fortress-palace of Traebarn as successive Governors had extended or enhanced the complex with new walls, apartments, towers, halls and keeps.

Now the fortress-palace was vast, a town within a city. The ever-practical Imperial government had turned the fortress-palace into a centre of regional administration and pulled within its walls all the offices of state that were required to manage the western region. At the heart of the complex stood the keep, large enough to be considered a major castle in its own right and housing the private apartments of the Governor. Two concentric walls encircled the keep, each containing the barracks, armouries, stables and forges needed to sustain the fortress-palace in the event of a siege.

Not that a siege was likely, not here, so deep within the Empire. There hadn't been an attack on Esterengel for over a hundred years but Imperial planners and engineers had long memories and planned on even longer timescales. Traebarn had been built for a future where it might stand alone against an invader or, though the thought was never spoken, against a rebel army intent on raising a new Emperor.

The palace was not all fortress, though. Amongst the fortifications were gardens for private or public entertaining, fountains and shaded paths for relief from the heat of the long summer months, elegantly trained climbing plants whose scents and colours softened the military bearing of the fortress. Each successive Governor had tinkered with the palace, tearing down only to rebuild as fashions or technologies changed. Ballrooms, apartments, dining halls, pleasure gardens; all had evolved over the decades as tastes changed and the Governors increasingly saw Traebarn as a home to be enjoyed rather than a remote posting to be endured.

The growth of the palace had mirrored the increasing size and importance of the city itself, which was now second only to Khemucasterill, the capital, in terms of population and wealth. The city crowded around the outer wall of the palace and was itself protected by two long walls punctuated with gatehouses and guard towers. As the population had grown and space within the walls had become ever more scarce, new houses and tenements had been erected outside the walls, extending the suburbs of the city and slowly swallowing the small villages that had dotted the plains.

By the time the courier from Heberon crested the final hill above Esterengel and rode down into the valley it was late evening and the sun was sinking through red-tinged skies. He had ridden hard and made excellent time, changing horses at the regular waypoints along the road and stopping only briefly for food and water, so that a journey that would normally take four or five days had been completed in only twenty-six hours. He was exhausted.

His tired horse trotted along the road toward the southern gate in the outer wall, slowing to a walk as the road grew busier and houses began to cast long shadows. Most of the farmers, hauliers and travellers had already returned home or reached their destinations but the roads were now filling with people looking for entertainment. The main road was crowded with people heading for inns and taverns and on the few public spaces and parks between the buildings tumblers, musicians and strolling players performed, hats or instrument cases set before them to catch coins tossed by their amused audiences.

Through this light-hearted crowd, the courier guided his horse, eventually passing under the inner wall as the sun disappeared behind the western hills. He dismounted and led his horse along the main avenue to the Traebarn palace, heading for the modest gate used by guards and servants. Here he stopped to show his badge of office to the men on watch before finally leading his horse into the fortress where he was able to pass it to a stable boy. Around the yard and along the walls lamps were being lit as the long day ended. Those who had been on duty for much of day were retiring for their evening meal; the night watchmen and guards who would stand duty overnight were moving purposefully around the fortress, securing the smaller gates and checking that all was as it should be.

The courier hefted his bag on his shoulder and followed the path to the main part of the fortress. The corridors through which he stalked were empty except for a few servants still running errands and he made his way quickly to the administrative offices in the keep where the clerks worked. During the working day, these areas of the fortress would be busy with men and women performing the myriad tasks required to manage the city and its province but at night the rooms were mostly empty. The courier had to search through several offices before he found a secretary, yawning over an accounts book as he worked through a stack of receipts and invoices.

The courier leant against the frame of the open door. There was a clerk sitting at a small desk, dressed in the sober blue and grey uniform of the Imperial civil service, scratching away at a paper. The courier paused for a moment to see if he had been noticed, knocked on the wooden panelling when it became clear that he hadn't. The clerk, startled by the unexpected visitor, looked round sharply and knocked a pile of papers onto the floor.

"Now look what you've made me do," he complained, moving to collect the fallen documents, "what are you doing wandering around at this time of night?"

"I have an urgent message for the Governor, from Heberon."

"From Heberon? Nothing urgent ever comes from Heberon - it's all receipts and reports and boring, boring notices." The clerk looked with distaste at the letter held in the courier's hand and sighed.

"Don't tell me, let me guess," said the clerk, "are the sheep rebelling again? Or maybe there's been a rain of frogs?" he asked, searching the courier's face for any hint of humour. He sighed.

"Does it need a reply tonight or can it wait till morning? You can see how much work I've got to get through and if I have to start disturbing people at this time of night..." he tailed off as he caught the look on the courier's face.

"When did you say you left Heberon?"

"I didn't. I left yesterday evening," said the courier wearily, "I changed horses five times and rode through the night because the Captain told me to get the message here as soon as possible. He was very definite about that. No stops, not even to sleep. And I haven't eaten since this afternoon."

The clerk sighed again.

"Right, fine. I'm Krant, by the way. I can't get you to the Governor but we can try to find her private secretary, Rincon. Will that do?"

He stood up and stretched, hands on his hips as he twisted back and forth.

"I'm a martyr to these chairs, you know, dreadful! Like little wooden torture devices designed to break the spirit of man. They'll be the death of me one day."

The courier stood at the door, a complete lack of sympathy showing on his face. He waved the message tube at Krant.

"Ah yes, sorry."

Krant stretched once more, then squeezed past the courier into the corridor.

"Secretary Rincon's office is this way, although he may well be somewhere else."

Krant led the way down the corridor and into a larger hallway where he stopped before a set of double doors. He turned back to the courier.

"Are you sure you want an audience? I could just take it in for you? No? Right, well, here we go."

He knocked on the left-hand door and pushed it open, stepping through into a large chamber, plainly furnished. The courier followed him in to find a man of medium build and indeterminate years sitting behind a desk, reading; Secretary Rincon, he assumed. The man looked up as Krant moved to stand in front of the desk.

"My apologies, sir, but there is an urgent message from Heberon," he said, flapping his hand at the courier. The man scuttled forward and placed the message tube on the desk in front of Rincon.

"From Administrator Nison, sir."

Rincon looked at the message tube with a certain lack of haste before waving Krant and the courier back.

"Wait over there. Is the Administrator expecting an immediate response?" asked Rincon. When the courier shook his head, Rincon picked up the message tube and broke the seal with his thumb. He pulled out the message, broke the second seal and quickly scanned the contents.

Then he stood up so fast he knocked over his chair, startling Krant, who took another step back. Krant had worked in the offices at Traebarn for almost four years and this was the first time he had ever seen Rincon react to anything. It was a deeply unsettling experience.

"This is dated yesterday; when did you leave Heberon?" said Rincon, almost shouting.

"Yesterday evening, sir. It's been a long day."

"You've done well to get here and you have my thanks. Krant, see that this gentleman is fed and watered and alert the Guild that we will have more messages to despatch shortly. Go, go!"

Rincon swept around the desk heading for the door and ushering them from the room. He locked the door behind him and almost ran down the corridor, leaving Krant and the bewildered courier standing alone.

"Well, I suppose we had better make a start. I'll show you to the kitchens, although what Cook will make of you I don't know."

Krant sighed again, squared his shoulders and struck out back along the corridor to his office.

"Come on, it's this way."

Rincon hurried along the corridor, the message grasped in one hand. He wasn't prone to self-doubt - nobody at his level of the Imperial civil service could afford the luxury and the long years tended to weed out the weak or easily stressed - but he stopped at one point to read the message again. It looked no different, and no better, on second reading:

I regret to inform you that a transport ship, The Gilded Branch, foundered five days ago off the coast at Heberon. The only passenger was Abaythian Marrinek. Reports suggest he is alive and has escaped west to the town of Catshed. His location is unknown.

It was signed 'Adm. Nison', a name familiar to Rincon through his steady stream of tedious, workmanlike reports. Solid, reliable and not given to flights of fancy; a man unlikely to write until sure of his facts. A man, in short, who couldn't easily be dismissed or ignored. Dammit. What with reports of skirmishes on the north-western borders of the province and the Emperor's continuous demands for additional troops and resources to accelerate his eastward expansion plans, this sort of embarrassing failure was really very inconvenient.

He hurried on, heading for the private quarters of Lady Camille von Crarne, Governor of the western province and the Emperor's direct representative. He swept past the guards at the entrance to the royal apartments, entering the part of the palace set aside for the Governor and, should he happen to grace the city with his presence, the Emperor and his entourage.

The contrast between the functional layout of the administrative wing and the decadent opulence of the private royal apartments could hardly be greater. The polished wooden floors of the clerk's offices contrasted strongly to the thick carpet of the apartment, warmed from beneath by a network of lead pipes carrying hot water through power-crafted stonework. The plain oak-panelled or white-washed walls of the working areas of the fortress were here replaced with alcoves lit by charmed lanterns cunningly concealed to illuminate without intruding and housing elegant power-wrought sculptures of stone or beautiful vases of paper-thin ceramic on finely turned pedestals of exotic hardwood. Paintings and tapestries hung on the walls between the alcoves and the ceiling was decorated with more charmed lanterns so that it seemed to glow, casting a gentle light over the corridors, stairways and public hallways between the private suites.

At the top of the stair near the Governor's suite Rincon passed a delicately ornate tea service displayed in a cabinet that rose almost to the ceiling, a gift from the Emperor and newly arrived with a company of soldiers from the far south-east of the empire, site of the army's most recent conquest. Rincon shared Lady Camille's obsession with fine porcelain and it was only today that the cabinet had been installed and the set displayed. He barely noticed it as he hurried down the corridor, so disturbed was he by this evening's news.

He eventually stopped outside Lady Camille's suites and spoke to her bodyguards.

"Is her Ladyship free?" From behind the door came the muffled sounds of music and laughter.

"I believe she is entertaining some of the musicians from this afternoon's command performance, sir, along with some of the local, ah, nobles." The guard seemed a little embarrassed, although Lady Camille's pleasures were neither secret nor unseemly. Rincon paused, nodded, then knocked on the door. The guard opened it just far enough to allow Rincon to slip into the outer chamber before he closed it quietly.

Rincon stood for a moment, orienting himself within the normally familiar room. For this evening's party, the high ceiling had been hidden under great sweeps of brightly coloured material. The walls were hung with more of the same fabric and the carpets that normally covered the floor had been replaced by a number of huge overlapping rugs. Dozens of silk cushions arranged in piles at various places had replaced the everyday chairs and furniture that were usually present. The overall effect was to give the chamber the appearance of a tent in the style of the southern desert traders, albeit on a rather larger scale than might normally be expected and without the sand and the camels.

Rincon made his way across the room as quickly and politely as he could manage, manoeuvring carefully between the groups of nobles who were clearly enjoying the selection of food and drink being distributed from trays by servants dressed in uniform flowing robes of grey and red.

Some of the nobles may have been surprised to see him, a mere civil servant, intruding into the party but they were quick to smile and bow and make space for him; in the complex world of court politics, Rincon had both power, as the gateway to her Ladyship, and influence. None of the nobles here this evening could afford to incur his displeasure.

On the far side of the room, Lady Camille was lying under a shade on a huge pile of cushions. Two servants in grey and red stood to either side and cooled her with huge fans made from bamboo and the features of an exotic bird. Lady Camille was holding a glass of white wine in one hand and picking dates from a glass bowl with the other, popping them daintily into her mouth while around her sprawled her closest friends and admirers. Rincon bowed when he was eventually able to stand before her and flicked a discrete coded hand signal to indicate an urgent, but not immediately dangerous, situation.

For the benefit of the guests, he said, "My apologies, my lady, but something... unusual... has come to my attention."

"What ho, Rincon." she said in a jolly voice, saluting him with her wine glass. Rincon kept his face straight but inside he groaned. Lady Camille rarely drank enough for it to affect her behaviour but tonight, in familiar company and the presence of several very old friends, she had clearly decided to enjoy herself. She clicked her fingers and waved at Rincon.

"Take a glass, Albert, and pull up a cushion or three. Here," she said, pushing the glass bowl toward him, "have a date. They really are very good."

Rincon took a glass from the tray and sipped the wine. He flicked the hand signal again, hoping this time that she might notice, but she was already turning back to her conversation. He sighed.

"It is a matter of some urgency, your ladyship."

"Can't it wait till morning?" said one of the men lying on the cushions just outside Lady Camille's shade.

"My lord, I'm sorry, but I do not believe that it can."

Rincon turned back to Lady Camille and flicked his hand signal for the third time.

"Please, my lady, if I might just have a few minutes of your time?"

She sighed and looked around for somewhere to put down her glass. A servant stepped in smartly from behind her and relieved her of it before stepping back out of the way.

"Very well, Rincon," she said, finally acknowledging his hand signals with one of her own, "let's step next door. Philip, be a dear and help me up." Philip, lord of a considerable manor to the east of Esterengel and enormously wealthy, stood quickly and held out his hand to help Lady Camille clamber to her feet.

"Thank you. Keep things going, I'll only be a few minutes."

She straightened up and focussed on Rincon.

"Lead the way, my good man, lead the way." She followed Rincon across the floor, exchanging brief words with several of her guests on the way, then passed into her private office as he held the door open.

He followed her into the room then closed the door quietly behind them, dulling the sounds of the party. Lady Camille sat down at her desk and focussed her will to cause several more lamps to begin to glow. When she was happy with the brightness of the room she sat back and waved Rincon into the seat opposite.

"You look very serious, Albert," she said, scratching at her ear with a long finger before folding her hands on the desk, "I think you had better tell me what is worrying you."

"Thank you, my lady. This note arrived maybe half an hour ago from Administrator Nison in Heberon."

Rincon passed over the note then waited while Lady Camille read and absorbed its contents.

"Nison's reports are generally very dull," said Rincon, "but he is a highly effective administrator and not, I think, given to wild surmising or overreaction."

Lady Camille stared at him over the top of the note, her eyes slightly dulled by alcohol. Then she took a few deep breaths and pinched the bridge of her nose.

"You're happy that the note is genuine and its contents believable?"

Rincon nodded.

"It was sealed with Nison's personal seal and yes, I think that the contents are believable, much though we might prefer them to be otherwise. I think it very likely that Nison impressed a very great sense of urgency on the courier, who left Heberon late yesterday afternoon and must have ridden like the wind to have arrived here so soon."

Lady Camille read the note again, then put it down on the desk and closed her eyes.

"This was not the sort of news I had wanted to receive during a party, Rincon, especially after spending a couple of hours getting into the spirit." She sighed and opened her eyes.

Rincon said nothing. It wasn't the sort of news anyone in the Imperial Government would want to receive at any time. They sat in silence for some moments before Lady Camille spoke again.

"You were right, of course, this couldn't wait till morning, although the gods alone know what we'll need to do to make this right. I certainly don't."

Rincon looked across the desk at her.

"I gave this matter some thought on my way over, my lady. I believe we need to send word to the capital."

Lady Camille looked at him, then stood and walked to the side table to pour herself a glass of heavily watered wine. She raised the jug toward him but he still had his glass from the party. She walked back over to her chair and sat down, sipping her drink.

"Right, yes, send word to the capital. And to the Governor of Malteron prison - that was where the Traitor was imprisoned, wasn't it? - to find out how this happened. I'll see someone hang for this and it might as well be him. If he put Marrinek on an ill-maintained ship..."

"Yes, my lady, although a summer storm might over-whelm even the most seaworthy of vessels."

"Pah! Storms, maintenance problems, bad navigation. Who knows? It might just as well have been sea monsters or pirates or ship-worm. Maybe Marrinek conjured a giant squid to pull the ship under the waves and release him!"

She was angry now that the alcoholic haze had cleared enough for her to appreciate the situation. She picked up the note, read it again, then threw it back down on the desk in disgust.

"His Majesty will be spectacularly displeased. Actually, that might be an understatement."

She sipped at her drink, then drained the glass and set it back on the desk.

"Right. Summon the Council, Rincon, I want them here first thing in the morning. Tell them nothing about this - I don't want anyone to know what's happened, although the news will leak as soon as we begin discussing things tomorrow. Who else knows?"

"Only you and I, so far. I don't believe either the courier or Krant, the junior clerk who brought me the message, know what it contains, although Krant will be able to work it out if rumours start to fly."

"Good. Is Krant trustworthy?"

"I believe so, my lady, although he is very junior and only moderately talented. Smart and reasonably competent, he probably has a long career ahead of him if he can learn to control his whining. He was the only clerk in the building when the courier arrived, working through the night to make up for some, ah, failings earlier in the week."

Lady Camille paused, thinking hard about her next move.

"Send the courier back to Heberon with instructions for Nison to scour the countryside and to search the coast, just in case they've missed a corpse; that'll keep them busy and might actually be useful."

"And Krant?"

"Yes, Krant. We need to keep him busy as well. Roust him out and use him to draft all the messages we send on this topic. Keep him close, for the moment. Don't let him out of the building and leave the other clerks in the dark." She stood up and walked around the desk to stand before a six-foot square map of the province and surrounding areas which hung on the wall. She stared at it thoughtfully, her chin cupped in her hand.

Prepared by the Guild of Cartographers, it was the most detailed and the most accurate map in the city but she was painfully aware that it was vague in places and wildly inaccurate in others, especially to the west beyond the Empire's borders. Each year the Guild sent her a new map and each year's map was a little more useful and a little less decorative. The area was so large, though, that in many places the map showed little more than forest or plains or swamp and she was sure that even those vague descriptions were not all correct.

Lady Camille found Heberon on the south coast and traced the route to Catshed to the north-west. The roads around in this area were poor, as were most of the people. There were few towns and no cities of any size.

"Where would he go, where would he go?" muttered Lady Camille, staring at the map. She didn't believe for one moment that the Traitor would stay in Catshed. The map showed a small walled settlement hardly big enough for two inns and a cooler and far too close to the Empire for a fugitive.

"Where would you go, Rincon, if you escaped just west of Heberon but wanted to get as far from the Empire as possible?"

Rincon walked to her side and stared at the map.

"The note says he went there, to Catshed," he said, pointing, "which is at the end of the Scla mountain range. To the north of the mountains on the other side of the river is what's left of the former kingdom of Sclareme but there's nothing there now. I can't imagine he would go that way," said Rincon.

"And if he heads east, he quickly arrives back in the Empire. If he had wanted to return home he wouldn't have gone to Catshed at all," said Lady Camille, "so let's rule out east as well."

"He could go upstream," said Rincon, "follow the river or take passage on a trading boat and head for the kingdoms to the north of the Toothnail mountains. Plenty of work up there for a man of Marrinek's talents."

"Plenty," agreed Lady Camille, "and they're a tough people but somehow I don't think so."

She traced the line of the river Guiln southward from Catshed until it hit the Vensi, the mighty river that drained snow melt from the Scla mountains into the Tardean Sea, striking the coast at the city of Vensille.

"Vensille," whispered Lady Camille, tapping at a city marked at the extreme south western edge of the map, "from Catshed, the easiest settlement to reach of any size is Vensille. He could just float down the river, maybe take a barge all the way to the coast and lose himself in the biggest city within, what, three hundred miles?"

"Maybe more, my lady," said Rincon, nodding, "the city has grown markedly in recent decades."

She found Vensille on the south coast, not all that far from the Imperial town of Heberon or, for that matter, the prison island of Ankeron West. Not that the prison was mapped, of course. The island was shown, some thirty miles off the coast, but it was unnamed and she was able to identify it only because she knew what was there.

She traced the links between Heberon, Catshed and Vensille, running her elegantly shaped nail across the map's surface. The cross-border roads were poor in this area but she knew that traders regularly travelled between the towns and not always by sea. She squatted down so that she could squint at Vensille but it was little more than a generic walled city on the river. Then she stood up.

"Yes, Vensille," she said with more confidence than was truly justified, "if I were Marrinek, in Catshed after escaping from an Imperial prison transport, I would head to Vensille."

Rincon looked doubtful.

"Is that not too obvious, my lady? Might he not have

chosen to go upriver, to try his luck in the northern kingdoms?"

Camille shook her head. The more she thought about it, the more she was convinced she was right.

"No, Vensille. It's a large trading city, easily reached from his last known position and convenient for further flight. From there he could take a ship to anywhere around the Tardean Sea or beyond."

"I suppose he could even settle there," conceded Rincon, "maybe make charms for a living, or serve in the Watch or something."

He stopped talking under Lady Camille's highly sceptical gaze.

"I agree, my lady, that those aren't likely outcomes, but they are not impossible."

"Maybe not, but either way, his future employment doesn't need to concern us. What's important is that we know where he is," she paused, then corrected herself, "or rather, we know where he is likely to be, having deduced it from a series of logical analyses."

"Vensille or Catshed, he is still in Duke Rhenveldt's territory," observed Rincon.

There was a pause for a few moments as Lady Camille stared again at the map.

"Do you wish me to do anything about your party, my lady?"

"Hmm, what? No, let them be. But find Philip, Lord Adraude, and bring him in here while he is still sober." Rincon nodded and disappeared through the door, returning a few minutes later with Lord Adraude.

"Thank you, Rincon. Find Krant; I think we'll send him to Vensille; you can begin the preparations. Be back here before the next bell." Rincon nodded and slipped out through the door.

"Take a seat, Philip," said Lady Camille, waving him toward a chair before turning away from the wall map and taking her own seat behind the desk.

"How many troops do you have under your command at the moment?"

Lord Adraude looked surprised but he saw the serious look on Lady Camille's face and decided that this was probably not the time for jests.

"Here in Esterengel, my lady, we have around four thousand soldiers, mostly foot but also a few companies of cavalry. Across the rest of the province, another few thousand but those are spread widely and it would take time to gather them. The nobles have more, of course, but getting control of them would be tricky." Lord Adraude looked at the map, then back to Lady Camille.

"You have something in mind?"

Lady Camille ignored the question.

"What of the Specialists, Lord Adraude? Where are they now and do we have access to them?"

Lord Adraude hesitated, his mouth open, as he considered the question.

"Specialists, my lady? You mean the Shock Corps?"

She nodded.

"No, we don't have access to them. They were Marrinek's troops and when he fell the regiment was broken and dispersed. Several, those most closely associated with the Traitor, disappeared. Others were sent to regional units but most are with the Imperial armies in the east. There are none in the west, that I know of."

Lady Camille looked again at the map then back at Lord Adraude.

"Hypothetically, if we needed to capture, say, Vensille, do you have enough troops?"

Lord Adraude shifted nervously in his seat and grimaced. He put down his glass and leant forward, thinking hard.

"Hypothetically? No. Vensille has strong walls and Duke Rhenveldt has, by all accounts, done an excellent job of making the city defensible. We would need to surround it on land, cut off the river and blockade the harbour. Even with all the soldiers in the province, including the levies and the nobles, we couldn't storm the city while it was defended and without a naval blockade, a siege would be ineffective."

Lord Adraude fell silent, then said, "Are you planning to invade Vensille? There are surely easier targets if expansion is desirable. Maybe we could look at some of the northern kingdoms..." He fell silent again as Lady Camille shook her head.

"Forget all that," she said, "military action was something I wanted to rule out, not an option I wanted to pursue. Discovering that the military option isn't an option at all merely forces us to look for other, more peaceful, more imaginative, solutions. It's probably for the best."

"Might I ask, my lady, why you need options at all? I wasn't aware of any particular threats or plans; your questions suggest you have something in mind, or that something is worrying you."

Lady Camille looked at him again, weighing her words. The effects of the alcohol were wearing off and she had the beginnings of a mild hangover. She sighed; she really ought to know better at her age but sometimes it was nice to relax and spend an evening drinking with friends as she had done in her youth.

"Yes, Philip, something is worrying me. We will talk about it tomorrow at the Council meeting."

"Tomorrow? I don't think there is a meeting scheduled until next week."

"Tomorrow. You'll have a message later this evening. In the meantime, go home and get some sleep. Talk to nobody about this, not even your wife."

"I understand," said Lord Adraude, although Lady Camille was quite certain that he did not since she had carefully and deliberately avoided giving him any useful information, "until tomorrow, my lady."

Lord Adraude stood, bowed, and left through the door, making his way through the continuing party and out of the Governor's apartments.

Lady Camille sat alone for a few minutes, then stood up and walked over to a solid cabinet on the opposite wall. The heavy doors were locked but there was no visible keyhole. Lady Camille found the chain around her neck and gently pulled the thin charm, about the size of her little finger, from its hiding place. She held the charm against first one door and then the other, focussing a little power into the charm as it rested against the wood. There was a clunk and the tall doors swung slowly open. A final touch of power and the charmed lamps within the cabinet began to glow, illuminating the contents.

Lady Camille's collection of charms was extensive and most of them were kept within this cabinet, protected both by the locked and hardened doors and a particularly unpleasant trap that would seriously inconvenience anyone attempting to gain entry by force. She selected two of the more discreet rings and slipped them onto her fingers. She never went anywhere without a selection of both defensive and offensive charms but this evening's news had set her on edge and she felt the need to augment her not inconsiderable abilities.

Her hand hovered over the sword but it would have seemed odd worn against her dress - she wasn't ready yet to abandon all sense of style - and she selected instead a slim wand of polished wood which she slid into her hair. It was less powerful than the sword, true, but also much less obvious. Satisfied, she closed the door and used the charmed key to lock the doors.

She sat down at her desk and drummed her fingers on the surface as she thought about her next move. Then she opened a drawer, took out pen, ink and paper and began to write. After a few minutes, she stopped, satisfied that she had completely described the situation and her intended actions. She read through the short report once more, signed it and rolled it into a steel tube, sealing it with a brief focus of power and attuning the lock to the Emperor so that only he could open it; if anyone else tried to force the lock their power would now subtly alter the tube, recording their attempt and making obvious to the Emperor that someone had tried to access his personal mail.

She laid the tube on the table as Rincon came back into the office. The sounds of the ongoing party were suddenly loud through the open door before being muffled almost to silence as the second man closed the door behind him. Rincon stopped in front of the desk.

"This is Master Krant, my lady. The courier from Heberon has been given a bed in the guardhouse of the royal apartments and will be sent on his way at dawn. He is being watched by people I trust."

"Good. Welcome, Master Krant. You'll find pen and paper at that desk." Lady Camille gestured at second desk, located against the wall and at right angles to her own.

Krant nodded and bowed nervously, "Yes, my lady." He sat down at the desk and pulled a fresh piece of paper toward him then grabbed a pen from the pot. In his haste, he knocked over the pot, sending pens flying across the desk.

"My apologies, my, my, my lady," he stammered, grasping at the pens and stuffing them back into their pot. He returned the pot to its station, smoothed his paper and turned back to face Lady Camille.

"Krant," said Lady Camille. Krant looked up, face radiating enthusiasm and confusion borne of his sudden elevation from junior clerk to the Governor's scribe.

"You are here because you know that an urgent message from Heberon has been delivered. Are you aware of the contents of that message?"

Krant shook his head then remembered who was asking the question.

"No, my lady."

"You have heard of Abaythian Marrinek?" said Rincon.

"Yes, sir. The Traitor. In prison."

"No, Krant, not in prison. Not anymore. He has escaped," said Lady Camille leaning forward, "and this information must go no further. If you mention it outside this room, if you even hint that it might be true or lend credence to a rumour, I'll have your tongue. Is that clear?"

"Yes, my lady, perfectly."

Krant swallowed, his face grey. Rincon couldn't tell if it was the news about Marrinek or fear of Lady Camille that had most affected him.

"Very well."

She settled back in her chair and glanced at Rincon before fixing her gaze on Krant.

"Let's make a start. First, a letter to Duke Rhenveldt of Vensille."

She steepled her fingers and laid her head against the chair's backrest so that she was looking up at the ceiling, then dictated a letter to the Duke that set out the position in broad terms.

"We very much wish to recover the traitor Marrinek and I trust that you will lend whatever aid you feel is appropriate should he be found within your borders. Signed Lady Camille etc. etc."

Krant completed the letter, sprinkled sand on the parchment to dry the ink then passed it across the Lady Camille. She scanned it quickly.

"You have a neat hand. A tidy hand speaks of a well-ordered mind, I think, and that may well be useful. Tell me, what do you know of Vensille and its dukedom?"

Krant seemed rather surprised to have been asked.

"Er, well, my lady, it is, er, the er, major city of the south coast and the first of the independent city-states that you would reach if you travelled west beyond our borders. The er, major exports are manufactured goods, wine and foodstuffs from the surrounding plains but the true wealth of the city comes from the tax levied on the trade passing northward through the city and along the river or southward to the Tardean Sea."

He paused, waiting to see if more was expected.

"The Duke has fortified the city to deter what he perceives to be Imperial aggression, expending vast sums of money on the walls and other defences. The population is largely supportive of their Duke, seeing in him a person capable of defending both their freedoms and their way of life. The streets, although less well-ordered than those of an Imperial city, are generally safe and relatively clean."

He paused again then said, "Should I go on, my lady? I have read extensively on the subject so if there was a particular item about which you were curious..." He stopped, fidgeting with the ends of his sleeves.

Rincon cleared his throat.

"Thank you, Krant. I would not have seen you as a student of either economics or politics. Looks can be deceiving, I suppose."

Lady Camille was clearly reaching a decision.

"Yes. Yes, I think you'll do. Good. Well, let's get on. We have more letters to write, Mr Krant."

Krant nodded and turned back to his desk, shuffling papers and preparing to take dictation. Lady Camille looked at Rincon.

"And you need to complete the preparations we discussed earlier," she said, nodding meaningfully at Krant's back, "tomorrow, mid-morning at the latest I think."

"Yes, my lady, that should work nicely. I will make the arrangements."

"So. First, we need to call the Council to attend me tomorrow morning."

She dictated a brief note.

"Four copies, to be sent to the Council members as soon as we've finished here tonight."

She dictated another note to be sent to the High Council in Khemucasterill, the capital, then one for the Emperor himself.

"Find a courier to leave first thing in the morning to take this message to the Emperor. This is a sealed tube to be delivered directly to the hand of the Emperor, wherever he may be." She reached out to pass the tube to Krant but held it as he took the other end.

"Don't let me down, Krant," she said, looking into his

eyes, "you have heard the stories, I suppose? About what happens to people who let me down?"

He had heard the stories, of course, everyone had, but he had never really believed them, dismissing them as old wives' tales or make-believe, the kind of things you told your children if you wanted them to behave properly and grow up in fear of a bogeyman. Till now, while he was just taking dictation, he still hadn't believed them. Now, under the direct gaze of the Emperor's most trusted servant, the Governor of the Western Province, the stories suddenly seemed far less amusing. He nodded dumbly.

"Good," she said coldly, "that saves me explaining what happens if you don't do what I want or if you fail me in some small way."

She released the message tube and sat back in her seat. Krant placed the tube on his desk next to the other notes and letters and took up his pen.

"What is your full name, Mr Krant?"

"Ezbedah Krant, my lady"

"Ezbedah. Unusual name. Another note, I think. 'I, Lady Camille Nydaekon, Governor of the Western Province, do hereby request and require that you should allow the bearer to pass freely without let or hindrance and to afford the bearer such assistance and protection as may be necessary.' Pass that over."

She took out her charmed wax holder as Krant sprinkled the note with sand. After scanning it quickly, she dripped green sealing wax onto the bottom of the page and pressed her ring into it before signing her name above the seal and handing the note back to Krant.

"That's everything I think, Master Krant. Find a message tube for that and keep it safe. Rincon will make the rest of the arrangements."

"My lady? What arrangements?" Krant looked confused.

But Lady Camille was already thinking about the next question and didn't answer him directly.

"Let's send Master Krant home for the moment, Rincon, he'll need his sleep."

Rincon nodded.

"That will be all, Krant. We won't need you again this evening. Report to my office once you have breakfasted tomorrow morning. Goodnight."

"Yes sir, thank you, sir. Goodnight, my lady."

Krant, still looking confused but unwilling to push his luck by asking further questions, made his escape before something even more unexpected happened. Once the door had closed behind him Lady Camille said, "He'll do nicely. Just smart enough, I think."

"Yes," said Rincon, "although maybe not smart enough to deal with Duke Rhenveldt. I have heard that he can be particularly persuasive and Master Krant, while tolerably clever, is neither wise nor experienced enough to handle him."

"Well, that at least is a risk we might be able to mitigate by providing the right companion. They might even stumble across the Traitor, although that's probably too much to hope for. Who do we have who could accompany Mr Krant?"

Rincon gave her a mirthless smile.

"Mr Gavelis is, I think, between engagements after returning from the northern borders with a most satisfactory outcome. I believe he might be prevailed upon to play the part of a personal servant and that Master Krant, appointed to be your personal representative, could be tasked with delivering a message to the Duke. The presence of Mr Gavelis would lend gravitas to the young Master Krant and, together, they might gain useful access to the Duke's court." He paused while Lady Camille thought about this. The court of Vensille was a place where secrets were easily uncovered but within which Lady Camille had not yet succeeded in placing or turning agents. The chance to insert Mr Gavelis into the court, however slim and even within the context of the wider disaster, was not one she was keen to miss. "And, as you say, they might even unearth the Traitor," said Rincon, which seemed to clinch the matter.

"Excellent. The capture or termination of Marrinek, will of course be most desirable, but the opportunity to put one of the Emperor's specialists at the centre of Vensille presents a wealth of further possibilities. I shall ponder them overnight and confirm my wishes tomorrow morning before you brief Krant."

"Very good, my lady. I will speak to Mr Gavelis and brief him on the wider situation."

Lady Camille grimaced slightly but Rincon was right. Briefing Mr Gavelis, now that she knew he was in the city, was necessary even if he wasn't directly engaged in the matter.

Rincon stood up and bowed.

"Good night, my lady."

"Bright and early tomorrow, Rincon, bright and early." The door closed behind him and she was alone again with her worries.

14

Marrinek found Floost and Darek sitting side by side on a small settee in the sitting room across the hall from Madame Duval's study. Darek was sporting an ugly black eye but other than that they appeared to be unharmed. They looked up when he came in but didn't seem overjoyed to see him. Neither of them said anything as he sat down in the chair next to them and leant his head back against the wall.

"I told you I would look after you while you were my apprentices and I meant it. Gander will not bother you again. Madame Duval and I have reached an arrangement; Hitton will compensate her for Gander's fraud but you are still my apprentices and so you're coming with me. Are you alright?"

They stared at him for a long minute, then Darek said, "What about Pratek and the rest of the North End gang? Are they going to bother us? Maybe we'd be better off without all of you, we've coped so far." Floost said nothing, she just watched Marrinek with big, suspicious eyes.

"Leave if you want to. I'll release you and you can find

your own way in the world, but the training I offer is not something you will find elsewhere. I promise, in two months you will know enough to be able to deal with the likes of those thugs from the alley. In two years, if you work hard, you'll be amongst the most dangerous people in the city, if that's what you want to be. By the end of your apprenticeship, assuming we all live that long, you can go your own ways and make a good living amongst the noble families of the Empire or the city states or anywhere else you choose."

Floost and Darek looked at him dubiously.

"Why should we trust you?" said Floost, "How do we know you didn't sell us to Gander?"

Marrinek sighed and ran his fingers through his hair.

"Gander is dead. He worked for a man called Hitton and he's someone I still need to talk to. After that I may have to deal with a few more of the North End gang but I don't think they will be a real problem."

Marrinek stopped and looked at their shocked faces.

"What? Did you think I would let someone kidnap my apprentices and sell them into the flesh trade? That there would be no consequences? Gander and Pratek were boasting about it in the Snarling Goat, boasting to my face when I confronted them. I don't think they knew what they had done."

Floost and Darek shared a glance

"You really will teach us?" said Floost.

"Yes. Now listen. Trust and loyalty work in two directions. I've given you food and money for clothes and promised to teach and protect you. I have secured your release from Madame Duval and provided board and lodging. But now we need to go. I have things to do and that includes beginning your education. This will only work if you trust me and follow my instructions."

Marrinek stood up and walked to the door.

"Are you ready?" he asked.

Floost and Darek glanced at each other again. It wasn't that they trusted Marrinek, not really, but what choice did they have? They followed him out onto the street and hurried after him as he strode through the crowds, heading for the Jewel.

"Did you get everything I asked you to buy this morning?" asked Marrinek, stopping outside a charm supplies shop.

"Most of it. We got bags and some clothes and shoes," said Darek, holding up his new bag as evidence.

"And I got a cloak," said Floost, "but we didn't find one for Darek."

"We didn't get the iron either," said Darek.

"Right, in here," said Marrinek. He held open the door and followed them into the shop. A counter ran lengthways through the small room and the three of them stood, slightly cramped, facing a wall lined with drawers and cupboards of various shapes and sizes. The room was lit by the sunlight coming in through the small windows at the front of the shop and by charmed lamps on the walls, which gave off a soft yellow light similar to a candle but brighter and more constant. The shop was cool after the warmth of the street but Marrinek couldn't see quite why that might be so. On a stool at the far end of the store sat the owner, who looked up as they came in and smiled.

"Good afternoon sir, young master, mistress. Welcome to my humble shop. My name is Eaves. How may I be of assistance?"

"Good afternoon, Mr Eaves," said Marrinek, "I'm Bay and these are my apprentices. Very new apprentices." He frowned at Darek, who was leaning his elbows on the counter, and raised an eyebrow until Darek noticed and stood upright.

"That's better. We do not lounge, Darek; stand up straight, pay attention and wait quietly."

Marrinek turned back to the shopkeeper.

"I need basic supplies. A pound of lead and two rods of wrought iron. A reel of copper wire. Eight short ash or oak staves." The shopkeeper bustled around as Marrinek listed his requirements.

"What does that come to so far?"

"Let me see, let me see. The staves are a penny for four, the iron tuppence for two, the copper wire is four pence so with the lead a shilling and a half, sir."

"Do you have tungsten or iridium?"

Mr Eaves paused and Marrinek could see him calculating the potential value of his newest customer.

"I have a little tungsten sir, a very little, but even the amounts I have will be in excess of forty shillings."

Darek's mouth dropped open and he started to say something until Marrinek glared at him.

"Those are expensive items, young master, very rare and very expensive. Forty shillings is a fair price. The iridium is even more."

"Well, even at half that price my funds would not currently stretch so far."

Marrinek looked back at the shopkeeper who was now eyeing him warily. He laughed.

"Fear not, my friend, I can cover these few items."

He pulled coins from his purse and laid them on the counter.

"I will want iridium, though, as soon as I have secured funds, and possibly tungsten as well. How much would you be able to supply?"

The shopkeeper tilted his head to one side, thinking, evidently not convinced that Marrinek was an entirely trustworthy client.

"I don't keep iridium in stock, sir, since there is so little demand, but I have a supplier who visits every week or so and can supply maybe an ounce or two. Tungsten is easier, I can get maybe four or five ounces within a fortnight. But I would need payment in advance."

Marrinek nodded.

"Those quantities would be useful. Tell me, if I visited any of your competitors, would I be likely to find stock of either of these metals?"

"In all honesty no, sir. Mostly we cater for the everyday requirements of the small number of crafters creating household items or modest tools. I'm not even sure that the Duke's own household would have these metals in stock, such is the cost. And when someone such as yourself has a need for these materials all of my competitors in the Guild of Artificers," he nodded at the coat of arms over the door, "are likely to obtain their supplies from the same source. I'm sorry, sir, these things just can't readily be found in Vensille."

"Very well," said Marrinek, "I will return once I have refilled my purse. In the meantime, the only other things I need, if you have them, are a copy of Jensen and one of Sturge's Discussions. Do you have them?"

"Yes, sir, although they are not new copies and they may have been annotated by previous students. Four shillings each, I'm afraid."

Marrinek weighed his purse.

"Hmm. Six shillings only, I think, and a promise that I'll return to patronise your store again at a future date."

"Thank you sir, and while I look forward to your future

custom I'm afraid your promises are of small value to my landlord. Seven shillings for the two, that's the best I can do."

Marrinek sighed and emptied his purse on the counter. He flicked through the coins, counting.

"Looks like six and ten is the best I can do, I'm afraid."

"Very well, sir, since I can see that this is important to you, I will take six and ten." The shopkeeper scooped the coins quickly into his own purse and produced the books from a locked cupboard under the counter.

"Yes, well, this copy of Discussions is almost as old as I am," said Marrinek, leafing through the faded pages, "but I suppose the contents aren't likely to have changed over the years." He smiled at the shopkeeper.

"Thank you for your assistance and until the next time we meet, good day."

He waved at Floost.

"Pick-up our things." He gave a short bow, picked up his staff and stepped out onto the street. Floost and Darek followed, stuffing items into their bags as they went.

"Follow me," said Marrinek, leading the way back to the Jewel. When they reached the inn, they entered through the side door and climbed the stairs to their new suite. Marrinek opened the door and strode across the compact living area to one of the other two doors, peering into the room beyond.

"This will be my room. You two will share the room through that door. Set out the items we have just bought on the table and dump your clothes in your room."

He closed the door behind him and sat down on the bed. It was roughly made and the mattress was stuffed with straw but the room was clean and dry and perfectly accept-able for a few days. He pulled off his boots and massaged his feet, then rinsed his hands and washed his face in the bowl under the window. He stood for a moment, looking through the small panes at the street below, then he rolled his head around his neck and splashed more water on his face.

In their own tiny room Floost and Darek were arranging their new possessions. Floost hung her cloak on a hook on the back of the door and then re-packed her other clothes in her pack. Darek was also re-packing, remembering the times they had been moved on by the watch or stable owners or innkeepers, leaving quickly and carrying all they possessed.

When they had finished, they left their packs on the floor at the foot of their bed and went back into the living room. Marrinek was already there, sorting through the crafting supplies they had acquired between them. He looked up as they came in and gestured to the bench.

"Sit down for a moment while I sort through these things." It took him a few minutes to arrange everything to his satisfaction then he pulled a chair over to the table and sat down facing the twins.

"I said yesterday that using power to charm items or through a charmed item, would lengthen your lives and this is a fundamental truth of the world. It shapes everything - family, relationships, politics, economics, war, religion - everything. There are many people of talent whose lives are unnaturally long, but there are far, far more people without talent, or with a talent too weak to extend their lifespan. What do you think that means?"

The twins were quiet for a moment, then both spoke at once. Marrinek held up a hand and they fell silent.

"One at a time. Floost, you first."

"The talented are rich 'cos they live a long time and get lots of stuff."

Marrinek plucked at his shirt and produced his purse, spilling his last coins on the table.

"All I own is what you see before me. Am I rich? Darek, what do you think it means?"

"If you're talented everyone else has to do what you tell them. You can make them do what you want."

Marrinek snorted.

"If only. You saw how those two thugs behaved when they grabbed you on the street? I had to use violence to make them leave you alone. No, talent doesn't allow you to force people to do what you want." He paused, then added, "well, it does, but it's difficult and anti-social." He shook his head. "Forget about that for now and we'll come back to it in a few years.

"The big difference between the long-lived talented and everyone else is that everyone we know and love, everyone we grow up with, everyone we meet on the street or in a shop or at a ball, everyone will die before us. Most of the powerful and talented people in this world spend their time accumulating wealth and hobbies and knowledge to counter the dreadful, terrible loneliness that comes from being the oldest person they know."

He paused again to let that sink in.

"Let's consider Duke Rhenveldt. He's very strong but not yet very old, around a hundred and thirty, I believe. He has ruled Vensille for over a century and the city has grown around him, bending to his designs. He's a clever man but like all talented people he has few children. For some reason, we just aren't able to produce babies very often. And so instead of family he focusses on the city, building its strength as an independent state. He gathers around him advisors who are talented and strong enough to help him rule the city but not so strong that they can threaten him.

"When he dies, it is likely that one of them will seize his throne unless he is killed beforehand by an interloper, someone of even greater talent who can wrest power from him and take control of the city. He knows this, as does the Emperor to the east and all the other kings and queens and princes and dukes and rulers. Anyone who governs must tread a fine line between finding the greatest talents to help them rule and doing what is necessary to maintain their position. Only those of moderate strength, or those with special abilities or sound political instincts, survive much longer than untalented people."

He paused and picked up an iron rod from the table.

"The world of the powerful is very different to the one in which you have grown up so far. Talent can bring you power and wealth and give you influence amongst the powerful and wealthy but it won't save you from a knife in the back. Stay loyal to your friends, and to each other."

He waited a moment for that to sink in before continuing.

"Now, let us consider something more practical. There are two primary ways to use power. The first, and by far the most common, is to apply power through a specialised charm and thus to change the world."

He hefted the iron rod, then picked up the small fire charm.

"This is charmed iron, housed in wood. It's a tool, used to make flame."

He demonstrated, focussing his will so that a small flame appeared at the end of the tool.

"You can use this to light candles or to light a fire. Or, if you exert yourself, you can use it to find your way in the dark." He pushed, adding power to the charm until the flame grew until it burned white and was painful to look at.

The flame when out and he laid the charm back on the table.

"To use this tool you must be calm, focussed, patient. You will use it as a practice tool but be careful, since too much power can be dangerous. Now, close your eyes and breath slowly and deeply. Relax. I'm going to light the charm; raise your hand if you sense anything."

Marrinek waited, then lit the charm. Floost raised her hand and opened her eyes.

"I felt it!" she said, exhilarated, "It was like a sucking feeling, as if the air was being pulled around."

"Good. Now close your eyes again and keep them closed. Raise your hand if you feel anything, lower it when the feeling goes away." He lit the charm again, then dimmed it, then lit it. Floost's hand rose and fell with the charm's light but Darek didn't move.

"Darek, count slowly to ten, breathing in on the even numbers, out on the odd numbers."

Darek's breathing slowed a little and Marrinek lit the charm again. This time Darek's hand rose as well and he couldn't help opening his eyes.

"I felt it that time," he grinned at Floost, who had also opened her eyes, then at Marrinek.

"Very good. This is the first lesson; being able to sense those around you when they use power to achieve an effect. The closer you are to a practitioner or the more power they are using, the more likely you are to be able to sense their activity. Over time you will become more sensitive. Close your eyes again and we will practice."

For the next hour Marrinek drilled them, moving around the room, varying his distance from the twins and changing the brightness of the flame until they were able to sense his actions wherever he was and however little power he used.

"Good. Now we'll try something slightly different. Over time practitioners become so used to sensing flows of power that it becomes instinctive but our needs, yours and mine, are best served I think by teaching this skill now."

He gave them each one of the oak staves and picked up one of his own, holding it in his left hand with the fire charm in his right.

"I want you to balance the stave on the palm of your hand and count backwards from one hundred."

Marrinek shifted his grip on his stave so that it was balancing on his palm then he lit the fire charm.

"You can see the charm; can you sense the flow of power?"

The twins shook their heads, staves wavering as they concentrated on keeping them upright.

"Then let's keep going."

After another hour, their arms tired from balancing the staves and their concentration dwindling to nothing, Marrinek ended the lesson. Neither of the twins had been able to detect the flow of power in the charm while they were balancing and counting and the delight of their earlier successes had given way to despondency. Marrinek, however, was pleased with their progress.

"We will repeat this exercise tomorrow morning. And as many times after that until you master it."

"But why," asked Floost, "what's the point?"

"The point?" said Marrinek, "Well, there are two points. Firstly, and most importantly, you will learn this skill because I have decided that now is the time for you to learn it. Secondly, do you not think it might be useful to know if people around you are using power?" He looked from one twin to the other.

"Talent attracts enemies, some of whom will be dangerous and may be prepared to use power to attack you. Knowing what they are doing can be useful."

He stood up and stretched his back, leaning from side to side and running his hands over his head.

"Enough for now. Darek, find a servant and ask them to bring us food for our evening meal. Floost, tidy everything away please."

Once they had eaten and the room was tidy Marrinek sat down at the table and picked up the lead. He beckoned the twins to join him at the table.

"If you want to use your power to affect the world around you it is almost always necessary to use a charm of some sort."

He removed the second of the five charm tools, Quill, from its place in the storage roll.

"Take this tool, for example. You can make it from wood and iron and power, you don't need anything else, but it's much easier and quicker if you already have another tool, like this one."

He pointed at the third tool in the roll.

"If you have a discrete piece of material, like that rod of iron, or an oak stave, or a piece of lead, you can transform it with power if you have enough time and strength and skill and if you know what it is you are trying to achieve."

Darek raised his hand.

"Is that how the walls were made, with really large versions of tools like these?"

Marrinek was surprised.

"Good question, but no. Stone is different. Stone you can work relatively quickly, if you have the knack, and there's something about the material that helps. Once you get started the stone becomes its own tool allowing you to use one piece of stone to work the next, and the next and so on. It's still slow but it allows the mason to bond together huge pieces of rock and harden them into the shapes of the walls around the city."

He paused and looked at Bone Dancer, leaning against the wall.

"Bone Dancer has copper netting coiled around its length, from the far end where the plates are all the way down to the butt. Now, sit quiet, don't interrupt me, and focus on what I'm doing. You can ask questions when I'm done."

The twins sat, transfixed, as Marrinek picked up the rough lump of lead and switched to Blunt, the largest of the five tools. He paused, briefly, wondering if he would be able to focus enough power without triggering the nausea he'd felt earlier in the day. Then he shook his head, pushing away the fear.

Holding the tool against the surface of the lead he focussed power, and then even more, until finally, after several minutes' effort, the lead began to change shape, slowly shifting from an amorphous lump into a short rod. When he was happy with the shape, Marrinek laid down the tool and picked up the lead, feeling its surface with his fingers.

Then he picked up one of the oak staves and used Chisel first to cut it in half and then to slice away surplus material until he was left with a cylindrical wand of wood about six inches long and an inch across. Then he drew Chisel along the length of the wand, opening a long channel in the core of the wood. He dropped the lead into the wood and closed the opening, working gently on the wood to cause it to flow softly around the lead until the surface of the stave was whole and smooth.

He put down the tool and picked up the heavy stave.

"So," he said, rubbing his eyes and stretching his neck, "what did you notice?"

Floost was bouncing in her seat.

"I could see the power, so much of it, but the lead just seemed to absorb it." Marrinek nodded.

"But the wood was different, as if it was being guided by the power rather than just absorbing it," added Darek. Marrinek nodded again.

"Good. Yes. Lead, like all the heavy metals, can store power, gathering it like a pool in a dammed stream, then release it quickly when you need it. That's very useful for certain applications but it makes working the lead very difficult because most of the power you push into it is simply absorbed. The heavier metals are even slower to work but they hold more power and release it faster." He turned the stave, feeling the difference the lead had made to the balance.

"We use a copper net to gather power, harvesting it from the atmosphere and pushing it into the lead which acts as a reservoir. The stored power can then be drawn back out to achieve some useful effect, such as lighting a room or generating heat," he said, hefting the stave, "this isn't useful yet, it's just a teaching aid, but maybe later we'll do something else with it."

He picked up a fire charm and focussed power, pushing it into the charm's small reservoir.

"Can you see the power flowing now?"

The twins nodded.

"It's flowing from you into the charm. The copper and the lead are glowing," said Darek.

"It's beautiful," added Floost, her eyes wide, "as if the fire charm was alive."

"Which it is not, of course, and a good thing too, since that would be very distressing," said Marrinek, "I will teach you to handle charms and to work metal, wood and stone but not today."

He pulled the two battered books from their resting place in the pack.

"These are student texts, useful starting points for anyone of talent. They are dull and worthy and long but they contain much information that you will need. Jensen is a textbook on the uses of power with a number of practical exercises and examples. Read the first few chapters and we will talk about them tomorrow. Discussions is a more general text on society and the impact of power."

He turned the book over, flicking through its pages.

"It's basically an instruction manual on how to survive amongst other talented people. This world is superficially similar to the normal world, the one you've lived in so far, but those similarities hide real and dangerous differences. Understanding those differences and learning to exploit them are key to survival. Pay close attention to the contents of this book."

He set the books down on the desk.

"If I am not here to teach you and you have no other chores, you are to study these books until you know their contents intimately. Once you have understood all that they contain we will progress to more advanced texts."

Floost and Darek looked somewhat sceptical, not to say downright rebellious.

"Can't you just tell us what's in them? I don't see why we have to read them ourselves..." said Darek, staring at the books with a degree of distaste.

Marrinek stretched his neck muscles and wondered if he might have been a bit hasty in apprenticing the twins. It was more than fifteen years since he had last had an apprentice and that had ended badly for all concerned. The twins, lacking the formal schooling or environmental background from which talented children usually benefited, were likely to prove difficult students. He sighed and resigned himself to a long effort.

"You read them because studying is an important part of learning. Later, you'll need to absorb information or discover it yourself and this practice will help. And the faster you master this material the sooner you can move on to more interesting lessons."

The twins sat in sullen silence for a few moments, staring at the books. Then Floost looked up.

"You said there were two ways to use power. You've told us about charms. What's the other way?"

"Ah, yes. Charms are common. Once you learn to recognise them you'll be able to spot them when they're used or even when they're inactive, if they're connected to a power reservoir. What you'll find is that they're everywhere. Most people know that charms exist and some have a rough idea about how they work. Almost nobody knows about the second way, which we call Flow."

Marrinek paused for so long that Floost thought he had forgotten they were there. She was about to ask another question when he looked up again.

"Flow is far more difficult to use and vastly more dangerous and versatile. It takes many forms and can do many, many different things. Most talented people lack the strength to make use of Flow and even amongst those who have the strength, many can't master the fine control required to affect the world around them. Whether or not you two are able to use Flow remains to be seen but we will get to that later, once you have mastered the basics."

Marrinek picked up one of the oak staves.

"For now, though, if you'd rather watch me work..."

The twins' faces brightened and they leant forward, the books forgotten.

"Right. Same as before, no interruptions." He took out Quill again and focussed his will through it into the oak. After a moment, the wood fell neatly into two pieces and Marrinek was left holding a four-inch-long stub of wood. Switching to the third tool, Twig, he formed a channel lengthways through the wood, three inches long with three holes to the surface and a wider chamber at the bottom. He worked quickly, now that he had a feel for the tools again, anxious to complete the work before the nausea returned, and settled a small lead reservoir into the chamber.

He picked up one of the iron rods and rolled it in his hands, getting a feel for the metal.

"Iron can be worked directly, if you have the strength. Nobody really knows why this is true of iron and not, say, lead, but there it is."

Again he focussed and the metal smoothly changed shape, flowing gently and dividing in two so that Marrinek was left holding a narrow three-inch stub of grey iron. He picked up the oak and slotted the two parts together. Happy with the fit, he held up the item and displayed it to the twins.

"What do you think it is for?"

Both twins shook their heads.

"Is it a key?" asked Floost.

"No. Darek?"

"A fire charm, like the one you showed us earlier? Or maybe a knife, except it's blunt, of course."

"Trick question, I'm afraid. At the moment it's just shaped wood and metal. But 'knife' was a good guess. Watch closely."

He slid the iron out of the wood and picked up Needle, delving deeply into the structure of the iron, causing the atoms at the end of the rod to ripple and shift before forming a precise pattern within the metal, just like the pattern he had made in Bone Dancer.

"Stand clear," he muttered, pointing the rod of iron across the room and pressing his hand to the patterned end, hoping that this work wouldn't trigger the nausea. He pushed power into the iron, more and more, until suddenly it caught. There was a loud bang which made the twins jump and cover their ears. Across the room, a fist-sized dent three inches deep had appeared in the wattle and daub wall.

Marrinek grinned and inspected the metal, which now had the same intricate pattern running all the way through it. He slid the iron back into the wooden casing.

Then he picked up the fourth tool, Chisel, and focussed power through it. He twisted the alignment of the wood to bond it to his touch and then twisted it again to fix the iron in place. He opened three holes in the wood and used Needle to embed a copper net under the surface, wiring it to the reservoir with copper wire. The actuators slipped neatly into their holes so that they stood just proud of the surface and he then linked them to the iron and the reservoir.

Swapping hands, he held the wood as he might hold a knife and then used Twig to close the remaining channels and holes and to raise subtle peaks and troughs to fit his fingers so that the tiny actuators sat comfortably under his thumb, one, two, three.

"Almost done," he muttered, reaching for the finest of the tools, Needle. He swapped hands again and focussed directly on the wood itself, brushing the tool over the surface until it was smooth and regular and the deep dark green of Bone Dancer. Finally, he held the tool like a pen above the wood and, using the same elegant, flowing script with which he had named Bone Dancer, etched a single word, 'Drake', into the hardened surface of the wood. It glowed brightly against the green of the handle then faded.

"This," he said, holding up the finished item, "is an altogether nastier piece of work. It's called a shock cannon and, once powered, it produces a blast that can incapacitate or kill. I've aligned this one to me so only I will be able to use it."

He paused, pondering.

"Or, I suppose, someone of very considerable strength, if they could break the alignment, but that's risky and difficult."

He held the weapon at arm's length and pointed it at the wall, pushing power into it to charge the reservoir. Then he pressed the first of the three actuators. There was a dull 'whump' noise and the twins jumped again.

Floost glared at him, hands on her hips.

"Why would anyone want to make such a thing? What is it for? What are you going to do?"

"Do? Maybe nothing, but I need to speak to Hitton, privately, and Bone Dancer is a little too conspicuous for subtle work."

Marrinek just slipped the shock cannon into his pocket. Floost was still glaring at him as he strapped on his sword.

"What, nothing to say about the sword?"

"That's different," she said, "at least a sword is..."

She stopped as Marrinek drew the sword and held it up in the pale lamplight.

"Different? Civilised? Familiar? Yes, you're partly right."

He sheathed the sword and unbundled his hair so that it fell naturally, covering his shoulders. He picked up his cloak and fastened it around his shoulders, twisting beneath it until cloak, sword and hair were arranged to his satisfaction.

"Think about this. The sword is an ancient weapon made only to threaten or kill people; it has no other purpose. It maims and destroys and corrupts. Anyone can use a sword but most people who try will die at the hand of someone faster, more skilled, more experienced or more desperate. For some, the sword becomes the embodiment of their purpose, the reason for their existence. Think carefully before picking up a weapon but especially one as obvious as a sword."

He pulled the shock cannon from his pocket and held it up so that he could inspect it.

"This is the same, of course, except it can be used with finesse so that, with a delicate touch, it isn't necessary to kill or to maim. It's a more humane weapon, if such a thing can be said to exist. And the range is short, so you have to get pretty close to your enemy and look him in the eye." He hefted the cannon, thinking, then he nodded. "You're right, though. It's a nasty little weapon, more dangerous than a sword in the right hands and easier to conceal."

He replaced the shock cannon in his pocket, paused, then added the fire charm and slung his empty pack over his shoulder. He opened the door to the corridor.

"I'm going to talk to Madame Duval and then I'm going to visit Hitton. Lock the door, keep quiet and make a start on your reading, I'll be back later."

And with that he closed the door and was gone, leaving the twins alone with only their books for company.

15

Marrinek ambled down the steps at the back of the Jewel, thinking through the plan for the next few hours. He had been tempted by Hitton's job offer - it would have provided a useful route into the gang and a lever he could have used to further his schemes - but the death of Gander had probably closed that opportunity. Not that Marrinek was particularly upset about either the death or the missed opportunity, it was just frustrating to have a perfectly good plan destroyed so soon after its inception.

He reached the bottom of the stairs and slipped out through the back door into the alley behind the inn. Even late in the evening there were still people on the streets, making their way home, searching for entertainment or, like Marrinek, looking for new opportunities. He joined the steady stream of people, pulled his cloak tight around him and, with his hood up, wound his way through the streets toward the house of Madame Duval.

The street outside the House of Duval was even busier and more crowded than it had been earlier in the day. Clearly the people of Vensille took great delight in both the bath houses and the establishments selling other, more specialised, services in the surrounding streets.

Marrinek walked up to the green door and stood, side on, in the light of the oil lamps, watching the street. He knocked on the door and after a few moments a small hatch popped open and Shad's face appeared, round and sweaty.

"Oh, it's you."

The hatch closed and bolts slid back on the inside of the door before it opened just enough for Marrinek to slip into the hallway. Shad closed the door quickly, ramming home the bolts and dropping a bar into a discreet set of supports on the walls either side of the frame.

"You don't seem to be welcoming many guests at the moment," said Marrinek, gesturing at the empty sitting rooms.

"We're closed for the evening, Madame's orders. She's in her study." Shad nodded toward the door at the end of the corridor and sat down heavily on the chair at the foot of the stairs.

"Right," said Marrinek, moving past Shad's chair and knocking on Madame Duval's study door.

"Come in," said a voice from within and Marrinek pushed open the door, finding himself again in Madame Duval's study. The candles were lit, casting a pale glow over the room, but the window was shuttered and heavily barred. A long knife rested on the desk and Madame Duval's hand hovered over it as Marrinek came in and sat down in the chair next to the fireplace.

She relaxed a little when she saw who it was but it was clear that the day had been trying. Madame Duval was sitting at her desk where Marrinek had left her earlier in the day but she had changed at some point and was now wearing a plain dress cut from nondescript brown linen.

Her hair was different as well and she looked very plain without her jewels and make-up; still striking but now more like a peasant woman dressed for field work or a housewife ready for the market.

"I didn't think I'd see you before tomorrow. Weren't you going to speak to Hitton?"

"Soon. I have a few questions first," said Marrinek, pulling his head off the chair to look at Madame Duval.

"Go on then, what do you want to know?"

"What can you tell me about Hitton? All I know is that he is moderately talented and that he runs his gang from the Snarling Goat. Where does he live?"

"Moderately talented? Is that how he seems to you?" she asked, eyebrows raised in surprise.

Marrinek just stared, saying nothing.

"Well to those of us not blessed with the power, even a 'moderate' talent can be very intimidating. We've all heard tales about what you Agers can do if you put your mind to it."

She sighed and rubbed her temples, trying to soothe away some of the pains of the day.

"Hitton's been here a few times, as a customer, but I stay well clear of him and just make sure he gets what he wants. He's a thug, a bully," she said, "he intimidates people with his talent and his reputation but I've never seen him actually doing much more than light candles. That's scary enough if you've heard the stories they tell about him."

Marrinek pulled the fire charm from his pocket and focussed a little power into it to produce a small flame.

"He does this - I've seen it. Does he do more?"

"No, that's all I've ever seen him do, but who knows what other skills or charms he has hidden away out of sight? They say he rarely leaves the Snarling Goat, and certainly not after dark. When he's here, which isn't often, it's always in the early afternoon and he doesn't stay long. Whatever business he does, he does it from his booth in the corner on the first floor of the Goat. You know the one?"

Marrinek nodded and Madame Duval went on.

"He comes here but his gang use the cheaper houses down the street. They boast, of course, and the girls gossip all the way down to the river and back, so if you keep your ears open you hear all sorts of things." She paused for a moment, thinking, and Marrinek waited patiently. Then she went on, "They say he sleeps in a room at the top of the Goat on a pile of silver and gems. They say he has the dried ears of the people who have tried to relieve him of his wealth nailed to the walls of his room. They say he has traps and magic locks and all sorts of things. Most of it's rubbish, of course. I don't believe in the piles of gems or the magic locks but the ears," she paused again and shuddered, "the ears I can believe. He probably thinks they deter burglars."

She stopped again and Marrinek took the opportunity to ask a question.

"Is he the type to fear assassins or other night-time intruders?" he asked.

She giggled, and an edge of hysteria crept into her voice as she answered.

"Assassins? Dear god if he finds out I've been talking to you, if any of them find out, they'll burn my house to the ground and I'll be lucky if they just kill me. Assassins? I don't know, but Hitton's an arrogant swine and he's been running that inn and that gang for a long time, decades maybe. I've never heard of anyone assaulting him or even thinking about it - his reputation is protection enough, I think, and his boys look after him."

Marrinek nodded, thinking it through.

"He lives in the Goat and hardly ever leaves so that's where I'll need to go to talk to him. He has been there a long time and may have defences embedded in the structure of the building so I'll need to be careful. He's arrogant and probably not worried about thieves or other intruders. Thanks, that's a great help."

He stood up and walked to the door then turned back to Madame Duval.

"I'll go back to the Jewel after I've spoken to Hitton so I won't see you till tomorrow. The twins and I will need somewhere else to live soon, somewhere safe and comfortable. Find us somewhere near here so that I'm on hand if you need me."

Madame Duval opened her mouth to say something snappy about taking advantage and making assumptions but Marrinek just shook his head and said, "You won't need to run," he waved at the travelling bag beside the desk, "but we'll need to work together if we're to make the most of the situation. You know the city and the people, so find me somewhere safe and close."

He closed the door behind him and walked down the corridor, prodding Shad to open the front door for him.

"I'll be back tomorrow. Stay alive, eh?"

He grinned at Shad, who tweaked his flabby lips into a rough smile.

"Sure, you too. Good luck."

Then he closed the door, slid the bolts across and dropped the bar.

Marrinek stood for a moment, alone on the streets with his thoughts, then he rolled his shoulders and stretched his neck from side to side. He pulled his cloak around him and headed toward the Snarling Goat.

As he entered the area of the city known as The Narrows, Marrinek slowed his pace, hunched his back and broke his stride, taking on the slight shuffle of the vagabond. His cloak didn't quite fit the disguise - it was too new, too clean, too complete and it lacked patches, stains and holes - but he didn't think anyone would notice in the dim light of the streets. And even if they did it wouldn't matter, as long as nobody recognised the tall stranger who had made such a mess in the Snarling Goat earlier in the day.

He shuffled along, keeping out of everyone's way, until he reached the row of buildings where the Snarling Goat stood. He leant against the wall of a closed shop opposite the inn, fading gently into the shadows, watching people come and go and feeling the mood and atmosphere of the street. People were passing in and out of the inn at a slow but steady rate; Marrinek couldn't be certain but it looked like a normal evening's trade, customers coming and going as the fancy took them.

He turned to look at the buildings around the inn. Entry through the front door would not be a smart move - his disguise wouldn't stand close inspection by someone who had seen him before, especially if he had to lower the hood of his cloak - but maybe he could gain access through the stables next door. After a few more minutes, it seemed that the stables were quiet except for the occasional snorting and neighing of the horses.

Decision made, Marrinek shuffled across the narrow street to the gate at the entrance to the stable's courtyard. He reached out gently with his power, sending thin tendrils of flow to feel for people or animals inside the courtyard. He could sense the slow thoughts of the sleeping horses and, above one of the stables, the fast urgent thoughts of a pair of lovers. In the courtyard itself, there were no people, as far as he could tell, but there were definitely at least two guard dogs sleeping just inside the gate. He paused. The gate was locked and bolted, too high to climb without attracting attention from passers-by.

Marrinek turned away and walked along the front of the building until he reached the corner, where an even narrower alley led between the stable block and a tenement building. The upper floors of the tenement were built out over the alleyway so that they almost reached the stable. He reached out again, ever so gently, and found within the tenement the signs of multiple people, mostly sleeping or dozing, filling the tiny rented rooms. He nudged open the front door, moving quietly into the dank and narrow hallway beyond.

With the door to the street closed the hallway was almost completely dark. He stood for a few seconds to allow his eyes to adjust but it didn't help much. Marrinek grunted to himself, slightly frustrated at the paucity of the tools available to him. He made a mental note to begin crafting a full set of equipment as soon as he could acquire the requisite resources but, for now, he would have to make do. He pulled out the fire charm and brought forth the smallest glow he could, just enough light to show him the stairs.

The attic space at the top of the building, three stories up, was open and half full of sleeping bodies. A shuttered dormer window let in a little air and Marrinek picked his way carefully across the floor, stepping between rough mattresses and over piles of possessions to reach it. He eased open the window, which ground on its hinges and squeaked, but nobody in the room woke. Anyone living in a place like this quickly learned to sleep through the building's strange noises.

Marrinek extinguished the fire charm and put it back in

his pocket. He pulled himself out through the window and onto the roof of the tenement. There he stood for a moment, balanced on the pitched roof of the building, staring out across the rooftops. From here he could see only a short way towards the centre of the city but he had a clear view to the river and the warehouses on the other side. The docks were full, crowded with river barges waiting to travel inland. To the north, along the line of the river, were the closest of the massive towers that ringed the inner city, the lamps on their ramparts casting thin streaks of light down the inner walls.

Even now there was traffic on the river as barges loaded or unloaded at the docks. Two of the huge river vessels were loading supplies and cargo, judging by the noise and move-ment, preparing to set sail as soon as there was enough light. There was activity in the streets too, as revellers made their way to the next pub or party and workers made their way home to bed.

A sudden noise in the alley below him brought him back to the present and he crouched low to the roof, looking around at the nearby buildings and rooftops, checking that nobody had seen him. After a few moments he relaxed again. There were no shouts of alarm, nobody knew he was there, he was safe for now.

He edged around the roof until he was opposite the stable then stopped, sitting low against the roof of the tene-ment. Again he reached out gently, sending tendrils of flow through the nearest part of the stable, searching for anyone who might be disturbed by his unexpected arrival. Again he found only sleepers and, a little further away on the right, the pair of lovers still working urgently in the hay loft.

Satisfied, Marrinek stood and stepped lightly between the roofs of the two buildings then began working his way around to the Snarling Goat. A few more minutes of quiet, careful creeping and he was able to climb up from the stable to the roof of the inn. He stopped again, pausing to catch his breath and to check for sounds of alarm but still there were none. He laid back against the rooftop of the inn, resting for a few minutes, and made another mental note to get more exercise; his time in prison had done nothing for his overall fitness.

As the Watch called midnight Marrinek edged around the roof of the inn, searching for a way in. Eventually he found a shuttered hatchway that opened into a loft space of some sort. He reached out gently, oh so gently, with his power and tested the sky light for traps or alarms; nothing. He searched the floor below the window and then the room beyond; still nothing. Happy that there were neither alarms nor traps nor people, he slid his knife around the window frame and flicked open the catch, lowering the sky light into the room. He squeezed through the frame and slid quietly to the floor of the cramped room, hardly breathing as he lowered his feet to the boards.

He waited for long minutes, frozen in the gloom, then gently searched the area around him for charms or people. Again, nothing, so he crept over the floor, between crates of old clothes and pieces of broken furniture, until he reached the door. It opened onto a tiny staircase that led down to a large, dimly lit landing with two doors and a second staircase leading down to the first floor. Marrinek reached out, trickling power outward toward the doors in search of charms and this time he found one, a trap, on the left-hand door. He moved to stand before the door and carefully sent delicate tendrils of power into the room beyond; nothing. It seemed that everyone was still downstairs in the common room.

He focussed on the trap, a cunningly wrought fire

charm, powered by a lead reservoir, that would have been triggered if he had opened the door. He trickled power out and around the charm, isolating it and temporarily disabling it, then he checked the floor, ceiling and walls, just to be sure. Again nothing, and he was just about to open the door when he felt a second, far more subtle charm hidden in the woodwork near the hinges. This one wasn't a trap but an alarm, linked to some other object, that would have sounded silently if he had opened the door and somehow avoided the trap. He stepped quietly away from the door and turned down the landing to the second room. There were no traps or alarms on this door and he quickly opened the door and stepped inside.

A store cupboard, shelves lined with candles, linen and other practical items necessary for running a home within an inn. Safe, but not very useful. Marrinek reached out toward the other door, trickling power towards it, then he twisted sharply and triggered the alarm. He settled deeper into the store cupboard and pulled the door closed, waiting.

The response was rapid. Hitton came quickly up the stairs, sword in one hand, charm in the other, and went straight to the door. Marrinek, watching through a gap between the warped cupboard door and its frame, saw Tam following a few paces behind, also with sword drawn. Interesting that they both led with swords, he thought.

Hitton stopped in front of the door, clearly confused, having expected to find someone caught in his trap.

"What the..." he muttered, "what tripped the alarm?" Tam said nothing, sheathing his sword and turning to go back downstairs. Hitton stood a few seconds longer before sheathing his own sword. He checked the alarm again and the trap, then he muttered to himself and stood there, shaking his head. Still muttering, he followed Tam back down the stairs to the first-floor gallery. Marrinek waited a few minutes then triggered the alarm again.

Again, Hitton came quickly up the stairs, still leading Tam, both with swords drawn. Hitton stood again outside the door, frowning, but Tam just shook his head and went back downstairs, leaving the confused Hitton to stare at the door frame on his own. After a few seconds Hitton disarmed the trap and opened the door. He stood in the doorway with his back to Marrinek's cupboard, inspecting the alarm.

Marrinek nudged his door open a few inches, pointed the shock cannon at Hitton and pressed one of the trigger buttons. The shock blasted Hitton him from his feet and through the doorway. Marrinek charged out of his cupboard and into Hitton's room, cannon held before him ready to fire again, but Hitton had struck his head on the floor and was out cold. Marrinek rolled him onto his back, checked that he was still breathing, then quietly closed the door and reactivated the trap with a trickle of power. Then he looked around the room for something he could use to restrain Hitton, settling on a sheet and a heavy Captain's chair. He manhandled Hitton into the chair and tore the sheet into strips to secure his wrists and ankles then added another length around his head as a gag. He set a second chair opposite the first and began to search the room.

In a small chest, hidden beneath a false base in the wardrobe, Marrinek found Hitton's stash of silver and a few modest gem stones. He stuffed them into his pack, put the chest back in the base of the wardrobe and continued searching. In the trunk beside the bed, under a pile of heavy winter clothes, he found a bag with almost an ounce of gold and maybe four ounces of tungsten. Marrinek raised his eyebrows, surprised that someone with Hitton's relatively modest talent would have been able to gather such expensive materials. Then he wrapped the metal in the remains of the sheet and put it in his pack next to the silver. He was searching under the bed and probing the floorboards when Hitton groaned from behind his gag

Marrinek walked back to the empty chair and sat down, facing Hitton but with the back of the chair between them. The shock cannon he held loosely in one hand and with the other he reached out to slap Hitton once, twice, then a third time. Hitton jerked awake, eyes going wide as he realised that his hands were tied to the chair. He looked down, trying to work out what was going on, trying to pull away from the chair, then he looked straight ahead and Marrinek felt him begin to gather power.

"Don't," said Marrinek, slapping him hard enough to break Hitton's concentration and waving the shock cannon in his face, "just don't. Let's talk about your two thugs, Gander and Pratek and how much you're going to pay me in compensation for their offence."

Hitton struggled again, pulling on the ties, then tried to shout through the gag. Marrinek slapped him again, then again, quick, hard blows that stung his hand. Hitton's head lolled but he stopped struggling, blood trickling down his chin. Marrinek pulled the gag down roughly and Hitton spat blood on the floor.

"You don't know what you've got yourself into, boy, I'll..." but Marrinek slapped him again.

"No threats, just answer my questions. Your men stole my apprentices and sold them to a whorehouse. I've taken your silver and your heavy metal. Is that enough, do you think? Hmm?"

Hitton stared at him as if he had gone mad.

"Enough? What the fuck? I'll kill you, you fucking shit, you're dead, do you hear me? Dead!" and he threw himself to the side, toppling the chair onto the floor and shouting at the top of his voice. Marrinek kicked out, catching Hitton in the chest and winding him. Hitton stopped shouting and focussed on trying to draw breath as he lay on his side, hands still tied to the arms of the chair.

Marrinek stood up and moved his chair to one side, then squatted beside Hitton and placed the shock cannon against his temple, pressing down gently, forcing the man's head down against the floorboards.

"I said 'no threats'. Where do you keep your charms? I think I'll take those as well."

"I'm not fucking telling you anything," said Hitton through gritted teeth. He spat blood onto the boards again and coughed.

"Really? Nothing at all? Well, sorry, but that's not going to be good enough. I'll need..."

There was a sudden creak on the landing outside the room. Marrinek slapped his hand over Hitton's mouth as the gangster tried to shout.

"Boss, are you in there?" said Tam from the landing, knocking on the door. Hitton struggled violently, screaming incoherently from behind Marrinek's hand.

Suddenly the door crashed open and Tam charged into the room, sword drawn. Marrinek dropped to the floor, shock cannon still resting against Hitton's head, but he needn't have worried; Hitton's trap, triggered by the opening of the door, fired as Tam crossed the threshold. There was a violent flash of yellow light, a great wash of heat and a soft fleshy thump. Tam's momentum carried him into the room but his eyes were glazing even as he stumbled to a halt, the sword falling from his hand. He turned his head toward Marrinek with a confused look on his face then, with blood bubbling from a fist-sized hole in his chest, he collapsed next to Hitton and lay still. Hitton and Marrinek stared for a moment, then Hitton drew breath to scream and Marrinek fired the shock cannon, punching a neat hole right through Hitton's head and the floorboard beneath him.

For a few seconds, Marrinek lay next to the two corpses. Then he pushed himself to his feet and stuck his head around the doorframe, peering at the stairs and along the corridor. There was a lot of noise from the floors below but nothing more than the normal sounds from an inn full of drunk people; nobody moved on the stairs down to the next floor or on the landing below. Marrinek pushed the door closed and looked around the room. He searched Hitton's jacket quickly, relieving him of a purse, some rings and a few small charms. There were probably others hidden somewhere in the room but the opportunity to search for them had passed and in any case the smell of burnt flesh was nauseating. Time to move.

Marrinek threw everything into his pack, slung it over his shoulders and stepped back out onto the landing. He thought about taking the trap - the lead could be reused in his own charms - but it would take time to dig it out of the wall and he had a feeling that time was now in short supply.

He closed the door behind him. The trap was old and inefficient and it took a few tense moments to focus enough power into the reservoir to reset the trap and charge it for another blast. Then he climbed the narrow stair back to the attic and picked his way carefully across the floor to the shuttered window.

Marrinek had reached the roof and was closing the window behind him when there was a scream from the floor below Hitton's rooms. The words were lost, muffled by the walls and floors, but it sounded like blood had been noticed as it dripped from the ceiling into the room below. Oops.

Heavy boots pounded up the stairs to Hitton's floor. Several men, lots of shouting from the landing. They called out to Hitton and Tam, then one of them pushed open the door and triggered the trap.

More screaming, more shouting. Someone said something about the roof and then there were more boots on the stairs to the attic. Marrinek moved up the roof till he was behind the dormer then paused, waiting, shock cannon in hand. More voices from the attic and the landing - this was becoming a bad place to be - then someone shouted again, clearly this time, "Just get out on the roof and check. Stop fucking around, just bloody do it!"

Marrinek tensed as the window was thrown open and someone climbed out nervously onto the roof of the inn. A man shuffled out and stood carefully, holding the edge of the dormer with his left hand and peering gingerly over the edge of the building toward the street three floors below. Marrinek paused, waiting for the right moment, then he thumbed the low power actuator on the shock cannon and blasted the man's leg.

The man yelled in shock and stumbled as his leg gave way. His fingers lost their grip on the dormer and he scrabbled desperately as he slid down the roof. Then he rolled over the edge and disappeared from view, screaming all the way to the ground.

There was more yelling from the attic and someone peered out of the window.

"Fuck! Shank! What happened? Fuck, he's fallen off the roof!"

The shutter slammed closed and the boots charged back across the attic and down the stairs.

Time to go. He edged carefully around the roof of the inn, back toward the stable. More people were shouting now, the clamour growing as the news spread. Marrinek hurried down onto the roof of the stable and, crouching low, made his way back to the tenement. He stepped onto the roof but noise from within the attic made him pause; he would need another way down. He circled around the roof, listening for signs of life, until he was able to step across another alley onto the roof of the next building, some sort of storehouse. From there he dropped down onto a walkway around the edge of the building where he finally paused to let the trembling in his legs subside.

By the gods, he was tired. Too much time spent locked in a small room with bad food and not enough exercise. He shook his head and vowed to spend more time training.

While he rested he slowly pushed power into the shock cannon's reservoir, filling it so that it was ready to be used again. By the time it was full, his legs had recovered some of their strength. He lowered himself quietly down into a narrow side street, straightened the pack on his back and tightened his cloak.

Then he walked calmly away from the Snarling Goat on a circuitous route back to the Jewel.

16

The road from Esterengel went due west for many miles, a great stone highway that climbed hills and cut through pasture and forest. The Imperial engineers had built stone bridges along the route of the road, elegant structures that carried the road across the rivers of the western province in graceful soaring arches. The network of roads that criss-crossed the Empire was one of the wonders of the age but few travellers appreciated the efforts that had gone into its construction. Fewer still, as they made their way slowly along the road from Esterengel in a great stream of people and carts and animals, felt the sheer majesty and power of the road network and most simply didn't think about the road at all, except maybe to curse the odd pothole or missing cobble.

Ezbedah Krant, newly elevated personal envoy of the Lady Camille, Governor of the Western Province, certainly didn't see much appeal in the stone road. He didn't see much appeal in the horse he had been given either, still less in the quiet companion that Rincon had foisted upon him. In fact, there was almost nothing about his current situation that pleased Krant, whose comfortably anonymous position within the Traebarn Palace had been rudely disrupted by the untimely arrival of the Heberon courier. To Krant, the unfamiliar road was a cruel and unusual form of punishment that continued unabated as it carried him ever further from his peaceful existence in the city into the wilds.

"Nothing urgent ever comes from Heberon," he had said to the courier, naively, and he had always believed it to be true. He was forced to admit, however, that the news of the escape of the traitor Marrinek was, if not important to Krant himself, at least of urgent importance to his masters. He couldn't really see the point in travelling to Vensille to deliver a message that could have been sent far more quickly, and with far less disruption, by courier.

He shifted in the saddle, trying to find some way of sitting that would relieve the pain in his lower back and relax the cramping in his legs. He scratched at his neck, loosening his collar in a vain attempt to circulate some air in the unrelenting heat of the mid-summer sun. He switched the reins from one hand to the other and back again, stretching his fingers and rolling his shoulders, but he couldn't work the stiffness from his arms. He looked over his shoulder, past his new servant, and back down the road they had travelled from Esterengel but the city was still there, only a few miles away as they climbed the low hills that covered much of the western province. He sighed and resigned himself to a long, uncomfortable, profitless, unnecessary journey.

At some point, and without stopping their slow plod westward, they ate a meagre lunch of bread and cold meat washed down with a thin beer that had grown warm in the sun. Krant's servant, Gavelis, doled out the food from a bag on his saddle having apparently decided that it was time to eat. He had then re-packed his bag, again without stopping, and fallen in behind Krant to follow at a respectful distance.

Around them the caravan they were following trundled slowly westward at the speed of the slowest animals. Krant counted the milestones and estimated their speed at no more than three miles an hour. He wasn't a keen horseman but he was finding the journey tedious, even on the first day, and he was beginning to wonder if they might not move rather faster, and thus get home rather sooner, if they rode ahead at their own pace.

Three milestones later, as they finally crested the hill and left the valley of Esterengel behind them, he was sure that he would die of old age before they reached Vensille and that something had to be done. He steered his horse to the side of the road and slowed until Gavelis came alongside.

"It's slow going, Gavelis, very slow."

"Yes sir. Very slow."

"Well, let's hurry things up a bit, shall we? I would like to get to the next town in time for supper."

"I can't advise it, sir. Two men alone in the countryside with horses and travel gear would be tempting targets for bandits or highwaymen."

Krant gave him a look.

"Surely we are safe here, barely twelve miles from Esterengel?"

Gavelis smiled but did not seem happy.

"I fear not, sir. The people travel together for security, sir, not entertainment. When we get closer to the town I will ride ahead to secure lodgings for the night, sir, and you should be safe to follow with the packhorse when you see the spire of the town's temple."

"The spire of the temple? But that could take hours!"

Krant was indignant. If there really were bandits in the countryside then Gavelis was probably right to be cautious but would they really be so bold as to attack the Governor's envoys so close to the city? He doubted it and said as much to Gavelis.

"I think, sir," said Gavelis in a low voice, "that even the Governor's envoys, if they were in fact travelling this road," he paused, meaningfully, and raised a cautioning eyebrow, "would ride with a caravan amid a cloud of anonymity." He looked around, checking for accidental eavesdroppers, then added, "And I think, sir, that we should stick to our cover story for as long as possible and remember the instructions given to us by 'your father' before we departed." He gave Krant a meaningful glare from beneath raised eyebrows.

Krant sighed. He had not forgotten the lecture that Rincon had delivered that morning but he had hoped to find a little more leeway in the interpretation of its contents. Gavelis seemed to have a different idea, apparently intent on following the instructions closely despite being merely servant employed to help facilitate Krant's mission.

The road took them past another village and Krant spent a few minutes watching the peasants weeding the fields and tending their animals. Theirs was a dull life, miles from the nearest town in a village with neither inn nor bath house. Krant couldn't imagine ever choosing to live in a rural village but he supposed that maybe some people liked it. He shuddered at the thought of giving up his familiar city comforts, then groaned with self-pity because that was exactly what he had done when he agreed to act as the Governor's envoy.

"How will you know when it is safe to ride on to the town?" Krant had asked at one point, desperate for anything to break the monotony of hills and farms and fields and orchards.

"I have travelled this way before, sir, many times, and there is a toll bridge over a small river four or five miles east of the town. I will ride ahead once we have cleared the toll bridge, sir, and find lodgings for us at an inn on the market square. There is, if memory serves, an inn called the Golden Perch where we might secure a small room."

"Many times? Why, what is so interesting that you would travel this road 'many times'?"

"Family, sir. Some of my extended family farm the land some miles north west of the town of Averley, through which we will pass in the next few days. I try to visit them at least once a year."

"Oh. Well, yes, that sounds, er, nice."

Krant wasn't sure what to say. The idea of visiting family members that not only lived outside the city but that also worked the land filled him with horror.

"And, er, do your relatives ever visit you in the city?"

"Yes, sir, but rarely because it is difficult for them to be away from the farm for very long and they can normally find all that they need in Averley. Sometimes the younger family members travel to the city in search of work or adventure but it is not a regular occurrence."

Krant wasn't sure what more he could say. He knew little of the countryside and nothing of farming but he didn't want to appear ignorant before his servant so he was reluctant to ask further questions. Instead, he lapsed back into silence and watched the hills and farms and fields and orchards slide slowly past as they made their way steadily toward the next town.

Around mid-afternoon they reached the toll bridge, a stone structure with a gatehouse at one end through which the narrowing stream of travellers was slowly easing. Krant and Gavelis made their way up onto the bridge where two gatekeepers were taking pennies from everyone crossing and tuppence from those with a cart or animal. Krant pulled his purse out and flicked through the various coins but the gatekeeper seemed to recognise Gavelis and just waved them through. As they passed over the bridge, moving more quickly now that they had cleared the melee at the gate, Krant stopped fiddling with his money and put away his purse, confused about what had just happened.

On the far side of the bridge Gavelis walked his horse onto the muddy edges of the road and dismounted so that he could unhitch the packhorse from his saddle. As he was tying the rope to Krant's saddle, Krant suddenly asked, "Might it be better for us to travel this next stretch of the road together so that we reach the town sooner?"

Gavelis finished securing the packhorse before answering.

"No, sir. Two men travelling with a packhorse might draw unwanted attention. One travelling alone will move more quickly and appeal less to bandits."

Gavelis swung back into his saddle.

"If you follow on with the caravan, sir, I will meet you in the market square outside the Golden Perch." And with that he kicked his horse into a canter and rode off down the road. Krant watched until Gavelis disappeared from sight then walked his horse back to the road and re-joined the informal caravan of travellers.

Another hour without interest or entertainment dragged slowly by.

Krant, ignored by his walking companions and unable to bring himself to talk to the cart drivers, found himself constructing ever more elaborate revenge fantasies featuring Lady Camille, Rincon, the awful courier from Heberon and his jumped-up servant Gavelis. His most cunning and desperate efforts, though, were reserved for the traitor, Abaythian Marrinek, whose crimes and subsequent implausible escape from justice had led directly to Krant's current discomfort. Krant was busily imagining an underground torture labyrinth filled with obscure mythical creatures (the study of myths and legends was one of Krant's few pleasures, a leftover from a childhood spent in the company of an eccentric uncle with an eclectic taste in reading material) when he was interrupted by the sight of a tall spire emerging from behind the low trees at the side of the road.

Finally, finally he was able to nudge his horse away from the crowd and kick it into a brisk trot. The packhorse followed gamely behind and together they chopped and bounced their way along the final stretch of road at the greatest speed they had reached all day. They slowed at the edge of the town where a bored watchman waved them through an ancient gatehouse and then Krant was at last able to feel that he had successfully navigated the wilds of the countryside and returned, a hero, to civilisation.

Actually, though, when he looked around, it was clear that this wasn't quite the same level of civilisation that he was used to. The buildings were smaller and less grand, the roads narrower and unswept, the alleyways darker and more obvious, the people poorer and less fashionably dressed. He followed the main road as it kinked through the small town, peering cautiously at locals as they went about their business and waving away vendors, beggars and small children by the score. The exhilaration of the last mile of the open road, crowded and busy though it had been, faded as he struggled to make headway through the mass of people and animals crammed into the small town. By the time he reached the market square and caught sight of the Golden Perch, he was definitely feeling the stress of the last mile of travel through a crowded and unfamiliar town.

At last he was able to steer his horse into the inn's court-yard and escape the crush. His relief at seeing Gavelis standing at the door with a stable boy ready to take his horse was far greater than he would have imagined possible. The news that there was a small hot bath waiting for him in the inn's modest bath house almost reduced him to tears. He thanked Gavelis, gladly handed the reins of his horse to the stable boy and headed straight for the bath.

An hour later, the pains of the day's riding had been soothed away along with the dust and grime and sweat of the journey. Krant, dressed in fresh clothes laid out for him by Gavelis, sat down in the common room to a supper of bread, cheese, potatoes and roasted beef. Later, alone in the small room he was to share with Gavelis, Krant thought back over the events of the day and tried to fit all he had learnt into his established world view.

Firstly, he had confirmed that he was neither horseman nor countryman. This was not a good sign for the days ahead, when it might be necessary to travel through areas that lacked towns or even inns. It might, Gavelis had warned, be necessary occasionally to beg lodgings at a farm-house; Krant shuddered at the thought and remembered with some degree of embarrassment the horror he had experienced at the suggestion. He had been sure that Gavelis was enjoying the situation and he half wondered if maybe it was something he had said just to see the reaction from his supposed master.

Secondly, he was definitely not used to having a servant and he wasn't really sure how to behave. He had plenty of experience with the servants in the palace, of course, but they had tended to regard the junior clerks with a mixture of amused contempt and pity. The experience of having someone who was, nominally at least, his to command was new and not entirely pleasant. Unfortunately, the only person Krant could talk to was also the one person whose advice he couldn't ask on this particular problem. He filed it away for further consideration at a later date.

Finally, he was forced to admit that without Gavelis he would have been at something of a loss today. Travelling between cities, which he had done only once before as a small child in the company of his parents, was considerably more complicated than he had remembered. He didn't like having to rely on someone as completely as he was relying on Gavelis but maybe tomorrow he could assert himself a little more and get involved in the planning of the next stage of the journey.

Happy that he had brought a little sanity and control back to his life, Krant laid down on the bed and was asleep within moments.

The next morning, when Gavelis gently shook him awake, all thoughts of a happy day's travel were pushed quickly from Krant's head by the terrible pains in his back and buttocks and shoulders and legs. It occurred to him then, as he struggled to sit up, that he had never in a day ridden one fifth as far as they had done yesterday and that, if you counted the return, they were barely a twentieth of the way through the journey.

He groaned and forced himself into a sitting position. Gavelis passed him a tray of breakfast - bread, boiled eggs, cold meat - and then said, "I'm sorry to wake you, sir, but today I fear we must make haste if we are to reach the next town before nightfall. The weather has changed and the locals are predicting rain this afternoon."

"Oh god," wailed Krant, "how far today?"

"About forty miles, I'm afraid sir, rather more than we did yesterday. But at least the roads should be a little less crowded, meaning that we should make better time."

Krant groaned again.

"You are a hard man, Gavelis, a tyrant."

Krant picked at his breakfast, his arms aching, then he set the tray to one side and slid out of bed.

"Aargh!" he opined, as he staggered from his bed, "Why aren't you suffering, Gavelis? What is your secret?" he demanded, leaning against the wall like an old man.

"A lot more riding, I'm afraid. Another week or so and the pain should have faded."

"A week? Dear god, why does anyone ever leave home?"

Krant stretched, dressed and finished his breakfast as Gavelis packed their things. Gavelis went ahead to prepare the horses while Krant stumbled down the stairs, clutching at the handrail and almost falling at the top step. By the time he reached the courtyard the stable boy was holding his horse and Gavelis was tightening the straps of the bags on the pack horse and checking that the riding horses were correctly saddled.

Krant hauled himself into his saddle and sat gingerly while Gavelis fussed around the courtyard. A few minutes later they were on the move, Gavelis leading both Krant and the pack horse out of the courtyard and across the market square. They stopped just outside the gatehouse so that Gavelis could talk to the watchmen, apparently questioning them about other travellers on the road.

"They say, sir," said Gavelis, once he had re-joined Krant, "that there is a group of merchants carrying linen and wool and various other goods about half an hour ahead of us. There have been no reports of trouble on the first few miles of road for years so we should be safe to ride after them. We should catch them within an hour."

He pulled his horse around.

"Are you ready, sir?"

Krant looked at him, unamused.

"Highwaymen again, eh?" he said, sighing, "very well, if we must."

He kicked his horse into a canter and they set off, the rising sun warming their backs and casting long shadows on the road in front of them.

That first ride on their second day of travelling was amongst the worst experiences of Krant's life. The pain in his thighs and back and buttocks from the previous day's riding was amplified by a brisk canter along the road in pursuit of the safety of the caravan. By the time they caught the slow-moving mass of people and carts, Krant was in such discomfort that the thought of a highwayman's arrow held considerable appeal. The casual grace with which Gavelis rode and his obvious lack of suffering simply highlighted the gulf in practical ability between them and enhanced Krant's feelings of disgust with both himself and the journey.

The rest of the day passed in a blur of pain and milestones, which Krant counted to distract himself from the awful motion of the horse and the endless boredom of the ride. By the time they had reached the second town Krant was ready to hurl himself into the nearest river to end the suffering but Gavelis insisted that this would only make it more difficult to complete their mission. Krant relented, but he didn't stop complaining.

The third day dawned hotter than the previous two and

without a hint of cloud in the sky. Boredom, exhaustion and unrelenting heat meant that the day dragged, the miles seeming to pass ever more slowly as the sun beat down, flattening the atmosphere. Gavelis pointed out the towers that marked the western edge of the Empire as they passed them late on day three but Krant barely noticed, entirely absorbed by his own suffering and misery.

Days four and five were much the same and Krant now rode automatically, hardly thinking about where the horse was going or what he should be doing to guide it. The pain in his legs and lower back was as bad as ever and five days tramping through the heat and dust of the summer roads had pushed Krant to his limit. His attempts to talk to Gavelis had petered out when he realised the older man wasn't really interested in conversation and shared none of his interests.

Finally, late in the afternoon of the fifth day, the weather broke and a sudden thunderstorm rolled in from the north bringing variety, if not relief, to the lives of the weary travellers. Clouds raced across the sky, dark thunderheads chasing away the bright summer sun and when the rain arrived it fell fast and heavy. Large droplets splattered noisily on dusty road, dusty animal and dusty person alike and within minutes the road surface was slick with mud. Krant was soaked through in minutes. His coat, so elegant on the streets of Esterengel, had offered no more than a token resistance and now leaked at seams and collar and cuffs.

Much as he had cursed the heat of the summer, the sudden downpour was worse. The temperature had dropped markedly and Krant shivered as he sat on his horse, watching morosely as the scenery passed slowly by.

At some point, as the rain came down in sheets and the road grew every muddier, Krant found himself alone on the road; Gavelis had disappeared. He must have ridden ahead with the packhorse to secure their lodgings for the night but Krant honestly couldn't say how long he had been alone, hunched over the neck of his horse and barely noticing the other travellers on the road. The storm eventually passed and the rain stopped just as Krant reached the edge of the town of Rayvale. He looked around, suddenly aware that he had no idea where he was supposed to be going or what Gavelis had told him about the night's accommodation.

He stopped the horse, panicking slightly, his mind racing through the awful consequences of being separated from his servant so far from home and outside the Empire. He had only a little money, no spare clothes and no idea at all about how to get to Vensille.

Krant was wet and cold and tired and he didn't even know the name of the town, let alone the names of people who might be prepared to help him. He snatched at the reins when his horse started to make its own way along the street, walking with the flow of people. He was about to turn around, thinking maybe he could retrace his steps to the edge of the town, when someone grabbed the bridle.

Startled, he jerked around. A man leered up at him, smiling out from under an oiled leather hood.

"Are you looking for an inn, sir?" asked the man in an ingratiating tone, "Somewhere dry and warm to stay the night, maybe? Somewhere you can get out of those damp clothes?"

"Er, what? No, I er, just need to find my, er, servant," said

Krant, looking around and tugging on the reins but the man held tight to the bridle and the horse declined to move.

"Why don't you come this way, sir," said the man, snatching the reins from Krant's distracted hands and turning to lead the horse through the crowd, "I've got a nice room you can have where we can take care of you and your horse."

Krant made a grab for the reins but missed and almost slid from his saddle. He threw his arms around the horse's neck to keep his seat and the man said, "Don't be like that, sir, we'll look after you. Oh, yes we will."

He leered up at Krant again and turned off the main road onto a side street, dark with overhanging buildings.

"Gavelis," shouted Krant, "help, Gavelis!" He twisted in the saddle, searching desperately for someone who might be able to help but his cries were ignored as his treacherous horse carried him further into the gloomy alleyway.

Then the man pulled the horse's head around and punched Krant hard on the leg.

"Shut up," he snarled, pulling the horse further into the alleyway. Krant scrabbled for his dagger but the man just slapped it out of his hand. Krant squealed as his was grabbed by the collar and dragged from his saddle. Krant yelled out in shock as he slid into the mud and muck, falling heavily on his shoulder. The man kicked him in the chest, knocking him onto his back, then turned back to lead the horse further from the main street. Krant groaned and rolled over, grasping at the man's rancid cloak and trying to pull him back.

The man staggered as Krant tugged on his cloak, then he turned back, yanked the cloak free. Then he drew a knife.

"You scrawny little runt!"

He kicked again as Krant tried to scrabble back, catching

him in the chest. Krant screamed as a rib cracked and then the man kicked him again and again.

"Stay away from me you little prick and keep your hands to yourself," he yelled, punctuating his sentence with more kicks.

Then the man turned and collected the reins, pulling the horse further into the alley.

Krant, lying on his back and struggling to breath, could do nothing but watch as his horse abandoned him to his fate. The man gave a final sneering look at Krant as he lay on the ground, then there was a noise like a side of beef flopping onto a butcher's block and the man stopped. He dropped the reins and poked briefly at a strange hole in the middle of his chest, then he collapsed into the mud and lay still.

"Let me help you up, sir," said Gavelis to the astonished Krant.

Gavelis helped him first to sit and then to stand. Krant stood, propped against a wall, while Gavelis retrieved his horse. Gavelis didn't even glance at the corpse, he just led the horse back to Krant.

"I just happened to pass the mouth of the alley, sir. I became worried when you didn't arrive at the inn and, knowing that this town is a little on the rough side, came looking for you. It seems I was just in time."

Krant, his eyes wet with tears from the pain of his snapped ribs and the humiliation of being robbed in broad daylight, said nothing. Clinging to his servant for support, he staggered the short distance to the inn and collapsed onto a bench in the courtyard. Gavelis handed the horse to the stable boy then helped Krant inside and up to their room.

Later, bathed and fed and with his wounds bound and

dressed, Krant sat on the bed while Gavelis busied himself around the room.

"Your intervention, Gavelis, was very much appreciated," said Krant, wincing and gasping at the pain in his chest, "and you have my thanks."

"You are most welcome, sir, but I blame myself. I think we must journey together from now on to prevent further mishap."

"That sounds like a very good idea, Gavelis," said Krant, lying back on the bed and closing his eyes as the wine dulled the pain in his chest, "and then you can tell me all about that little toy you have and how it works."

Gavelis said nothing and seconds later Krant began to snore.

17

M arrinek pushed open the apothecary's door and walked in to the small shop. It was crowded with shelves of drawers and jars and it smelt of a dozen different herbs and spices.

A tall, thin woman of indeterminate age sat at a counter at the back of the shop, reading a small book. As Marrinek approached, she closed the book and stood up.

"Good morning, sir, how can I help you today?" She spoke quietly in a voice that seemed strangely educated and out-of-place amongst the grim and crowded streets of the Narrows. Marrinek looked at her, unable to gauge her age, and decided that she was definitely a woman of talent.

"I have a problem of a somewhat delicate nature," he said, leaning on Bone Dancer, "and I hope you will be able to give me something for it."

She took a deep breath and settled her expression into one of polite and neutral interest.

"Take a seat," she said, pointing at a stool beside the counter, "and tell me all. There are certainly things I can offer if you are having difficulties in the bedroom."

"The bedroom?" Marrinek was briefly confused, "Ah, no, not that sort of 'delicate' problem. It's more, well, maybe I should just tell you."

He sat down on the stool, leant Bone Dancer against the counter and then turned to face the apothecary.

"Can I trust you to be discreet?"

"Of course. Everything you say here will be in complete confidence, unless I think you're planning an evil act or have committed some heinous crime, in which case I'll incapacitate you and summon the Watch." She smiled, all innocent, as she said it but Marrinek didn't doubt her sincerity.

"It's nothing like that," he said, hoping to reassure her, "well, not quite. I'm not really sure how to put this but I was, er, well. I was arrested and imprisoned - falsely, I promise - and they fed me something in my food to suppress my talent."

The apothecary looked at him, peering closely at his eyes.

"When did you last take the drug?"

"About a week ago, maybe nine days. I'm fine most of the time but then, every now and again, I try to focus a little power and the nausea returns. Sometimes it's so bad I can't stand and I see spots before my eyes."

"You don't know what it was you were fed?"

Marrinek shook his head.

"Sorry, no. Does that make a difference?"

The apothecary sucked at her teeth.

"Maybe. Don't know. It would be better to know for sure. How long were you forced to take this substance?"

"About two years, give or take."

"Two years? That's a long time to take a drug like this. Some of these substances can have permanent effects on the body or the mind. Have you been able to use your talent since you stopped taking the drugs?"

"Yes," said Marrinek, now severely worried, "but sometimes it just doesn't happen the way I expect it to."

"Doesn't matter," said the apothecary, shaking her head, "if you can still access your talent then the damage probably isn't permanent."

She looked at him for a long moment then leant over the counter to pull up his eyelid.

"Look down at the floor," she instructed.

Marrinek looked at the floor as the apothecary inspected first one eye then the other.

"Focus your talent, draw as much power as you can then release it."

Marrinek took a deep breath and did as she said, drawing and holding as much power as she could.

"Whoa, I felt that," she said quietly, and now when Marrinek looked at her he could see fear in her eyes, "who are you?"

"It doesn't matter," he said shaking his head, "please, can you help me?"

He released the power and looked at her hopefully, fearing that she might give him more bad news. She stood there for a long moment, then shook her head.

"I don't think I can," she said, then held up her hand as Marrinek opened his mouth, "no, listen. I don't think you need any help, I think you'll be fine, you just have to give it time. If we knew what you'd been fed then we might have options. I could give you Hensleaf to counter Redstar or Baron's Mixture if you'd taken Foxbane. I have a dozen other things that would counteract various inhibiting substances but without knowing what you've taken we would be gambling and the odds would not be good. Take the wrong counter and you'd probably be worse off."

She shook her head again.

"I'm sorry, but sometimes the best thing I can offer is a reassuring word. Modern medicine has its limits and this is one of them."

This wasn't the answer Marrinek had hoped for and he didn't even try to hide his disappointment.

"So there's nothing I can do? I just have to live with this? For how long?"

She shrugged.

"Don't know. Sleep, exercise, eat well. Look after yourself, in other words. Exercise your talent. You'll probably find that the bouts of nausea become less severe and with longer gaps between attacks but it might take weeks or months for them to disappear completely."

Marrinek stood up and took a deep breath.

"Thanks. I suppose I should be grateful that it isn't worse. What do I owe you?"

The apothecary shook her head.

"I only charge for prescriptions and you, whoever you are, don't need anything I sell."

"Again, thank you."

He bowed then turned to leave, collecting Bone Dancer on his way, and stepped back onto the street, heading for the Jewel.

"So why can't we just force things to change? Why do we use charms?" said Floost, frowning at Marrinek from where she sat cross-legged on the floor of their suite at the Jewel.

"You can," said Marrinek, "the use of charms is entirely optional. The problem is that the whole process becomes vastly less efficient to the point where you achieve ten or a hundred or maybe even ten thousand times as much with a charm as you could without one. So you pull more power, and more, until either you achieve your aim or you burn out your ability. Or worse."

He paused briefly to let that settle in.

"Burnout would be a major topic if you were being formally trained but you're strong and I haven't time to go into the details." The twins looked at him, clearly unconvinced and unhappy. Marrinek sighed.

"You have to be careful. If you pull too much power, too quickly, you can burn out your abilities. It happens sometimes, if people lose control or try to do too much without a charm. Effects range from immediate death to coma to simply destroying one's mind or ability to focus power."

The twins stared, looks of horror on their faces.

"And that's why we use charms. They're very efficient, so you use less power and avoid the risk of burnout. You don't have to use charms, if you don't want to, it's just much, much safer."

Marrinek held up his fist.

"Think about the other disciplines. You've seen masons at work?"

The twins nodded. The city was alive with masons working stone to construct, repair or extend walls or buildings. The Duke's programme of building and fortification was vast and ongoing and a constant stream of men and material flowed into the city to keep it going.

"It's the same for them. The quality and type of the tools used make a big difference to the speed and quality of the work. Masons have small chisels for fine lettering and big heavy cold chisels for breaking rocks. They could use the lettering chisels to break rocks but it would take days instead of minutes. It's the same for us. You could force enough power into something to change it without using a charm but it's much easier to use a charm that's appropriate to the task."

"But we could do it, if we wanted to?" pressed Darek, leaning forward.

"Theoretically, yes, but for all normal applications it just isn't practical. It will almost always be faster - and safer - to find a charm, or make one from scratch, than to work without one. The exception is Flow but that's a subject for another day."

Marrinek pulled out the flame charm.

"The next question is 'how do we make a charm without tools?' and it's a good one. The simple answer is that, in general, you don't, because it's just not necessary and it takes too long."

"But if it was necessary, how would you do it?" said Floost.

Marrinek paused to think.

"Right. Let's imagine you've got a piece of wood that you want to harden, like Bone Dancer. The best way is to find a tool, like Chisel or Twig from the tool roll, and use it carefully to focus power into the wood, causing the structure to alter so that the wood becomes a lot harder. If you don't have a tool - pass me that length of oak - it can be done but it takes a lot longer and you have to focus a lot more power."

Marrinek put down the flame charm and held the piece of oak in both hands.

"Watch the power."

He focussed, drawing power until he had enough to begin altering the wood. After a few minutes, he stopped.

"What did you see?"

Floost said, "The power was just flowing into the wood,

like a river falling into a cave. Did that harden the whole piece?"

Marrinek smiled and shook his head.

"Not even close. That was a lot of power and all it did was harden the last inch or so." He rapped the foot-long piece of wood on the floor.

"Now let's see what happens when I use a tool instead."

He pulled Chisel from the roll and held it over the oak, focussing power. This time he moved the tool quickly over the surface of the wood, directing power into the oak through the charm. He stopped when he had worked the length of the piece several times with the tool and held it up for the twins to see.

"That's done the whole piece, although if I spent more time on it I could make it harder still. This is why we use tools."

He tossed the oak to Floost and picked up the fire charm, making it glow gently.

"Find a piece of wood, Darek. We will practise sensing the flow of power."

The twins groaned but Marrinek just raised his eyebrows and looked down his nose at them.

"Begin. Tell me if you sense the power."

For an hour they practised but without success. Finally, Marrinek called a halt.

"We will practise this again tomorrow but now I want you to try to light the fire charm."

The twins sat up, their interest renewed at the suggestion of practical activity.

"To produce a flame, you must pull power and focus it into the charm. This simple exercise will teach you the rudiments of power manipulation. Once mastered, you can proceed to learn ever finer degrees of control, and once you

reach a certain point you can begin to learn more complicated and demanding applications. Everything, though,
comes down to focus and control; you must learn to feel the
power and direct it. Without focus your will draw no power
and achieve no effect and without control the power you
draw won't do what you want it to do."

Marrinek held up the fire charm, focussed, and
produced a small flame.

"To do this I focus a small amount of power. If I want a
larger flame," the flame grew as he spoke until it was six
inches tall and bright enough to cast shadows, even in the
daylight, "or a brighter light I focus more power. If I want a
big flame and bright light I change the way I focus the
power, and if I want heat without light I change again."

He extinguished the flame and handed the charm
to Darek.

"Clear your mind. Close your eyes and picture a blank,
empty space in your mind. Breathe deeply and slowly. You
too Floost - this is an exercise you can practise without
having a charm."

Darek sat cross-legged on the floor next to Floost, the
charm held out in front of him, breathing deeply with his
eyes closed. Floost copied him. Marrinek kept talking in a
slow, low, comforting voice.

"Breathe evenly, be calm and at peace. You remember
what the flow of power felt like when I focussed on the
charm? Empty your mind and picture the fire charm in your
hand. Feel the fire charm, remember the feel of power
flowing into the charm, feel a trickle of power flowing again
into the charm."

When the clock on the nearby guild house struck
midday Marrinek held up his hand.

"That's enough. Floost, you take the charm and try."

For another hour they repeated the exercises, Marrinek talking quietly, the twins trying to feel the power flowing into the charm.

"Right, we'll stop there," he said eventually, "I will buy another fire charm today so that you can both practise at the same time."

He stood up and stretched, easing his sore muscles.

"We're going out. I need to speak to Madame Duval and we need to make some arrangements. Tidy your things away, you're coming with me today."

While the twins tidied the room Marrinek transferred some of the coins he had taken from Hitton to his purse then packed the rest into his bag. Carrying them all was a risk but so was leaving them in the room and at least while carrying them he wouldn't have to worry. When the twins had finished their chores Marrinek held up a small piece of metal.

"This," he said, "is tungsten, sometimes known as power stone." He handed the nugget to the twins.

"It's heavy," said Floost.

"Heavier than gold and almost as valuable. Easier to obtain, almost, but prized for its ability to hold power, to store vast quantities in fact, and then to release it very rapidly. Like the lead I added to Bone Dancer, but much more effective. With this you could power a charm so that even an untalented person could use it. You could work it into a building to power a lamp or into a fireplace to provide heat. With the right charm and a power net this metal can do almost anything you can imagine."

He placed it on the table and pulled out the small nugget of gold, setting it down alongside the tungsten.

"Not as dense as tungsten but still an excellent reservoir of power. The reason gold coins are so rare is that it is too

valuable to use as mere currency. Most gold that comes out
of the earth ends up in weapons like Bone Dancer or other,
more exotic tools."

He put both nuggets into his purse.

"And here's the clever bit. Copper can be used to pull
power from the atmosphere. If you attach a net of copper
wire to a nugget of heavy metal - lead, gold or tungsten, for
example - it will siphon power into the metal where it
remains until you pull it out again. The bigger the net, the
more power it draws. Very useful."

Marrinek stood up and checked his dagger, then picked
up the shock cannon, Drake and stuffed it into his pocket.
He slung his pack over his shoulder.

"Right, let's get going. In public, you need to behave like
respectful apprentices, so walk just behind me and if I call
for you or tell you to do something you do it right away. No
messing around."

He opened the door and led them out onto the hallway
then down through the inn. The lunchtime trade was in full
flow and the common room was filling with hungry and
thirsty people. Outside, the street was busy with the usual
mix of people and market stalls and animals. Floost and
Darek fell-in behind Marrinek, bouncing along at his heels
as he made his way through the crowd. Progress was rapid;
Marrinek's unusual height, the staff he carried and the
bizarre way that he wore his hair marked him as a foreigner
and even in this cosmopolitan trading city the crowds often
parted ahead of him.

As they drew close to the House of Duval he stopped
and turned to speak to the twins, drawing them under the
overhanging roof of a tailor's shop.

"Keep your eyes open while we are here. Make a note of
everyone who comes and goes, their class and clothes,

wealth and bearing. Madame Duval will help us while her interests align with ours but she isn't a friend."

The twins nodded

"Is it safe?" asked Floost uncertainly.

"Yes, mostly," said Marrinek, already turning to head back onto the street, "insofar as anywhere is safe."

He led them onto Eastside Bath and along the street to Madame Duval's.

Shad ushered them into the hallway and closed the door carefully behind them. The house was quiet - no music floated down the stairs, there was no laughter from above, not even the floorboards creaked - and even the sounds of the street were dulled as Shad barred the door.

"Madame Duval is in the back room," said Shad, leading the way down the hall and through the door at the end. He stopped outside another door at the end of a short corridor lined with oak panels, quiet and dark. He knocked twice, then opened the door and ushered Marrinek in.

"You two stay out here," said Marrinek, gesturing at a pair of tall chairs, "and keep out of trouble. Read something and practice your exercises." Then he stepped through the doorway and left them alone. Shad looked them over, then retreated back to his chair in the hallway.

In the back room, Madame Duval sat on a small mat in the middle of the floor, her eyes closed. She opened them and looked up as Marrinek raised an eyebrow.

"Meditation," she said by way of explanation, "I find it helps me to think and today I have done a lot of thinking."

She stood and pulled a bell cord by the fireplace.

"Tea?" she asked, sitting on the edge of a low sofa under the window.

Marrinek sat down in the armchair opposite Madame Duval. He fished in his purse and tossed the nugget of gold to Madame Duval, who caught it with her left hand before it could reach the floor.

"Compensation, as promised."

Madame Duval looked at the nugget as it sat in the palm of her hand, weighing it carefully, her mouth suddenly dry. She looked up at Marrinek and there was doubt in her eyes.

"This is more than I paid for the twins, Bay, far more. My whole house is worth less than this nugget even if I add in the girls."

"More than you paid, maybe, but less than they are worth. Be careful how you spend it and even more careful when you fence it. Do you have someone you can trust?"

"Yes. Well, maybe," she said, nodding slowly, "if I break it up into pieces first." She looked up at him.

"I'll find a way. What do you want in return?"

"Your help, like I said. First, tell me what you've heard about the Snarling Goat."

Her eyes went wide and now she seemed truly fearful.

"That was you? Four people dead was what I heard, including Hitton and Tam. Five if you count that bastard Gander. The North Enders are out for blood but they don't know whose."

She closed her fist then stood as the door opened and Nandy came in with a pot of tea.

"Thank you Nandy, on the table please. I'll pour. Oh, and find something for the twins," she looked at Marrinek again, "I assume they're here?"

Marrinek nodded and smiled at Nandy, who curtsied before leaving. Madame Duval's hands shook as she poured the tea. Marrinek leant forward to take a cup.

"To be fair," he said by way of justification, "the evening

didn't play out exactly as I had planned. Hitton proved to be less amenable to persuasion than I had hoped and Tam was rather more incautious than I had expected. If he'd stayed downstairs they would probably all still be alive. Well, mostly. I'm not sure Hitton would have held to any promise he had made."

He sat back in the arm chair and sipped at his tea.

"Oh, very nice. A light Imperial tea. Was it difficult to find?"

"Damn the tea," said Madame Duval, anger chasing the fear from her eyes, "and damn you too. What the hell have you dragged me into, you bloody idiot! The North Enders have got people out all over the city asking questions, looking for the man who broke into the Snarling Goat, and here you are sipping tea like some effete bloody nobleman."

"Well, yes. Sorry. I can take the twins and the gold and leave, if you like, or we can work out what to do next and settle in for the longer game. I can promise more riches, if you take the latter route, enough to get out of the game and set yourself up as a minor noble house."

Marrinek sipped his tea again.

"This really is very good tea but a little cool for my tastes. Your girl needs to warm the pot and the crockery."

"Forget the bloody tea," said Madame Duval, putting down her cup with shaking hands, tea slopping into the saucer, "what do I tell the North Enders when they ask what I know? What do I tell them about you?"

Marrinek sipped his tea again, thinking.

"It's all about the money. Well, money and power. We need the former to buy the latter which in turns brings security. Nobody will just give me what I want so I plan to take it from the North Enders. What should you do? Tell them the truth, or some of it, at least. Tell them that I came here this morning, flashing too much money, and confessed all to one of your girls.

"Tell them that I boasted about killing their men, that I made wild threats, that I mocked their dress sense, if you like, but make sure they know who to blame. In fact, let's send them a message right now, before they have a chance to ask. Don't mention talent, or the twins, just tell them that you think they're looking for a tall thug with long hair and a staff who's been loose-lipped around your girls."

He sat back and finished his tea.

"I'll leave the twins here for now - you'll see that they're well cared for - and I'll pay another visit to the North Enders."

Madame Duval shook her head as she stared at him.

"You're mad, you know, totally mad. What do you hope to gain?"

Marrinek smiled.

"Well, I'd settle for an enormous sack of gold and a palace full of dusky maidens to do my every bidding but, lacking that, my plan is to take control of the North Enders, to squeeze out the other gangs and then use their combined resources to force my way into Vensille society."

Madame Duval gaped at him again, staring as if he had grown a third arm.

"You really are mad. You'll never be able to take control of the gangs and why would the nobles accept you, even if you had all the money in the world?"

"Oh, they won't accept me, not even slightly, but that doesn't mean they can't be persuaded to make themselves useful, and I have all sorts of plans for a long and pros-perous life. Now, what can you tell me about the rest of the North Enders?"

They talked for another hour or so, Madame Duval

laying out in detail all that she knew of the North Enders, their territory, leaders, habits and weaknesses. Marrinek nodded and asked occasional questions. By the time Madame Duval's lecture wound down, he had a good grasp on the local criminal scene and a decent knowledge of the city itself.

"So their leader is a man called Stern Fangfoss - ludicrous name - and he's a powerful practitioner as well as a brutal thug, is that right?"

Madame Duval nodded and poured more tea.

"But he's rarely seen outside Trike's, next to the Snarling Goat, where he has some sort of apartment or suite of rooms."

Madame Duval nodded again.

"Why is that? Hitton was the same - he stayed in the Snarling Goat when he should have been out running his men - what's the story?"

Madame Duval frowned and shrugged.

"I don't know all the details but a few years ago there was a clampdown. The gangs had grown bold, cocky even, and were running rackets across the whole city, fighting turf wars in the streets. It was bad for business, everyone's business, and the Watch hit them hard. They arrested all the gang members they could find, hanged the leaders and sold the rest to slavers from across the ocean. Then they let it be known that they knew who else was involved and they would be hanged as well if things got out of hand again."

"I thought Rhenveldt didn't like slavers?" interrupted Marrinek.

"He doesn't, hates them. Says they're a drain on a decent city, if you can believe it. The way I heard it, he sold the gang members to send a message. Seems to have worked.

"Since then it's been a lot quieter. The gangs still racketeer and smuggle and they run most of the cheaper bath houses but there are fewer of them and they settle their differences more discretely. And the leaders, especially the talented ones, stay out of sight. They're playing a long game, waiting for the Watch to calm down, to forget their threat, so that they can go back to the way things were before."

Madame Duval paused, thinking about how things had been.

"It wasn't a nice city, back then, it wasn't safe. The Watch made a big difference but I still pay protection, to them and the North Enders. Between them they make sure I never keep too much of my earnings."

Her voice had grown bitter and dark and she lay back on her chaise, staring up at the ceiling.

"I want out of the game and out of the city but I can't afford it. I have nowhere to go so I'm stuck here, running my House and trying not to upset anyone so badly they decide to make life difficult. This city is still a dangerous place, especially for untalented single women, and I don't think things are going to get better now you've killed one of Fang-foss's lieutenants."

"Well, at least I know where you stand," said Marrinek, "so let's get started and see if we can help each other. You have a room the twins can use for now?"

Madame Duval nodded.

"Good. They have their studies but they also need more clothes - nothing elaborate, just good quality everyday clothes suitable for the children of a successful merchant. Not flashy, but enough to discourage undue interest. Can you arrange that?"

Madame Duval nodded again.

"Great. Now, let's send a message to the Snarling Goat and see what floats to the surface."

Later that day, with the twins settled in a large room in the attic, Marrinek waited in the servants' corridor at the back of the house, idly running Chisel over the rear door and focussing power to harden the frame and the door itself. He was about to turn his attention to the bar and bolts and hinges that secured the door and held it in its frame when Shad appeared and beckoned him to follow him.

"Trusted Man from the North Enders just arrived," whispered Shad, "he's in with Madame D now."

Marrinek followed Shad back to the servant's door that led to Madame Duval's study. He leant Bone Dancer carefully against the wall and rested his head against the door to listen but he needn't have bothered. Madame Duval was really letting rip, denouncing him loudly, expressing her disgust at his boasts, insulting his manhood, appealing for help. Marrinek raised his eyebrows at one point and looked at Shad, who just shrugged and grinned. After a few minutes her anger wound down and she described Marrinek in some detail, throwing in more cheap insults to keep things interesting.

Eventually the man left through the other study door and passed quickly into the street. Marrinek opened the servant's door and went in with Shad. Madame Duval was sitting behind her desk, fanning herself as she leant back in the chair.

"Well he took the bait. God knows what'll happen now but I hope you're ready - they're all going to be looking for you soon."

"Good," said Marrinek, grinning, "time for me to do my part." He checked his sword and shock cannon, pulled on his cloak and picked up Bone Dancer.

"Are you sure about the cloak? It's not really the time of year for it..." said Madame Duval.

Marrinek just grinned and bowed and swept out of the room.

Back on the street, in the late afternoon sun, the cloak didn't seem like such a great idea but it hid his sword and most of his hair. It still wasn't a great disguise but hunched over with his head bowed he looked little like the tall, staff-wielding maniac that Madame Duval had described. He shuffled slowly through the streets toward the Narrows, pushing gently through the crowds until he was able to slouch against the wall opposite Trike's.

It looked much like every other inn in every other city Marrinek had ever visited. The first and second floors jutted out into the street, shading the door. A sign hung over the door but the paint had pealed leaving only the carved triangles behind to announce the inn as Trike's. The door swung freely as people entered and left and the noise from inside was loud.

Marrinek stretched his neck, loosened his sword in its sheath, rolled his shoulders and strode across the street into the common room. Inside it was much the same as the Snarling Goat. A gallery ran around the first floor but where the Goat had booths, Trikes had open space filled with tables and chairs. And drunks, it appeared, which explained much of the noise.

Marrinek, still hunched, lurched unsteadily across the room and up the stairs to the first floor. Even at this early hour the gallery was busy with people and the air was thick with pipe smoke. He found a small table in a corner and settled down to wait. A passing barmaid brought him a small jug of chilled wine and he sat back to enjoy himself, watching the room and the people and sipping at his drink.

It didn't take long to spot a pattern. Every few minutes a tall thin man with an extravagantly twirled moustache would emerge from a door near the top of the stairs on the first floor and either walk around the gallery or down to the common room, apparently looking for specific individuals. Each time he found one he would lean down and whisper in their ear then return with them through the door on the first floor. A few minutes later the chosen individual would re-emerge and head out of the inn, sometimes taking one or two other people with him. After he had seen this happen half-a-dozen times, Marrinek decided he had seen enough to know what was going on.

He stood up and stretched, abandoning his hunch. He tossed a few coins on the table then walked across the gallery to the door, timing his arrival so that he got there a few seconds after the door had closed behind the mous-tached messenger and his latest guest. Marrinek paused briefly then pushed open the door and passed through into the room beyond.

As he closed the door behind him he found five men looking at him in surprise in a large room that seems to run most of the length of the inn. Along one side were shuttered windows looking out onto the street. Two of the men sat quite close by at a bench under the windows. Another, presumably Fangfoss, was lounging at a table further into the room. The moustached messenger was standing in front of the table with the fifth man, his latest guest, a heavyset thug with a multitude of scars and tattoos. All of them stared at Marrinek.

"Well," said Marrinek, "this is awkward."

He strode into the room, walking toward the fifth man until he stood a few feet in front of the table.

"I don't believe we've been introduced," he said to the seated man, "I'm Bay and you have many things I want."

"Kill him," said the seated man to the room in general. The two men on the bench stood slowly, drawing swords and edging forward. The story of Marrinek's activities the night before, told and retold throughout the day, growing larger and more violent with every telling, had made them wary. Moustache, less worried by incredible stories from unreliable witnesses, whipped a pair of knives from his belt and turned quickly toward Marrinek only to find himself blocked by Tattoo, slower on the uptake than the others and standing motionless as he tried to work out what was going on.

Marrinek grinned at the seated man and undid the clasp of his cloak with a flourish, letting it fall to the ground. Then he pulled out Drake and held it loosely in one hand.

"Last chance," he said, "why don't we..."

Then Tattoo charged forward, swinging his knives.

Marrinek took a step back and triggered Drake, hitting Tattoo with a diffuse low-power blast that knocked him off his feet. Marrinek swung round and blasted Moustache as well then kicked Tattoo between the legs as he tried to stand.

Moustache was struggling upwards, a confused expression on his face. Then he pulled another knife and advanced again toward Marrinek, teeth bared.

Marrinek triggered Drake a third time and knocked Moustache back down then he spun round and used Drake to hit both the men behind him, stepping forward to kick one in the jaw before he could rise. The second man scuttled away on his backside, face white with fear.

Marrinek turned back and found Tattoo climbing to his feet, meaty hands clenched into fists, face red with rage. He raised Drake again and triggered another pulse, knocking Tattoo back into the long table. Then he stepped forward and punched the man in the face before he could regain his balance. Tattoo's head whipped back, smacking hard against the table, then he slid to the floor and lay still.

Moustache came forward again, faster this time, fresh knives in each hand. Marrinek blocked one cut, dodged another then felt a third slice thinly across his arm. He yelped and punched out, missing Moustache but forcing him backwards so that he stumbled over Tattoo's feet and fell in a heap on the floor. Marrinek released a final blast from Drake, emptying the reservoir, and smashing Moustache's head heavily against the floorboards.

Marrinek swung round to face Fangfoss and pointed the depleted shock cannon at him.

"That's enough," said Marrinek firmly, "the next person to do anything violent, dies. Got it?"

Fangfoss, stationary for the duration of the fight, cleared his throat.

"Got it," he growled. Only one of Fangfoss's thugs remained conscious and he lay on his side clutching at his bruised ribs, unable to do much more than groan.

"You!" said Marrinek, pointing at the last man standing, or rather sitting, "Get out of here and take them with you." He waved his hand at the fallen fighters as the man scrambled to his feet and began dragging his colleagues to the door.

"Right, let's talk." Marrinek pulled up a chair and sat down at the table opposite Fangfoss.

"So it's like this," said Marrinek, "your gang controls much of the northern end of the city, right?"

Fangfoss nodded, eyes narrow, shoulders tense, waiting patiently for his opportunity.

"Here's my offer. I'll take half of your profit from now on, you'll pay weekly, starting now."

Fangfoss stared at him for a few moments, then threw his head back and laughed. Marrinek sat for a few seconds, then slapped his hand down on the table, Drake beneath his palm. Fangfoss jumped, then laughed even harder. Finally, tears in his eyes, he regained enough control to speak.

"And it might be worth the money just to hear your jokes. Half, he says. You really have no fucking clue, do you?" Fangfoss shook his head as the last of his thugs was dragged from the room.

"You might as well have a mug of wine while you're here and still able to drink it," said Fangfoss, reaching around to the table behind him to collect two mugs and a jug of wine. He filled them both and pushed one toward Marrinek.

"Your good health, short though it might be."

Fangfoss drank deeply then set down the mug and looked at Marrinek.

"You think you can just walk in here and take half my profits? Well, yes, of course I'll give you half," he said, sarcasm heavy in his tone, "why wouldn't I? But you'll be dead before sunrise."

"Frankly, I don't really care how you run my gang," said Marrinek, "as long as you pay. For now, I'll take whatever you have stashed in your apartment - upstairs, right? If you make me kill any more of my men," he leant forward, "I'll take your legs and ears and one eye."

He sat back and picked up his wine and raised the mug in a mock salute.

"I think we can work together, you and I. You just continue to do what you do but now, instead of paying the

Watch, you'll pay me. I'll handle the Watch and soon you'll be able to walk freely around the city again," said Marrinek, sipping at his wine, "and you can call me Bay."

"Bay? That's where they'll find your stinking bloated corpse you fucking cretin after I've taught you a lesson."

Marrinek could feel Fangfoss sucking in power as he spoke, focussing it on some sort of small but dangerous fire charm held beneath the table in his hand. Marrinek threw himself sideways as Fangfoss released the charm, directing a gout of blue-tinged flame toward the now empty chair. It burned straight through the back of the chair, setting it alight, then went out. Fangfoss swung round toward Marrinek who rolled away and back to his feet, eyes on the charm.

"That's me just getting warmed up," said Fangfoss, focussing more power into the small charm. Marrinek backed rapidly away and drew his sword. Fangfoss snorted and released the built-up power through the charm to send another gout of flame at Marrinek, who leapt back just in time to avoid the searing heat.

"Keep jumping, little man, keep jumping," said Fangfoss, gathering more power into the charm.

"Oh, what's the point?" said Marrinek to himself. He backed off some more then tossed the sword to the floor. Fangfoss smiled.

"I'm going to enjoy this. Come into my inn, assault me and my men, try to rob me blind, eh?"

He released the charm, shooting another gout of flame toward Marrinek.

Then he stopped as he felt Marrinek drawing power, a great deal of power, and pushing it into the charm he held in his hand. Alarm showed on Fangfoss's face as Marrinek raised his hand and then suddenly he was bowled over by a strong punch to the shoulder as a small part of the charm's power was released in an unfocused blunt attack. He rolled across the floor and scrambled to his feet, swinging his arm to bring his fire charm to bear.

Too slow, far too slow.

Marrinek triggered the shock cannon fired again and Fangfoss was knocked back down, landing heavily, the fire charm flying from his hand and rolling toward the corner of the room.

Fangfoss scrabbled after it then flipped himself onto his back so that he could see Marrinek advancing across the room, shock cannon raised.

"Help, help!" he shouted, still scrabbling backwards, eyes wild and afraid at the sudden turn of events.

Marrinek, still focussing power into the shock cannon, pointed it at Fangfoss's head.

"Shut up or I'll kill you now," he said quietly, waiting to see if Fangfoss would follow orders, "get up. You look pathetic, crawling on the floor like some sort of coward. Sit back down at the table and remain silent."

As Fangfoss took his seat the door burst open and Moustache came back in, knives drawn, teeth bared, blood running down the side of his head. He looked around the room until he saw Marrinek, still standing by the table with the shock cannon in hand. Moustache moved forward cautiously, eyeing the charm in Marrinek's hand, rolling his wrists and slashing at the air.

"Time to die, fucker."

Marrinek swung the shock cannon around and hit him with a low burst of power, like the ones that had felled Fangfoss. Moustache staggered back but didn't fall. Then he came forward again, lip curled in a sneer, so Marrinek hit him again, harder. This time Moustache went down, dropping his knives as he was knocked over backwards.

"Get him under control or I'll kill him now," Marrinek snarled at Fangfoss.

The gang lord raised a shaky hand towards Moustache as he struggled to stand.

"It's alright, Chickie, we're just talking. A misunderstanding. Get up, man," he said, annoyed now, "and get someone to send in some more wine and some food."

Chickie stood slowly, wincing at the pain in his ribs, and scooped up his knives. He glared at Marrinek.

"You sure, boss?"

"Just go," said Fangfoss, wearily.

Chickie waited a moment longer then sheathed his knives and backed out of the room, face full of suspicion.

Marrinek picked up his sword and sat down. He laid his sword on the table in front of him and set the shock cannon beside it.

"I'm not really a fan of fire charms as weapons. They can be effective, undoubtedly, but they lack finesse and their effect is just too obvious to be hidden. This, though," - he picked up the shock cannon again - "is quiet, discreet and controlled."

He set it back down on the table.

"What do you want?" said Fangfoss, his eyes on the shock cannon. He forced himself to look back at Marrinek, tearing his gaze away from the weapon on the table. He'd never heard of anything like it and he wanted one, seeing in it a way to dominate his gang for years to come.

"I told you. I want half. I have plans for which I need funds; you're going to provide them and then, when I'm done, I'll leave the city in your hands. I might even leave you a shock cannon," he gestured at the charm on the table, "or two."

Marrinek could see from the expression on the face of the gang leader that he had found a price that would secure his cooperation, at least for a short while. Cooperation would be sufficient, for now.

With Fangfoss still glancing at the shock cannon, Marrinek began to give him instructions.

18

Lady Camille swept into the council chamber of the Traebarn Palace, skirts flying as her heels clicked across the marble floor. She strode past the elaborate furnishings, the tapestries depicting famous scenes from Imperial history, the finely decorated chairs, the exquisitely painted statues, sparing them not a glance. Instead she flung her gaze across the assembled councillors then took her place at the head of the great table. Rincon took the seat to her left, setting the curled message from Administrator Nison in front of him.

Lady Camille gestured to the councillors, two men and two women.

"I'm sure we all have things to do so let's make this quick. We will continue this conversation in private," she said, gesturing to Rincon, who dismissed the guards and clerks so that the councillors were left alone in the chamber, "and no minutes will be kept."

"That is somewhat irregular," said the Lord Justice, Lady Clara Fiethien, sitting furthest from Lady Camille as was her habit, "I seem to remember that the last meeting we conducted without minutes resulted in decisions we later came to regret."

She stared hard at Lady Camille, who stared back, stony faced. The silence dragged for a few awkward seconds before Lady Camille spoke.

"Yes, well, whatever the outcome of the previous meeting, in this instance you will at least want to hear the news before we decide how to continue. Rincon, please read the message."

Rincon cleared his throat and picked up the message.

"This was received late last night from Heberon, the new port town on the south west coast. Administrator Nison, the man overseeing the construction of the town, sent this to us by courier as soon as the news reached him. The message reads, 'I regret to inform you that a transport ship, The Gilded Branch, foundered five days ago off the coast at Heberon. The only passenger was Abaythian Marrinek. Reports suggest he is alive and has escaped west to the town of Catshed. His location is unknown.'"

He put down the message and looked up at the councillors. Lady Fiethien lent back on her chair, staring at the ceiling. Lord Adraude looked slightly ill. Lord Trerrakath, the Lord Chancellor, and Lady Drocia, the Lord Spiritual, were staring, both aghast, at Rincon and Lady Camille respectively.

"That," said Lady Fiethien, "is unwelcome news."

Lord Trerrakath snorted.

"Unwelcome?" he said loudly, "Unwelcome? A tax audit is 'unwelcome'. A dose of the clap is 'unwelcome'. An inappropriate suitor for your youngest daughter is 'unwelcome'. This is catastrophic."

"Steady on, my lord," said Lord Adraude, weakly, "there's no need to despair."

He paused, thinking.

"Not yet, anyway. There's no reason to believe Marrinek will come here or that he will in fact bother us at all. I wouldn't be at all surprised if he's decided just to get as far from the Empire as he can."

Lord Trerrakath looked at him as if he had sprouted horns and wings.

"Are you mad? He's an insane, power-hungry traitor whose lust for blood and death are well known. How can you possibly think he won't want revenge after all that has happened?"

Lord Adraude opened his mouth but Lady Drocia leant forward, speaking in an unusually harsh voice.

"Revenge? Upon whom would he take revenge, exactly? The Emperor, hundreds of miles away and surrounded by his armies? The High Chancellor or the Council, safe in Khemucasterill? The provinces themselves? You? Us? We may need, as the closest Imperial seat of Government, to be professionally concerned about Abaythian Marrinek but I don't think you need to worry unless you were the one who betrayed him to the Emperor."

She stopped, aware that everyone was watching her, and relaxed back into her chair with visible effort.

"Marrinek may have had many failings and problems but an irrational preoccupation with revenge was not one of his flaws."

Lady Camille smiled grimly, her interest piqued. Lady Drocia's history was long and varied and her career before she became the Lord Spiritual of the Western Province had been illustrious. She had played the role of a caring, loving and supportive Lord Spiritual for so long that it came as a shock when she spoke with such forthright passion. Lady

Camille found it strangely refreshing and just a little unnerving.

Lord Trerrakath sat back, also surprised by Lady Drocia's outburst.

"Who knows what effect two years of imprisonment and solitary confinement have had on him? I might be tempted to behave differently if I'd just escaped from a life sentence on that god-forsaken rock in the sea."

"About that," said Lady Fiethien, "is there nothing in the message to say how he escaped? Do we really know nothing more?"

"That's your area, I think, Lady Fiethien," said Lady Camille, smiling without a hint of warmth as she said it, "personally, I'd like to know why adequate precautions weren't taken to prevent his escape."

Lady Fiethien bristled.

"Are you suggesting some fault or error on the part of myself? I can assure you that no efforts are spared and no failure is tolerated in the transportation of dangerous prisoners. Whatever happened won't have been because of a fault in our procedures or people."

"That statement would seem premature," said Lord Trerrakath coldly, "given that we have no information at all about how he escaped."

"Quite," said Lady Drocia, "but so is the apportionment of blame. A full investigation, conducted quickly and discreetly, would seem to be desirable."

"I agree," said Lord Adraude.

"At least then we would know who to execute," said Lord Trerrakath, glaring at Lady Fiethien.

"I think," said Lady Camille, raising her voice slightly to forestall further argument, "that we will leave the question of executions to one side for the moment."

She gave Lord Trerrakath a hard look.

"Investigation first, please, Lady Fiethien. I'd like to know who oversees prisoner transportation and how the ship came to founder. Was it seaworthy when it left port, did it sail into a storm, was it taken by pirates? Did we have enough guards on board, was one of them bribed? Was it bad luck, incompetence, deliberate act or something else? Find out, Lady Fiethien, find out."

She turned back to the rest of the council.

"For now, keep this news close. I have sent messengers to the other provinces and to the Emperor. News will leak soon enough but for now I would prefer to keep it from the streets and the nobles. I particularly do not want Marrinek's former associates to hear the news before we have had time to control the situation."

Lord Adraude shook his head.

"I'm not sure that will be possible. As I said before, the soldiers under Marrinek's command were widely dispersed when he fell. The regiments were broken and spread around but many soldiers left the army or took posts with the nobles. Sooner or later they will hear just because people talk, and people will talk about this everywhere, when the news leaks."

They talked around the subject for another hour or so before Lady Camille brought the discussion to a close.

"That's enough for now. It will obviously take some time for the message to reach the Emperor and probably the same again to receive a response, although I think we can all guess what his response is likely to be. I want to know everything about the escape, Lady Fiethien, before the Emperor asks for details. I want to capture or kill Marrinek before he can do any more harm; Lord Adraude I want options for the pursuit of Marrinek by tomorrow."

She looked around the council, wondering whether to tell them about Krant and his message to Duke Rhenveldt, then decided against. There would be time to share that news later, if anything came of it.

"Is there anything else?" she asked.

Nobody said anything.

"Right. Get to it, then."

She stood up and the councillors followed suit, filing out of the chamber as Lady Camille stood at the head of the table.

"Lady Drocia, a word, if you please," she said, still standing in front of her seat. Lady Drocia pushed the door closed and, leaning heavily on her stick and slightly hunched with age, turned back to walk slowly to her seat, lowering herself gently down onto the cushion. Lady Camille sat down, waiting for Lady Drocia to settle down before speaking.

"Adraude is very good with his men and clever on the battlefield but you have the experience and you knew Marrinek. What will he do now?"

Lady Drocia sucked her teeth.

"What do you want me to say? That Marrinek will forgive and forget and crawl quietly away to build a new life for himself as a shepherd somewhere far beyond our borders? I don't think that's likely, whatever I said to that fool Trerrakath."

"But you knew him, you were a soldier, what will he do? How does he think? Where will he go?" Lady Camille pressed.

"Ha. I haven't been a soldier for over two centuries. Might as well ask Trerrakath's opinion for all I know. Yes, I knew Marrinek, but that was before his disgrace and arrest. Could he seek revenge? I have no idea. Would I, in his place?

Maybe, but maybe not," she paused, then said, "where is his wife?"

Lady Camille slumped back in her seat.

"That I don't know. Fiethien might know but I'm not sure she'd tell me. There were rumours that she had been taken by the Inquisition at the same time that Marrinek was arrested but as far as I know nobody's heard from her since then."

"I heard those rumours. I knew his wife better than I knew him. She was tough and smart. Very smart. And very talented. She would have made a hell of a fuss if the Inquisition had tried to snatch her, so either they did it very discreetly or they missed and she's in the wind."

"How talented, exactly?" asked Lady Camille, not quite achieving the nonchalance she was aiming for.

"Very. Not as strong as Marrinek, of course, nobody was, but still very strong. I wouldn't want to face her in a fight and I wouldn't want to upset her. She was loyal and honest and reliable but she had no time for traitors or fools and her patience could wear thin very quickly," said Lady Drocia smiling to herself, "I remember her losing her temper once with one of her husband's friends over some piece of political trivia. She laid into him with such venom and at such length that nobody dared visit for a month. Marrinek was furious - he was in the city for a rare visit and they had to cancel all their engagements until, finally, she relented and apologised to her poor victim. A strong woman."

Lady Drocia chuckled to herself. Lady Camille pursed her lips.

"Yes, insightful undoubtedly, but not useful for the problem at hand."

Lady Drocia pulled herself back to the present.

"My apologies, my lady, a fault of the very old. Reminiscing at inappropriate times, I mean. Even the near past often seems better than the present, at times."

"Yes, well. Something we all have to get used to, I suppose. Did she believe the accusations against her husband?"

"I don't know, for sure, but I very much doubt it. I saw her a few days before the storm broke but once Marrinek had been arrested I didn't see either of them again, except him, briefly, just before he was shipped to the capital. From her I haven't heard a word."

"Theories? Where would she have gone? Were there particular friends or favourite places to which she might have gone? Can we find her and use her to help trap Marrinek?"

"Loyal, remember? She had a wide network of friends. She was popular and travelled far, both inside and outside the Empire."

Lady Drocia paused, considering.

"No, you couldn't use her to trap Marrinek, unless you plan to force him into some sort of rescue attempt and I think that would be foolhardy in the extreme. If the Inquisition don't have her then finding her would be difficult. I'm sure she will have left the Empire, if she had the chance."

Lady Camille sighed and stood up.

"Never mind the wife, then. That was always going to be a long shot. I have other irons in the fire."

Lady Drocia raised an eyebrow at this, but Camille ignore her expression of interest.

"We'll just have to hope that we find something through another route," said Lady Camille.

With that she stood and walked to the door of the chamber.

"Thank you for your help, Lady Drocia. Until tomorrow, I think."

And she swept back out of the council chamber leaving Lady Drocia alone at the table.

The temple complex that made up the official residence of the Lord Spiritual of the Western Province was only a little distance from the Traebarn Palace but Lords Spiritual didn't walk the streets of the city like ordinary citizens. Lady Drocia made the short journey in a plain coach unmarked by either the arms of her office or her family. She was so deep in thought when the coach stopped outside her formal residence that her footman had to cough politely to attract her attention. She snapped back to the present, slightly surprised to find herself in her own courtyard, then, still acting the old woman, she stood and shuffled carefully out of the coach, walking stick clicking, and into the hallway of the house.

Inside her maid, Ame, waited to take her summer coat and to help her through the residence to her study, which looked out over the small formal garden at the centre of the building. As soon as the door was closed Lady Drocia straightened her back and stretched to work out the kinks. She strode across the floor, rolling her shoulders to loosen the muscles as Ame fussed with her coat and stick.

"You were limping on the wrong foot this afternoon, Mother," said Ame, "it was the left that was giving you problems this morning but the right when you returned from the Palace. I don't think anyone noticed."

Lady Drocia, grimaced.

"Blast. Playing an old woman," she paused, then corrected herself, "an even older woman, seemed like a good idea when I started but I'm beginning to wonder if it's really worth the effort. Maybe, once things settle down a bit, I'll suffer a miraculous cure and cast aside the stick."

She thought about this as she searched her desk drawer for the leather pouch that held her charmed key.

"Yes, a miracle of healing in the Grand Temple, something beyond even the finest healers, something to convince the congregation that even the sufferings of the very ancient can be overcome with sufficient piety. That might be just the thing to fill the donation plates at the winter solstice."

She found the pouch and pulled it out of the drawer.

"In the meantime, I think a light lunch with some watered wine, please Ame. I'll take it here at my desk. And see if you can find Coewia, will you? I have letters to write."

"As you wish, Mother."

"And send word to The Farm that I plan to visit tomorrow. I may stay a few hours or a few days; I haven't decided yet. Have the coach prepared so that we can leave shortly after dawn."

"Yes, Mother," said Ame, closing the door behind her.

Key in hand, she walked to the ornate cupboard that displayed some of her lesser charms and her collection of porcelain dragons.

"Now, then," she said quietly to herself as she ran her eye over the accumulated items, "ah, there you are."

She opened one of the doors and pulled out a tiny cylindrical charm, no larger than her little finger, from where it rested against the tail of a yellow two-headed dragon figurine. She slipped it into a pocket in her skirt and closed the cupboard door. Then she pressed the key into a nondescript section of the moulding and focussed a tiny flow of power to activate the charm. There was a click and a section of moulding hinged open.

After a second press of the charm against another section of moulding and another tiny flow of power she pulled the secret door open so that she could slide out the shallow drawer that lay hidden behind it. Inside, nestled in cavities lined with red velvet, were six charms of varying sizes and shapes. She quickly removed all the charms then slid the drawer closed and locked the door.

Back at her desk she laid out the six charms from the drawer and the one from the cupboard, then she reached around to open the taller cupboard behind her desk where she kept her walking sticks. She shoved the ornate stick she had used to visit the palace roughly into the cupboard and pulled out a far longer staff, plain but beautifully made. It would be less useful as prop for her 'old woman' routine but its other properties would be valuable and with Marrinek once again in play she didn't intend to take any risks.

Finally, she sat down at her desk and surveyed the seven charms arranged across its surface. She rolled up her sleeves to expose her forearms. On the desk there were two slim short-range shock cannons, one shaped to fit her hand - she slid that one into the pocket of her robes - the other fitted with straps of supple calfskin - she strapped this one to the inside of her wrist where it would be hidden by the long sleeve. The two guards, made from lightweight leather with iron cores, she strapped to the outside of her arms before rolling down her sleeves. The ring she slid onto a finger on her right hand, the necklace she hung from her neck. That left only the seventh charm, which should be safe in her pocket. She stuffed it back into the pocket of her robes alongside the shock cannon then returned the charmed key, now back in its pouch, to its hiding place in the desk.

With her charms in place she stood and walked to the window, leaning the long staff against the wall. She focussed tiny trickles of power into each of the charms in turn, checking that they still worked and that she had remembered their functions. Eventually satisfied, she walked back to her desk and sat down just as there was a knock at the door and Coewia came in clutching a satchel.

"You sent for me, Mother." she said, approaching the desk. She was a timid creature and Lady Drocia found her manners extraordinarily annoying but she had a neat hand and was a reliable secretary, even if Lady Drocia trusted her with only the most public of secrets.

"Sit down girl," said Lady Drocia, irritably gesturing toward the small writing desk where Coewia customarily sat to take dictation, "and, we'll start with replies to this morning's messages."

She laid out the papers on her desk as Coewia flattened a clean sheet of paper and prepared her pen.

19

The fire charm flickered, giving off a small light no brighter than a candle as it was waved around the cellar. A little more power and the flame grew until it stood maybe six inches tall and lit the whole of the damp, dreary room. Part of the ceiling had caved in so that the rooms of the ground floor were visible through a gaping hole between the joists. Water dripped steadily into the cellar, falling on the remains of the ceiling and a thick carpet of leaves, carried in with the rain that poured down and was blown into the house through the gap where the front door had been. The cellar stank of damp and mildew and rotting vegetation but bizarrely, amongst the mess and destruction, a rack of bottles stood dry and untouched in one corner.

The fire charm floated across the room as its owner moved to examine the bottles. He ran his long fingers over the necks and peered at the corks. He grabbed one at random and pulled it from the rack, holding it up to the light of the fire charm and blowing dust and muck from the glass. Satisfied, he stuffed the bottle into a leather bag that hung at his side on a long strap slung over his shoulder.

Then he plucked a couple more bottles from the rack and loaded them into the bag as well.

He turned away from the rack and looked over the rest of the cellar again but there was nothing else worth seeing so he headed back to the stairs and climbed carefully up to the ground floor.

Upstairs the house was in worse shape than the cellar. Much of the roof had gone and decades of rain had made a mess of the interior. It had been a large house, a mansion for a wealthy merchant, maybe, but the fine tapestries had long since vanished, the furniture was riddled with rot and everywhere the creeping tendrils of ivy and other climbing plants could be seen. Another few years and the house would collapse and disappear, consumed by the forest that was taking back the whole town.

The man tugged his hood up over his head as he stepped out onto the street from the meagre protection of the house's porch. Here too the wild was reclaiming its territory, tearing apart the streets and pulling down walls. The cobbles were fighting a losing battle against grass, shrubs and small trees, all of which were growing thickly between the buildings. The man kicked his way across the street, hacking a path through the more stubborn shrubs with a long heavy-bladed knife, and walked into a larger stone building that had kept most of its roof and wasn't as badly decayed as its neighbours.

"Hello," shouted the man as he climbed the steps, shaking rain from his cape and hood as he crossed the open threshold into the relative dry of the building's main entrance hall. He crossed the hallway, boots booming on the floorboards, and entered the dining room. There was a small fire in the hearth and someone had pushed the table to one side to make space for the group's kit. The man extinguished his fire charm and looked around at his companions, although only three were present.

"Where are the others?" he asked, squatting down on the floor next to his wife, Farwen, and setting his sack carefully on the floor, "I thought everyone would be back by now."

"They are," said Farwen, leaning over to kiss her husband, "you're the last. Thaurid and Ediaf are rummaging through the library upstairs, although there's not much left to see. Looks like the place was thoroughly cleared out years ago. Stydd is checking the horses and we've just been sitting here working on our kit." She held up her knife, sharpening block in the other hand.

Gwilath looked round at Gendra and Theap, the two hands hired to do whatever rough jobs they were given. Gendra was checking the fletchings of his arrows, something he seemed to spend every free moment doing, and Theap was oiling and sharpening her knives. Both looked at him but neither said anything.

"Well, this might cheer you up," said Gwilath, pulling out one of the bottles from his sack, "found these in a cellar across the street. Can't tell what it is but I plan to find out."

Theap grunted and went back to examining her knives. She had many blades of various lengths and weights and, like Gendra with his arrows, she checked them obsessively - cleaning, sharpening, polishing, oiling - an endless cycle of maintenance and preparation. Gwilath had tried to make a joke of it shortly after they had left Riverbridge, asking if maybe she rattled as she walked. Theap had just looked at him, totally unamused, before stalking off along the path they were following. He hadn't tried again.

Gwilath pulled out his own knife and set to work on the cork, eventually levering it out of the neck of the bottle before tossing it into the flames. He sniffed at the bottle then took a cautious sip, then a larger swig.

He spluttered a little and thumped his chest, then passed the bottle to Farwen.

"It won't win any medals," he said, "but it's probably not poisonous."

Farwen looked sceptically at the bottle and doubtfully at Gwilath, then took a swig herself. She coughed, covering her mouth with her free hand, then offered the bottle to Gendra. He shook his head and focussed on his arrows but Theap, apparently happy with her blades, stood up and took the bottle from her. She took a long swig, shrugged indifferently, and passed it back to Gwilath.

"Did you find anything else?" said Farwen, "anything of value?"

"Nope," said Gwilath, "just a load of that stuff in a corner of the cellar and piles of rotten vegetation. This came from the house over the street and it has lost most of its roof. The years haven't been kind to it and most of the rooms are covered in creepers or piles of rotting timber. What about over here; anything?" He took the other two bottles from his sack and placed them on the floor.

"I think Ediaf is hopeful of the library but then he always is. Thaurid went with him to keep him company but this place is just too close to the river and too easy to find. We'll have to head further west, maybe turn north or northwest, to find anything worth finding, I think."

Gwilath pursed his lips. They hadn't expected to find anything of great value here but it was still a little disappointing. They had been travelling roughly westward for almost two weeks and he had hoped to have moved into virgin territory by now. He put the bottle down on the ground and pulled a leather roll from his backpack, spreading the map it contained on the table they'd been using to store their gear.

"We're here, Little Moss," he said, jabbing a long finger at the map and muttering to himself as the others went about their chores, "and Lankdon Gate is here. We know that pretty much every band of hunters stops here on their way west," he took another swig from the bottle and wiped his mouth then turned his attention back to the map, "so we need to head further out."

He ran his finger over the map, mumbling the names of the towns, reviewing the route they were taking and where they would be heading tomorrow.

All the towns and villages marked on the map, even the cities, had been abandoned decades ago when the kingdom of Sclareme had fallen. The Disaster, as it was known, had started slowly. At first there were just a few isolated reports of remote farmsteads and small villages being abandoned, apparently without reason. Travellers or traders would arrive one day to find the village or area was empty, its people vanished, their homes and farms and businesses abandoned and falling to ruin. Sometimes, if the abandonment was recent, visitors might find corpses on the ground or fires still burning in the hearths but always it was the same; the people simply vanished, their possessions left behind, their animals starving in the fields.

The city dwellers and the townsfolk paid little attention. Everyone knew that living in the country was a hard, unpredictable life, especially in the north. People up there were a little cracked, they said, a little wild from living at the edge of the kingdom. In the foothills of the mountains the life was tough and people even tougher; who knew what might get into your head as the cold winter winds blew down from the north?

But as the number of deserted villages grew and a pattern emerged, the people in the towns began to feel uneasy. Eventually even the cities started to pay attention. Lords were petitioned, rousing speeches were delivered and eventually a small military expedition was sent to ride the borders and seek out both the missing people - for where could they have gone except to the border? - and whatever enemy had forced them to leave their homes.

Weeks passed but no word came and the expedition did not return. More villages were deserted, more farmsteads abandoned. The King and his Lords grew uneasy, maybe feeling the long fingers of Death himself tugging at the collar of their realm. And then the first large town fell to a night-time attack by an unknown invader.

For the first time there were survivors, people who by luck or happenstance or skill had escaped and made their way south. They told tales of painted figures looming out of the dark with swords and spears and pain, of vicious attacks and inhuman cries, of horror and fire and death.

Everyone agreed that something had to be done before the whole of the western region was overrun. The King and his Lords, shaken by the stories but confident in their martial prowess, gathered their armies at the northern fortress city of Lankdon Gate then matched westward to recover the lost territory and to seek out and destroy their enemy.

For weeks they searched, combing the hills and the forests and the plains of the western counties. They found survivors, terrified individuals who spoke of night-time attacks and of foraging for berries in a land stripped of people. They found villages and towns and mining settlements, all abandoned, some destroyed by fire or weapons of unknown design. They sent back to Lankdon Gate a continuous stream of progress reports along with accounts of the ongoing desertions and descriptions of all that they had found.

And then one day, after searching for nearly two month, the reports stopped coming and the King, his Lords and their army was never heard from again.

In Lankdon Gate there was panic and the trickle of people fleeing southward became a flood. Within a week half the population had fled. A week later the gates of the city closed for the last time and no further news or people had ever emerged from Lankdon Gate.

After the fall of Lankdon Gate the Disaster claimed more and more settlements, spreading ever wider across the country. Villages, towns and even cities were abandoned as people headed east to escape across the Guiln or south to the newly assertive coastal city states. In less than a year, the entire kingdom had been abandoned or lost.

Gwilath knew all this. The history and collapse of the kingdom of Sclareme had been a favourite late-night topic of debate at university, where students of history and archaeology, or some of them, dreamed of heading west to unravel the secrets of the Disaster.

"Or we head northward towards Lankdon Gate itself. Not many people go that way," muttered Gwilath, "not many people at all."

"Yes, we know," said Farwen, "but we've been over this before and people don't go near Lankdon Gate because anyone who does is never seen again."

"It might be worth going to have a look, though," said an excited voice from the door. Ediaf came into the room carrying a small pile of books and a map in a leather case.

"You found something useful in the library?" asked Gwilath.

"Yes. Well, no, not in the library, as such." He stopped next to Gwilath and placed his charges carefully on the floor.

"What he means," said Thaurid, following in behind Ediaf, "is that there was a cupboard hidden in the panelling. It was lined with stone so that if you tapped the wood, it sounded like the rest of the wall but the damp must have got to it over the last season and warped the door."

"And so nobody else had found it," finished Ediaf, spreading one of the maps on top of Gwilath's and weighting the edges with pieces of wood, "which means we're the first people to look at this in maybe seventy years."

"Look," he said, pointing at the map, "Lankdon Gate is marked, here, about eighty miles northwest of Little Moss." Interesting but not very helpful. Everyone knew the location of Lankdon Gate, the fortress-palace of the kings of Sclareme, but everyone also knew that the city's wealth - powerful charms, a hoard of precious metals, great weapons and marvellous gems - weren't in the city itself but in a lost room hidden in the labyrinthine dungeons beneath the palace.

"Great," said Gwilath, "so how does this help us?"

"Bring the light," said Ediaf, flapping his hand toward one of the charmed lamps they had bought at great expense in Vensille, "look here, you see these faint lines under the main map? I think this is a route through the labyrinth, a route to the treasure rooms of Lankdon Gate."

Everyone was listening now. Nobody had entered the labyrinth of Lankdon Gate and returned in at least fifty years, as far as anyone knew, possibly longer. A document purporting to offer a route to the vaults was by far the most valuable thing they'd found so far.

Farwen gave the map a jaundiced glance and snorted.

"If it's real. What are the chances of finding a genuine treasure map in an abandoned town that's been searched a hundred times before?"

"I don't see there's any need to take that tone, Farwen," said Ediaf, evidently put out that someone was doubting the provenance of his discovery, "you can see just by looking at it that its old."

"Old, maybe, but so what? You're old and you can't lead us to the vaults; why should we think this map can?"

"It doesn't matter," said Thaurid, trying to be reasonable, "all we have to do is persuade someone that it's genuine and take their money. Easy."

That sparked an argument. Ediaf said it was their duty to take valuable antiquities back to the university in Vensille and Farwen countered that the map was valuable only if it was genuine, which she doubted. Thaurid stuck to his belief that a sale would be easy given the value rumoured to be held in the vaults and Ediaf expressed his horror at the awful materialism of his younger colleagues.

Gendra and Theap, mere employees on this expedition, just looked at each other then went back to their chores to wait for the argument to die down.

Eventually Gwilath grew bored of the discussion and spoke over them all.

"None of this matters because we're not going to sell it and we're not going to put it in a museum." That shut them all up and they turned to look at him.

"Farwen's right that it's worthless if it's a fake; Thaurid is right that we could probably sell it even if it is a fake; Ediaf's smoking something if he thinks we're just going to stick it in a museum." Farwen and Thaurid sniggered a little, Ediaf glared angrily at Gwilath and started to open his mouth to object.

"No," said Gwilath, holding up his hand, "don't argue. We're going on. We'll head north and find Lankdon Gate, enter the labyrinth and, using the map, find the vault. We'll take home as much of the treasure as we can carry then go back for more with a larger, better funded, party next season We'll be rich and famous and we'll never need to work again."

Silence greeted this, broken only when Gendra started laughing. They all turned to look at him and that just made him laugh harder. Nobody said anything while they waited for him to calm down.

"Your faces when Gwilath suggested going to Lankdon Gate."

Gwilath grabbed the bottle from the table and took another swig. He grimaced and set it back down by the map.

"Early start tomorrow. It'll be hard work trekking through the forest, harder than it has been so far because not so many people travel that way."

"And none come back!" said Thaurid, cutting to what he felt was the heart of the debate, "Look, we've got the map and the books," he pointed at the small pile of books Ediaf had found with the maps, "let's just go home and use what we have to raise funds for a bigger expedition. The Duke will bite, you know he will, and we can come back next year, in the spring, when the weather is better and we're properly supplied."

Gwilath curled his lip.

"Are you scared, old friend?" he asked.

"No, not scared, but..."

"But you want to go home? But you don't like being out here in the forest? But you miss the city? Boo hoo. You may be ready to head home with an old map and a handful of worthless books but I'm not. We press on together or you go home, alone. Which will it be?"

More silence and this time nobody laughed. Thaurid looked at Farwen and Ediaf but there was no help there. The late-night discussions about solving the riddle of the Disaster had driven them to this point but it was a fantasy that Thaurid found he no longer wished to pursue. He desperately wanted to go home but the thought of trekking scores of miles alone filled him with dread. He hated himself for caving in to Gwilath - again - but he just couldn't face the alternative.

"On," said Thaurid, his voice quiet with fear and frustration and resignation.

Gwilath grinned, triumphant, and slapped Thaurid on the shoulder, all smiles now that he had what he wanted.

"Great, that's settled, then. Early start tomorrow, time to turn in."

He picked up his kit and made his way over to the corner of the room that he and Farwen had staked out for themselves. Thaurid glared after his friend and seethed but he knew when he was beaten.

20

News in Vensille travelled quickly, spreading across the city as market gossip, elaborated stories, overheard conversations or even, sometimes, deliberate report. Sooner or later, any news that was worthy of the name reached the ears of Lord Pieter Mantior, Duke Rhenveldt's personal secretary. From his study in his family home, Stant House, or his private apartment in the Palace of Sails where he was currently working, Mantior reviewed reports from contacts and agents across the Dukedom and from correspondents further afield.

Today he was working his way through a tedious set of reports on the agricultural development of the western Imperial provinces, sent by a merchant in Esterengel whose ambitions included a position within Vensille's court. Mantior's mind wandered onto other subjects as he tried for the third time to read a torturously constructed paragraph about the coming apple harvest and the possible impact on the availability and cost of cider. A reduced wheat harvest might have been interesting but apples? Mantior couldn't bring himself to care and could see no threat to Vensille.

He set the report aside and moved on to a transcript from a secret meeting of the guild of charm makers. The major concerns seemed to be about the ongoing difficulties of procuring gold and tungsten for use in private commissions. Mantior smiled; his agents had been stockpiling the metals for some months and the price had risen steadily as supply had tightened. The Duke's auction of new mining rights in the closely regulated hills thirty miles north of the city should fetch a good premium when they were announced in a few weeks' time. The news that some amongst the charm-makers were looking for illicit sources of metal from across the ocean was less welcome but not wholly surprising. Mantior made a note to investigate further. Neither smuggling nor the commission of smugglers was going to be tolerated if it threatened the Duke's revenues.

The third document was an estimate of the cost of extending the city walls to encircle the slums that had grown up outside the eastern walls. The costs themselves didn't interest Mantior - the treasury would handle that aspect of the project - but extending the walls involved clearing a large area of the slums, demolishing parts of the existing walls and redistributing parcels of land from the squatters currently living on them to the Duke's supporters and friends. The project was complex and risky but the rewards would be significant.

The document contained several things that worried Mantior and he made notes in green ink as he read. The increased risk of crime from people displaced by the slum clearance would need to be addressed by the Watch. Then he reached a brief paragraph describing how part of the old wall would be removed before the new had been built and he frowned. Weakening the city's defences, even if it allowed the stone to be reused and kept down costs, was not going to work. Green ink flowed as Mantior, aware that the city was already monitored by Imperial agents, struck out much of the offending paragraph and added some detailed instructions.

The Treasurer would complain about the expense, of course, but he would complain a whole lot more if the city suddenly had to fund an army to fend off an invading neighbour, tempted by the appearance of a breach in the otherwise excellent city walls. Mantior shook his head at the short-sighted naivety of the planners, even though they were likely ignorant of Imperial activities and ambitions.

The final report in his pile was a description of a disturbance late the previous night at the Snarling Goat. An incident that had claimed the lives of four of the North End gang, including one of the senior lieutenants, was unusual. Mantior frowned. This level of violence hadn't been seen in recent years and there was nothing in the report to explain how it had come about. Adding in the fight from earlier in the day, rumours of which had reached Mantior late the previous evening, and it seemed that the North Enders had lost five men in just a few hours. Strange, although there was nothing that linked the two incidents.

Mantior examined the coded signature on the bottom of the report. It was from a source at Trike's, one close to the leadership and always reliable in the past. He re-read the report then decided that maybe he should be paying a closer eye to the activities of the North Enders. It would not do for them to get too cocky and to restart the anarchic conflicts he thought had been decisively ended a few years ago. He made a mental note to tighten the screw on Fangfoss to remind him where his loyalties, and his best interests, lay.

As he stared out of the window onto the private gardens at the Palace of Sails, Mantior's thoughts drifted to the grim period a few years before when he and his Watch officers had acted to stem the rising violence amongst the gangs. The trigger had been the murder of a well-connected and talented merchant, assassinated by members of the Flank Side gang as punishment for unpaid "protection" money, or so it had seemed at the time. The subsequent collapse of the Flank Siders, under direct and unrelenting pressure from the Watch, was something of a victory and had brought a measure of peace to the city but Mantior had subsequently wondered whether the death had, in fact, been ordered by the Flank Siders.

It had been almost eight years since the clampdown and the city had prospered in the relative security that had followed. The largest of the remaining gangs, the North End gang, was involved in a variety of activities too numerous to mention but as long as they threatened neither the peace of the streets nor the safety of the talented, Mantior was happy to allow them continue. In a very real sense, their existence acted as a buffer preventing other, less agreeable, organisations from seizing their niche.

Mantior dragged himself back to the present and forced himself to review the list of supplicants to be presented to the Duke. By tradition, anyone living within the Duke's lands could petition for an audience to plead for justice or aid or favour. In practice, most of the cases were heard by the Duke's Chancellor, a man not known for his sympathetic outlook but able nonetheless to handle cases quickly and efficiently. That thought brought forth another frown from Mantior. The Duke's Chancellor, capable though he might be, did not always deliver the judicial outcomes that Mantior, and the Duke, preferred.

Mantior went back to the lists, searching for a few straightforward cases for the Duke to hear. His criteria were simple; he wanted easily resolved stories that would play well to the public gallery. Honest peasants toiling through adversity, bereaved wives desperate for help raising their broods, destitute traders laid low by the villainous actions of their competitors. Anything, in short, that could showcase the Duke's legendary generosity and greatness of spirit, building his image in the eyes of his people and cementing his position as grand protector of the realm.

That was the plan, at least. It worked best when the case was relatively simple and the Duke could cut decisively through the argument to punish or compensate or reward. Today's list was the usual mix of disgruntled tenants, defrauded traders and unhappy spouses but nothing interesting or politically useful. There was little enough to keep the Chancellor busy and nothing at all worth bothering the Duke about.

Mantior dropped the list back on the pile and strode to the window. The gardens of the palace, laid out to form a map of the city, were peaceful in the midday sun, bees floating around the blossoms doing... Mantior paused. What did bees do? And why did they spend so much time buzzing at flowers? Then he shook his head and cleared his frown. What did he care for the activity of insects? He walked back to his desk, checking the rings on his fingers as he went, and picked up the report on Imperial agriculture.

The paragraphs on cider production were no more interesting the fourth time around so he tossed the report into the filing tray and collected his cane from its place near the door. After a last look around the room to check that he had everything he needed, Mantior opened the door and stepped out into the corridor. He closed the door behind him and pressed one of his rings into an indent in the lock. A brief focus of power through the ring and the lock closed, securing the room. Then, cane swinging, he walked down the corridor and made his way through the building to the Duke's private courtyard.

Today the Duke, wearing a fencing jacket, helmet and padded gloves, was practicing the Ethrani short sword. It was a style of fighting that Mantior didn't really like. To him, it seemed to involve a good deal of flamboyance and noise for precious little effect. Using two blades, one long and slender for fast lunges and stabbing attacks, the other short and curved for parrying and occasional off-hand ripostes, seemed excessive.

The Ethrani instructor, brought across the ocean at great expense specifically to demonstrate this obscure art, parried the Duke's long sword, catching the blade in the guard of his short sword. He twisted his wrist, trapping the Duke's blade, and deftly landed the point of his own blunted long sword on the arm of the Duke.

"Two to Master Lojacono," announced the adjudicating guard officer, as the two men stepped apart, "salute, and resume."

The Duke swept forward, feet dancing, reaching around with his long sword. Lojacono parried and riposted, keeping his right foot forward and his short sword in a high guard. Back and forth they went, each looking for an opening that would allow a direct strike with the long sword or a capture and disarm with the short sword. Both men were sweating as the bout dragged on. It was clear that Lojacono was a master swordsman, highly accomplished in his speciality and fast on his feet. The Duke's lack of experience in this particular form was showing but his long practice with many other styles of fighting was helping him to push Lojacono.

Eventually, though, Lojacono's evident skill prevailed and he trapped the Duke's long sword again, flipping his wrist to lock the blade harmlessly to one side. He reached over to poke the Duke in the chest, his long sword deftly avoiding the Duke's wild attempts to parry with his own short sword.

"Three to Master Lojacono, who wins the bout, three points to one."

The Duke stepped back and saluted, sheathing his swords.

"Well fought, Master Lojacono, well fought. I thought I had you for a moment, in that last point, but then you trapped my sword again."

"Thank you, your grace. Your improvement over the last few days has been remarkable. With a little more training, I think I would be very hard pressed indeed to resist your attacks."

"Pish, Master Lojacono, but it is kind of you to say so."

Mantior caught the Duke's eye.

"But I can see that affairs of state are calling. Until tomorrow, Master Lojacono."

The fencing master bowed and the Duke waved him away, taking a flannel from a tray held by a serving boy to wipe his face and brow. He tossed the flannel away and walked over to where Mantior stood, shielding his eyes from the sun.

"Well fought, your Grace. You almost had him in that last point. He's very quick."

The Duke looked around then laughed.

"Ha. Yes, he is extremely good," said the Duke, stepping closer and lowering his voice, "but he's quicker when he practices with my officers and quicker still if he hasn't been out all night whoring and drinking."

Rhenveldt stepped back and spoke in a more normal voice.

"And what brings you out of your den today, Pieter. Good news, I trust?"

"Apart from the joy of watching you lose a bout to an imported fencing master?" said Mantior, grinning. He had known the Duke a long time and was well aware of exactly how far he could push their relationship in private.

"I thought a walk in the gardens might help me to reach a decision about how to deal with the North End gang," he said finally, returning to business.

The Duke turned to walk along the path, away from the fencing ground and toward the open gardens at the centre of the palace. Mantior followed.

"I thought you were happy with the way things were going? That the current 'arrangement' with the gangs was working for everyone. Are you worried that this might not be the case?"

"Yes, I was happy," said Mantior, "and yes, I'm now worried. The North Enders suffered an unusual spate of deaths yesterday, which may suggest something has been brewing unseen and is now coming to a head. At the very least, I'm going to tighten my grip a little, have my informants squeezed to see what squeaks. I'd prefer not to lose the current setup, if we can preserve it, but all things pass in time."

"Hmm. Well. Do what needs to be done, Pieter, as usual. I'm still happy for the current arrangement to continue - it seems to deliver a reasonable degree of security - but I won't let things slide. It's just not good for business and, ultimately, that isn't good for any of us. Keep me informed."

They reached the end of the short gardens and turned to retrace their steps, heading back to the fencing ground.

"I will do that, your Grace. And if it looks like things might spiral out of control I'll let some blood and break some skulls. Well, I'll arrange for blood to be let; obviously I wouldn't want to do the actual bloodletting myself, nasty business, too much risk of actual bodily harm."

"Pieter, you're waffling. Stop it." The Duke stopped walking so that he could watch Lojacono fencing with the guard officer who had been keeping score. The officer was truly awful and Lojacono was scoring point after point, hardly making an effort.

"Look at this, Pieter. Where do we find our officers, eh?"

The Duke shook his head.

"Jab, man, Jab," he shouted, "and keep your short higher if you want to... oh, never mind, another hit."

Rhenveldt and Mantior walked back into the palace leaving the fencers to fight on.

"Do we still teach fencing to our officers, Pieter? Maybe we should invite our guards and our watchmen to compete in a fencing tournament, see if we can't improve the standards, eh?"

"Well, it has been a while since we last ran such an event. Fifteen years, maybe?"

"That settles it. On the strength of that display our officers could only impede an Ethrani attack by dying in an awkward spot and tripping them as they pressed forward. Let's put up a hundred shillings and a promotion as the prize for the winner and invite all of our forces to participate. Final bouts to be held in the main square in front of the palace. In fact, let's open it up more widely and allow anyone in the city to compete."

"Very well. I will make the arrangements," said Mantior,

"shall we plan for a ball in the evening, maybe invite the last sixty-four and their spouses?"

"Yes, yes, let's do that as well. I'll leave the details to you, Pieter."

They had reached the door to the Duke's private apartments. Rhenveldt turned, his hand on the door knob.

"I don't like the idea that the North Enders might be losing their grip on things, I don't like it at all. Let me know as soon as you have news, Pieter."

"Yes, your Grace. We should know more by tomorrow."

"Very well. I'm going to change before this afternoon's meeting. Was there anything else?"

"Not at the moment sir, no."

"Good."

Rhenveldt opened the door and disappeared into the room beyond.

Mantior stood in the corridor for a moment then walked slowly back toward his own office, thinking about how best to organise a fencing tournament. By the time he reached his study he had made some decisions and he spent an hour making notes and writing instructions for his staff. Once those had been passed along he turned back to the problem of the North Enders. Like the Duke he was worried that the gang was in danger of collapsing; losing five members in a single day was unheard of in recent times. He sat thinking for a while longer then reached a decision.

He pulled the bell cord by his desk and waited until one of his staff appeared through the door from the anteroom where they worked.

"Ah, Funteyn. Can you please find Commander Astiland and ask him to attend me at his earliest convenience?"

Funteyn curtsied and ducked back out of the room, leaving Mantior alone again with his reports. He turned briefly back to the report on Imperial agriculture then decided that life was simply too short for such matters and decided instead to review again the gaming board set on the small table behind his desk.

He played against an old friend who lived some leagues outside the city, exchanging moves by letter. This game had been in play for some months and was nearing a climax. Mantior had been hopeful during the middle stages of the game but those hopes had now waned in the face of an unforeseen and relentless assault along the right-hand side of the board. He was now fighting a desperate defensive battle but, all too soon, he would be forced to concede defeat. He could concede now and begin a new game but he had a stubborn streak and he liked to play to the bitter end.

He was still pondering the board, groping his way toward a move that might delay the inevitable for a little longer, when Commander Astiland knocked on the door and came striding into the study. A tall man, Astiland was the very model of a city Watch Commander. His uniform was spotless, his breastplate shone and his moustache was immaculately waxed. He stopped in the middle of the room and clicked his heels.

"Good afternoon, my lord. I understand you wished to see me?"

Mantior, still pondering the gaming board, said "Good afternoon, Commander. Thank you for coming so promptly. Take a look at the board, Commander. What move would you recommend?"

Astiland looked briefly surprised then strode over to stand beside Mantior, leaning forward to peer down at the board. After a long pause he said, "Well, I hope you're not playing white. I would say that black is pretty much guaranteed to win from that position." He straightened up.

"Unfortunately, I am indeed playing white. I have one trick left but my opponent has the advantage and probably won't make a mistake now."

Mantior took his seat behind his desk and gestured for Astiland to take the chair opposite.

"Tell me, Commander, do the North Enders still make the agreed payments?"

Astiland shifted in his seat.

"You know that I'm uncomfortable with this arrangement, my lord. I would prefer simply to remove the rest of their leadership and," but Mantior cut across him.

"Yes, yes, I am indeed familiar with your opinions, Commander, but what I care about at the moment is whether the North Enders are paying their dues."

Astiland took a deep breath, not used to being interrupted.

"Yes, they are paying. Things have been generally quiet in recent months, no big changes to speak of, no unusual complaints or problems, no mess or fuss on the streets."

"Until yesterday, it would seem, when they lost five of their members including Hitton, who ran the Snarling Goat."

Astiland furrowed his brow, his face showing scepticism.

"Five? All dead within a single day? I have heard nothing of this and certainly we haven't yet found any more bodies than we might normally expect at this time of year."

"Yes Commander, five. All dead. In one day. So, I ask myself, what has changed to trigger such an upsurge in violence? And who has caused the change? And what," said Mantior, raising his voice slightly, "are the City Watch going to do about it?"

Astiland sat back, stroking his beard and thinking hard.

"My preference would be to raid the North Ender's base

in The Narrows and arrest Fangfoss so that we could ask him directly," he looked at Mantior for feedback on that suggestion, "but I suspect that would be dangerous and diffi-cult and in any case, it breaches the terms of our agree-ment," he concluded, spitting out the last word like an insult.

"Barring that, our best option is probably to pick-up a couple of the mid-level enforcers, Old Ned maybe, and see what they know. That shouldn't be too risky and if they don't have what we need they can at least carry messages back to Fangfoss and his surviving lieutenants."

"Very well," said Mantior, "let's see what Old Ned has to say on the matter. But be discreet. I don't want to disrupt the agreement or bring unnecessary attention to our rela-tionship."

Once Astiland had left, Mantior turned back to the gaming board. He didn't like to lose and he certainly wasn't keen to surrender. He stared at the board for more than an hour, considering, pondering, imagining, trying to think his way into his opponent's mind. Eventually he smiled to himself and made a move, happy that he now had a plan, a way forward, something that might even deliver him the game. He wrote the move on a fresh piece of paper, added a somewhat downhearted appraisal of the state of the game, then sealed and addressed the letter before tossing it into his out tray.

21

By the time Marrinek returned to the House of Duval, the party was in full swing. Elaine let him in through the front door and he quickly walked down the hallway to Madame Duval's study, passing the sitting rooms to either side of the staircase where clients were being served wine and food as a prelude to their main entertainment.

Madame Duval was waiting for him in the study, sipping a glass of red wine as she sat behind her desk.

"I was wondering how much longer you might be. I had started to think you might not return."

Marrinek grinned at her then grimaced as he raised his arm and felt again the cut from Chickie's knife. He flopped into a chair by the fireplace and examined the cut. It was not deep and had scabbed over already. He forgot about it and turned back to Madame Duval.

"It turned out they were open to persuasion, eventually. Tomorrow should be interesting."

Madame Duval raised her eyebrow.

"Did you kill anyone? Throw them from a balcony, maybe, or tip them into the river? Maybe you set fire to them and sent them dancing down the hallway?" She poured him a measure of wine and held out the glass to him.

"No, it was very quiet, very easy. Well, fairly quiet; some blood, many bruises, no broken bones, no deaths. And I think we will get what we need from Fangfoss."

Madame Duval kept her thoughts to herself. Marrinek could say 'we' and talk of them working together or having common objectives as much as he liked but she was still suspicious, still doubtful that anyone might offer so much in return for so little. She would play along while he kept his end of the bargain but she was prepared and ready to act when he eventually showed his true colours, whatever they might turn out to be.

"And I see you decided to reopen the house," said Marrinek. Madame Duval hesitated, suddenly worried that she might have missed part of the conversation while her attention was elsewhere.

"Er, yes," she said, taking a sip of wine to cover her momentary confusion, "it seemed like a good idea if you were going to have the North Enders under control. And if not, a full house makes it harder for them to act and easier for me to slip away in the confusion. Anyway, the regulars were starting to complain, which is never a good sign."

"Good," said Marrinek, sipping his wine, "makes a lot of sense. And I think The North Enders are fairly well cowed, even though some of their members may need a little more persuasion tomorrow. I've set them some tasks and we will see how they get on and what shakes loose. Did the twins give you any problems?"

"No, they appeared briefly to eat but other than that they've been very quiet."

Marrinek stood and retrieved Bone Dancer.

"Good. I plan to spend a couple of hours with them but

maybe you and I can speak again later. There's something I want you to do for me." He opened the door to the servant's area and climbed the back stairs to the attic, leaving Madame Duval to nurse her wine.

When he reached the room where the twins were staying he knocked on the door before entering and was a little surprised to find Darek and Floost standing in the centre of the floor, waiting for him.

"We were watching for you from the window," said Darek by way of explanation, "Watch."

Floost held out the fire charm and concentrated. Marrinek could feel her focussing power into the charm and was delighted to see a small flame appear at its tip. Floost held the flame for a few moments then extinguished it and passed the charm to Darek, who repeated her trick.

"Excellent," said Marrinek, impressed, "that really is very good indeed."

The twins smiled and relaxed, evidently pleased.

"Tell me what you have learnt today," said Marrinek.

The twins stumbled over themselves to explain how they had mastered the technique, how Darek had first produced a spark and then together they had worked until both could achieve a full flame.

"It's all about confidence, isn't it?" said Floost, "If you believe and you can see it happening then it happens. Seeing Darek make the spark allowed me to really believe and from there it was easy to see how to focus the power into a flame."

"And we found an exercise in the book, Jensen, that helped us understand how to focus. It really helped." Darek was clearly enthused by their success.

Marrinek fished in his pockets and produced a second fire charm.

"I want you to practice a few exercises to strengthen your abilities and help you to focus power whenever you need it." He described the exercises in some detail, working through an example until both twins had seen enough to be able to follow the instructions.

"But don't get ahead of yourselves. These charms are serious tools, just like hammers or swords; if you fail to take the necessary care you can focus too much power and produce a huge flame, like this!"

And suddenly the room was full of heat and light and flame, driving away the shadows and making the twins jump back in surprise and sudden fear. As quickly as it had appeared the flame was gone, leaving behind bright images and hot, hot air.

"You see? Very dangerous in a wooden building with furniture and fabric and flammable people wandering around. Take care not to focus too much power." The twins nodded, both white-faced, and Marrinek tossed the charm to Floost.

"Good. Practice the exercises that we've covered from Jensen. Now that you can both produce a flame I also want you to practice the awareness exercise we did in the inn. That's as important as producing a flame; more so, in fact, since detecting other people's flows is the key to mounting a successful defence."

"How?" said Darek.

"Oh it's obvious," said Floost, exasperated at her brother, "if someone's standing outside focussing power into their fire charm then feeling the flow allows you to do something about it. Right?" she added, a little uncertainly.

"Yes. At the very least you might move away from them.

I've got some other things to show you as you progress but, right now, the thing to concentrate on is detecting the flow of power even when you're doing something else. Once you've mastered that, and it might take a while because it isn't easy, we'll move on."

They spent the next couple of hours practicing the exercises as Marrinek lectured them on technique, principles and the framework within which power could produce action. Eventually he called a halt.

"That's enough for today. We'll stay here tonight. Make yourselves comfortable," he gestured at the beds against the wall, "and we'll move somewhere more permanent tomorrow, hopefully. I'm going to retrieve the rest of our stuff from the inn. I'll be back in the morning."

Floost yawned but Darek frowned.

"And what about us? We've been stuck here all day. Can we get out somewhere tomorrow?"

Marrinek looked at them from the door.

"Practice again tomorrow morning, then you will have the rest of the day free. Sleep now." The door closed behind him, leaving the twins alone again.

Marrinek descended the stairs from the attic of Madame Duval's house slowly, deep in thought. The twins were progressing more quickly than he had hoped and far faster than most students. They had achieved in days a level of control that most people would reach only after many weeks, or sometimes months, of training. At this rate, he would need a tutor and lots more books to keep them occupied. He grinned to himself; this wasn't something he had foreseen but it was definitely going to make life more interesting.

At the bottom of the stairs he stopped. The hallway was quiet and Shad's chair was empty. He padded softly to the sitting rooms; also empty. No sign of Elaine, either. Suspicious, he draped his cloak over a chair and walked back to Madame Duval's study, Bone Dancer in hand. He pushed open the door and stepped into the room.

"Bay!" said Madame Duval, relief and fear and concern in her voice, "I was just explaining to these, 'gentlemen', that they needed to talk to you about this week's payment." She was standing with her back to her desk while two men poked around, evidently looking for something of value. A third man stood, hand on the hilt of his sword, watching Shad and Elaine as they sat on the sofa in front of the window.

"This ain't your business, friend," said one of the two men, "so just fuck off back the way you came." He turned back to Madame Duval and said, "Where's the money? You know what happens if you don't pay."

Marrinek closed the door behind him and grounded Bone Dancer.

"The arrangements have changed," said Marrinek in a low voice, "who do you work for?"

"This is Sergeant Snitz of the city Watch, Bay, he..."

"Shut it," said Snitz, interrupting Madame Duval and turning to Marrinek, "I work for Captain Paltiel. What are you going to do about that, eh?"

Marrinek smiled at Snitz.

"Thanks. I will speak to your Captain tomorrow. Right now, you need to leave. You won't be taking payment this evening and if you return," he stepped forward half a pace, looming over Snitz and pushing Bone Dancer forward to rest gently on the man's shoulder, "if you return I will be less polite. Do you understand?"

Snitz stared at Bone Dancer, a creeping horror showing on his face as he felt the wrongness of the staff. Marrinek pressed a little harder and Snitz took a quick step backwards, bumping into his colleague who had stopped searching and was watching the confrontation.

"All right," said Snitz, his voice shaky as he looked from Marrinek to Duval, "we're leaving. But we'll be back. I ain't forgotten what you owe."

He circled around Marrinek, staying as far from Bone Dancer as he could, and backed toward the door. His men stood as if rooted to the floor, clearly surprised at the turn of events. Snitz opened the door.

"Out," he snapped, holding the door while his men filed out into the hallway.

"You'll regret this," said Snitz to Marrinek.

But he moved quickly down the hallway to the front door when Marrinek stepped forward, still smiling, Bone Dancer bobbing in the candlelight.

When the front door closed Marrinek turned back to Madame Duval who was standing in the doorway to her study.

"That problem can wait till tomorrow," he said, "I need to get my things from The Jewel and tomorrow I need you to find me a house and a tailor."

Madame Duval looked at him.

"A house? Anything in particular? Some sort of palace, a small fortress, maybe a converted abbey with nuns as servants?"

"Something nearby. Clean, spacious, well-furnished, presentable. Minor nobility, that sort of thing. Nothing too ostentatious, just big enough to impress. Can you do that?"

She stared at him, mouth open.

"You don't want much," she said, shaking her head in

amazement, "but I'll ask around. I think the house behind this one might be free. It's certainly big enough - used to belong to a successful merchant, before his ship sank - would that do?"

"Sounds perfect. Arrange that tomorrow and I'll move in with the twins. We'll need servants, a housekeeper, butler, that sort of thing."

"I'm not your bloody slave," she said, getting angry now and planting her fists on her hips, "and I've got my own business to run. How do you expect me to arrange all that, just magic a bunch of servants out of thin air?"

Marrinek grinned at her, completely ignoring her anger.

"You're a resourceful woman, use those resources."

He fished around in his pack and took out a roll of silver coins, part of the wealth he had liberated from Hitton. He tossed the roll to Madame Duval.

"That should cover expenses for a while. I have more if you need it," he hefted the backpack, "but I wonder," he stopped, thinking, "actually, just take the lot."

He passed over the rest of the silver and the gem stones he had taken from Hitton's stash, keeping in his bag only the rings and charms.

"That ought to be enough to buy the bloody place. Spend what you need but please, get a decent bargain."

He looked at her, then reached out to tilt her head back so that he could look into her eyes.

"I can trust you, can't I?"

She nodded, not wanting to speak while she held so much money in her hands.

"Good. Use the silver, hold the gems. Fencing them today might be risky and I've got an idea that some of them might come in handy."

He adjusted his near empty pack so that it hung almost

flat against his back then he flung his cloak around his shoulders and picked up Bone Dancer.

"That staff," said Madame Duval, a tinge of horror in her voice, "there's something odd, something wrong, about it. How do you stand it?"

"Bone Dancer?" said Marrinek, tilting the staff toward Madame Duval, "Yes, you're right. Want to hold it?"

He offered her the staff but she backed quickly away and Marrinek grinned, a strange expression on his face.

"If it helps, think of it as a magic staff, dark and dangerous, angry and unforgiving. It won't bite, it just feels to you like it might."

He grinned again and rested Bone Dancer on his shoulder.

"I'll be back in the morning. Have fun. And don't worry about the Watch, I'll deal with them tomorrow."

Marrinek opened the front door and stepped out into the warm night air. There were fewer people on the streets now but the area still bustled. The doors along the street were open and brightly lit, welcoming customers and throwing little patches of golden light into the dark. Only Madame Duval's door was closed but even as Marrinek watched from across the street it opened and Elaine stepped out, ready to greet patrons.

He turned and headed down the street, away from the bright lights and towards The Jewel. Lost in his plans, he didn't notice the men following him as he entered an alleyway. It was darker here and the ground was shadowed so he didn't see the step that caught his foot and sent him stumbling suddenly forward into the deeper dark of the alley. And it was just luck that he stumbled out of the way of the club, which caught him on the shoulder instead of the back of the head.

Marrinek yelped, staggering forward and turning to try to get his attacker in view. He backed away down the alley but all he could see was the outline of dark shape. Several dark shapes with stealthy feet. He swung Bone Dancer one-handed as the first dark shape fell toward him. Something wooden cracked against the staff and he backed away, off-balance, toes aching from catching the step, hand ringing from the half-caught blow. Another shadow moved quickly forwards. Something else moved, half-seen, swung rapidly towards his head and all he could do was fall backwards out of the way.

He landed on his arse and pushed backward with his heels, still holding Bone Dancer in one hand. He could see them now, dark figures dimly outlined against the clear night sky. The lead figure, still swinging his club, with two more following dark shapes just behind. He scrabbled further back, Bone Dancer waving in front of him like a shield.

"What do you want?" he shouted, his shoulder aching where the first blow had landed.

"Captain wants a word so you're coming with us, mate," said the lead figure. The voice was recently familiar.

"Snitz?" said Marrinek, peering into the gloom. His back hit a wall and he pushed himself quickly to his feet, Bone Dancer held out before him like a talisman.

"That's right," said Snitz, "but it's Sergeant Snitz to you. Are you coming quietly, or do we get to break some bones? Captain won't care either way." Marrinek, his eyes finally adjusting a little to the dark, could see Snitz hefting his club and behind him his two fellow watchmen, both with swords drawn.

"I think quietly," said Marrinek, rolling his shoulder to test for damage, "although, and for this I apologise, not right now." He dropped Bone Dancer until her head was pointing at Snitz's chest and flicked the control sliders to the lowest intensity setting. The shock wave knocked Snitz backward and he backed into his companions.

"What the hell...?" he said. He rubbed at his aching chest, confused, then Marrinek hit him with a stronger shock, knocking him to the floor of the alley where he collided with his colleague, taking him down in a clatter of falling weapons. The other watchman rushed forward, swinging his sword. Marrinek switched his grip on Bone Dancer and stepped away as the watchman attacked. He leant back to let the sword whistle harmlessly through the air in front of him then surged forward, smashing Bone Dancer into the watchman's arm. There was a sharp crack of breaking bone and the sword fell to the floor from the man's suddenly useless fingers. As he drew breath to scream Marrinek flipped his staff again and took the man's legs out from under him, dumping him onto the ground next to his colleagues. The man yelled as he fell on his broken arm, rolling away to take the weight off it.

Marrinek took a step forward to stand over Snitz as he struggled to push himself upright. He pushed Bone Dancer into Snitz's chest and forced him back down to the ground so that he lay tangled in the legs of his uninjured companion.

"Don't follow me, Snitz," he hissed, leaning forward to put more weight on Bone Dancer. Snitz groaned as he struggled to breath but Marrinek ignored him. He glanced at the other watchman, frozen between his sergeant and his injured colleague, then he turned to look at Snitz again.

"And if I hear that you've been anywhere near Madame

Duval I shall be violently displeased. Do you understand?"
He pushed Snitz again for emphasis.

"Stay out of my business, Snitz," said Marrinek, then he
stood up straight and took Bone Dancer with him. Snitz
drew a ragged breath and stared at Marrinek. There was
fear and hatred in his eyes but he didn't try to get up.

Marrinek turned and walked away down the alley.

"This ain't over, Bay," said Snitz as loudly as his crushed
lungs would allow. But he didn't follow Marrinek onto the
street.

The Jewel was mostly quiet by the time Marrinek reached
the back door of the inn. A solitary maid was still tidying up,
yawning as she worked, but the last of the day's guests had
left and the common room was empty. Marrinek picked up
a candle from the behind the bar then took the stairs one at
a time, sending subtle lines of power ahead of him to search
for intruders or other assailants. He reached the door to the
suite without incident and lifted the latch, entering noiselessly. It was empty and quiet, just as he had left it that
morning.

By the light of the candle he packed his possessions and
those of the twins, checking that he'd got everything. Once
he was happy with the pack he went through to his room,
leant Bone Dancer against the door and flopped down on
the bed. He stared at the wall for a few minutes, thinking
over the events of the day, then he extinguished the candle
and went to sleep.

The early morning sounds of the kitchen coming to life
woke Marrinek shortly after dawn the next day. He lay still

for a few minutes then he rolled out of bed. There was a jug of water outside the door to the sitting room and he used it to freshen up before changing his shirt. He ran his hands over his beard and peered at his reflection in the water bowl; tired but free, so he was better off than he had been last week.

He picked up his kit, checked that he hadn't left anything behind, then stuffed his cloak into his pack and threw it over his shoulder. He patted his pockets, grabbed Bone Dancer from its resting place against the wall and stepped out onto the hallway.

Downstairs the kitchen was buzzing as the innkeeper and her staff baked bread, tended the ale, turned the cheese and generally prepared for the day ahead. Marrinek filched a loaf that was cooling on a rack by the door and strode out into the inn's courtyard, where the stable hands were feeding the animals and tidying up.

Marrinek walked quickly through the waking city, heading for The Narrows and the dubious attractions of Trike's. He stopped at the window of a small bakery to buy a mug of weak ale and one of the local dishes - a hot roll stuffed with cheese and some sort of white fish - and stood for a few minutes eating his breakfast.

Trike's was quiet when he arrived, shutters down, doors closed, fires unlit. The streets and alleys of the Narrows were busy with early-morning traders and workmen but the inn itself was strangely subdued, almost as if it were hibernating. Marrinek walked to the back of the building and let himself in through the kitchen. In marked contrast to the bustle of The Jewel, Trike's kitchen was quiet and dark and empty.

Marrinek wandered around the back rooms of the inn, inspecting the brewery, such as it was, the pantries and the storage rooms. It was clear that Trike's wasn't aiming to support travellers or serve discerning diners; it was a gang meeting place serving simple food and a single style of light beer. He grabbed a candle from the common room and headed down the stone stairs from the room behind the kitchen.

In the cellars Marrinek found what he had been hoping for; a locked and guarded door. He set the candle down on a barrel and examined the door. Both lock and guard were charms, the first requiring a matching key, the second a pair of nasty traps similar to the one that Hitton had used on his room door. Marrinek set down his bag and leant Bone Dancer against the wall beside the door, then squatted in front of the first of the two traps.

He used slender tendrils of Flow, carefully directed to investigate the nature of the traps. They were not subtle or even carefully hidden. The first would produce a sudden flame at chest height if the door was opened without being correctly unlocked. The second would send more fire at anyone still eager to enter the room after being singed by the first trap. He widened his search to look for further traps, monitors or devices and was about to begin work disarming the first of the traps when he noticed something suspicious in the ceiling.

He stepped backward, away from the locked door, and focussed on the ceiling itself, using his power to feel his way through the plaster and paint. He found an iron wire running through the ceiling, just under the surface of the plaster, and forming a circle maybe four feet across above the spot where he had stopped to examine the door. Sitting just outside the circle of iron was an even thinner copper wire. The two wires were linked by a large piece of lead installed between the joists of the inn's floor. Another trap

Marrinek stepped further back and checked carefully for more metals; nothing. He checked again until he was sure that the only charms in the room were the lock and the three traps. He looked again at the third trap, which was unlike anything he had seen before and far more cunning than the two very obvious traps in the wall.

He raised his eyebrows in surprise and not a little admiration when he saw how the three traps worked together. The first two were placed not only to prevent access by untalented burglars but also to present an obvious target that would become the immediate focus of any talented intruder. Focussing power to disable the first two traps would have triggered the third, producing a downward shock that would have killed anyone standing in front of the door. Clever.

Marrinek stepped further away from the door and checked again for hidden metal. When he was sure he was safe he pulled out his dagger and jabbed it into the plaster of the ceiling to make a hole he could fit his hand through, then he pulled out the block of lead, yanked it free from the copper wire and tossed it into the corner of the room. He looked at the copper wire, dangling free from the ceiling, then gave it a sharp tug and pulled it out onto the floor. A small cloud of plaster dust came with it.

He walked back to the door and focussed on the first two traps. They were simple enough devices, both powered by a net of copper and a block of lead. He disabled them swiftly then turned to the lock itself. The easy option would be to use Bone Dancer to destroy the whole lock but the noise would certainly be heard upstairs and, in any case, he rather wanted to leave most of the cellar intact. Instead he placed his hands on the lock and focussed, concentrating until he could see the underlying nature of the materials used in the charm. He searched slowly through the lock until he found the part that would respond to the key, then he pushed and twisted, forcing the lock to operate. It clicked

Marrinek opened his eyes and pulled handle so that the door swung gently open.

"I'm impressed," said a voice behind Marrinek, "but you could just have asked for the key."

Marrinek spun around to find Fangfoss standing in the shadows behind him, leaning against the wall.

"How long have you been there?"

"Only just arrived. Saw you open the door, missed the rest, although I can have a guess at what you've been up to," said Fangfoss, gesturing at the ruined ceiling, "I think you're the first person ever to open the door, let alone get through the doorway."

Fangfoss stepped forward and pushed the door fully open. His fire charm lit the first few feet of the room.

"I hope it was worth the effort."

Marrinek grunted and lit a lamp from the shelf inside the store room then looked around. It was a long, low room lined with shelving along both sides. At the near end the top shelves held a few dusty bottles - spirits, by the look of them - and boxes of what appeared to be cigars. Beneath this were small chests of silver coins - a modest fortune but of little interest to Marrinek. Further in, Marrinek was surprised to see shelves of weapons; swords, daggers, a few spears, shields and various bits of armour.

"You're expecting a fight?"

Fangfoss scratched at his chin through his beard.

"Well, more sort of planning for one. This city has a violent history and I'm a careful man."

Marrinek grunted again and kept looking until he found the small chests he had been searching for. They were locked but Fangfoss offered him the key without being asked. Inside he found gold and gems. He looked at Fangfoss.

"Is this all of it?"

Fangfoss snorted.

"Of course not. Like I said, I'm a careful man. This is all I keep in the inn but I have other caches and other properties."

Marrinek nodded.

"Good. I need funds but I actually don't want to bankrupt you or destroy the gang. I'll take some of this now and leave the rest for later."

He picked out some of the smaller gem stones then closed the lid and handed the key back to Fangfoss.

"I'm going to take some of the silver as well, but I expect you can replenish that quite quickly."

Fangfoss shrugged, aiming for casual disinterest but not really succeeding.

"I'd rather you don't take anything at all but you're the boss."

He was clearly not pleased but Marrinek wasn't going to lose any sleep over a gangster's discomfort.

"And if you come through with your side of the bargain it'll be worth the cost," he said, trying to find a bright side to being robbed blind. He stopped, scratching at his chin again.

"And I suppose I can always take it off your worthless corpse if something happens to you in the meantime," he added, somewhat more happily than Marrinek would have liked.

Marrinek pushed past Fangfoss back to the entrance of the room. He grabbed a large bag of silver coins and added that to his pack. Behind him Fangfoss sighed.

"Occupational hazard, in my line of work, but getting robbed while you're in the room is a new experience for me. I wish I'd stayed upstairs."

Marrinek turned to face him.

"About that. How did you know I was here? There were no monitors, no further traps and the lock wasn't rigged as an alarm. What did I miss?"

Fangfoss shrugged again.

"Nothing, it was blind luck. I came down to grab some cigars - I have them shipped in from a small farm I own up the coast - and I arrived just as you were doing your lock-picking trick. How did you spot the trap in the ceiling?"

Marrinek raised his eyebrows.

"Luck, eh? Seems we were both lucky today, then. I was about to start disarming the traps in the door when I felt the ripples of the copper pulling power into the lead. Very subtle, that third trap, very nasty. Good bit of work."

"You felt that?" said Fangfoss, eyes wide, clearly impressed, "How? I've never heard of anyone being able to do that, not even the Duke."

Marrinek settled the pack on his shoulder and shrugged.

"It's all about strength and training, sensitivity and prac-tice. Trust me when I say that you really don't want to get on my bad side."

Fangfoss nodded.

"I'd pretty much worked that out for myself but if you can sense the copper wire pulling power into the lead then I think I'll just play along with whatever you've got planned."

"Wise man. And speaking of plans, how are things going with the Flank Siders?"

Fangfoss scratched his head.

"Shall we go back upstairs? I could use a drink and something to eat if we're talking business."

Marrinek stepped out into the cellar and waited while Fangfoss locked the door and reset the two remaining traps. He sighed.

"I'll have to fix that later, then get someone down here to re-plaster the bloody ceiling," he said, shaking his head, "I'll get you a key to the door. No sense in you wrecking the joint every time you want to rob me."

Marrinek grinned at him.

"You're taking this better than I had expected. Better than Hitton did, certainly."

"Let's talk upstairs," said Fangfoss, "where I can't see the mess you've made of my cellar."

Fangfoss led the way out of the cellar and back up the stairs to his room on the first floor, collecting a large jug of ale from the kitchen on the way through.

"Between you and me, Hitton was not one of life's great thinkers. He was a decent organiser but his loss won't really slow us down. I'd like to believe I might be a bit more flexible, a bit more, well, realistic."

He poured ale into two mugs and sat on the bench near the window, sipping.

"I've been here a long time. I'll probably be here long after you've gone. I might lose a bit while you're here but I might gain a bit of something else. I've always known this life wouldn't last forever, that I'd need to move on. Maybe your arrival will bring that forward a few years."

Marrinek sat down at the other end of the bench and sipped his beer.

"I like a man who can see the opportunities that lie beyond his present difficulties. It suggests a degree of intelligence. Tell me about the money. How fast is it coming in and from what sort of activities?"

Fangfoss sat back, leaning against the wall and stretching his legs out in front of him.

"The money? Well, the value you 'liberated' from the cellar is about three months' profit from our work across the northern end of the city. We have other interests in the surrounding towns but those are rather less profitable and we don't bring the money into the city. Smuggling is a big part of it but we also run some bath houses and inns, some gambling dens, fight pits, a few loans and various other little bits and pieces. The Duke's river taxes and duties have been good for us, since there's now plenty of room for smuggled goods."

He paused to fill his mug. He waved the jug at Marrinek, who shook his head.

"What about the nobles. Any action with them?"

Fangfoss grimaced.

"Tricky. Risky and dangerous. Some of them like to gamble and some struggle to pay their debts but we have to tread carefully when collecting. Anyone else who doesn't pay gets a beating but the nobles have their own protection, so mostly they pay with little favours. You know, they turn a blind eye to something or bring in some contraband from the country. The Duke knows about it, I'm sure, but he just doesn't care as long as the city is peaceful."

He finished his ale and set the mug down on the table, then walked back to the door and called downstairs to the maids. He closed the door.

"And obviously we have to steer clear of the Aviary. Can't afford to attract their attention."

Marrinek raised an eyebrow.

"The Aviary? I haven't heard that one before."

"Yeah," said Fangfoss, "I'm not surprised. The Duke has a secret police force, very small, very close. They sit within the City Watch but run their own games. Mostly they keep an eye on the nobles - make sure none of them are getting too close to the Duke's throne. They run a network of spies across the Duke's territory and sometimes they stumble onto something we're doing. That can be awkward; we pay off the City Watch to make sure we're left alone; the Aviary is something else entirely."

"They can't be bought?"

Fangfoss shrugged.

"Individually, maybe, but they would be expensive and just as likely to break a deal as keep it. Better to stay away. We just drop anything they stumble into and back off. You really don't want to get dragged into their dungeons beneath the Palace."

"And the Flank Siders. What about them?"

Fangfoss made a face.

"Tough bunch, not that I'd say that to my guys. They run most of the same gigs we do but on the other side of the river. We steer clear of them."

"What about the brothels? The houses on Eastside Bath. They run them too?"

Fangfoss spat on the floor and looked Marrinek in the eye.

"You know about that? Yes, they run the brothels. Not all of them, we have a few of the smaller, crappier ones, but all the big houses are theirs, everywhere you might actually want to go if you have enough coin."

"Even on this side of the river?" asked Marrinek, although he already knew the answer from Madame Duval. Fangfoss paused and grimaced before nodding.

"We discussed this with them a few years ago," said

Fangfoss bitterly, fingering a long scar on his arm, "and they won. Now we stay off Eastside Bath and leave the top of the market to them. They either own the houses or they take a cut. We don't get a look in."

"How do they do it, if that's their only action this side of the river?"

"Like I said, they're tough." He was silent for a moment, as if making a difficult confession. "They've got a couple of talented enforcers and they're not scared to use them, out on the street."

Marrinek waited while Fangfoss wrestled with his pride.

"We've just got the edges, right? The small fry. I talk the talk but the Flank Siders have the best gigs, best brothels and that gaming den, the one that stands next to the bridge on the west side. Huge place, lots of people, lots of money, lots of profit. They really don't give a fuck about us as long as we stick to our side of the river and stay off Eastside Bath."

"How many people do they have?"

Fangfoss raised an eyebrow.

"Really? You want to take them down?" Marrinek nodded and Fangfoss shook his head. "I don't think it's possible. They've got a couple of hundred all told, maybe more, and the Watch is on their side. They outnumber us, and some of them are real nasty."

"And this gaming den. What's it called?"

"The Palace of Providence, if you can believe it, but it's known as the Lighthouse 'cos of that damn great spire and the lantern they keep burning in it. You can see it for miles outside the city, or so I'm told. That's where they run all the good stuff. And that's where they make all the money."

"And everything else?"

"A pub, the Groaning Platter. Much like here, really.

They run all their small stuff from the Platter. A dozen enforcers, maybe, and a load of thugs. Nothing smart or clever about it, just business, like we do only with the prospect of promotion to the Lighthouse if you're smart enough."

Marrinek leant back in his chair, thinking. Then he nodded.

"Just the two bases?" Fangfoss nodded.

"Yeah, one high-end, one low. If they've got other stuff going on it's so small that we haven't heard about it, and we hear everything that goes on, sooner or later."

"So the Lighthouse is the key, yes?"

Fangfoss nodded wearily. He didn't like the way this conversation was going, not at all. He'd known Bay was mad as soon as he'd seen him but this was a whole other level of delusional detachment.

"Are you sure you want to do this?" asked Fangfoss running his hand through his hair. Marrinek nodded and Fangfoss just shook his head. "What you did here, to me and my crew? It ain't gonna be like that over there. You're not gonna just walk in and threaten them into submission." He shook his head again and leant forward, as if passing a secret.

"Lorn Artas is stronger than me," he hissed, "stronger than you too, maybe. His friends are stronger too and he has the nobles." Fangfoss leaned back in his chair. "You know why they leave us alone? Because we're strong enough to hold off the competition but too weak to challenge them. We're their buffer, their shield against other gangs. We do the nasty work, down in the gutters, keeping the pests under control so that Artas can pull in the big money. Our stash downstairs is nothing compared to what they've got at the Lighthouse."

Marrinek nodded and grinned.

"You're fucking insane," said Fangfoss, pouring more ale, "the Aviary will be all over you if you try this, and the Watch. The nobles, too, and they're not without resources, if you know what I mean. It's suicide."

There was a pause. Marrinek said nothing while Fangfoss sipped at his ale, letting him work through the problems in his own time. Eventually Fangfoss sighed and put down his mug.

"I can't help with the Lighthouse. I'm known, marked. So are all my crew and everyone who works for me, even down to the pot boys and the bar maids. None of us is getting close to the Lighthouse, let alone inside. They have people watching, serious people, making sure that people like us stay away from the nobles."

"I don't need help with the Lighthouse," said Marrinek, hoping that he wasn't underestimating the scale of the challenge as Fangfoss raised his eyebrows in surprise, "I have a plan. Instead, I need you to focus on their wider network. They run everything out of the Groaning Platter?" Fangfoss nodded. "So take it down. You know what to do." Fangfoss nodded again, although he wasn't enthusiastic. Marrinek leant forward. "If this works, we both win. You'll be rich." Fangfoss still wasn't convince and it showed on his face.

Marrinek dealt his final card.

"And the same deal applies, of course. A share of the profit from the Lighthouse will be yours, starting with a portion of the contents of their vault if you pull off your end of the plan."

And that was it. Greed trumped caution and Fangfoss nodded, a broad grin spreading across his face.

"Right," said Marrinek, leaning back and sipping at his beer, "so here's what I want you to do." The plan was simple and Fangfoss nodded as Marrinek laid it all out for him. By the time they'd finished their beers, Fangfoss was completely sold on the idea and had even contributed his own suggestions. They spent another half hour thrashing through the details then, satisfied that they had a solid, if massively risky plan, Fangfoss summoned some lunch.

A maid arrived in a few minutes with a tray of bread and fresh cheese, which she laid on the table. As she bustled around clearing the empty mugs, a tall woman with dark hair tied back in a long braid came into the room and stood just inside the door, leaning against the wall. She kicked the door closed behind the maid and pulled a chair across the floor, spinning it so she could sit facing Marrinek and Fangfoss but lean her elbows on the back of the chair.

"Isn't this cosy," she said, her smile suggesting anything but warmth, "are you recruiting from outside the city now, Fangfoss? Local talent not up to snuff so you're hiring Imperials?"

She glanced at Marrinek, running an appraising eye over him in much the same way that a farmer might gauge the quality of a goat offered for sale in a market. For reasons he couldn't quite explain, Marrinek found her gaze unsettling in a way that wasn't at all pleasant.

Marrinek returned the appraisal. The woman was tall, almost as tall as Marrinek, and she sat with the easy grace of the long-lived. Her clothes were practical and simple but well made from high-quality material. She wore a sword at her hip and moved easily with it, as if she had long carried it and was used to having it around. A fighter, of some sort, then, with power and money and talent.

"Bay here is my new," Fangfoss paused, looking thoughtfully at Marrinek, before continuing, "how shall we put it?

My new business partner. We're going to be working together on a few projects."

"Advisor, really," said Marrinek, by way of clarification, emphasising his Imperial accent, "an associate, rather than a full-time partner."

"Really? And on what will you be advising, the latest in fashionable court wear?"

She smirked, clearly amused by Marrinek's poor quality boots and ill-fitting shirt.

"Your beard is at least tolerably well-trimmed, so maybe you'll be helping Fangfoss with his. Looks like a badger died on your chin, Stern, old friend. You really should get it seen to. Or maybe you could just give it a decent burial."

"Oh ha, ha," said Fangfoss, "Bay, this is the Lady Mirelle. She does... things... for the Duke. She probably knows more about me than I do," Fangfoss sighed. Not for the first time he found himself wondering if being involved in Lady Mirelle's schemes might be bad for his health.

Mirelle looked at Marrinek again.

"What about you, then? Imperial citizen, former soldier, talented, recently fallen on hard times or," she glanced again at his boots, "so staggeringly out of touch that you just don't care about style. Probably both. I'd say you know how to use that stick but you've probably got other things squirrelled away for emergencies."

She beamed at him.

"How did I do?"

Marrinek sucked his teeth and fixed an expression of polite, even courtly, disinterest. He stood and gave Mirelle an elegant bow, sweeping low to flatter.

"A pleasure to make your acquaintance, my lady," he said, then he collected Bone Dancer and left.

Mirelle turned back to Fangfoss when they were alone.

"Talkative, isn't he," she said,

Fangfoss sighed again.

"What do you want Mirelle? It's damned early, the day has started badly, I have things to do and it's not like you've just dropped in to chat with the staff or take tea with my new partner."

She leant forward, all hint of a smile abruptly gone from her face, as if the humour had blown away like fallen leaves in the first storm of autumn.

"What do I want?" she asked, sneering at Fangfoss, "I want to know what the hell is going on and why the streets are littered with the corpses of your idiotic gang members."

"Ah," said Fangfoss, "that."

He tried a faintly sickly half smile just to see if she was maybe still in a joking mood but her face just hardened further and he quickly dropped the grin.

"There was a falling out, a disagreement amongst thieves, if you like, over a game of cards and it er, escalated. All sorted now, though, no more trouble, back to business as usual, laughs and smiles all round."

She stared at him, clearly not believing a word he had said.

"Four men dead over a game of cards. Is that the story you would have me pass on? That's the story you're going to lean on if someone suggests it's time for a change? Really?"

"Actually, it was five, if you include Gander. Although that was a totally separate matter," Fangfoss added quickly, his own face hardening as he caught a grip on the changing atmosphere, "completely unrelated to the other four. He crossed the wrong person, did some things he shouldn't have done and handled the consequences poorly. Definitely no more to worry about from that direction."

Mirelle just stared at him, wondering if she ought to

push it further. Eventually she decided she'd got what she really wanted, even if the truth of the matter was still shrouded in fog. She pushed herself up from the chair and stood up. Tugging down her jerkin she looked at him unhappily.

"Well, I don't know what to make of this, Fangfoss, I really don't, but if those men died over a game of cards then I'm a baked potato."

She jabbed a finger at him.

"We have a deal, Fangfoss. Five men dead in a day isn't part of that deal. Keep your house clean, keep the corpses off the streets and don't do anything to bring me back here in a hurry."

Fangfoss just nodded, although he had no idea how he was supposed to keep control of a psychopathic and homicidal former Imperial soldier with top-grade fighting skills and enough power to level buildings. He raised his mug in salute and gave her a confident grin as she opened the door to leave.

"Always a pleasure, my lady. And don't worry, we'll keep things tidy."

She looked at him and snorted in disgust, then swept out of the room.

22

Lady Drocia woke before dawn and lay for a few minutes listening to the muted early morning noise of the city. She planned out her day as she washed, using her established morning routine to settle her mind and help her achieve a degree of inner calm and focus after yesterday's disturbing news about Marrinek. That little snippet of gossip had threatened to disrupt some of her long-running plans and today was going to be long and busy; she needed time to think and consider.

Fortunately, as supreme spiritual leader of the province, she had both considerable resource and a wide degree of freedom within which to act. Her position meant that she was technically the third most powerful person in the Empire, after the Emperor himself and the Lord High Council. In practice, she was guided and bound by the decisions of both the provincial Council and the High Council in Khemucasterill, as well as the requests of her peers. It was, to her mind, an almost perfect balance of influence and responsibility.

The main benefit was that Lady Drocia's position gave

her the freedom to go where she wanted and do what she wanted, as long as she appeared to stay within the somewhat arbitrary limits imposed by her clerical order. It was just over a week to the Summer Solstice, the next major event on the religious calendar, so she could spare a few days for a visit to The Farm even though the timing of the trip might be viewed by some of her more conservative staff as controversial.

Established shortly after the founding of Esterengel by her predecessor (in what Lady Drocia couldn't help but think was an unusually forward-thinking move), Yirdale Seminary and the estate that surrounded it had grown considerably over the last two hundred years.

Known universally by its less formal name, The Farm now served as a spiritual retreat, a school and a secure rural base for the Lords Spiritual in addition to its role in the production of foodstuffs for the temple complex in Esterengel. The seminary accepted students from across the Empire, taking enthusiastic and other-worldly applicants and turning them into effective clerics and administrators before spitting them back out into the world.

The training that students received during their five years at The Farm was tough and varied, going far beyond the skills traditionally associated with clerics. Lady Drocia had personally overseen the re-development of the education programme shortly after she had assumed her position. Under her direct instruction, the areas of study had become more numerous, far broader and much tougher, with the result that graduates were highly skilled in a number of areas that lay well outside the traditionally religious. For the very best and most talented students, their training was interspersed with regular placements within the temple complex, working directly for Lady Drocia.

So successful was The Farm's programme that its graduates were in demand across the Empire, allowing Lady Drocia to install her protégés in both public office and the private chapels of the elite. Over the last fifty years she had placed hundreds of clerics and her near obsessive letter writing allowed her to trade news and information with most of them. Every few years the temple would hold a gathering, bringing together as many clerics as possible for a spiritual retreat at The Farm, renewing their friendships and reasserting Lady Drocia's dominance of the wider church.

Today she would make the short journey to The Farm to inspect progress on the latest student intake. Each year the number of applicants grew as The Farm became increasingly popular as the dumping ground of difficult second children or talented troublemakers rejected by the more conventional Universities. For many of these individuals, The Farm's specialised and sometimes harsh training acted as a focal point in their lives, helping to give them purpose and meaning in an otherwise dull world.

She dressed conservatively in simple white travelling robes. These too had changed over the years of her office, from the straight, heavy, unflattering and largely unadorned woollen robes worn by her predecessors. Today she wore loose-fitting linen trousers with an elegant but sensible smock that hung to her mid-thigh. The badge of her office was embroidered discretely on the breast of the smock, which was cut to be comfortable but not at all revealing - some things even Lady Drocia was not able to change. The relaxed dress rules, although not popular amongst some of the older clerics and the more hidebound nobles, meant that she could move freely within comfortable and functional garments - a huge boon for a former soldier more used to sudden violence and then extended bouts of peaceful contemplation.

She checked her charms and reviewed her appearance in her hand mirror, patting her hair back into shape, then stepped through to her study. Yesterday's letters had gone, taken away to be filed by the efficient Coewia. Today's letters had not yet arrived - they'd be here sometime around mid-morning - but there were a few late messages in her in-tray. She skimmed through them - mostly minor updates about temple administration, things her staff thought might interest her - then took a large notebook from the desk drawer. She set it carefully on the desk and from another drawer took a small charm in the form of a stylised panther. She focussed a little power into the charm - a diviner - and ran it carefully over the top of the notebook, feeling for the tell-tale hints that would indicate someone else had been reading the book. As suspected, her "private" notebook had been inspected. Somebody had flicked through the pages, focussing on the latest entries and leaning heavily on the page to do so.

She sat back, thinking. There was nothing secret in the notebook - it was merely a record of her appointments with a few predictable, non-controversial observations about the people she had met - but the fact that it had been read confirmed some of her suspicions. She grinned and slid the notebook back into its place in the drawer. The task now was to work out which of her staff was spying on her, and for whom; she loved a challenge.

She pulled her key charm from its hiding place in the desk and used the diviner again. Nobody had touched the key. She considered moving the key to a new hiding place or taking it with her but that would risk alerting the spy. Or spies, she thought, grimacing. The temple staff was large and fluid. She was sure of her aides, her personal servants and most of the cardinals but the real affiliations of the rest of the staff, particularly the ever-changing secular servants and the soldiery, were unknown and untested.

Lady Drocia stood up from her desk and collected her staff. She stopped at the door, trying to remember which leg she'd been limping on the day before, then pulled open the door that would take her to the main complex and stepped out, pulling on the habits of a tired old woman like a cloak as she went. Staff tapping, she walked slowly to the quadrangle and walked several times around the cloisters, ostensibly for exercise but mostly so that everyone saw that she was awake and moving. From the cloister she walked slowly down the stairs to the kitchens, busy even at this time of the morning, and along the corridors past the store rooms. Servants, maids and cooks alike curtsied or bowed as the approached. Only the guards at the gate that separated the private areas from the public ignored her, standing tall with eyes straight ahead as she tapped her way towards the public temple.

A pair of junior clerics, recent graduates from The Farm, bowed their heads. Lady Drocia inspected their appearance as they prepared for the early morning service then said a few words of encouragement to one, of mild chastisement to the other. She tapped her way along the central aisle of the temple to the huge front doors, closed now but soon to be opened to admit the faithful. She pushed open the small postern door and let herself out onto the steps of the temple. Even at this early hour, a crowd of worshippers had formed, attended by the ever-present sellers of pies and beer.

As she sat at the edge of the steps, unrecognised without the gaudy gowns and accoutrements of office, her staff beside her on the steps, the sun finally crested the roofs of the houses on the other side of the square to cast its light on the front of the temple. When the sunlight had crept down far enough to light the dawn window, the clerics waiting inside opened the great doors to admit the public and Lady Drocia sat quietly as they streamed past.

As the rush cleared, the sun finally reached the steps upon which she sat. She closed her eyes and enjoyed the feel of the sun as its warmth seeped into her bones; she might act the old woman and exaggerate her frailty but there was no escape from the effects of her terrible age.

She waited a few minutes, basking like an ancient lizard in the dawn light, then she stood and shuffled with the trickle of the faithful into the chamber of worship.

She smiled to herself, still grateful for the fortune that had gifted her one of the most powerful positions in the Empire, and mused on the irony that she should hold this position without entertaining any of the supernatural beliefs of the order she led. That didn't stop her from engaging in the order's regular bouts of introspection and doctrinal argument, of course, but it did allow her a certain perspective that some of her more devout cardinals lacked. Even amongst the cardinals there were non-believers, people holding their position through habit and a stubborn refusal to admit their real beliefs, or at least to face the likely consequences. Much like herself, in fact, a thought that brought another smile to her face.

She left the faithful filing dutifully to their pews or to the servery, where the junior clerics were offering the customary bread and honey, and tapped her way back across the temple towards the cloisters. In the refectory, the lay staff were serving a full breakfast of bread, fruit, cereal, pastries and preserves for the temple staff. She sat with a small group of slightly overawed groundsmen, making light conversation about the care of the rose bushes in the quadrangle and eating a bowl of porridge sweetened with raspberry jam. When she had finished, she walked slowly back to her private apartments to find Ame waiting for her.

"Good morning, Mother," said Ame, as Lady Drocia close the door of her chamber behind her and stretched to ease the tension from her back.

"Good morning, Ame. Is that coffee I see in the pot?"

"Yes, Mother. Let me pour you a cup."

Ame poured and Lady Drocia accepted gratefully, wrapping her hands around the cup.

"The coach will be ready within the hour, Mother, and I've packed clothes for a week, just in case. Will you want me to accompany you today?"

"Yes, Ame. And dress... cautiously."

Ame looked surprised.

"Cautiously? Are you expecting trouble, Mother? Should we warn the Guard?"

"Not expecting, no, but for the next few weeks it may be sensible to take extra precautions."

"Very well, Mother. In that case, I should return to my quarters to gather some things."

"Yes, do that. Meet me at the coach."

Ame left and Lady Drocia took the opportunity to retrieve her key and check her notebook for interference. Nothing, which was welcome news; she had not wanted to suspect that Ame might be spying on her. If she was lucky, the spy would check the notebook while she was at The Farm and she could shorten her list of suspects.

She finished her coffee then checked her charms again, making sure they were settled and safe. When she was satisfied that everything was as it should be she collected her staff and began to make her way to the stable yard. The coach wouldn't be ready yet, of course, but it didn't hurt occasionally to show up early and keep the staff on their toes.

The ride to The Farm was uneventful but it seemed to Lady Drocia that it took longer every time she made the journey. Maybe that was her age but it was also true that both the city and the surrounding towns and villages had grown significantly in the last fifty years. Where once the coach would have rattled along at a fair pace, it now spent hours trundling slowly behind animals being driven to market or carts loaded with produce. Even with members of Lady Drocia's personal guard riding ahead it was still almost mid-morning before the coach broke free of the traffic.

The road out to The Farm was much quieter and the coach made rapid progress. Lady Drocia had continued her predecessor's policy of buying parcels of land around the Farm as they became available and so now the seminary was both secluded and quiet. The hamlets and farms within two miles of the complex had been quietly absorbed into the estate to both buffer the school from the secular world and provide for its material needs.

About a mile out from The Farm they slowed for the outer gatehouse, a modest structure set in the six-foot-high stone wall that ran for almost four miles around the complex. One of the guards rode on ahead to identify the party and by the time the coach reached the gate the road was clear. It swept across the short bridge, under the arch of the gatehouse and into The Farm proper.

They followed the road for another quarter of a mile before clearing the forest and breaking out into the plains that surrounded the seminary itself. The coach slowed slightly as it began to climb the long gentle slope that led up to the broad plateau on which The Farm had been built. Lady Drocia loved coming here in the summer when the trees were in full leaf, the grass was green and the warm breezes gave the estate a wonderful feeling of safety and contentment and peace.

The feeling faded slightly as they pulled across the bridge and under the second gatehouse into the outer court-yard of the seminary itself. There were still trees and flowers here but against the grey stone of the buildings they seemed somehow less natural, less carefree. It was all an illusion, of course; the woods on the estate might appear natural but most of the trees were less than a hundred years old and they were carefully managed to provide wood, timber, fruit and charcoal to The Farm.

Lady Drocia looked around the courtyard as she stepped down from the coach. There was a serenity about The Farm, a quietness, that Lady Drocia found comforting. Away from the bustle and the energy of the city, the seminary was a place of reflection and learning with an atmosphere that had been carefully cultivated, at least in the more public areas, to impress upon visitors the aura of quiet study and scholarly effort.

More illusion. The public areas, the library, the study rooms, the apartments and the lecture theatres were peaceful and scholarly. The inner buildings and the under-croft, where some of the more specialised courses were taught to the senior students, were anything but peaceful.

Lady Drocia was met in the courtyard by the Principal, Cardinal Jendryng. A tall, hard man with a scarred face and short-cropped hair, he looked very much like the former soldier he was. He twitched his scars into a smile as he strode quickly across the courtyard to Lady Drocia, taking her hand to kiss her ring of office.

"Mother, it is good to see you," said the Cardinal, his voice deep and respectful. He bowed again then stepped back.

"And you, Cardinal, and you."

Lady Drocia offered her arm and the Cardinal moved to her side to help her into the main building, leaving Ame to supervise the unloading of the coach.

"We'll go to my study, Mother. There is much I must tell you."

"And much that I must tell you, Cardinal."

She hobbled slowly along the hall ways of the seminary, staff tapping, as Cardinal Jendryng walked carefully beside her. Here, out of the sunlight, the world seemed even quieter. Students, staff and servants hurried through the corridors, stopping briefly to bow or curtsey. Jendryng led Lady Drocia up the main stair case, helping her gently up each step and waiting patiently at the halfway landing while she caught her breath. Eventually they reached the Principal's study and Cardinal Jendryng helped her to a large armchair with a view out over the courtyard.

"You can leave us, Trahan, but have cakes and coffee sent up," said Cardinal Jendryng.

Trahan stood from his desk in the corner and bowed low.

"Yes, your Eminence," he said, bowing also to Lady Drocia, "Mother."

Then he backed away and left the room, closing the door quietly behind him.

Lady Drocia waited for Trahan's footsteps to recede.

"Come, sit, Franz. We have much to discuss. Tell me your news."

Cardinal Jendryng sat in the armchair opposite Lady Drocia and stretched his legs out in front of him.

"I'm not really sure where to start, Mother. Most of our news you will have had already from the weekly letters. What you won't have heard, because I wanted to speak to you in person, is that..." he stopped as there was a knock at the door.

Ame came in carrying a tray of coffee and cakes. She curtseyed to Cardinal Jendryng then put the tray down on the table between the armchairs and poured the coffee, handing one cup and a slice of fruit cake to Lady Drocia. The Cardinal waved away the cake but accepted the coffee.

"Thank you, Ame. Wait outside; make sure we are not disturbed for an hour or so and keep away anyone who looks like they might be eavesdropping," said Lady Drocia.

"Yes, Mother."

Ame curtsied again and left the room, closing the door carefully behind her.

Lady Drocia balanced the plate of cake on the arm of her chair as she sipped her coffee, then she sat back.

"Go on, Franz. What did you want to tell me?"

Cardinal Jendryng grimaced as if chewing something sour.

"It's more of a feeling than a certainty, Mother, but I've noticed that in the last few months some of our new intake seem to be unusually quick learners, as if they've had training elsewhere before being sent here."

Lady Drocia frowned.

"And you wouldn't be telling me this if you weren't worried. What do you fear?"

Jendryng grimaced again.

"Honestly, Mother, I'm not sure. Most of our students, I'm sure, are exactly what they appear. They arrive, they study, they're trained, they leave, they serve. Some, though," he paused to sip his coffee, "I think some, two or three, maybe, have been planted. They've been trained elsewhere and sent here to spy on us. I worry that someone has grown suspicious about our programmes and our success, that they may be conducting an illicit investigation."

Lady Drocia put down her coffee and picked up her plate, prodding at the cake with a fork.

"Someone suspects something. Someone able to insert students into our intake. I worry, Mother, that someone in the capital has seen a pattern in our placements, has grown worried about our plans and motives, and is preparing to move against us."

Lady Drocia considered this. Political intrigues and games were everywhere within the Empire. Almost all the long-lived talented, the Ancients, played the great game, manoeuvring carefully amongst their peers for relative position, personal gratification and Imperial favour. The games tended to be long, drawn-out affairs, utilising all the tools and resources that the talented could gather over centuries of work and effort.

The Emperor knew, of course. He had his own resources - spies and informants, specialists like the Kareethi, the civil service, several armies - with which to counter or confound the schemes he didn't like. Sometimes he would simply disrupt the plots of people who had fallen out of favour or whose embarrassment might be particularly entertaining.

Most of these schemes would fizzle out or fail quietly, some would run for years as the players moved and counter-moved, a few would explode into hugely embarrassing or damaging scandals. The rest? It was impossible to say for sure but for each plot that was seen or known or uncovered there were probably a dozen others that nobody ever knew about.

Uncovering or exposing other people's plots was almost as good as having one of your own come to fruition. Information she received from her carefully cultivated networks had allowed Lady Drocia, on occasion, to cause significant embarrassment to some of her most ancient rivals. At other times, she had been able to subvert their schemes to deliver an outcome more in keeping with her overall aims. She was good at the great game and, like all good players, she took seriously any hint of a threat to her power.

"Two or three, you think?"

The Cardinal nodded.

"Well, it's only a surprise that nobody became interested before now. Let's see... Knowing that there are spies might be useful, if we can find out who they're working for. Do any of them show particular promise?"

"There is one, yes, who might be called highly promising, Mother. The other two are more dull, more every day, at least in our terms. They'll make adequate clerics but not great leaders."

"Well, keep an eye on them but don't scare them off. I want to know who they're working for and why the sudden interest. Intercept their messages, if you can, and make sure they aren't able to leave The Farm."

Cardinal Jendryng nodded.

"Yes, Mother. Is there nothing else you'd like me to do?"

"No, not for now, just keep me informed."

Lady Drocia took a fork-full of cake and chewed thoughtfully.

"Although maybe we should shake things up a bit, keep them moving around. Yes, let's offer all the students an opportunity to come to the city for the Solstice and see who decides to go and who stays. That might be informative, don't you think?"

Jendryng grinned.

"That sounds excellent, Mother. I'll make the announcement at supper."

He sat back and picked up his coffee, clearly much relieved to have spoken of his fears and to have agreed a plan.

"Now, to my news," said Lady Drocia, "a report reached Esterengel yesterday that the ship transporting Abaythian Marrinek to Ankeron West foundered, about a week ago. Marrinek is believed to have escaped and headed west toward Catshed then probably south toward the city state of Vensille."

She paused to eat another piece of cake while Jendryng sipped his coffee and digested the news.

"Escaped? Interesting. I wonder how he did it?"

"Nobody seems to know. Or care, at the moment. The Council is investigating, of course, and the Lord Justice is desperate to prove that she wasn't at fault, but that's all we know for now."

"She'll have to be told," said Cardinal Jendryng, pouring fresh coffee for Lady Drocia and then himself.

"Quite. How is she? Keeping busy?"

Cardinal Jendryng sipped his coffee.

"You knew her better than me, Mother, but I hear good reports from the other instructors. And she has been teaching her courses now for more than fourteen months. I would say she has settled into her new life, although I'm not sure she has quite accepted her changed circumstances."

"Good. Acceptance would imply permanency and I don't think any of us would want to wish that on her. Summon her here, I will talk to her myself."

Jendryng nodded and walked to the fireplace to pull the bell cord that would summon a servant. He turned back to Lady Drocia.

"I would hate to lose her, Mother, but maybe, if we are being scrutinised, it would be sensible for her to..." he paused, choosing his next words carefully, "for her to consider spending time with her family, away from The Farm."

"Quite," said Lady Drocia, "I wouldn't be surprised if she decides to leave today, which might raise questions. Still..." she paused as the door opened to admit a footman, who bowed his head to Lady Drocia.

"Ah, Fernwright. I want you to find the Lady Aspene and ask her to attend me here at her earliest convenience. She may be teaching a class, in which case you should interrupt with my apologies."

"Yes, your Eminence."

Fernwright turned away, closing the door behind him.

"And now we wait," murmured Jendryn, finishing his coffee.

They didn't have to wait long. After a few minutes, there was a knock at the door and Fernwright appeared, leading a tall attractive woman; Lady Aspene. Fernwright bowed and left, closing the door behind him.

Lady Aspene strode confidently into the room and curtseyed to Cardinal Jendryng but her face turned white when she saw Lady Drocia sitting opposite him. Lady Drocia pushed herself upright from her chair and, leaning heavily on her staff, tapped her way across the floor to embrace Lady Aspene.

"Mother," said Lady Aspene, "I hadn't expected to see you here."

She trembled slightly as she took Lady Drocia's hand and bent to kiss it. Jendryng nodded to Lady Drocia and then left the room, closing the door behind him as he went.

"Sit down, child," said Lady Drocia, gesturing to the armchair vacated by Cardinal Jendryng, "you look well. The country air agrees with you?"

"Thank you, yes Mother. I have found a degree of peace, within these walls. And nobody has bothered me or asked difficult questions. It is an almost idyllic life."

Lady Drocia snorted.

"Rubbish. Don't give me 'idyllic'," snapped Lady Drocia, suddenly harsh and unsympathetic, "it's dull and boring. You're stuck out here, estranged from your social circle and cut-off from your former friends. You've been violently separated from your husband and forced into hiding because of his crimes. You're filling time training worthy students to be effective clerics but you can't wait to escape back to your former life. You must hate it."

Lady Aspene's face twitched with each sentence.

"I... yes."

There was no denying it. Teaching was rewarding, in its own way, but it didn't compare to the richness of her former life.

Lady Drocia leant forward and took Aspene's hand.

"I don't mean to dwell on your pain, my child, but it is important always to see life as it truly is, not as we might wish it to be, and you must remember that a disguise is not the same as a life, no matter how comfortable it might become."

She released her hand and sat back.

"Anyway, none of that matters now. Your husband has

managed to escape. The ship transporting him to Ankeron West foundered. He seems to have survived and fled west."

Lady Aspene closed her eyes and sat back in the armchair, breathing deeply. Only now, as the tension drained from her muscles and she relaxed into the chair, did she understand just how worried she had been for the last two years. There had been no warning, no hint of suspicion, no suggestion that he was to be arrested. The speed with which she had been ostracised by almost everyone she knew, even those closest to her, those she had thought of as loyal and lifelong friends, had been terrifying. The news, gleaned from a former friend too scared now to be seen with her in public, that she was sought for questioning by the Inquisition had triggered her flight from the court of Esterengel. She had gone first to the Temple, then to a small house in the countryside and finally, after weeks of hiding and jumping at shadows, she had found her way here, to The Farm.

The news that her husband was alive and free rather than caged in the living death of Ankeron West changed everything. She sat up and opened her eyes, looking straight at Lady Drocia.

"Thank you, Mother."

She flexed her fingers and looked at her hands. They no longer trembled.

"What will you do?" asked Lady Drocia.

Lady Aspene looked up from her hands.

"Follow," she said simply.

Lady Drocia nodded.

"Good. He will need your help and guidance, you need his support and strength. The report said he was in Catshed, on the Guiln, although God alone knows why."

"I suppose everyone will be looking for him?"

"Not yet. The Council decided not to release the news while they conducted their 'investigation' but that'll be cursory and short-lived at best. The Lord Justice cares only about defending her name, the others care only about deflecting the blame onto someone else, preferably someone far away from Esterengel. As soon as they think they have the results they need they'll loose the Kareethi, if they haven't already, and mobilise armies to recapture him before the Emperor finds out."

"Lady Fiethien," said Aspene, with real hatred in her voice, "always was a small-minded, self-serving, stupid little bitch. She did nothing, said nothing, when the Inquisitors took my husband."

Lady Drocia's face hardened.

"And rightly so, considering the rumours about the crimes for which he was arrested. Nobody was going to contradict the Emperor, not when he was so furiously certain. Even I could go only so far and that achieved precisely nothing."

"But you tried, Mother, and for that I am grateful. Others did nothing and said nothing. They circled like vultures while the Inquisition destroyed us then they swooped on our estates, our houses, our possessions. We have nothing left, Mother, nothing at all. They took everything we had, everything we had built. I cannot forget and I will not forgive."

"Nor should you, my child, but revenge can wait. You have other tasks to attend."

Aspene stood and straightened her clothes.

"I must go, Mother."

Lady Drocia stood awkwardly, leaning heavily on her staff. She pulled from her pocket the small charm she had taken from her cabinet and held it out to Lady Aspene.

"Do you know what this is?"

Lady Aspene looked at the tiny charm as it lay in her hand then shook her head.

"No, I hadn't really expected that you would. It belongs to your husband. Give it to him, when you see him. Will you continue to use the same name?"

"No, Mother. I think Aspene suits me and it has worked well at The Farm but it wouldn't do to carry it too far. I will write to you, something bland and innocuous, but you'll know it's from me."

Lady Drocia nodded.

"Very well. Probably better that I don't know for now anyway. You know where to find me."

She pulled a small purse from another pocket.

"This should cover your expenses, if you travel modestly, and I'll have Jendryng find you a horse. Hurry now, and pack what you need. Find me before you go."

They embraced, then Lady Aspene headed to the door.

"I've always thought very fondly of you, my child. I would be disappointed were something to happen to you now. Take care."

Lady Aspene turned toward her, hand on the door knob.

"You too, Mother. And thank you."

She stepped out of the room and closed the door behind her, leaving Lady Drocia alone again.

Lady Aspene stood outside the Cardinal's study for moment collecting her thoughts, then she noticed that Lady Drocia's maid servant was watching from across the hall. She pulled herself back to the present and walked down the corridor towards her cell, passing the theatres and classrooms where she used to teach. She paused, briefly, outside the double doors of the main lecture theatre, considering whether to go in and say goodbye. Then she shook her head; the time for sentiment had passed and now she had something real, something important, upon which to focus. She walked on.

Her cell, her home for the last eighteen months, was sparsely furnished and few of the things it contained were really hers. Even the robes belonged to the seminary. She dragged out from under the bed the pack she had acquired - stolen - in Esterengel as she had fled the city. Into it she stuffed the few items of clothing she had gathered during her stay at the seminary. She collected her knife from the bedside table and slipped it into her belt under her smock.

She was wearing the plain robes of a cleric, which ought to deter people from speaking to her without real need and might even prove useful if she needed a cover story. Clerics travelled often, even outside the borders of the Empire, so nobody would question her presence if they thought she was on temple business.

Finally, she flipped up the thin mattress and retrieved the small leather pouch hidden between the slats of the rough base. She opened it and tipped the contents into her hand, then stared for a few minutes at the ring that lay there. It was a thick ring - gold, mostly, worked in intricate patterns around a core of iridium and iron - and it was the only thing she had to show for decades of married life, the only possession she had carried with her when she had fled their home two years before.

She remembered the day that Marrinek had given it to her after the weeks he had spent acquiring the materials - long before his rise to fame and fortune - and crafting the ring in secret. Eventually, when she had started to worry that he had lost interest in her, he had presented it to her and asked for her hand. It was only once they were married that he fully explained the charms he had worked into the ring and the lengths he had taken to craft it. He had woven four metals and worked each over many hours to produce a powerful object, one fit for his wife-to-be and tailored to her particular talents. She slipped it back onto her finger, relieved finally to have it restored to its proper place, and tested the charms.

Satisfied, she spent a few minutes stripping the cell of everything that was hers and packing it in her bag. The room she left behind had barely changed; four whitewashed stone walls, a plain bed with simple woollen blankets, a small table and a three-legged stool. There was nothing left to suggest she had ever been there. She looked around the cell one last time, then decided that she would need the blankets more than her colleagues in the seminary. She rolled them quickly and tied them to the bottom of her pack.

She walked away from the cell and from her time as a lecturer without regret. Her life had been on hold for the last two years and now she felt that she was, finally, doing something positive that would again give her life meaning.

She paused briefly at the door that would take her to the stables, wondering if a quick exit might be preferable, but in the end she decided to seek out Lady Drocia again as she had requested, so she passed by the door and headed back to Cardinal Jendryng's study. Ame was still sitting outside so Aspene knocked on the door and entered. Cardinal Jendryng had returned and was writing at his desk while Lady Drocia sipped at a fresh cup of coffee, back in her armchair by the window.

"Ah, Lady Aspene," said Cardinal Jendryng, "I see you have packed already," he nodded at the pack on her shoulder, "and I'd like to thank you for all your help since you arrived here. I think the staff and students will miss you greatly."

Lady Aspene bowed.

"Thank you, your Eminence. Strange though it may seem, I have enjoyed being here and please accept my thanks for your hospitality. I understand the risks you have taken, and are still taking, by helping me."

Jendryng bowed his head to her.

"A calculated risk, my lady, and one that I bear happily as thanks for our long friendship."

Lady Drocia sniffed loudly.

"If you've quite finished, the girl has things to do. Let's move this along."

Jendryng coughed and looked slightly embarrassed.

"Yes, well. These are for you," he said, passing over a pair of leather saddle-bags, "a little food for your journey and some other items that may be useful on the road."

Lady Aspene accepted the bags graciously.

"Thank you, your Eminence."

She bowed again to Jendryng and to Lady Drocia.

"And thank you, Mother. I will write."

"Good. Now get along before the day is quite wasted. You should be well west of Esterengel by nightfall. It's only a matter of time before the Inquisition learns of Marrinek's escape and then, whatever the Council says, they'll be looking for you both. There may already be others hunting him, if I know how Lady Camille thinks. There's a horse waiting for you in the stable yard."

"Thank you again, Mother, Cardinal."

Lady Aspene threw the saddle bags over her shoulder and left the room quickly. Ame peered in through the swinging door then pulled it shut, leaving Lady Drocia and Cardinal Jendryng alone in the study.

"Well," said Lady Drocia, "we've done all that we can on that matter."

She looked at the Cardinal.

"Let's have a little lunch and talk again about how best to deal with your spies."

23

Marrinek waited at Madame Duval's back door until one of the servants heard him knocking and let him in. He hurried down the corridor to the study and let himself in but Madame Duval was not there. He swore quietly and stepped back into the hallway, heading for the stairs. At the top of the house he found that the attic room, where he had left the twins the day before, was also empty.

He glanced around the room but nothing appeared to be amiss. He dumped his bag on a bench and rummaged around for his charming tools, then he leant Bone Dancer against the wall, checked that his shock cannon was in his pocket and walked back down the stairs. He was heading for the kitchen when he bumped into Elaine.

"Elaine, morning. Where are the twins and Madame Duval? I've been to the attic and the study but there's no sign of them."

"Madame Duval has taken Shad and the twins shopping. She said something about new outfits for the twins. I don't think she was planning to return before noon."

Marrinek muttered something to himself and dumped his bag down on the floor.

"Sorry, Bay, didn't catch that. What did you say?"

"Nothing. I asked her to arrange new clothes for the twins I just hadn't expected her to start so early this morning. Is there any food? It's been a long morning."

Elaine looked at him, her head tilted to one side.

"Try the kitchen. They should be baking today's bread and cakes but if you were expecting something substantial you'll probably be out of luck."

"Thanks, I'll have a look." He walked the rest of the way down the corridor to the kitchen and pushed open the door. Inside, Cook and a maid were setting out loaves to cool and preparing trays of snacks and finger food for the day's clients. Marrinek grabbed a loaf and grinned at Cook as she glared at him.

"Thanks," he said, slipping back out through the door.

Elaine had disappeared so Marrinek headed for the back door, munching on the loaf as he went. He stood at the back door, staring at it for a few minutes, then he took out his charming tools, unrolling the leather case on the floor. He pulled out the largest tool and focussed a little power through it into the door frame, feeling his way around it to check his earlier work. Satisfied, he checked the door itself, hardening further in a few areas, before turning his attention in turn to the lock, the hinges the bar and the surrounding wall.

For two hours he worked, gradually hardening everything he could reach until the door was as secure as he could make it. He stepped back to admire his work; it wouldn't keep out a talented attack but any casual visitor would find it almost impossible to break down the door.

Marrinek gathered his tools and walked through the

corridor to the front door, where Elaine was talking to one of the bouncers.

"Business as usual today, yes, but keep an eye out for the Watch. Our friend here," she nodded at Marrinek as he laid out his tools on the floor, "seems to have a knack for acquiring enemies."

The bouncer, Trick, was a short, heavily muscled man with slicked-back hair. He was tidily dressed in short white shirt and black trousers and he nodded at Marrinek.

"The Watch can be tricky, if you're not careful. Best to keep them friendly, if you can."

Marrinek ran his hands over the door and frame.

"Some good carpentry here but also some that is not so good. Look, here," he pointed at a spot about a foot from the ground, "you can see where someone has patched up the frame and tied it back into the wall but they haven't done a good job. When was the door last kicked in?" he looked at Trick, who shrugged and looked at Elaine.

"About fifteen months ago. A couple of thugs from out of town tried to kick their way in after we turned them away. Shad broke noses and split lips and that was the end of it but they damaged the door."

"Leave me to work and I'll fix it so that the door can't be kicked in." He studied the door again while Trick moved to sit on the chair at the bottom of the stairs. Elaine stood watching him for a few minutes as the tool moved over the frame and wall, then turned to leave.

"I could do with something else to eat, if you're passing the kitchen. Maybe send one of the maids out for a pie?" said Marrinek over his shoulder.

Elaine looked at his back for a moment, then at Trick, who shrugged.

"I'll see what I can do. Don't scare away the punters."

She stalked off toward the kitchen leaving Marrinek to work on the door while Trick sat, watching impassively from his chair.

Marrinek focussed on the door, feeding power through the charm to harden the wood. He worked methodically, moving inward from the frame to the door and back again, hardening and strengthening the wood, the metal of the hinges and the surrounding wall. It took him another three hours to finish but, when he eventually sat back and put away his tools, the front door was as strong as the back door. He rolled his head from side to side to loosen the muscles of his neck and stretched his back.

Trick, silent for the last three hours, rumbled into life.

"Is that it?" he said, disappointed, "I was expecting something more impressive."

Marrinek snorted.

"Fire and brimstone, maybe? Bright lights and bangs? Try digging it with your knife."

Trick stood up and walked over to the door, pulling a short dagger from the small of his back. He gingerly touched the plain wooden surface of the door with his hand, then raised an eyebrow at Marrinek, who nodded encouragement.

"Well, if you're sure."

Trick brought the dagger down in a heavy over hand blow, ramming it's point at the door. The door banged in its frame but the knife just skittered over the surface of the wood leaving behind a shallow scratch. Trick grunted in surprise and inspected his knife, checking the blade.

"Hmm," said Marrinek, "you're stronger than you look."

He pulled out the largest charming tool and ran it again over the surface of the wood.

"I'll fix this - wouldn't want to leave a scratch on Madame Duval's door."

He focussed briefly and Trick's eyes widened as the scratch disappeared back into the wood.

"That's neat," said Trick, sheathing his knife, "what about the windows?"

Marrinek looked around the hall. There were windows on either side of the door and more in the sitting rooms. The back rooms had windows as well, so there were maybe ten or more on the ground floor alone. Marrinek put away his tools and stood back.

"It might take a few days to do the windows and I don't have the time. I think we'll pay someone else to work on the windows. In fact, I'll talk to Madame Duval about that when she returns."

He patted his pockets then opened the door to look at it from the outside. He rapped his knuckle against the wood, listening to the sound it made. After a few minutes, he stepped back into the hallway and closed the door, satisfied that he had done all that could be done.

"I'll leave you to it," he said to Trick as he walked down the hallway, "if anyone breaks down the door now, my advice would be to run away."

Trick nodded at Marrinek's retreating back and sat down on his chair, alone again.

Marrinek jogged up the stairs and dumped his tools on the bench. Madame Duval was still out with the twins but he didn't want to wait any longer. He thought about looking for them but discarded the idea quickly; he could speak to them again this evening and it would do them good to spend time with other people.

He stripped off his shirt and swapped it for a clean one - his last - then checked that his shock cannon was in his pocket. He emptied his bag onto the bench and cursed as gemstones and silver spread across the surface and coins trickled onto the floor.

"I need a chest or a lockbox of some sort," he muttered to himself as he collected the fallen coins.

He stuffed a handful of silver and a couple of the smaller gems into his purse and slipped it into his pocket, then picked up the empty bag and slung it over his shoulder. The rest of the gems and the silver he wrapped in his dirty shirt, leaving the bundle on the floor under the bench. Then he grabbed Bone Dancer and went back downstairs, stopping by the front door to tie back his hair. Marrinek nodded at Trick - still sitting patiently on his chair - and stepped out of the house.

The street was busy with people and traders, the normal mix of city dwellers and visitors, shopkeepers and craftsmen. Marrinek weaved through the crowds towards the charms shop, Bone Dancer tapping along at his side. The day was warm and the heat brought forth a strong and unpleasant smell from the city's drains. As he walked, Marrinek daydreamed about his childhood in Esterengel and the long summers he had spent running on the streets, hiding from the Watch and living off whatever he could steal. He grimaced to himself and pulled himself back to the present; the past held only pain and suffering and death and loss.

Eaves' charm shop was empty when Marrinek arrived and he stood for a moment holding the door, just looking around. It struck him that, as on his last visit, the atmosphere inside the shop was noticeably cooler and more pleasant the outside. Marrinek closed the door behind him and looked curiously at the window, the door and the walls but there was no obvious mechanism for cooling the shop. He ran his fingers over the door and wall but the wood was perfectly normal, not even hardened. Confused, he stepped back, turning around just as the shop keeper came in from the back room.

"Good afternoon, Mr Bay. How are you today?"

"I'm very well, thank you Mr Eaves, but in need of assistance." They discussed the general principles of building security and the hardening of windows and Mr Eaves opined that there were people within the Guild who might provide the services Marrinek sought, although he himself did not execute that type of work. They agreed that Mr Eaves would find someone discreet and arrange for them to call at the House of Duval at the earliest opportunity.

Marrinek pulled out his purse and removed two of the smaller gem stones that he had acquired from Fangfoss. He laid them on the table and prodded them towards Mr Eaves.

"I have a number of stones like this. I can't use them in my work and I wondered if you might be able to make use of them?"

Mr Eaves examined the stones, at one point producing a magnifying glass from under the counter to aid his inspection. Eventually, he put them back down on the counter.

"Yes, Mr Bay, I believe I can use these. And what might I offer in return?"

Marrinek leant Bone Dancer against the counter.

"Firstly, silence. Discuss my business with nobody and if anyone asks about me tell them that you know nothing about me."

Eaves looked surprised.

"But I don't know anything about you," he protested,

"except that you have twin apprentices and a ready supply of gem stones. What else might I tell 'them' and who might ask questions about you anyway?"

"Maybe nobody. If someone does come and they threaten you, tell them they can find me at the House of Duval."

"Very well, as you wish, the House of Duval if threatened," said Eaves, clearly unsure what to make of these instructions.

"Good. Secondly, I need a tutor for my apprentices. They're quick and smart but I don't have the time to spend with them. Can you recommend someone?"

"The Guild can certainly provide tutors but they would obviously insist on membership," he paused to look at Marrinek, judging, "and I imagine you might prefer to avoid that?"

Marrinek nodded.

"In that case, your options are limited but I might be able to find a few hours to give them general pointers and to show them the rudiments of charm-making, if that would be of interest?"

"Rudimentary charm-making would be perfect. I shall want to see results, mind."

Mr Eaves nodded, as if taking on illegal tutoring of twin apprentices was something he did every day and, obviously, their Master would want them to receive only the best training.

"Thirdly, I need more supplies. Two sets of charming tools for the twins, supplies for them to practice with and whatever other books you might have that would be appropriate for fast-learners."

Mr Eaves produced a notebook from under the counter and began to make a list.

"Sorry, Mr Bay, but I find that if I don't write things down I tend to forget almost everything."

He noted down Marrinek's requests so far.

"I have copies of Jensen's second and third volumes, which should be enough to keep them occupied for the next few years, but beyond that I am only occasionally able to acquire the more advanced treatises. Practitioners, in Vensille at least, tend to collect books rather than circulate them so old copies are seldom available and new books rarely reach this part of the world; most of the knowledge of power is passed from master to apprentice or from peer to peer, although in Vensille new discoveries are seldom shared."

"I'll take volumes two and three of Jensen, then, and anything you might have that covers the history of Vensille."

Eaves ducked into the backroom for a few minutes before returning with four books.

"Jensen volumes two and three, a short history of Vensille written maybe three years ago and this, which I thought might appeal to you. It describes a local martial art, Long Stick, that was briefly fashionable amongst the nobility in Vensille maybe eighty years ago. Given your apparent weapon of choice," he nodded at Bone Dancer, "you might find it interesting."

Marrinek took all four books, flipping open the slim Long Stick volume. He flicked through a few pages then looked up.

"Thank you, yes, I'll take all four," he said as he slipped the books into his bag, "and finally, for now, you could tell me about the temperature in here. How do you keep it so cool?"

Eaves smiled.

"You are not the first to ask, sir. It's a mechanism of my

own devising, powered by a net of copper wires and a large block of lead, which absorbs heat. It sits upstairs and the air it cools falls down a shaft in the wall and out through those vents near the ceiling."

He pointed to a set of wooden slats over a hole in the wall, high up behind the counter.

"It works well enough but it's not quite ready for sale. When it is perfected, I mean to sell it to the rich, become rich myself and retire from shop-keeping. Until then..."

Marrinek nodded.

"I understand - you'd rather not share your secrets. Very sensible. I may need a few of those mechanisms in my house - I find your summers a little too warm for my liking - so if you want somewhere else to test them, let me know."

"Thank you sir, I will bear that in mind, although summer hasn't really arrived yet. It'll get a fair sight warmer yet, I think. Now, let me find you those charming tools."

Eaves stepped into the back room again while Marrinek peered around the shop. Now that he knew there was a mechanism delivering cold air he could feel the gentle flow as it fell from the vent. Clever.

Eaves returned, placing two sets of charm tools on the counter along with an assortment of basic supplies, which he packed into a sack.

"Two sets of tools, a selection of iron rods of varying diameters, several lengths of copper wire, a variety of short kiln-dried ash and oak staves, a few blocks of beech, two pairs of heavy leather gloves."

He stopped, thinking.

"That should be enough for teaching the rudiments. Is there anything else you need, sir?"

"There is one more thing. I have a knack for making

enemies and I feel a need to enhance my personal protection. Do you have any charms of a martial nature?"

Eaves shifted uneasily from one foot to the other.

"You must understand, sir, that such things are closely regulated in Vensille. Only the Guild is allowed to sell such things but, sometimes, for special clients, there are opportunities to acquire a limited range of items. What, specifically, did you have in mind?"

"I'm looking for discreet items of powered armour. Arm shields would be best but if supply is limited I'll take anything that might be available."

"Ah, that is a little different. Weapons are very difficult but shields are rather easier. I carry no real stock in this area - there is almost no call for it amongst my customers - but I do have an arm bracer, if that would be of interest? It is small, designed to be worn under the sleeve of a fashionable shirt, but with sufficient power it should provide significant protection."

Eaves opened a small cupboard door under the counter and after moving aside a crate of oak staves he produced a leather bag about six inches long and laid it on the counter. Marrinek picked it up and loosened the drawstring, upending the bag so that the short leather and iron bracer dropped into his hand. He turned it over, examining the workmanship, and flexed it between his fingers to test its rigidity. Satisfied, he rolled up his left sleeve and laced the bracer to the outside of his arm then focussed a little power into it. Immediately a translucent disc about fifteen inches in diameter appeared in front of his arm, exactly where a traditional shield would sit. Marrinek twisted his arm and experimented with the amount of power flowing into the bracer until he was happy that everything was working as expected. He rolled down his sleeve.

"Perfect. I'll take it. And keep your eyes open for other pieces. I will probably take any quality pieces you can find."

"Certainly, sir. Will there be anything else?"

Marrinek hefted the sack then stuffed it into his pack on top of the books.

"No, I think that's everything for now."

He nodded at the gem stones.

"I'll trust you to track how much I'm spending; let me know when I reach the value of those stones."

He opened the door and slipped the bag onto his shoulder.

"I'll send the twins for their first session this evening. A note to the House of Duval will reach me, if you have need."

And Marrinek stepped out of the shop, closing the door behind him as he went.

Back at the House of Duval, Marrinek found the eponymous Madame in her study. She turned around as he came in but finished stowing her coins in a small chest before joining him on the settee. She handed him a parcel tied up in string.

"Fresh clothes. The trousers should fit better than those you're wearing and the shirts are clean and pressed. The tailor is coming tomorrow morning to measure you for coats, more shirts, trousers and so on, so by the end of the week you should have a halfway decent wardrobe."

"Excellent, thank you," said Marrinek, weighing the parcel then setting it beside him, "how were the twins?"

Madame Duval wrinkled her nose and waggled her head a little in frustration.

"I don't think they trust me. Hardly surprising, given the way we were introduced, but maybe things will improve. They behaved themselves, though, and they both now have much of what they need to pass as polite members of society. They've been measured so the rest of their clothes will be here later in the week."

Marrinek nodded.

"Good. Any other problems?" he asked as Madame Duval frowned.

"No," she said, "were you expecting something?"

"Not really." He paused, as if unsure about what he was about to say. Madame Duval looked at him expectantly as the moment dragged on.

"I have a plan for dealing with the Flank Siders, for getting you out from under their thumb," he said finally, "and there's a part for you, if you want it."

"If I want it? You mean I have a choice?"

"Of course," said Marrinek, surprised, "but it'll be more difficult if you say no, more risky."

She looked at him, face full of doubt, inviting him to say more.

"If it works, you'll be free and there will be a bonus, a big one."

"And if it doesn't work? What if it goes wrong?"

Marrinek looked away, briefly, as if hiding from an inconvenient question.

"If it goes wrong, we'll probably both be dead before morning," he said quietly, "but I don't expect it to come to that."

She raised her eyebrows.

"So you're not actually planning to get us killed, then. Is that supposed to inspire confidence?"

Marrinek sighed and shook his head.

"It's dangerous. I have to get close to Artas and the longer we leave it the more difficult it will become because they'll work out how I'm linked to Fangfoss and then I'll have to cut my way in. Very bloody, very dangerous, very difficult. We have one chance to keep things clean and easy." He paused to let her think about this. "Are you in?"

She looked at him and he could see the fear in her eyes as she thought it through. Then she gave a quick nod and an excited grin.

"Good. It's a simple plan but it starts with you in a fine dress, as revealing as you can manage in polite company. Do you have something suitable?"

Madame Duval snorted.

"Revealing dresses are pretty much my stock in trade," she said, "I'm sure I can find something that will suit."

"Right. Well, thanks. I'm going to bathe then pay a visit to our Captain Paltiel, give her a nudge in the right direction and see what she has to say about things."

He picked up the parcel.

"Are you sure that's wise? It might be better to let the Watch be. Paltiel has a reputation. Prickly, difficult. And that's without adding the Flank Siders into the mix."

Marrinek shook his head.

"Can't. I've already upset Snitz so it's only a matter of time before they come back in force. Besides, there are too many other things going on to stop now."

He stood up and opened the door before turning back to her.

"Anyway, it might be fun." He closed the door behind him and Madame Duval listened to the sound of his boots retreating down the corridor toward the bathroom.

Old Ned's day wasn't going at all well. They had grabbed him right off the docks and taken him to a Watch house somewhere on the east side, near as he could tell. When they'd finally taken the bag off his head he was in a cell lit only by a small grill set near the ceiling. Even at midsummer, the cell was damp and chilly and he could hear the rats running along the corridor and through the foul straw that covered the floor.

He shivered and kicked out at the rustling straw but he'd been arrested before and he knew the drill. Sit tight, find out what they wanted, say nothing. Eventually they'd get bored of having him around and throw him back out on the street.

At least, that's what had happened every other time he'd been arrested. Things had been quiet recently and he hadn't seen the inside of a cell for several years. This afternoon's grab had been a surprise. He kicked the straw around a bit in frustration then tried shouting and rattling the door, although he knew from long experience that nobody would take any notice. Still, for appearances if nothing else, he shouted and yelled all the obscenities he could think of. After a while he gave up and dragged his boot across the floor until he'd cleared a patch to sit on. With nothing to do but wait, he pulled his knees up to his chest and leant his head against the wall.

Time was the enemy. He tried to track how long he'd been in the cell by watching the shadows thrown by the grill, just to give himself something to do. The shadow hadn't moved more than a few inches across the floor before he heard someone coming down the corridor and the door to his cell was thrown open. A lantern came into the cell, preceding a man who also carried a chair. He hung the lantern from a hook in the ceiling and placed the chair down near the door, standing to one side as second man came in and sat down on the chair.

Ned frowned up at him from his spot on the floor. He knew most of the people in the Watch, at least vaguely. He recognised with an inward groan the man in the chair. Sergeant Snitz, a man of low character that he, Ned, would have crossed the road to avoid if they'd been out in the open.

"What do you want, Snitz? I'm busy."

Snitz looked around theatrically.

"Busy? Looks to me like you've got plenty of free time. Years, maybe, if we forget you're here."

Ned said nothing, waiting for Snitz to get to the point.

"Answer my questions and you'll be home before breakfast. What happened at the Goat the day before yesterday? Who killed Hitton?"

Ned gaped at him.

"Is that it? That's what you want to know? You're an imbecile, Snitz. I have no fucking clue who killed Hitton because I wasn't there. And I've been stuck in here most of the day so what the fuck do you think I should know?"

"Constable Boyer, help our friend remember."

Snitz gestured at Ned and the lantern carrier, Constable Boyer, stepped away from the wall with a grin and backhanded Ned across the face, knocking him onto his side. He bent down, grabbed Ned's shirt and pulled him back into a sitting position against the wall, then slapped him the other way. Boyer dragged Ned up again then stepped back to lean against the wall.

Snitz leant forward on the chair, leaning on his knees.

"Don't give me any of that 'I don't know nothing' horse shit. Just tell me what happened, now."

Ned spat blood onto the straw but said nothing. Snitz waited, then sighed.

"Last chance, old man. Who killed Hitton?"

Ned looked up at him and sneered.

"As if I'd tell you, even if I knew."

Snitz gestured again and sat back while his colleague punched and beat Old Ned, raining blows onto his head and legs and arms. Eventually Snitz raised his hand and the beating stopped. Old Ned lay on his side, wheezing badly and bleeding from cuts all over this face. Snitz stood up and moved over to Ned's side, crouching beside him in the filthy straw. He leant down so that he could whisper in Ned's ear.

"I'm going to leave you here. I'm going to forget about you while I eat your food and drink your beer and fuck your whores tonight. Somebody will talk, eventually, but this is your last chance of getting out of here alive. What happened?"

Ned just groaned and dribbled blood. Snitz grabbed him and pulled him up so that he was sitting against the wall.

"What happened in the Goat?"

Ned coughed, spraying blood across his shirt and the floor. Snitz stood up and walked back to the chair.

"You think Fangfoss cares about you? That your silence will count for something? That you're doing him any good and that he'll save you? You stupid old fucker."

Snitz walked toward the door and Boyer followed, picking up the chair as he went. Ned watched them go, then the door closed and the two men walked back down the corridor. Silence descended and Ned sank down into the rancid straw, cradling his head in his arms.

"He wouldn't talk, Captain," said Snitz, "he don't know nothing, or he ain't ready to talk. We could try him again in the morning?"

Captain Paltiel sat behind her desk looking up at the two men.

"Bring him up here. We'll see if he'll talk to me."

"Right you are, Captain, but I don't know it'll do any good." He gestured to Boyer, who slunk out of the office.

"Is there anything else, Captain?"

"Get back on the street, Snitz, and sniff around. Find out what happened at the Goat; somebody knows what went on."

"Yes Captain." He saluted raggedly and left, leaving the office door open. Paltiel sat down, leaning back in her chair and resting her feet on the desk. She waited only a few minutes before Boyer reappeared dragging the unfortunate Old Ned. He stumbled into the office and Boyer pushed him down into the chair opposite Paltiel's desk.

"Thank you, Constable, that will be all for now. Close the door and wait outside."

Boyer nodded and left, closing the door behind him and leaving Paltiel alone with Old Ned. She looked at him as he slumped in the chair, taking in the fresh cuts on his face and head and the bruises that were blooming across his cheeks.

"Well, you look like you're having a bad day, Ned. Could it be that you didn't give my Sergeant the information he required?"

Ned said nothing, keeping his eyes on the floor. Paltiel stood up and walked round to the front of the desk, leaning against it so that she stood just in front of Ned. She reached out and placed her finger under his chin so that she could gently tip his head back.

"Look at me Ned. Look at me!" she said, forcefully, focussing a little power into the charm on her finger. Ned looked up, meeting her eye for the first time. She smiled at him and pushed more power into the ring.

"Now," she said, quietly, "tell me what happened at the Goat so that we can get you out of here and let you go home. Who killed Hitton?"

Ned coughed and dribbled blood and spit onto his shirt then said, "New man, Imperial. Name's 'Bay'." He stopped to cough again. Paltiel pushed a little more power through the charm.

"Go on. How did it happen?" she asked.

"Don't know. Hitton went up to his room at the Goat, there was some sort of struggle, and they found him, dead, on the floor. There was a hole right through his head, large enough to stick your finger in."

"And the others, Ned. How did the others die?"

"Dunno. Tam and Chent by some sort of magic, maybe," he paused to cough, then said "but the other one, don't know his name, he fell off the roof while chasing Bay."

Paltiel sat back on the desk, letting Ned's head flop down onto his chest.

"And what about Gander, the man killed earlier in the day. How did that happen?"

"Wasn't there. Some sort of fight. Bay crushed his skull with a staff."

Paltiel walked back round to her seat and sat down, looking across her desk at Ned.

"When did Bay arrive in Vensille? I haven't heard his name before."

Ned lifted his head so that he could look at Paltiel again. One eye was closing and the rest of his face was a mess of blood and cuts and bruises. He looked at her with his good eye.

"Funny thing. He arrived the day before, off a boat from upriver, and I sent him to Hitton. Thought he might be a useful man."

"Useful, eh? Magic and killing. What does he look like?"

"Tall, broad. Soldier, maybe, long beard and hair. Carries a staff, knows how to use it."

"Hmm. And do you know where I might find this, 'Bay'?"
Ned shook his head slowly then stopped.

"Think he had a room at The Jewel, near the docks."

Paltiel smiled slowly to herself. Name, description, lodgings; all she needed, really.

"Boyer!" she shouted, "Get in here."

She waited until Boyer came in.

"Get rid of him," she said, nodding at Ned, "out on the streets." Boyer nodded and dragged Ned up by the armpits, forcing him to his feet and pulling him out of the office. Paltiel could hear the old man protesting and groaning all the way down the hallway as Boyer dragged him to the front door of the Watch House. Then the door banged shut, cutting off the noise.

Paltiel wasted no time. She strode out of her office and started issuing instructions.

"Boyer, find Snitz. Tell him I want you two plus six others ready to go as soon as I have briefed the Commander."

"You got what you needed, then, Captain?" asked Boyer.

Paltiel turned at the bottom of the stairs, one hand on the balustrade.

"I did, Constable, I did. Now go, and make sure Snitz knows to see me once he's assembled his squad."

At the top of the stairs Paltiel stopped briefly to straighten her tunic and arrange her armour, then she knocked on the Commander's door.

"Come in. Ah, Paltiel. What news on our mysterious killing spree?"

She closed the door behind her and walked into the office - a bright, well-furnished room completely unlike the dark, undecorated hole she shared with the other Captains on the ground floor - to stand before Astiland's huge desk. It truly was monstrous, a great slab of hardened mahogany, rumoured to contain a number of defensive charms and other nasty surprises for anyone mad or brave enough to confront the Commander in his own office.

"Old Ned gave me a name, a description and an address for the killer, sir. Seems it was an outsider, an Imperial newly arrived in the city."

"Newly arrived Imperial?" Astiland looked deeply sceptical, "Why would he just set about killing North Enders? What possible motive could he have?"

"Don't know, sir. Maybe his young family were killed by gang members and he came here seeking revenge." Astiland glared at her.

"Sir. Sorry."

"So where did he come from, this Imperial revenge-seeker?"

"Ned says upriver, arrived the day before the killings. Seems unlikely but Ned believed it was true."

"Well, nothing good ever comes downriver except wood and gold and iron, so maybe it's not completely false. Right, pick him up, bring him here. I want him in chains in the cells by morning. Try not to kill him but, if you have to, well, I don't think we'll lose any sleep over it, eh?" Astiland smiled at her and waved her away.

Paltiel took the hint. She saluted quickly and left the office sharply, heading back downstairs to find Snitz and his platoon. She found them gathering in the courtyard at the centre of the Watch House. There were eight of them and she was surprised to see Snitz and Boyer wearing heavy armour; the other six were only lightly armoured but all were wearing swords and shields as well as carrying their more usual truncheons.

"Are you expecting a war, Sergeant? This should be a simple arrest."

"Simple, Captain? He's killed five people, from what I heard, so I ain't taking no risks. Who are we after?"

Paltiel smirked.

"Have it your way. You should find him at The Jewel, you know it?" Snitz nodded.

"He's an Imperial, tall, broad, soldier maybe. Long hair, beard and..."

"...and he carries a staff. Green one, about so high," said Snitz, holding his hand up at about head height. He sighed.

"We met him yesterday at the House of Duval."

"What? You had him and you let him go?"

Snitz squirmed.

"Not exactly, Captain, no. We didn't know he was wanted but we tried to take him in 'cos he was, well, difficult, but he wasn't having any of it. He threatened us, Captain, on the street."

Captain Paltiel wasn't a woman given to fits of rage but as she stood there in the courtyard listening to Snitz she was getting pretty close to being furious. She walked up to him and prodded him in the chest with her finger.

"Threatened you? Did he use bad language as well? What are you, a bunch of bloody milkmaids? Get out there and find him, drag him back here in chains if you need to, but bloody get it done, Sergeant."

Snitz saluted.

"Yes Captain, right away." He turned and started shouting at his men, sending two of them to bring cross-bows from the armoury and Boyer to round up a few more constables.

Paltiel left them to it and returned to her office, still seething but unable to do much more. She considered accompanying Snitz but, ignorant though he might be, he was still a reasonably competent Sergeant and he should be able to handle an arrest, especially with seven or more constables in his squad. She sat down at her desk and picked up the report she'd been reading earlier.

The Watch were going to be a problem, Marrinek knew. If he couldn't put himself beyond their reach, and that was looking pretty unlikely at the moment, they were going to make life difficult for Duval and for him. He sat for a long time, thinking about the best way to approach the problem. Finally, he decided upon direct confrontation woven with elegant misdirection.

Grinning, he washed and dressed in the finest of the clothes that Madame Duval had so far acquired for him. With his hair tied back and his beard freshly oiled, he strolled out of the House of Duval looking for all the world like an Imperial nobleman taking his leisure. Bone Dancer tapped the road as he walked, heading along Eastside Bath to the main Watch house on the western side of the river. He stopped thirty yards from the entrance and stood for a few minutes in the shade of the overhanging first floor of a large house.

The watch house was a squat two-storey building set slightly back from the street behind a low wall of stone. An arched gateway led through to a courtyard. Then Sergeant Snitz emerged, leading a squad of maybe a dozen heavily armed guards onto the street. They marched quickly away, the crowds parting to let them through, and disappeared into the general hubbub. Now the courtyard and building were quiet, subdued even, as if emptied of their driving force.

Marrinek adjusted the set of his shoulders, gripped Bone Dancer lightly in one hand and sauntered daintily across the cobbles toward the gateway in the effete manner believed locally to be typical of Imperial nobles.

The courtyard was empty except for a pair of horses tied to a railing in the far corner. One side of the yard was clearly stables, the second appeared to be a dormitory of some sort. On the third side, to Marrinek's right, a wide door was propped open at the top of a short flight of steps and he picked his way carefully across the yard, avoiding the mud and manure.

Inside was bright, the hallway lit by tall windows opening into the yard, their shutters thrown back to let in the light. A corridor ran in both directions and, not knowing exactly where he was going, Marrinek picked a direction and began walking, looking for something that might guide him to Captain Paltiel.

"Oi, you," said a voice from behind him, "what are you doin' 'ere?"

Marrinek turned to find a young constable hurrying down the corridor toward him, a long truncheon held tightly in one hand. He coughed quietly then said in a heavy Imperial accent, "Officer, thank heavens you're here. I have an appointment with Captain Paltiel but I have completely lost my way. Would you be so kind as to direct me, please?"

The constable looked highly sceptical but he pointed along the corridor in the direction Marrinek had been heading.

"Captains' office is the last on the right. She's probably in there."

"Thank you, officer, you've been most helpful." Marrinek gave him a polite little bow and turned to continue along the corridor until he reached the last door. He knocked lightly then opened the door and went in.

"Captain Paltiel?" A short, blond-haired woman dressed partly in leather armour looked up from the document she had been reading and stared at him, open-mouthed, clearly surprised to see him.

"My name is Bay, Lord of Anceh in the Imperial Eastern Province. May I sit down?"

Paltiel, evidently unused to having wanted men present themselves at her desk, gestured vaguely toward the chair.

"Thank you." Marrinek moved to sit demurely on the indicated chair but stopped just short.

"Oh, my word! Captain, someone has been bleeding on your stone flags. I'll just move the chair a little..." He lifted the chair and carried it a foot closer to the door, placing it carefully back on the floor away from the small pool of drying blood. He took out a handkerchief and made a fuss of wiping down the arms and seat of the chair, then he sat down and looked at the Captain.

"Captain Paltiel. I am here on painful business, I fear you will not welcome my news."

Paltiel finally stirred and closed her mouth.

"Painful? I don't follow."

"Just last night I found one of your men, Sergeant Snitz I believe he was called, attempting to extort money from a close friend of mine. I very much fear that we exchanged harsh words during our thankfully brief meeting."

"'Attempting to extort'? What the hell are you talking about?"

"I believe it's a practice known as 'racketeering'. You are familiar with the term? It is, I understand, a most distasteful activity and one I am sure you will wish to stamp out amongst your fine body of officers."

"Protection money? That's it? That's what you wanted to talk to me about?"

"Why yes, Captain," said Marrinek, allowing his face to show surprise at her reaction, "that was all. Well, and to apologise, of course, for speaking harshly to your man. I am afraid I was forced to raise my voice to Sergeant Snitz before he agreed to leave. I very much regret that that was necessary, you understand, but he seemed committed to his course of action and was initially unwilling to deviate."

He paused, face radiating innocent concern.

"I'm sorry, Captain, were you expecting something more?"

"What about five dead men at the Snarling Goat, eh? What about the man you left dead in the common room after crushing his skull with that?" She pointed at Bone Dancer.

"Five dead men?" Marrinek looked shocked and contrived to sound shocked as well. "I am terribly sorry, Captain, but I think you must have me confused with someone else."

"So you weren't in the Snarling Goat the day before yesterday? You didn't strike down one man in cold blood then return later in the evening to kill the pub's owner and his bodyguard and two other men? You didn't throw someone off the roof of the Goat into the street forty feet below?"

"No, Captain, I did none of those things. I will admit to enjoying several drinks in one of the booths at the Snarling Goat. I must say I found it to be a fine establishment, a little rowdy at times, but generally most invigorating." He paused again to straighten his shirt. He stroked his beard absentmindedly.

"Tell me honestly, Captain. Do I strike you as the sort of

person who could kill one man, let alone five? I abhor violence in all its forms. I am a poet, an aesthete, an artist."

"And the staff? Is that an aesthetic accessory or do you use it to write your poetry?"

Marrinek gave a weak laugh.

"Aha ha, very droll, Captain, very droll."

Paltiel leaned forward and focussed power into her charm, pushing it toward Marrinek as she had done with Old Ned. She probed towards Marrinek with her power and then opened her mouth to ask another question.

"Oh no, Captain, I'm afraid *that* won't work at all."

Marrinek smiled and leaned forward a little, as if he were about to tell a secret.

"Where I come from the Watch does not extort money from innocent businessmen, respectable gentlemen are not accused of murder and nobody tries to coerce their guests, especially with charms so feeble that they are little more than children's toys. I am, quite frankly, insulted. I shall raise this matter with the Duke at our next meeting."

Paltiel looked at him in surprise, unsure of just what had gone wrong.

Marrinek flashed another quick smile then stood up and made to leave.

"Can I assume that you will deal with Sergeant Snitz and put an end to his racketeering? I would hate to think that this was something else I needed to discuss with his Grace."

Paltiel said nothing, still rattled by her failed attempt at coercion, and Marrinek took this to indicate assent.

"Good. Then our business here is concluded and I wish you a fine day. It has been a pleasure."

He offered her an elegant bow of the sort used in public between high-ranking equals of the Imperial Court. Then he swept out of the office, leaving the door open as he walked unhurriedly down the corridor, back toward the yard, staff tapping gently on the floor as he went.

Paltiel sat for a few minutes after 'Lord Bay' had left, replaying the interview in her mind. No matter how she looked at it, she couldn't make sense of what had happened. Then she shook her head and stood up. She walked quickly down the corridor and grabbed the first constable she found.

"Get down to the Jewel of Vensille, you know it?" she asked. The constable nodded.

"Find Sergeant Snitz and tell him that his man has gone and that he is to get his squad back here as quickly as possible. Got that?"

"Yes, Captain," said the constable, still nodding.

"Then go! Run!"

The constable ran through the watch house and disappeared while Paltiel went back to her office and sat down at her desk. For a few minutes, she sat with her head in her hands then she realised she was letting 'Lord Bay' get under her skin and she stood up, kicking the desk in her frustration.

She stamped around the watch house in a foul mood, waiting for Snitz and his squad to return from their aborted attempt to apprehend 'Lord Bay'. Was he a lord? She certainly didn't buy all that 'Knight Commander of his Majesty's third territorial infantry' rubbish. Whatever he was, he was bad news, and she wanted to know why he was in her city, when he would be leaving and what he planned to do in the meantime.

She stopped for a few minutes to watch another squad preparing for their patrol around the inner city, then found she was gripping the iron railings so hard her fingers were hurting. She released her grip, stretched her fingers and took a deep breath, trying to calm her thoughts.

Where the hell was Snitz? She had almost decided to go looking for him when he stamped back into the courtyard, leading his squad back in through the gate. He saw her, waiting for him, and came straight over, following her silently back to the Captains' office.

"What the hell is going on, Snitz?" she asked, as soon as the door was closed.

"Not sure what you mean, Captain," said Snitz, looking confused.

"Not five minutes after you'd left to pick up the suspect, he bloody turned up here, bold as brass. Sat in that chair and told me he was a poet, or some such rubbish, and didn't know anything about five deaths at the Snarling Goat."

"He came here? But why would he do that? He must have known we would be looking for him."

Paltiel sighed and some of her anger drained away.

"Apparently he came to complain about you extorting money from his friend. Madame Duval?"

Snitz nodded, slowly.

"That was the first time I met him. She would have paid if he hadn't been there."

"And when you met him, did he strike you as a sensitive soul, an artist or poet who might be troubled by a little blood on the floor?"

"No, Captain," said Snitz, shaking his head, "I thought he was a thug of some sort, a heavy that Madame Duval had hired to scare us off."

"Hired to scare us off? We're the fucking Watch! Did she think one man would stand in our way?"

Snitz thought back to the fight in the alleyway, playing it

over in his mind. How had the man dodged that first blow? It should have laid him out, nice and neat, ready to be dragged to the cells. And then there was the staff. He'd pointed it at them and knocked them all over, but how? Snitz cleared his throat.

"I think he has a magic staff." He sounded embarrassed, as if admitting the existence of such a thing might damage his image as a tough man of the streets.

"That great long stick he carries? Dark green wood, about six feet long, sharpened to a point at one end?"

Snitz nodded.

"It's a charm, a damn big one, so yes, he has a magic staff. But until he does anything with it nobody's going to object, right? It just looks like a normal staff."

Snitz shuffled his feet and grimaced, uncomfortably aware that the Captain was not going to be pleased.

"What? Do you know something else? Come on, Sergeant, spit it out."

"Well, Captain, it's just that we had a bit of a run-in with Bay and his staff in an alley when we first tried to arrest him. He sort of pointed it at us and knocked us all over."

Paltiel stared at him.

"He assaulted you with a charmed weapon and you didn't think to mention it?"

Snitz, not normally a man to hide from confrontation, leant back as Paltiel stood up from her seat, fists resting on the desk in front of her.

"He knocked you down in the street and walked away and you didn't think I'd want to know?"

Snitz squirmed but there was no way round it.

"Sorry, Captain, didn't want to trouble you," he said quietly. He was staring straight ahead now, using the blank expression of an experienced sergeant talking to his commissioned officer.

Paltiel stood stock still for a few more seconds then lowered herself slowly back into her seat. If she had known this earlier would it have made any real difference? She sighed.

"Right. So, he plays the tough guy on the streets and in front of his 'friends', he's familiar with violence and might have been a soldier, he has a charmed weapon that he isn't afraid to use and he can convincingly," she almost spat the word, "impersonate an Imperial nobleman when he wants to toy with the locals. We've been played, Snitz. I think he knows more about the deaths at the Snarling Goat than he's telling but we'll get nothing from him by going direct."

She paused to consider the next move.

"Get back out on the street, Snitz. Find out where 'Lord Bay' lives, where he eats, who he meets, where he gets his beard trimmed. I want him watched all day, every day, for as long as it takes. Make the arrangements and report to me each morning."

Snitz nodded.

"Yes, Captain. And should we arrest him?"

Paltiel paused again.

"If he steps out of line, yes. Otherwise, no, just let him run. And when we've got what we need we'll arrange a short trip to the execution yard for our 'Lord Bay'."

Snitz nodded again, smiling.

"Yes, Captain, and what about the payments we've missed? Should I visit Duval again?"

"No, we'll let him think he's won that one, for now. We'll take it all back, with interest, once we've dealt with 'Lord Bay'."

24

While Marrinek shopped, Fangfoss was having an entirely different meeting with his remaining lieutenants. They were in the room at the top of Trike's, sitting around a table set with beer and bread and beef. Marrinek and his demands were, of course, the major topic of conversation.

"Look, there's no way round it," said Fangfoss, "we either dance to Bay's tune or we get out of the game. He killed Hitton and Tam and three others without picking up a scratch and," Fangfoss paused and held up a hand to forestall the argument he could see Hines was about to make, "yes, I know, we've dealt with some mean bastards in the past but so fucking what? He's talented, right? He's," Fangfoss paused again, uncertain of how to continue before settling on, "very strong indeed."

"So that's it?" said Hines, in a disgusted tone, "We just give up and roll over, let him take what he wants and walk all over us?"

There was grumbling from around the table. Nobody

liked the course that Fangfoss was setting or the reasons for the change of direction.

"We've done well, these last few years. We've all got a bit put away, somewhere safe, right?" said Fangfoss. There was a general nodding of heads. They'd seen a lot of coin over the last few years, it was true, and all of them, even Chickie, had salted away a tidy sum, insurance against an uncertain future.

"But now things have changed and we've got to work at it a bit more. Frankly, I don't see an alternative, unless you want to take a stab at Bay directly. What would you say to that idea, Chickie?"

He looked at Chickie, lounging at the far end of the table, picking at his fingernails and occasionally eating pieces of bread smeared with beef dripping. Chickie looked around the table, the marks from his previous encounter with Marrinek showing on his bruised and battered face.

"I might pay to see it done," he said in a high pitched, almost comical voice, poking gingerly at his chin, "but only if I was damn sure it would get done and it wasn't going to be me that had to face him."

"But he's just one man! Why are we so scared of him? It makes no sense, no sense at all!" raged Hines, waving his plate-like hands in the air to emphasise his disgust.

"It makes perfect sense, dammit," said Fangfoss, slamming his fist on the table and making the plates jump and rattle. "Bay's fast and well-trained and talented. He's damn quick with that stick of his and he's bloody dangerous without it," Chickie nodded, rubbing his bruises again, "and he's got some sort of powered weapon that I haven't seen before. He used it on Hitton, drilled a neat hole right through his head, if you haven't forgotten."

Hines grumbled in his seat but didn't say anything else.

Hitton's death hung over the meeting like a bad smell, tainting everything. It wasn't just that Hitton had been popular or that he had made the Snarling Goat his own over several decades. It was that he had died in his own room where he should have been safe, killed by something none of them had seen before. The gentlemen's agreement with the Flank Siders and the Watch meant that they were all, generally, fairly safe if they kept things sensible. Hitton's death was the end of that agreement and they all knew it, even if nobody was talking about it.

Fangfoss looked around the table. Hines was the only one without talent but what he lacked in power he made for with muscle, a short temper and a genuine skill in non-lethal punishing violence. That was a skill that Fangfoss had ruthlessly exploited to build and maintain their current business empire. Hines was an excellent enforcer, untroubled by empathy or morality, but he was a middle-aged thug nearing the end of his useful lifespan. In the present company, surrounded by people much older than him who were likely to live for decades, possibly centuries longer, he seemed impatient, almost child-like in his naivety.

Trike, by contrast, was playing some sort of long-term game of his own that Fangfoss had never been able to understand. The bar was part of it but he had other hold-ings outside the city, just as Fangfoss did, and he would often spend several days or a week away from the city working on something that he wouldn't tell anyone about. Fangfoss half suspected that Trike had a family in one of the outlying villages but he just couldn't bring himself to believe it and Trike wasn't one for small-talk. It was clear that he wasn't pleased to be paying Bay but if it allowed them to escape the stultifying hand of the Watch he would follow the plan, especially as there wasn't an alternative at the moment.

Chickie, Fangfoss's second, was by far the most dangerous of the three. Deadly with knives and sword, he lived in the moment, spending much of his time gambling and whoring. He didn't so much plan for the future as charge headlong into it, screaming defiance and challenging it to disappoint. For all that, he was a realist and he could, on occasions, be patient if there was no other way. Giving up the gang's profits to pacify Bay was very much not what he wanted but after taking one beating he was reluctant to tangle again with the tall Imperial.

There was a lull in the conversation as all four ate. For a few moments, the only sounds were of men chewing and drinking. Then Fangfoss set down his tankard.

"Right. So we're agreed. Nobody likes it but we have to pay Bay until either he gets bored and moves on or we work out a way of killing him that doesn't put us all in the ground with him."

"Or we sell him to the Watch," said Trike, "whatever he's planning isn't going to go down well with Astiland, is it, so maybe we set him up somewhere public, tip off the Watch and let them deal with the problem."

Fangfoss looked at Trike, surprised. Trike never suggested things like this, he was more of a details person rather than a big picture man. If Fangfoss had suggested something Trike could be relied upon to tweak the idea till it worked but suggest the plan in the first place? No, that was not something that Trike ever did. This business must have upset him more than Fangfoss had imagined.

"It would need to be done with finesse. If it went wrong and he found out what we'd done..." Chickie didn't finish the sentence. They could all work out the likely consequences of failure.

Fangfoss thought about it for a moment before deciding against. Even if it was possible, he didn't want to do anything before he had his hands on the shock cannon. Until then he would play along, biding his time.

"Yes, well, we'll see what opportunities come along. In the meantime, let's just make sure we can cover our payments to him. As long as we give him enough to keep him happy we should still be able to make a decent living and with Hitton gone there are only the four of us dipping our fingers in the pot anyway. And if he can really sort out the Watch like he says he can..." he trailed off for a moment, thinking about a future where he didn't have to make huge payments to the Watch.

"Right, here's what I want you to do. Trike, keep the Goat running and make sure nobody gets any smart ideas about taking over till I say. Keep the Watch sweet, if you can, but don't pay them anything."

Trike nodded, although keeping the Watch sweet without giving them any money would be tough.

"Hines, Chickie. You need to keep on top of our people, make sure they're doing their jobs. If they're not bringing in enough coin, get them fixed or replace them. Squeeze them, make sure we're not missing opportunities. And get Old Ned and the other enforcers in here so I can speak to them."

He looked around.

"And then we have to work out what to do about the Flank Siders," he said, slipping it into a pause in the conversation like it was something easy, something he'd almost forgotten to mention, something nobody would really care about. There was silence, just for a moment.

"What about the Flank Siders?" asked Trike, his brow

furrowed like he was working at a bit of stubborn meat between his teeth.

Fangfoss looked away, embarrassed, and sighed. There was no avoiding it.

"Bay wants them gone."

"Gone?" said Hines sharply, "You mean dead?" He looked distinctly unexcited by the prospect.

"I mean gone, ended, absorbed, no longer active, consigned to history, unable further to trouble us," said Fangfoss, testily, his patience exhausted, "Bay wants us to take over their activities, all of them, put them out of business and run their rackets ourselves."

More silence, then Trike shrugged.

"Overdue, in my mind," he said lightly, "they're arrogant fuckers, up there in that gaming palace, lording it over everyone else like they was noble or something. Got them shitty little gigs on the west side, small-time protection and crap. Needs sorting, putting on the level."

Fangfoss stared at him for a moment.

"Apart from the gaming palace, how is their operation any different to ours, eh? What is it that makes us so great?"

Trike screwed up his face as if this was obvious.

"They're idiots," he said, you've 'eard the stories about 'ow they run their people, 'ow they keep things going. Not a patch on our lads, that's for damned sure," he finished proudly, as if pride was the most important thing in the world. Fangfoss raised an eyebrow but Trike just nodded and took a mouthful of beer.

"Right. Well, Bay can't take them out on his own," said Fangfoss, not believing it for a moment, "so we're going to help out. They work of out two bases, the Lighthouse and that crappy inn over on the west side, the Groaning Platter."

Trike snorted.

"'Orrible place, food's disgusting and you don't wanna know what they do to the beer."

"No, I don't," said Fangfoss sharply, "so shut the fuck up and let me outline the plan before we all die of old age." He took a deep breath and blew it out slowly. The others, long familiar with Fangfoss's temper and aware that he was close to the edge, stayed quiet.

"Right. Trike, get yourself over to the Flank Siders' palace tomorrow evening. Watch, don't enter, and make sure you've got a few bodies in case there're problems. Bay'll enter as a punter and start making threats. If it goes well, he'll just take over, no fuss, no blood, no problem. If not, well, we'll want to know that it's all gone wrong, right"

Trike nodded, already thinking it through, but Hines grimaced, not impressed.

"Can't we just leave him to it, boss? Maybe the Flanks'll do us a favour and kill the fucker."

"No," said Fangfoss, banging his hand on the table, "can you not think further than the end of the fucking day? Bay won't be here for ever. If he closes down the Flanks we'll pull double the cash or more and we'll all be better off. When he leaves, we'll be well set."

"How do you know he'll leave, though?" asked Hines, "What if he stays, leaching us dry forever?"

"Have you any idea what the Flanks pull in through that gaming hall? Even if Bay takes half, we'll still make at least twice as much," said Fangfoss, exasperated, "which means we're better off and we don't have to compete with those fuckers from the other side of the river." He looked around the table, daring anyone to object. "As soon as Bay enters the Lighthouse, we make our move at the Groaning Platter. That's up to you two," he said, looking at Chickie and Hines, "so take a few of the boys and squash the Flank Siders.

Break down their people, beat them, kill a few if you have to, but take control, yes? Run down their enforcers, make them offers and make sure they don't refuse."

"Got it, boss," said Chickie, nodding and smiling behind his moustaches, "consider it done."

"Right," said Fangfoss, somewhat relieved that at least one of his people was happy just to take orders, "well, that's it."

"Risky," said Hines, shaking his head doubtfully, "what if Bay fucks up while Chickie and Trike are breaking heads at the Platter?"

"Fuck risk," said Fangfoss, "we take risks every day. Get out there and get it done." He stopped and stared at Hines until the man nodded. Chair legs scraped across the floor as the four men stood up.

"And don't fuck it up," warned Fangfoss, wagging a finger at his lieutenants, "the stakes are high enough already and we've already lost Hitton."

Grim nods. They were a practical crew with long experience of the business but nobody liked to be reminded that Hitton had died at the hands of the new boss.

"Questions?" Nobody said anything.

"Right. Get going. And remember to get rid of the bloody corpses properly."

Fangfoss had been right. The Lighthouse was an impressive building, calling to mind in splendour, if not sheer scale, the pleasure palaces of Khemucasterill or the legendary love temples of Garrash Dar. It rose up from the streets, a building of dark stone chased with white marble and roofed in a mishmash of tile and slate. The doors and windows were decorated with intricately wrought iron from which hung lamps that burned in a dozen different colours. During the day it was a dull lump of a building but at night it came alive, lit from within and without by both everyday oil lamps and less common Powered lamps.

Marrinek stood for some time in the shadows of the buildings opposite, watching people enter the Lighthouse. A stream of well-dressed citizens made their way slowly past the door wardens, laughing and joking as they went. Some were followed by servants or bodyguards; none were alone, none carried weapons.

Eventually he nodded to himself and turned to Madame Duval, who waited patiently at his side, dressed in a fine, low-cut dress and wearing a net of pearls in her hair. She looked every bit a high-class escort, an obvious paid companion, dressed to impress and display. She looked at him and grinned, nervous and excited.

"Stick to the plan," said Marrinek quietly, "and don't worry about me if things get bloody."

She tittered, deep into her character.

"That's the thing about staking your life," she said quietly but in her normal voice, "there's really no need to worry about escape." She looked around then made a tiny adjustment to her dress, pushing her breasts up so that they were barely contained, then blew out a long breath. "I'm ready."

Marrinek nodded and held out his arm. Then he led them across the street, past the wardens and into the hallway.

They had only a moment to look around the dimly lit room before a hostess appeared in front of them. Dressed in an outfit that revealed far more than it hid, the woman ignored Madame Duval entirely and focussed on Marrinek.

"My lord," she said with a little bow, "is this your first visit to the Palace of Providence?"

Marrinek looked at her haughtily then let his gaze play across her body. He smiled.

"It is, my dear. I am newly arrived in town and seek entertainment."

The hostess smiled.

"We offer gambling of all sorts on the upper floor, fine food and wine on this floor and, downstairs, all the pleasures that might be brought from the flesh. I'm sure we have everything you need, Lord...?"

"Bay. Call me Bay. Gambling first, I think, then maybe the lower level, if you're going to be there?" He leered at her and winked.

"Whatever my lord desires," the hostess said with a friendly smile, obviously well-used to this sort of behaviour. For a moment, Marrinek thought he had made a winning impression. He almost smiled back, then he remembered where he was. He leered again instead and offered a lascivious grin.

"If you would step this way, my lord, we can setup your line of credit," said the hostess, leading Marrinek and Duval into a side room and closing the door behind them. The room was small with a single table against the far wall. On the table sat a large iron box with a fist-sized hole in the front face.

Marrinek peered at it suspiciously, suddenly worried that he knew what was coming.

The hostess stood beside the box and gestured toward the hole.

"The House of Providence values strength, my lord, and so we test every new visitor when they first arrive," she paused to glance at Duval, "every new visitor with talent, at least. The machine reads your strength, my lord, and we advance credit based on that strength. Please."

Marrinek eyed the machine suspiciously, his smile gone, his demeanour suddenly serious. Then he sighed and said, in heavily accented Gheel, "Well, if I must. How does it work?"

"Put your hand in here, my lord, and grasp the bar within. Then focus as much power as you safely can into the bar. The machine will do the rest."

Marrinek hesitated. This hadn't been part of his plan. Then he coughed, took a sudden step forward and thrust his hand into the box, grabbing the bar tightly. He screwed his face into an expression of extreme concentration and dribbled power into the bar, enough to light a fire charm. He held it for a few seconds then released as a wave of nausea washed over him. He staggered backward, not having to fake his sudden illness.

"Thank you, my lord," said the hostess with a slight smile, "if you just wait a moment while my colleague..." She paused, although Marrinek couldn't see why or which colleague they were waiting for. Then a hatch opened and a tray slid though into the room. The hostess plucked a slim card from the tray and held it out to Marrinek.

"There you go, my lord. This charm is keyed to you and will grant you access to your account at the Palace of Providence. You will be able to draw credit or access your funds at any time by focussing power into the charm to prove your identity." She smiled and gestured toward the hallway as the door silently opened.

"And now you are ready for the Palace, my lord. I trust that you will enjoy yourself."

"Are you alright?" hissed Duval as she and Marrinek sauntered casually down the hallway and into the hall beyond. Then she forgot all about her question as she looked around and took in the sights.

The room was part restaurant, part entertainment, part awe-inspiring backdrop to the rest of the activities. The ceiling was high, the floor low, and from the viewpoint at the top of the stairs that swept down to the main floor, Marrinek and Duval had a clear view across huge space.

Near the walls, diners sat at tables small and large. Waitresses threaded their way between the tables delivering food and drink. Musicians played on a little plinth at the edge of the stage that dominated the centre of the room, set even lower than the main floor. On the stage, tumblers bounced and leapt as above them artistes on trapezes swung and flew.

Around the room, galleried landings clung to the walls, filling the space and overhanging towards the stage so that even at the highest level, patrons could hear the music and watch the acts on the stage. Marrinek was impressed, despite his cynicism and his fear that Vensille might have little to offer by way of entertainment.

"Maybe Fangfoss was right," he muttered, "maybe this really isn't possible." There was a sharp pain in his ankle as Madame Duval kicked him vigorously.

"There's no backing out now," she hissed, "so let's just get on with it, shall we?"

Marrinek was still for a moment then he nodded. He took Duval's arm again and set his shoulders, tilting his head a little so that he looked down on everyone they passed.

"Come, my dear," he said in nasally accented Gheel, "let

us gamble and gambol." Then he led Madame Duval to the gaming floor.

Their first stop was the credit booth where Marrinek was required to produce his charmed account card. The cashier took his name and passed across a small pile of low-value chips.

"Compliments of the house, my lord."

Marrinek looked at the pile and sniffed.

"It would seem that my strength is poorly rated," he said, glancing disdainfully at the meagre value of his gaming chips, "but I trust I can buy more?"

"Of course, my lord," said the cashier nodding, "we can accept any readily exchanged medium."

"Silver," said Marrinek, pulling three tightly wrapped rolls of coins from a pouch at his belt.

The cashier unwrapped the coins, checked them quickly, then nodded and pushed across a rather larger stack of chips in a neat container of bamboo.

"And there's a small bonus in there, my lord, in appreciation of your first deposit with us. Good luck at the tables." He smiled as Marrinek scooped up his chips and weighed the bamboo box in his hand.

"Where first, my lord?" asked Madam Duval in a sultry voice, leaning her head in against Marrinek's shoulder as they turned back toward the gaming tables. They wandered for a few minutes amongst the other players, taking note of the games and watching how they were played.

Eventually Marrinek stopped at the edge of the gaming area and pulled Madame Duval close so that he could talk quietly to her.

"That one," he said, nodding at a table where players were watching a ball falling through a grid of pins and betting on which number it would land on, "put about a tenth of the chips on a number, any number, and increase the stakes if you win."

She nodded and took the chips from him. They strolled over to the table and she sat down in a vacant chair, Marrinek standing behind. She smiled at the croupier then spent a few moments arranging her chips before her on the table before placing her first bet.

"Green," she said, pushing a dozen chips into a coloured square. The croupier nodded as other players placed their bets then he flicked a lever to shoot a small steel ball into the top of the board. The players watched as it pinged across the board, falling steadily toward the numbered and coloured slots at the bottom. Madame Duval squealed in delight as the ball dropped neatly into a green number.

"Green and six," announced the croupier, scraping losing bets from the table and pushing small piles of winnings towards the lucky players. Madame Duval blinked as her stake was returned fourfold.

"Four colours, one hundred and four numbers, twenty-five of each colour and four numbers coloured black that can't be bet on," she muttered, looking again at the slots, "and so let's try green again."

She doubled her stake and stared at the board. Again the croupier flicked his lever and again the ball rolled and pinged and bounced across the board, falling steadily downwards until it landed, again, on green.

"Green and twenty-four," said the croupier, doling out more winnings. Madame Duval pulled in her chips and waggled her fingers with the sheer excitement of winning.

"Red this time," she said, pushing two dozen chips onto the red panel.

"And I think I'll join you," said the tall man seated to her left, "since with two wins in a row you're clearly onto something." He leant forward and pushed a rather larger pile of high value chips onto the red square, then he sat back and grinned. "Let's hope your luck holds, yes?"

The croupier stood before them, stony faced, as the other players laced their bets. Madame Duval was practically bouncing in her seat with the excitement, even though she knew that Bay was doing something to make the balls drop in their required places.

"No more bets," said the croupier, flicking the lever to begin the game. The ball curved around the board and fell toward the pegs, jumping and leaping and falling.

"Come on, come on," urged the tall man, his fists clenched as he willed the ball to land in a red number.

Madame Duval held her breath, almost too sacred to watch, until the ball fell, as predicted, onto red.

"Red and twenty-six," announced the croupier. The tall man grinned broadly and nodded as the croupier pushed his winnings forward.

"A tidy sum," said Marrinek, forcing the accent and smiling happily as Madame Duval chose her next bet. The tall man nodded, stacking his chips and preparing his next stake.

"Where next, my lovely?" he asked, glancing at Madame Duval as she prepared her own stake.

"Back to green, I think," she said, smiling as she pushed across three dozen chips. The tall man nodded along and added his stake. Again they watched the ball, again the croupier paid out heavy winnings to Madame Duval and the tall man.

Marrinek, standing behind, released the tiny portion of power he had focussed and looked around, wondering if anyone had yet noticed his cheating. There were no obvious signs but then he didn't really expect to see them, not yet, anyway. He watched Madame Duval place another bet and this time he kept his power to himself, letting the ball fall without diversion.

"I win again!" said Madame Duval, clapping her hands and dragging her winnings toward her rapidly growing stack of chips.

Marrinek looked away, grinning. Maybe this was going to be a lucky evening. He stayed out of the next round as well and Madame Duval lost, along with the tall man who was now mirroring her every bet. When he turned back, he saw the stakes had doubled again and the ball was already falling. He pulled a tiny portion of power, so small as to be undetectable to anyone standing even very close, and placed the merest slither of Flow onto the board so that the ball bounced at last onto a red number. Madame Duval again pulled her winnings into her growing stack.

The croupier swapped out her chips for a smaller number of higher value tokens and Madame Duval kept going, placing bets randomly on the four colours. Marrinek clapped along with the delighted crowd every time she won and commiserated when she lost but, as the evening wore on, the pile of chips grew steadily until she had before her a small fortune.

"Shall we take a break, my dear?" said Marrinek after the croupier had changed up their tokens for a third time. The table was busy now as other players crowded around to follow Madame Duval's bets and Marrinek was starting to worry that things might be getting out of hand. The tall man had left, taking his winnings and cashing out, but other players had replaced him and all were now nursing large piles of chips. "I could do with something to eat and maybe a drink."

Madame Duval sighed and reluctantly scraped her chips into a small bag then stood up from the table. She smiled at the other players and thanked the croupier then stepped away and took Marrinek's arm.

"That was fun," she said as they walked away from the tables and back toward the restaurant, "what's next?"

"Food," said Marrinek quietly, "and a little rest. This much success is exhausting."

They ate quickly at a small table with a distant view of the stage. The artistes still flew overhead but now their costumes had changed to become revealing almost to the point of not being present at all.

While they ate, Marrinek described his conversation with Captain Paltiel at the watch house.

"I think it's safe to say that she hadn't expected my visit. Not sure if it will have made any difference, though."

Madame Duval picked at her food, her appetite strangely absent.

"I'm surprised you think it's even worth the effort of trying. Everybody just pays the Watch and they leave us alone; you're the only person I've heard of since I've been in town who has refused to pay. Well, the only person who's still walking."

"Fun, isn't it?" said Marrinek, grinning.

Madame Duval shook her head, sadly.

"I know what you said and it would be nice to think that we could run an honest business without paying the Watch, but I still don't believe it'll happen."

Marrinek leant forward, serious now.

"Maybe, maybe not, but either way we're changing how things are done in this city. The North Enders, the Watch and now the Flank Siders."

"And after that? What will you do once you control both gangs?"

Marrinek ignored the question, watching as a new troupe of acrobats bounced onto the stage and began their routine.

"I'm sorry, what was that?" he asked suddenly, aware that he had missed something that Madame Duval had said.

"Never mind," she said, shaking her head, "it wasn't important."

They watched the show for a little longer, taking in the sights. It was a well done and Marrinek was impressed, even though he'd now had an hour to grow used to the dim light and to soak in the atmosphere. Madame Duval had also adjusted, no longer gazing around with wide eyes but looking more carefully and noting specific details.

"It's much like my own house," she said as a waiter cleared plates and delivered a fresh course of meat and fish, "although rather larger. They're selling sex and food and entertainment, that's all, but they're doing it on a grand scale."

"And at the top of the market," said Marrinek, watching as a group of young nobles strutted in from the street and headed straight for the gambling floors, their wealth advertised by their clothes and bearing.

"Have we got enough, yet?" murmured Madame Duval as Marrinek totted up their winnings, "It's not that I'm not enjoying myself, of course, but…"

"A good start but not even close. For this to work, we'll have to ramp things up a bit." He shoved the chips back into the bag and stood up, holding out his arm for Madame

Duval. Then they went back into the gaming hall, heading back to the falling ball game.

The crowd of players had changed and thinned and Madame Duval took a seat at the end of the row, nodding familiarly to the croupier. He eyed her warily but let her place her bet.

"Number twelve," she said quietly, pushing a quarter of her chips out onto the board. Marrinek raised an eyebrow in mock surprise, leaning forward as the other players laid their own bets.

"Are you sure, my dear? That's a rather large bet..." he said, just loud enough for the croupier to hear. Madame Duval laughed.

"Trust me, you'll see."

They watched as the croupier started the game.

"Red and fourteen," said the croupier, as Madame Duval's face fell. He scraped her stake across the table.

"Huh," said Madame Duval, daunted but not yet defeated. She carefully racked her chips, dividing them into three piles, then she pushed one of the piles across the table onto number forty-six.

"Are you sure, dear?" asked Marrinek, concern leaching into his voice. Madame Duval said nothing and together they watched the ball bounce and skip across the pins.

"Yellow, seventy-four."

Madame Duval coughed and looked over her shoulder at Marrinek. He shrugged and looked away. She turned back to the now clear table, set her shoulders, and pushed all her remaining chips onto number forty-six. Marrinek watched, focussing his power, then all eyes flew to the board as the ball was released. It fell, flicked across the board by the pins it struck, bounced on a random path by gravity and little pieces of wood, helped ever so slightly by minuscule pieces of Flow carefully positioned and quickly removed.

"Red and forty-six," said the croupier, eyeing Madame Duval's huge stake with open suspicion. Madame Duval shrieked with delight and turned to hug Marrinek, giving every impression of being utterly surprised. She kissed him hard, playing up to her role, then turned back to the table, flushed with the victory, as the croupier pushed across a stack of chips of the highest value.

Madame Duval pulled her chips into a pile in front of her and sat, staring at it. The value was colossal, a huge return on their initial stake, more than she had ever dreamt she might possess.

Around the table her fellow players clapped politely, buoyed by her success even if they hadn't backed the same numbers or colours. How much had they won? She sat out the next round, too busy admiring her sudden fortune to place a bet.

Eventually she felt Marrinek touch her on the shoulder and she turned.

"Let's take another break," said Marrinek quietly, and together they stepped away from the table, their winnings jingling in Madame Duval's bag and a crowd of disappointed well-wishers begging them to return. Marrinek laughed politely and gave them an elegant bow before turning away, his arm around Madame Duval's waist.

At the edge of the gaming floor, he pulled Madame Duval into an empty booth and tugged the bell cord to summon a waitress. They sat in silence until their drinks arrived, then Marrinek leaned over the table so that he could speak softly.

"We're being watched," he said, allowing a leer to creep across his face as he pretended to be captivated by Madame

Duval's bosom, "but don't look around," he said as a look of sudden fear crossed her face.

"Management's thugs, I think," he said quietly, "which means we're almost at the next stage. You ready?"

He looked at her as she sat, a little fearful, in the booth. Then she nodded, just a small jerk of her head.

"Good," said Marrinek, tossing back his drink, "because they're coming over."

A huge shape loomed suddenly in the entrance to the booth. Meaty hands fell on either side of the booth's entrance, blocking their escape, as the figure leant down to speak to them.

"My lord, my lady," a voice said politely as the heavy head nodded to each of them in turn, "Mr Artas, the proprietor, would like to speak to you. If you could come this way...?" The figure straightened up and stepped back, one arm outstretched to guide them away from the booth. Behind him, other figures lurked.

Marrinek glanced briefly at Madame Duval then stood up and affected a heavy Imperial accent.

"Well, I don't know why this Artas person wishes to speak to me," he said with an air of complete confusion, "but by all means, lead on."

He stepped out of the booth and waited for Madame Duval to take his arm. Then they followed their new acquaintance through a door between two booths and down a long flight of narrow stairs.

At the bottom, they turned onto a broad, dank corridor before stopping outside a large pair of double doors.

"Good luck," whispered their huge guide, who opened the doors and ushered them into the dimly lit space behind.

The doors behind closed and, for a moment, all was dark and quiet.

Then powered lamps were activated and a roar rose, as if from a hundred delighted throats. Madame Duval clutched at Marrinek in sudden fear.

"The pit," she hissed, looking around, eyes wide with terror, "they know!"

Marrinek looked around, searching for a way out. Then a gong boomed out across the huge space and the audience fell silent.

"Everyone is welcome at the Palace of Providence," came a loud voice from above. Squinting, Marrinek could just about make out a figure on a plinth amidst the audience where he might have a clear view of everything that took place below.

"Everyone is welcome," the voice repeated lightly, "everyone except cheats and thieves." The audience screamed their hatred and Marrinek looked around at the smooth stone walls that rose from the floor of the pit, ten feet tall. The pit itself was maybe thirty feet across with a second set of doors in the opposite wall and a floor covered in grubby sand. Marrinek scuffed at the surface with his toe and found hard wooden boards beneath.

"So now we play a different game," the voice continued, "a game where winner takes all when they leave the pit!" The audience roared their approval as Marrinek bared his teeth.

"I thought this sort of thing was outlawed?" he hissed at Madame Duval.

"It is! What difference does that make?" Her voice was small and angry and she clung to Marrinek, even as he struggled to remove his coat.

"There are no rules in the pit," the voice said, "except the survival of the strongest. Let the contest begin!"

Marrinek succeeded finally in pushing Madame Duval away so that he had time to throw off his coat.

Then the doors opposite opened and two huge men appeared, one armed with sword and shield, the other with a long spear. Both word helmets and breastplates of shining steep and the strode onto the sand as if they had been born to it. Their arrival was cheered by the ecstatic crowd and the two men played up to it, holding up their arms to the gallery and waving to elicit greater applause.

"Stay behind me," Marrinek said, shoving Madame Duval away from the circling men. He watched them for a few seconds as the voice droned on, introducing the house champions and listing their achievements in the pit. Sensing that his odds were rapidly deteriorating, Marrinek drew his knife, a pitiful thing compared to the long blade carried by the champion on the left, and threw himself suddenly forward.

The crowd saw immediately and the champions turned from their adoration to see Marrinek already close. The spearman turned quickly, more quickly than Marrinek might have expected from a man of his bulk, but not quickly enough to bring his weapon to bear.

Marrinek crashed into him and knocked him down. The man landed hard and the impact jolted the spear from his grip. Marrinek rolled desperately away and scrabbled for the spear, forcing himself up as quickly as he could. He backed away as the spearman levered himself to his feet, a look of rage on his face.

"First touch to me," said Marrinek, piling on the scorn and emphasising his accent. He danced backward, laughing and swinging the spear, before stopping in front of Madame Duval, spear set as if it were a staff, head facing forwards.

The swordsman screamed something from behind the faceplate of his helmet but the spearman stood as still as a statue, less confident without his weapon. He took a step to his left, maybe hoping to encircle Marrinek, but a sudden stab of pain made him stop. He reached around and found the handle of Marrinek's little knife jutting from the flesh of his lower back. The man yelled as he dragged the knife free and brandished it, foolishly. The crowd murmured their surprise then roared their support as the swordsman charged.

Marrinek jabbed with the spear and the swordsman pulled up short, swinging his weapon but not able to get close enough. The spearman screamed as he too ran at Marrinek but he hadn't circled far enough and the spear swung swiftly across to strike him on the side of the head as soon as he came close. Down he went again, sprawling in the sand at Marrinek's feet.

But that made an opening for the swordsman, who ran in swinging his blade. Marrinek dropped the spear and pushed power into his shield, catching the falling sword and pushing it away. The swordsman, off balance, staggered aside as the crowd gasped in surprise and shouted their anger.

Marrinek pulled more power and struck out with a thick cord of Flow, knocking the swordsman from his feet. To the crowd it seemed that the swordsman had stumbled and they yelled encouragement to their hero.

Marrinek scooped up the spear as the swordsman scrambled back, his face now showing fear. Shield up, he circled away from the jabbing spear, fending it off as best he could.

Marrinek pulled power to prepare another attack and suddenly the nausea was back. Head swimming, he staggered backwards and tripped on the outstretched legs of the spearman.

The swordsman, no stranger to taking advantage of sudden turns of fate, sprang quickly forward, sword swinging.

Marrinek shuffled back, spear abandoned, as the swordsman came on quickly. Roaring, the man slashed at Marrinek's legs, throwing heavy strokes that raised clouds of sand and splinters from the floor.

Then there was a yell, a new voice. The swordsman jerked around in surprise as Madame Duval swung the spear. The blow crashed into the man's upper arm and his numbed fingers lost their grip on the sword. The swordsman roared and switched direction, batting Madame Duval aside with the shield so that she fell against the wall of the pit, unconscious.

Marrinek stood now, fingers curling around the hilt of the sword, and he hefted it as the swordsman turned back to face him.

The spearman was also trying to stand, clutching at the sand as he tried to push himself to his knees. Marrinek kicked him in the face, snapping his head back. The man slumped back down again.

The swordsman circled around, eyeing Marrinek. Then, as the crowd roared, he charged, shield up. Marrinek swung the blade but his timing was off and it clanged uselessly from the man's shield. Then he was down, the swordsman on top, sword arm pinned to the floor beneath the shield and the man was punching him again and again.

Marrinek punched back but his blows were feeble and the man shrugged them off.

With a desperation borne of real fear, Marrinek snatched for his Power, grappling with it, wrestling it into submission. A stinging blow to the head rattled his teeth and caused him to see stars but then he had it.

With a roar, he shoved a sharp needle of Flow at the swordsman, once, twice, three times.

The punches stopped and the man peered down, confused. Then blood dribbled from his mouth and he collapsed, dropping his full weight onto Marrinek.

The crowd went silent, unable to see what had happened. Then Marrinek pushed the corpse off and it flopped onto its back, blood everywhere. He heaved himself to his feet, clothes scuffed and torn and covered in blood.

For a moment, nothing happened. Then, as the crowd cheered their new hero, Marrinek walked wearily across the pit, retrieving his knife on the way, to kneel by Madame Duval.

She groaned as he touched her face, then opened her eyes and sat up. She looked up at him for a moment, then turned away and threw up on the sand.

"Better?" asked Marrinek, helping her to her feet.

"What happened?" she whispered, leaning in close, ignoring the blood.

"You saved my life," said Marrinek wearily, "and now I think it's time..."

The double doors opened again and Marrinek swung around to face them, Madame Duval slipping behind him.

"Cheats cannot prosper at the Palace of Providence," said the voice as three more men, heavily armoured and with the look of professional soldiers, came onto the floor of the pit and spread out. The crowd didn't seem to like that so much and their cheers were interspersed with boos and calls to release Marrinek and Madame Duval.

Marrinek scooped the sword from the floor of the pit as the three men drew their own weapons and edged forward, shields raised. He stretched, standing up straight to emphasise his height, then pushed Power into his bracer and turned to face the three soldiers.

"Who dies first?" he said casually, rolling the sword in his hand. Then he lashed out with Flow, striking the soldiers on the left and right, knocking them from their feet before leaping towards the one in the middle. Startled, the man stepped back and Marrinek hooked his foot with another column of Flow.

All three men crashed noisily to the ground and the crowd laughed, unable to see how it had happened.

"Are these your best?" shouted Marrinek above the crowd's laughter, "I have had better threats from unpaid whores!" The crowd laughed again, even though the joke was weak. Marrinek flicked out more columns of Flow to knock the three men back down again then held up his sword. "Is this not victory?"

One of the soldiers tried to crawl away and Marrinek strolled forward and planted his boot firmly on the man's back, forcing him into the sand.

"With men such as these," he said, casually flicking a column of Flow into the shoulder of a half-risen soldier to spin him back to the ground, "who needs clowns?" He tossed the sword away and cut the power to his shield then kicked the legs from one of the soldiers and sent a column of Flow to knock the other two back to their feet, slamming their heads against the planks of the floor to keep them from rising again.

"Ladies and gentlemen," he said to the crowd as they quietened, "I thank you for your time and your kind attention." He gave them an elegant, courtly bow, turning to ensure all had been honoured, then he collected his coat from the floor, shrugged himself back into it and brushed off the sand. He smiled and held out his arm to Madame Duval, who took it with as much grace and poise as she could manage.

He walked toward the double doors and gave them a shove so that they swung silently open. Then they strode from the pit, the crowd's applause following them into the corridor.

"That's far enough," said the thug who had escorted them from the booth. He was standing in the corridor, a long blade clenched in his fist, colleagues behind him.

"The boss wants to see you," he said, before adding when Marrinek remained still, "I mean he really does want to see you." He waggled the blade. "It's that way. We'll follow."

Marrinek relaxed a little as they climbed up from the lower levels back into the main part of the Lighthouse. He'd come prepared for a scuffle but full-on fight-to-the-death in a gladiatorial combat ring was not something he had expected. Up here, where the bulk of the guests were, things were bound to be more civilised.

Eventually they came to a private hallway on the top floor where the music of the evening's entertainment could be dimly heard from below. Marrinek reckoned they were somewhere above the central stage, up beyond the crawl spaces and the finely decorated ceilings.

After a brief pause, the heavy doors opened and they were shown into the private study of Lorn Artas, leader of the Flank Side gang.

He sat behind a desk in the plushly decorated room, the very picture of a successful merchant, basking in great wealth and long-familiar power.

Artas leant back in his leather-bound chair as Marrinek and Madame Duval walked into the room. There were no chairs for guests so Marrinek guided Madame Duval to a long sofa set against a wall and laid her, still shaking, on its cushions.

"Lord Bay," said Artas, "what made you think you could steal from me?" His tone was casual, almost friendly, but there was steel concealed within. Marrinek had wondered, on the walk from the pit, how they had spotted his cheating but it didn't really matter.

"Let me tell you a story," said Marrinek in his affected 'noble' accent as he cast around for somewhere to sit. He settled on a heavy armchair, spinning it around to face Artas then draping himself across it, looking for all the world as if her were taking his leisure in a private club. The thugs shifted uneasily and one pushed himself off the wall where he stood, a long club dangling from his fist.

"Our hero, let's call him Edwin," said Marrinek, ignoring the thugs to focus on Artas, "comes to the city in search of wealth and happiness. He works hard and, from a low beginning, he prospers at his craft because demand is high and people find Edwin pleasant to work with. Soon, he has a house of his own and a growing business and his mind turns to the courting of the shopkeeper's daughter, who would, in Edwin's mind, make a fine wife."

Madame Duval lay on the sofa listening to Marrinek's tale, unable to see where he was going with it and too scared to interrupt.

"Well, Edwin's luck in love is as solid as his skill at business and within a few months the pair are wed. Their first-born arrives a year later, a strong boy they name Loft, after his maternal grandfather. Brothers and sisters follow and before Edwin knows it, he is the patriarch of a huge, sprawling family whose business interests span the city and spread their tentacles across the country.

"As the decades roll on, Edwin becomes Mayor and proved a capable, much-loved politician, equally adept in the council chamber as the counting house. He lives to see his city grow beyond all expectations as his benevolent rule and carefully husbanded wealth transform the lives of the people he knows and loves. When he dies, the city holds a great funeral for their beloved leader and the streets are thronged with mourners and well-wishers from across the country, all gathered to pay their respects to the great man and his still-beautiful widow."

Marrinek sat back, smiling, as his tale came to an end. He looked around at the blank faces of his audience and frowned.

"Do you not see?" he asked Artas, "Do you not understand the point I am trying to make?"

He looked around at the blank faces of the thugs then shook his head.

"Are you saying that you're this 'Edwin' character?" asked Artas softly, a frown on his face and menace in his voice.

"What? No, of course not. Do I look like a benevolent ruler?"

"Then who, me?" said Artas.

Marrinek snapped his fingers and grinned, a strangely worrying expression amongst the serious threats of Artas's thugs.

"Now he's getting there," said Marrinek happily, as if he were a teacher pleased at the progress of a troublesome pupil, "but no, you're not Edwin either," he said, now sad, as if his favoured pupil had suffered some tragic accident, "the point of the story is that you might have been Edwin, had your decisions not brought you here, to this point, instead. Now, though," Marrinek paused and raised his arms, shaking his head in sorrow as he contemplated the future.

"Your time runs short," rumbled Artas, scowling at Marrinek as he leant back in his chair. The wood creaked under his bulk as the ganglord stared at Marrinek, who lounged in his chair as if they were discussing a pleasant evening's gambling.

Marrinek stood up, wincing slightly from the pain in his battered ribs. Artas stood as well, moving lightly for someone so large. The thugs also came alert and the tension ratcheted upwards as hands crawling toward weapons that had never been far from reach.

"I'm going to make you an offer," said Marrinek, "it's a good offer, but I'll make it only once. Let's see where a little reasoned discussion might take us."

Long Carp was running for his life through the alleys of the west side of Vensille. He had absolutely no fucking clue why the North Enders were chasing him, or even what they were doing this side of the river, but chasing they most definitely were and he had no intention of hanging around to find out what they wanted. He barged past a vendor of colourful fruit - he didn't stop to check what sort as the man yelled abuse at his back - then lost his footing in the mud and crashed head first into a pile of assorted manure.

He heaved himself out of the mess and wiped some of it from his face before shouts from back down the alley spurred him on. The fruit vendor was laughing hard as Long Carp turned a corner and hared off, heading for the sleazy pub that was the base of the Flank Side Gang.

His pursuers seemed to be having no problems staying

upright and as he dodged along the alley he threw glances over his shoulder. He was younger and faster but in the tight twisted spaces between the houses he couldn't get clear. Head down, he charged along the alley, jumping from one side to the other in search of firm footing and splashing through the muck when he had to. He checked his lead as he reached the corner - better, but not good enough - then ran straight into a large man wearing a butcher's apron coming around the corner from the other direction.

Long Carp bounced off the butcher, who staggered back against a wall, and fell onto his backside in the dirt and slime of the alley. He looked back down the alley as the butcher loomed over him, then scrabbled desperately to get his feet under him as two men yelled and charged at him. Barely standing, he pushed past the surprised butcher, fingers of one hand grabbing at the wall as he tried to drag himself forward and into a full run. He slipped again in the muck of the open sewer that ran down the middle of the alley and fell flat on his face. Spitting muck, he pushed himself up and scrambled onto a low wooden bridge laid across the alley then stood up and looked back.

The butcher was still standing at the corner of the alley, just fifteen feet away, watching him and shaking his head when the first of Long Carp's pursuers came around the corner and collided with him, knocking him to the ground. The second came more slowly and managed to jump the two men sprawled on the ground, sliding to a stop at the edge of the sewer, halfway between the corner and the bridge. He saw Long Carp and held up his hand, palm forward.

"Just want to talk, friend, that's all. No need to go runnin' around all over the place."

The second man had disentangled himself from the

butcher and was moving up the alley to stand beside his friend. The butcher, having picked himself up, looked around unhappily before deciding he wanted no part of whatever violence was about to strike; he disappeared around into one of the houses and slammed the door behind him. Long Carp watched him go, wondering if his last chance of help had also just disappeared as well.

Long Carp edged backwards as the two men edged forward. He stopped when his heel reached the edge of the narrow bridge.

"Go on then, talk," said Long Carp, eyes darting from side to side as he tried to watch both of the men in front of him and look for a way out of the alley, "What've you got to say?"

Pursuer One smiled, displayed two rows of rotten brown teeth.

"Not here, lad, somewhere more private. Why don't you come to the Snarling Goat and we'll have a nice chat over a mug of beer."

Long Carp goggled at the man. Cross the river to drink in the Snarling Goat? The man must be mad if he thought he'd get Long Carp over the river and into the stronghold of a rival gang for a 'chat'.

"Yeah, right, just give me a moment," said Long Carp, then he turned and jumped off the bridge, landing in a rare dry patch. He sprinted down the rest of the alley for all he was worth, the sounds of swearing and continued pursuit coming from behind.

At the next corner, he grabbed at the edge of a house and swung around into an even narrower alley, maybe three feet across and dark from overhanging buildings, then he bounced off the walls and took the next left to burst into the small square outside the Flank Siders' main watering hole, the Groaning Platter. He would find friends here and show these two North Enders what a mistake they'd made by chasing him so far into his own territory.

But the man sitting outside the pub on a chair, looking very much at ease with a mug of ale in one hand and a cold meat pie in the other, wasn't one of usual toughs who worked the door. And the dozen other men drinking with him also weren't Flank Siders. Long Carp skidded to a halt in front of them, stopping just a few feet from the bench they were using as a table. He could see that the man with the pie was tall, even though he was sitting down. He had a long moustache, oiled and twirled to fine points, and he was dressed in clean trousers and shirt; this wasn't a man who had been chasing people through the mud and dirt of the west side of the city.

Long Carp turned as his two pursuers came around the corner and stopped just behind him. They were too close, now; no escape that way. He sighed.

"Fuck."

"Gave you a good run, did he?" said Moustache to the men now standing behind Long Carp. One of them, bent almost double and leaning on his knees with his head down, just waved a hand and focussed on his breathing. The other, younger and in better shape but still spattered in filth from the alley, nodded.

"He's quick. Maybe you'd like to run after him for a bit, Chickie, see how much fun it is."

"No no," said Chickie, raising his mug in mock salute, "I'll leave that to you chaps and just concentrate on my pie and beer, thanks all the same." He turned back to Long Carp, looking him up and down. What he saw was a man in his early twenties, tall, medium build, long dark hair, poorly dressed and covered head to toe in shit and mud and muck from the alley.

"And what a sight you are," said Chickie to Long Carp, chuckling, "looks like you've led my friends on a right old chase. Is there any shit left in those alleys or did you use your shirt to clean them out?"

Long Carp swallowed and straightened up. He looked around but there was nowhere to run and there were no friends in sight.

"I'm Chickie. I'd shake your hand but, well, maybe I'll wait till you've had a bath. What's your name, son?"

Long Carp looked around again. He knew Chickie by reputation, had even seen him from afar a few times, but to say he was surprised to find him here was an understatement. However it had happened, it was bound to be bad news for the Flank Siders.

"Name's Long Carp," he said, flicking indescribable muck from his fingers and running them through his hair.

"Long Carp?" said Chickie, incredulously, "Dressed like that you look more like Long Crap," he said, and the North Enders laughed heartily. Long Carp grimaced weakly.

"Ha bloody ha. What do you want?"

Chickie took a long pull on his beer then put the mug down on the floor next to his chair. He took a bite of his pie and chewed while he stared.

"Well, it's like this," he said finally around a mouthful of food, "life is full of choices, mostly shit ones. And opportunities, although mostly they're shit as well. I'm here to make you a one-time-only offer to join the North Enders. Throw your lot in with us, as it were. What do you say?"

Long Carp looked around, unsure.

"Can I think about it? Sleep on it, maybe? Chat it over with friends?"

Chickie sucked in air through his teeth and shook his head sadly.

"No, 'fraid not, need an answer now, so no sleeping on it. And can't think you've got many friends left, if I'm honest. Most of your gang have opted to join us already, those that we've found. You might ask the ones who declined but you'd have to find 'em first and, to be honest, they ain't likely to do much answering."

And that clinched it for Long Carp. Better alive amongst a bunch of unfriendly cut-throats than dead and fed to the pigs, or whatever it was that the North Enders did with corpses.

"Well, since you've asked so nicely, I accept," said Long Carp weakly, wiping his hand on his filthy trousers before sticking it out. Chickie stood up from his chair and stepped forward as if to shake it.

"On second thoughts, no, I'm still not shaking your hand. Welcome aboard. Dear god but you stink. Is your stuff inside?" Long Carp nodded. All that he owned, apart from the remnants of the clothes he stood in, was in a small cupboard in the first-floor dormitory of the pub.

"Right. Get yourself cleaned up," said Chickie, looking at Long Carp's filthy clothes and hair, "we do have standards, you know? Then we'll have a proper chat."

Later that evening, Marrinek sat in the Snarling Goat with Fangfoss, nursing his ribs and pot of beer.

"Artas proved immune to your charms?" asked Fangfoss, barely concealing his disappointment that Marrinek was still amongst the living, "can't say I'm surprised."

Marrinek shrugged and grimaced slightly at a twinge of pain from his back.

"Doesn't matter now. His second, Martha Gauward, was more amenable, although that might have been because we discussed her opportunities in a room full of corpses." Marrinek sighed. It had been a bloody day's work, by the end.

"I know Gauward. She's a complete bitch, especially if she catches you staring at her tits, but she practically runs the Lighthouse for Artas. Or ran it for him. If she's on-board, we're home and dry."

"Good. I want you over there first thing tomorrow," said Marrinek, tossing back his beer as Fangfoss looked on in alarm, "take Chickie and make sure the place is secure. Gauward gave me a tour and it's an impressive operation but I don't trust her, not yet." Marrinek didn't trust Fangfoss either but at least his motivator was clear. Gauward wasn't anywhere near as transparent. "She'll need a bit of slack to run the Lighthouse effectively but if she slips the leash we'll be back to square one. I want to know that Gauward is doing what she's supposed to be doing." He stood up, stretching a little to try to pull some of the pain from his ribs.

"I don't really go out, as a rule," growled Fangfoss, his displeasure evident.

"Tomorrow you go out. Can't trust anyone else with this, it has to be you. If we don't put our stamp on the Lighthouse quickly it'll drift away from us and I'll have to slap them down again. Take control, Fangfoss, and do it tomorrow. I'll drop in as well, make sure nobody needs kicking."

He tossed a velvet bag onto the table.

"First payment from Artas, courtesy of his vault. More to follow once we've got everything under control."

And then he was gone, leaving Fangfoss to grind his teeth and complain into his beer.

A little while later Long Carp emerged from the inn a new man. He'd scrubbed himself clean in the inn's tiny bath-house, changed into fresh clothes and washed most of the muck from his boots. He was almost presentable. He carried a stool out of the inn's common room and sat down at the bench opposite Chickie. A couple more Flank Siders had turned up and were also seated in the small courtyard, eating pieces of pie that they cut from the plate set on the bench. Long Carp joined them, cutting himself a large slice - he felt he was owed it after the events of the morning - and pouring himself a large mug of beer.

"What do you do for a living, son?" said Chickie when Long Carp had settled down.

"I'm a Collector. Debts, rent, fees, favours, that sort of thing."

"Good, good," said Chickie, nodding, "and you bring it all back here, the stuff you 'collect', right?"

"Yeah, that's right."

"So here's what we want. You keep doing what you do but instead of handing over to, who was it, Lorn Artas?"

Long Carp nodded.

"Instead of handing it to him you pass everything to Hines, here, who'll be taking over. Understood?"

Long Carp nodded again. That didn't sound too oner-ous; business as usual but with a new boss. The Flank Siders were used to those sorts of changes.

"And you're gonna have to work a bit harder as well," continued Chickie, "on account of there being fewer people on your crew, now, and higher expectations of profit."

Long Carp frowned. That didn't sound so good.

"How much higher?" he asked, although he had a feeling he didn't really want to know.

"Ah, that's what I like; a man who focusses on the important things. Basically double, and as you've lost about a third of your crew I reckon you three will have your work cut out. In fact, I really don't understand why you're sitting here in the sun drinking my beer and eating my pie when you've earned me no coin."

Long Carp joined Flat Cap and John the Bush in goggling at Chickie.

"Double?" said Flat Cap, his bass voice rumbling, "How are we supposed to do that?"

Hines leant forward from his place next to Chickie.

"What am I, your mother? This is your patch, round 'ere, get out there and work it."

"Just remember that you have a loving, supportive team back here at base waiting to feed and water you as soon as you've done something worth rewarding," said Chickie, "or you could try your luck with the Watch, if you'd prefer, or fuck off to some other city."

There was silence for a few moments. Long Carp could tell that Flat Cap was weighing the odds but eventually he just straightened his cap and stood up. The tension that had kept Long Carp's heart hammering drained out of the atmosphere like pus from a wound and he stood up as well.

"Better make a start, then," he said, "John, you ready?"

The little man looked at Long Carp and Flat Cap towering over him, then at Hines and Chickie relaxing opposite him.

"Sure, why not. Beats floating downriver or feeding the pigs."

The three of them slunk off round the corner and Chickie sat back in his chair.

"That seemed to go well. I think those lads have a bright future ahead of them," said Chickie, pulling out a pipe from his shirt and fishing around for his tobacco.

"Brighter than Faran's, that's for damn sure," said Hines, "although his pigs are fattening up nicely."

"Any more of these guys left, or have we spoken to all of them now?" asked Chickie, lighting his pipe with a small fire charm.

"That's the last of 'em, I think. They had about thirty working out o' this place, I reckon, and we've spoken to twenty-four so far. Eighteen have come over to our way of thinking, a couple made a run for it and could be anywhere by now."

Chickie hooked Long Carp's stool with his foot and pulled it over then, legs stretched out and feet comfortably resting on the stool, he puffed on his pipe contentedly.

"A good day's work, then. I'll just finish my pipe then saunter on back to Trike's to report to Fangfoss. I guess you'll need to stay here to clear things up and make sure there's no backsliding. Wouldn't put it past them to try something tonight or tomorrow morning."

"Yeah, I'll handle it," said Hines, standing up. He stretched his arms and cracked his joints.

"Maybe I'll pick out one of the whiners this evening and give him a good beating, out in public where everyone can see. That ought to help settle things down a bit."

Chickie took his pipe out of his mouth and waved it at Hines.

"Just make sure you pick a useless one, someone without friends, and keep these guys," Chickie waved his pipe at the other North Enders lounging in the sun, "around just in case things go south."

"Aye, you don't have to tell me that."

"No, I guess I don't. Have we found Faran's stash, yet?"

Hines looked over at one of the other North Enders, a short, thin man named Lacey, who looked up from his whittling when he heard a question that might be for him.

"Nothing worth 'aving so far. There's change in a box under the counter and a bit o' silver in a draw in the back office. That's about it so far."

Chickie frowned.

"That ain't right, there must be more hidden somewhere. What about the cellars? Anything down there?"

Lacey shook his head.

"A couple of barrels of beer, a stack of wood for the fires, a still where they made some sort of apple brandy from a cheap cider they brought in from the countryside somewhere. Nothing of any real value. One o' them said they sent the days' takings to the gaming palace so's nobody'd be tempted to pinch it."

Chickie considered this as he puffed on his pipe. Maybe it was true, maybe they just hid their stash well. Or maybe the Flank Siders just didn't take any real money around here but that didn't seem likely. The west side wasn't poorer than the east side, just different. There were plenty of opportunities for men who knew how to exploit them.

"Well, maybe they were just shit at managing business. You'll have your work cut out turning this mess around," said Chickie, "and Fangfoss'll want profits from tomorrow, you know that."

Hines grunted but didn't say anything, as if he'd expected the Flank Siders to be difficult and all this was just another way for them to cause him problems.

Chickie finished his pipe and stood up.

"Right. Time to head east. Till tomorrow, Hines."

"Aye, till tomorrow."

Chickie banged out his pipe on the bench and strode off, disappearing quickly into the shadows of the alleys.

Hines stood up as well and gestured at Lacey.

"Let's go through the cellars again, make sure we haven't missed anything. You lot keep an eye out for trouble," he said, nodding at the other North Enders, "check round the back as well, make sure everything's ship-shape."

They nodded seriously but didn't move until Hines kicked away the stool that the nearest man was resting his feet on.

"Bloody get on with it," he said, a touch of anger showing in his voice. They got on.

Back at Trike's the atmosphere in the room that Fangfoss used for his meetings was busy with excitement and activity.

News of the day's events and of Marrinek's activities at the Lighthouse had shot through the gang faster than a greased pig through a crowd and now everyone wanted to know what would happen next.

The common room downstairs was even more full and rowdy than normal as the enforcers came through, dumping the pooled share of their weekly take on the table before heading back downstairs to drink and gossip and gamble. Chickie was checking the money as it came in, ticking off the deposits against a list he kept in a small black notebook.

"That's everyone," he announced, as the last of the money was counted and stacked in a small chest, "except Hines, who won't be producing anything till at least next week, and Old Ned, who hasn't showed up."

Fangfoss frowned at Chickie.

"That's unusual. Ned's a scruffy bugger but he's reliable, always pays his dues. Send someone down to the Crown to roust him out; can't let things slide, even for Ned."

Chickie nodded and closed the lid on the chest.

"Pretty good week, though, considering. We're down a bit overall but with Hitton out of the picture we're doing all right and that ain't counting what we'll pick up from the Flanks." He stood up and walked over to the door but as he stretched out his hand the door opened and Old Ned almost fell into the room. He grasped at Chickie's arm to hold himself upright then staggered over to the table where Fangfoss was sitting and collapsed into a chair. The room was silent for several seconds before Fangfoss spoke.

"You know I like a big entrance, a bit of drama and some blood, a nice pratfall or maybe a joke, but you've taken it to extremes, Ned. What the hell happened to you?"

Ned coughed and closed his eyes briefly as he clutched his ribs. Then he raised his head and looked at Fangfoss through his good eye.

"Paltiel dragged me in for questioning, boss, wanted to know about your new best friend, Bay."

Fangfoss sat up at the news.

"Bay?" he said sharply, "Why was she interested in him?"

"It was about what happened at the Goat. She wanted to know who did it and where they could find him. I kept quiet for a while but..." he trailed off, waving a hand at his smashed-up face.

Fangfoss grimaced. Paltiel had a reputation for getting information from people, even people like Ned who knew better than to talk to the Watch or answer their questions.

"What did you tell her?" asked Fangfoss in a weary voice.

"Pretty much everything," said Ned, resigned to his fate but choosing honesty because it seemed like the only option, "although she only asked about Bay and the Goat, nothing else. They gave me a beating in the cell then she did something else, felt like she was squeezing my mind, and when she asked questions I couldn't not answer. I told her Bay was at The Jewel, 'cos that's where Trant sent him when he first arrived in town; don't know if he's still there, though."

"And did you come straight here after they let you go?"

"Almost. Stopped at The Crown to get this for you." He pulled a small purse from his pocket and tossed it to Chickie, who checked the contents then made a mark in his notebook.

"Good man," said Fangfoss, nodding.

"Do you want to warn Bay?" said Chickie as he added Ned's silver to the chest.

"Warn him? Sure, why not. Send someone round to The Jewel but if the Watch are already there, so be it."

Chickie nodded and stepped out of the room to find a messenger.

"Course," said Fangfoss to Ned, "might be that our warning arrives too late and Paltiel'll have him in chains before our messenger arrives. That'd be a shame, losing our new 'partner' so soon after acquiring him, but Bay's a big lad, I reckon we can trust him to look after himself."

"Mind if I go, boss?" said Old Ned, "I need food and sleep and maybe a couple of shots of brandy to dull the pain."

"Sure, get out of here. And I 'preciate you bringing your dues round in person. Most wouldn't have bothered or would have sent an excuse, and I value reliability."

Ned nodded at him, unsure if his reputation for reliability was really worth the pain he'd suffered getting here from The Crown, then he stood up and shuffled back downstairs, holding the door for Chickie as he went out.

"Runner's gone, boss."

"Get over there, Chickie, and keep an eye on what

happens. I want to know if the Watch take Bay and what sort of fight he puts up. I'll want to know if he ain't there, too."

"Right you are, boss. Sure you don't want to come along? Could be fireworks if Bay's as tough as he seems."

Fangfoss pretended to consider it then shook his head.

"Think I'll just stay here, thanks. Never did like walking the streets if I could avoid it."

"Right. I'll be back as soon as things quieten down," said Chickie, slipping out the door.

25

Lady Adrava rode away from The Farm without a backward glance, leaving behind both her home and the alias - Aspene - that she had used for the last year and a half. The horse, a chestnut mare called String, was strong and Adrava let her run for several miles along the almost empty roads that led away from the seminary. When they reached the main road to Esterengel she slowed to a moderate pace that was more in keeping with her image as a low-ranking cleric; it would not be seemly for her to gallop everywhere and in any case, she had a long way to go.

String seemed happy to go at a fast trot and they soon settled into a mile-eating pace which would see them well west of Esterengel before nightfall. Adrava intended to reach Catshed as quickly as possible but not at the expense of her horse so she took care to walk, water and rest String whenever it was necessary.

The main road ran straight through Esterengel and although it was probably the fastest route to the west she didn't want to take the chance, however slim, that she might be recognised. Instead she skirted the city, cutting south a few miles short of the outermost slums and taking String on a roundabout tour of the towns, small villages and farms that surrounded the city.

Stopping only once to buy bread and cheese and a skin of watered wine from a small inn in one of the larger villages, Adrava made good time and by mid-evening, with the sun still well above the horizon, she was a good distance beyond Esterengel and approaching a small town. The evening was warm and there was no sign of rain so she decided to camp in the wilderness rather than risk being recognised in the town and so she turned off the road onto a small track and made her way south, looking for a secluded spot where she could spend the night.

She found a small clearing a short distance from the track and, she estimated, maybe a mile or two beyond the western edge of the town. She hitched String to a tree at the edge of the clearing and removed the saddle and bags. Once String was settled, Adrava gathered firewood and settled down herself, lighting a fire using a small charm.

Warmed by the fire and wrapped in a blanket, Adrava turned out the contents of her saddlebags, which she had not yet had time to inspect. She spread out her second blanket and tipped out the saddlebags. It seemed that Cardinal Jendryng had been very generous, a trait that she had not previously seen in him, although maybe Lady Drocia's patronage had helped in that regard.

The bags turned out to contain many of the things she might herself have chosen to pack had she had time to plan and consider. There were a pair of powered arm bracers made of leather and iron which she strapped on with considerable relief; travelling without armour was, she now found, something of a worry. The shock cannon in a holster of supple calfskin was something she hadn't expected but which she was delighted to find - she fitted it to her belt where it would be easily reached but also hidden by her tunic. She spent a few minutes fiddling with the sliders - it wasn't clear from the markings which control did what - and checking that she could reach and holster it quickly and discretely.

A small pot of honey and several other minor luxuries went straight back in the bag; nice to have but not things with which she needed to do anything now. Likewise the dagger and fire charm, which would serve as useful backups in case she lost her own.

A roll of charming tools was a thoughtful inclusion and might be useful but her skills in this area were limited. She didn't have the patience for anything but the most rudimentary of charms and she doubted that she would find much use for the tools. Still, nice to have, just in case.

Finally, she unwrapped a small leather case and opened it to find a charmed monocle. Intrigued, she set it in her eye and focussed power into the charm to see what it would do. Immediately the darkened forest around her became visible and she found that she could see clearly through one eye even as the sun dipped fully behind the horizon. She had heard of such things but never had one to use before and she spent several delightful minutes experimenting before re-wrapping it in its case. She was about to put it away when she realised that simply hanging it around her neck on the attached necklace would be a better idea.

Her investigations complete, she ate half the loaf of bread and a good chunk of cheese, washing it all down with a generous mouthful of the rather sour wine. Then she stoked up the fire a little, checked on String and wrapped herself in her blankets before settling down for the night.

The next day, Adrava was up at first light and on her way

within minutes, aiming to get many miles behind her while the light and the weather held. She ate as she rode, walking String frequently so as not to tire her and in this way she made rapid progress. Her early start allowed her to make good use of the road before it became busy with the day's traffic and by late afternoon she judged that she had was now approaching the western edge of the Empire. This part of the province was unceasingly rural with farms and small villages covering the hills and plains. Occasional small towns - mostly just large villages - were distinctly provincial and although they buzzed with people the focus was on farming and trade; Adrava was unlikely to be recognised this far from the city.

She was tired after two long days of riding, an activity she was unused to after months of virtual isolation at The Farm, and so she decided to try her luck at a roadside inn in a small village. Her clerical garb should deter most people who might otherwise be tempted to pay close attention to a woman travelling alone and, with luck, it would be enough to get her a small room to herself.

She guided String into the inn's stable yard and handed the reins to a boy who came running over, tipping his hat in respect for her office. She gave careful instructions for String's care and then, taking the saddlebags with her, went in search of the innkeeper.

The inn's common room was about half full, mostly of locals - farm hands, foresters, a blacksmith and his apprentice - but there were also a few travellers making their way home from the big city. The innkeeper, a large, no-nonsense woman in her mid-fifties, looked Adrava up and down, clearly not believing that she was a cleric.

"I'm just a student, really," she said, hurriedly, weaving her apparent youth into the cover and sucking at her lower lip to emphasise her vulnerability, "not yet an ordained priest. I'm travelling home to see my mother, who is very ill," said Adrava giving her name as "Gwycia". It seemed to work and the innkeeper warmed to her a little, coming over all matronly despite being at least thirty years her junior.

"A pretty young girl like you shouldn't be travelling alone, miss, not all the way out here. It's not safe on the roads, especially at dusk. Can't have in you the dormitory, either, not with the crowd we've got staying here tonight, but we've got a small room we keep for special visitors. It's extra but it's all I've got and I'll throw in a spot of dinner. I've always said it was good luck to have a priest in the building," said the innkeeper. She chattered on, rabbiting away about nothing of any real interest while she steered Adrava through the inn, eventually depositing her at a tiny room with scarcely enough room to stand beside the bed.

"You'll be wanting a bath, no doubt, so I'll have the maids prepare one for you and find you something to wear if you'd like your clothes washed. I always find the smell of horse gets stuck in my nose, after a while, can't wait to get rid of it." She smiled and disappeared down the corridor, clucking as she went. Adrava removed her arm guards, slipping them into her saddle bags, then laid her knife on the bed beside the bags. She took her shock cannon from its holster on her belt and was still holding the short charm in her hand, half hidden by her sleeve, when the maid arrived carrying a heavy woollen dressing gown and some towels. Adrava followed her to the bath house where a warm bath was waiting and allowed the maid to help her undress, slipping the shock cannon into the bath water before climbing in herself. The maid disappeared, promising to return her clothes, washed and dried, before morning.

Adrava relaxed in the bath until the water grew cool,

allowing the aches of the ride to soak away, then she dried herself on the towels, slipped into the dressing gown, fastened the cord tightly around her waist and made her way barefoot back to her room. When she got there, she found a tray of bread, cheese and sliced meat had been left for her on the bed and she ate quickly, washing it down with the remains of her wine skin.

"Why Catshed?" she muttered to herself as she drank. It was a question she had pondered, on and off, since Lady Drocia had first mentioned the town. She just couldn't see why Marrinek would be interested in the town - he had no family there, no friends, no contacts at all. As far as she knew, he had never even been to Catshed, so why go now?

She paused as a sudden thought struck her. Maybe the report wasn't wrong, maybe it was just incomplete. The report had said that Marrinek had gone to Catshed but that didn't mean he had *chosen* to go there; maybe he had just washed-up there after escaping his pursuers. Maybe they hadn't been able to follow him further and had simply reported it as his destination?

Another thought occurred. Catshed was a trading town, close to the border; what if it was just a waypoint, a stop-off on the way to somewhere else? She sat up, excited now, feeling that she might finally be asking the right questions.

Catshed was on the river. It was good for trade but it was small and Marrinek would want crowds to hide in, resources to work with and places to hide, especially if he thought the Kareethi were following him. If he had moved on - and she could no longer believe that he was still in Catshed - where would he go?

Not east, toward the Empire. Of that much she was certain. She wracked her memory for details of the area.

Was there anything west of the Guiln? She couldn't remember and she shook her head in annoyance.

Then it hit her and she sat back, a daft grin spreading across her face.

"Vensille," she whispered, "he's heading for Vensille."

It made sense. Vensille was outside the Empire and it big, rich and strong. It would be a perfect hiding place for a wanted man. The more she thought about it, the more it seemed the only logical, the only possible, destination. She went to bed still thinking about it but ever more convinced that she was right.

The next morning she again rose early, keen to resume her journey before the roads became busy. She found her clothes - washed and mostly dry - on a peg outside her bedroom door and she dressed quickly, strapping on arm bracers and holstering her shock cannon. She repacked her saddle bags and then slipped down to the common room where the innkeeper was already busy tidying and sweeping and making good after the previous night.

"Up so early, miss? Did you sleep well?"

Adrava nodded.

"Very well, thank you." She dropped coins into the woman's hand and said, "might I trouble you for some bread and beer for the day ahead? I have a long way to go and I won't stop if I can avoid it."

"Certainly miss. Come with me down to the kitchen and we'll get you sorted out." She waddled off down the corridor and Adrava followed, trailing behind like a duckling following her mother.

"Meg," said the innkeeper in a loud voice as they reached the kitchen, "Meg. Drat it, where is that girl?" She bustled around the kitchen but Meg didn't appear.

"Well I don't know where she's got to, I really don't, but

here, take this loaf and some cheese." She passed the items
to Adrava then turned around to find a young girl standing
behind her.

"Oh Meg, there you are. Fill this with beer for the lady,"
she said, handing over the wine skin.

"Is there anything else you need, miss?"

Adrava made a show of thinking about it for a few
seconds.

"No, thank you, you've been very kind."

"Well, I hope you have a good journey and that your
mother isn't too ill when you arrive. Here's your beer," she
said as Meg ran back into the room with the filled skin.

The innkeeper walked her to the stable yard and waited
while String was saddled and made ready, then she waved
as Adrava mounted and rode out of the yard. Adrava
returned the wave from the road before pointing String
westward and kicking her to a quick trot, her back to the
rising sun.

By mid-evening, with the road almost deserted, she had
covered a good number of miles and both she and String
were flagging. She turned off the road where it forded a
small brook and headed upstream for a little way, looking
for somewhere sheltered to make camp.

She settled on a small grassy area above the stream and
surrounded by tall oak trees. She tied String to one of the
trees and gave her the last of the oats that she had brought
from The Farm. A short while later, while String munched
contentedly on her nosebag, Adrava had started a small fire
and was enjoying her own dinner as she looked west over
the stream toward the setting sun. A real bed with clean
sheets might have been better but she wasn't about to

complain about a night in the open when she had food, warmth and peaceful surroundings.

She was finishing her food when she heard sounds of movement, of people heading towards her from the road. Then three men emerged from the woods on the opposite side of the fire. One took String's reins and started to talk to the horse while a second just stood at the edge of the clearing watching her and the fire. The third moved close to the fire and crouched down, making a show of warming his hands even though the night was still mild. All of them were roughly dressed, unshaven and armed with swords and bows; outlaws, of some description.

Number three, a thin wiry man with a bald head that Adrava decided to name 'Baldy' looked at her and grinned, his eyes gleaming in the firelight.

"Well. You're a long way from home, miss. What are you doing out here, all alone?"

Adrava smiled back at the man, hoping that a little politeness might encourage a friendly response.

"I'm on my way to meet my husband," she said, opting for the truth, "and you? What's your business in the woods at this time of night?"

"Oh, this and that. Looking for opportunities, food, money, horses, that sort of thing. So you're meeting your husband, eh? He's not here at the moment, then?"

Adrava shook her head.

"No, he's many miles away, unfortunately, somewhere out west, beyond the Empire's borders."

The other men were paying close attention now and the leader was grinning ever more widely.

"Out west, eh? That is sad. Isn't that sad, lads? The poor lady priest, out here in the middle of the woods, all alone..." his voice trailed off but his eyes stared at Adrava.

"I do hope I can trust you gentlemen to behave honourably," said Adrava wearily, not for one moment believing that their intentions were even pleasant, let alone honourable, "it would be so disappointing to spoil a fine day with something distasteful."

Baldy raised his hands, palm upward.

"Well, pleasant means different things to different people, don't it, now." He leered at her again, not even bothering to try to look at her face.

"You give us what we want, all of us, and maybe you'll still get to meet your husband."

"But you might walk a bit funny," said the man standing by String. He clutched at his crotch, just in case she'd missed the joke.

Adrava sighed.

"Is there anything I could say that might make you forget that I was here and continue your journey?"

The leader laughed and his colleagues laughed with him.

"Oh, no miss, nothing at all. So be a good girl and just slip out of them clothes so we can get started." He was staring hungrily now, licking his lips in anticipation, his hands twitching. Behind him the man holding String was rubbing at the bulge in his trousers.

Adrava stood slowly and Baldy stood as well. She raised her left hand to her neck to unfasten her tunic and Baldy took half a step forward.

"Is it just the three of you?" she said in a nervous tone, left hand paused at her throat, right hand by her side.

Baldy just grinned and then, too late, she heard someone moving behind her. Before she could move a huge arm grabbed her around the neck and she was dragged up and backward. She clutched desperately at the arm with both hands but he was very strong and very much bigger than her. Baldy grinned as Adrava's captor grabbed her breast with his free hand, squeezing.

"No miss, I'm afraid there are four of us," Baldy grinned again as she squirmed and struggled, then added, "and when we get back to camp we can introduce you to the rest of the gang."

Behind her the big man was laughing, one arm clamped around her throat, the other wandering freely across her body. She struggled harder as he pawed at her clothing but his grip didn't loosen and now she realised that she had misjudged the situation. Growing slightly desperate, she changed tack and stopped struggling, going limp in his arms.

"That's better miss, much easier all round. Put her down there, Tink, and let's get a closer look at her."

Tink half-carried her back towards Baldy and then let her go, pushing her down to her knees. He kept one heavy hand on her shoulder while Baldy undid his belt and came forward, then stepped away.

Adrava wasn't slow to seize her chance. She threw herself to her left, away from the fire, and rolled quickly to her feet, crouching in the darkness with her knife in her left hand. Baldy hooted with laughter and stumbled a little as he dragged up his trousers. Adrava stood slowly, keeping the knife between her and the four men, and slipped her shock cannon from its holster.

"Grab her, Tink, and don't let go of her this time," said Baldy, grinning but watching the knife as it glinted in the firelight. Tink lumbered forward, arms spread wide to encircle Adrava, eyes on the knife but no hint of fear on his face.

Adrava backed away slowly, painfully aware that the

clearing was small and that if she turned to run they would be on her in moments.

"Last chance," she said, "please don't make me..." but Tink was already moving, rushing forward far more quickly than someone of his bulk ought to be able to move. Surprised by the suddenness of his charge Adrava didn't have time to do more than stab her thumb at the shock cannon's actuator as it pointed in Tink's general direction. The cannon, set for high power, punched a neat hole, as broad as a man's thumb, in the flesh of Tink's thigh. He stumbled, his shoulder catching Adrava and knocking her backwards as he tried to stay upright on a leg that was suddenly not working properly. She spun around him, rolling with the impact, and brought the knife down as he fell past her, catching him in the arm or back or shoulder - she couldn't tell exactly - and losing her grip on the handle.

Tink felt the knife go in and roared in pain. The momentum of his charge carried him past Adrava and into the low bushes surrounding the clearing. He tried to turn back to face her but there was something wrong with his leg and he slipped over, crashing onto his side and rolling onto his back. He screamed again as the knife was driven more deeply into his shoulder.

Baldy, his face now contorted in anger, pulled his sword and snarled at Adrava.

"I'll gut you for that you fucking whore!" He came forward quickly but Adrava had his measure, now. She stepped back and to one side, raising the shock cannon and fiddling with the control sliders. She stabbed the actuator and stopped Baldy dead with a diffuse blow to the chest. The man looked confused and pained but he came on again so Adrava nudged the slider and hit him again, harder. Then she hit him a third time, harder still, knocking him over, breaking his arm and dislocating his shoulder. Baldy screamed and let go of his sword as he thumped to the floor of the clearing.

Adrava glanced at Tink but he was still on his knees, trying to pull the knife from his shoulder and hampered by the hole in his thigh. She turned back to the other two men, who had drawn swords and were approaching warily, neither of them keen to get too close.

"I warned you," she said, "I asked you to leave, to walk away, to avoid any unpleasantness."

Behind her, Tink whimpered and crawled away from the fire, heading for the safe darkness of the forest.

Adrava now had the feel for the shock cannon and the time to use it properly. She flicked the sliders to boost the power and tighten the area of effect then raised her arm and pressed the actuator twice, punching fist-sized holes in the chests of each man, one after the other, more quickly and easily than butchering meat. They fell almost noiselessly, dead before they hit the ground.

She turned back to Baldy who was trying to clamber to his feet.

"I haven't finished with you." She raised the cannon, fingers moving deftly over the sliders, and hit him with a blast that knocked him back to the ground. Baldy screamed again but he stopped trying to stand.

Adrava looked over at Tink just as he finally managed to haul himself upright, his weight entirely on his undamaged leg, the other hanging useless from his hip, his meaty right hand wrapped around a tree branch for support. He'd managed to pull the knife from his shoulder and he held it in his left hand, blood dripping from the blade. He waved it uncertainly towards Adrava as the blood ran from the hole in his leg and soaked his trousers and the forest floor. They stood like that for a few seconds, each just watching the other, then the big man seemed to sag and his good leg failed him, pitching him forward onto the floor of the clearing. The knife fell from his hand and he lay still.

Adrava looked around the clearing then fitted the monocle and looked again, focussing a little power through the charm until the forest was exposed as if it had been noon. Satisfied that there was nobody nearby, she holstered her shock cannon and turned back to Baldy, who was lying on the ground and trying to protect his damaged arm.

She walked over to him and used the toe of her boot to flip him onto his back. Baldy screamed as his broken arm flopped against the ground. Adrava knelt beside him and plucked his knife from his belt, resting it against his neck. His screams stopped quickly, replaced by a ragged, fearful, breathing.

"You could have walked away, you know. I would have let you go if you had only taken the chance. What should I do with you now, eh?" She stroked his cheek with the flat of the blade. Baldy tried to edge away from the knife but she moved it back to his neck and he stopped, barely daring to breathe.

"No, don't try to move. Let me have a look at your arm. Oh dear, that's a nasty break. And is there something wrong with your shoulder?" She poked at his upper arm and it was all Baldy could do to hold in another scream.

"I think you're probably fucked," she said, "all alone, at night, in the woods, miles from anywhere."

"Not alone," hissed Baldy through gritted teeth, "others, nearby." He swallowed as she rested her knee gently on his broken arm.

"Others? How many, where?" Her tone was polite,

conversational, friendly almost, but Baldy gasped as her knee weighed a little more heavily on his arm.

"Twenty, twenty. Please stop, please."

She pressed harder and Baldy shuddered in pain.

"Where?"

"South-west, two miles, maybe."

Adrava eased back off Baldy's arm and he almost fainted in relief. She edged back from him and sat on a log, thinking quickly. She had to get away from here before the rest of the gang could stumble upon them and that meant moving through the night. She stood up and began to repack her things, stuffing them into her saddle bags and re-saddling String. Baldy watched her carefully, cradling his arm and slowly edging himself into a sitting position with his back against the trunk of a small tree.

Adrava ignored him while she packed her kit and readied String. With power flowing continuously to the monocle she could see everything in the forest around her; she would not be caught unawares again.

She finished packing and checked the straps on the saddle then turned back to Baldy. He had managed to get to his knees and was trying to use a long branch as a crutch to get him to his feet. She shook her head and walked back over to him, standing behind him as he struggled. When he finally made it to his feet she stepped forward and stabbed him twice with his own dagger, neat strikes into the back of his thighs. Baldy screamed again and fell back to the floor, rolling away from his broken arm and whimpering, lying on his good shoulder, legs bleeding heavily.

"Yes, you're completely fucked." She retrieved her knife from the ground where Tink had dropped it and cleaned it on his jerkin, then slipped it back into its sheath. Baldy's knife looked almost like a small sword in her slender hand, far too large for her to carry even if it hadn't been crudely made and spotted with rust. She looked at it dispassionately; a crude weapon that matched its owner. She tossed it away into the bush and drew her own knife then knelt down beside the fallen man.

"Is there anything else you can tell me? Anything I might need to know?"

Baldy, breathing heavily, stammered, "N-n-no, nothing, I've told you everything."

"Then goodbye. It wasn't a pleasure, in the end, but we don't always get what we want." Her arm darted forward, faster than a snake, and Baldy hadn't even time to draw breath before his life was snuffed out.

Adrava sat there for a moment, looking at her hand and examining the edges of the blade where they met the ruined jelly of Baldy's eye, then she pulled the knife free and cleaned it carefully on the man's shirt. Then she sat back on the floor as her legs suddenly gave way, shivering despite the warm night, and threw up.

She wasn't sure how long she sat there but by the time she roused herself the fire had died to glowing embers and the air had chilled. The shock had passed but now she shivered with cold, her teeth chattering under the clear skies.

"Get up, get up, get up," she muttered, urging herself to action. She forced herself upright, trying not to look at the corpses spread around the clearing, then kicked dirt over the fire to put it out completely. One last glance with the monocle to check that she had left nothing behind, then she untied String from the tree and picked her way carefully out of the clearing.

A narrow track wound broadly south and west and Adrava followed it cautiously, looking for the camp that Baldy had mentioned. Attacking a band of outlaws hadn't been part of her evening's plan but she wasn't about to leave them completely free to operate on the road behind her if there was something she could do about it.

String wasn't too cheerful about being led through the dark, especially as the moonlight was dim beneath the tress, but the monocle allowed Adrava to see exactly where she was going. After an hour's slow progress along the narrow track she caught the first sounds of human activity - men singing a raucous tavern song - and she stopped to tie String to a tree. Another hour's wait and the sounds died away.

With String safely tethered Adrava crept toward the camp, scanning the forest for guards or sentries as she went. It had been a long while since she had practised her bush-craft and her lack of recent experience almost got her killed when, despite the monocle, she almost walked into a sentry crouched under a cloak in the lee of a tree, bow in hand.

Adrava froze in the darkness, barely daring to breath, but the man was clearly asleep. She waited for a few moments as the sentry's soft snoring drifted over the sounds of the forest. Beyond him in the clearing there were maybe twenty men, all asleep. There was no sign that they had noticed her and it looked, from the discarded wine skins, as if they'd drunk themselves to sleep. What to do next, that was the question. She needed to get past these men without alerting them to her presence. Time to move.

She took a deep breath to steady herself then took a careful step backward, edging away from the sleeping men. Then she circled the camp until she found the gang's horses, all conveniently corralled together for the night. There were two dozen animals tied to line strung between the trees and Adrava smiled to herself in the darkness as she cut them loose. Then she slipped back into the under-growth, watching through her monocle as the horses began to explore their new freedom, searching for grass to nibble.

She circled back towards String so that the outlaws' horses were between her and the outlaws, then she spent a few moments looking at the nearby trees before finding one that suited her purposes - an elm, about fifty years old. Adrava backed away about ten yards and crouched down behind a broad oak. Then she focussed, drawing a huge amount of power which she dumped straight into the elm.

Immediately the tree exploded, showering splinters across a wide area as super-heated sap expanded and rushed through the wood. The noise was tremendous and the horses, as she had hoped, took off in all directions, spooked by the sudden violence and determined to get away. The men were equally shocked, waking to a night-mare of noise and screaming horses, and they shouted wildly and charged around the clearing as they tried to work out what the hell was going on.

Adrava smiled to herself and walked calmly back through the forest to where String was still tied securely to her tree. She reached up to comfort the mare, patting her nose and speaking softly to her, then she untied the reins and led her away through the forest, disappearing into the dark and leaving behind the sounds of men shouting at each other and at their fleeing horses.

After an hour of walking she decided it was safe to stop and she made a cold camp, wrapping herself in blankets and trying to snatch a few hours' sleep. Dawn, when it came, found her shivering and poorly rested, tired and hungry. She packed quickly and led String away from the rising sun, picking her way through the undergrowth and looking for the westward track.

When she eventually found it, she mounted String and

headed west at a fair trot, anxious to put as much distance as possible between her and the events of the previous night. Around mid-morning she was passed by a pair of men on horseback, going hard along the road. Roughly dressed and carrying bows, they looked a lot like Baldy and his companions. Adrava watched them go then hurried after them, aiming to reach the next town before the two men turned around and decided that she was the only person travelling the road.

But it was worse than that. When she reached the edge of a small town an hour later both men were sitting at a table at the side of the road outside a small inn. They exchanged meaningful glances as she rode toward them and one of them stood as she got close.

"Camping out, were we?" he shouted at her.

She ignored them and guided String past the inn toward the town gate.

"It was you, wasn't it, at the camp?"

She stopped and turned, looking back at the two men.

"I don't know what you're talking about," she said, but she could see that they didn't believe her and one was staring at her feet. She glanced at her boots, dark spots of blood standing out on the pale leather, unseen in the pre-dawn light when she broke camp, and when she looked up again the man was triumphant - she'd given herself away. He smiled grimly at her and nodded but made no move. Too many people around, too public even for an outlaw.

She swore under her breath and nudged String onward, leaving the two men behind.

"We'll be waiting for you," said the bandit, "we've got questions." She pressed on ignoring him, forcing String to go a little faster even though the road was narrowing.

"Four questions. Four, you hear me? Four," shouted the

man, "and we want the answers."

Adrava slid from her saddle and tugged String deeper into the town, searching for an inn or a temple or somewhere she could find refuge. In the main square she found a large inn and she led String into the yard. She couldn't see the bandits in the square or on the streets behind her but she didn't doubt that they were following, waiting for their opportunity to ask their 'questions'. She stepped quickly into the inn once String was stabled and sought out the innkeeper.

"You'll have to sleep in the common room with everyone else, miss," he said, apologetic but disinterested, "I don't have any rooms available."

She sighed, annoyed, but nodded agreement and paid the fee. The common room was all but empty when she went in and she found a quiet corner in which to sit. She pulled spare clothes from her pack and changed discretely, careful to avoid attracting attention, then she sat down to wait, her bags on the floor at her side.

By late evening the rush had passed and the common room was beginning to quieten. Adrava, having seen no sign of the bandits, had started to relax. She had eaten two good meals and washed them down with several mugs of weak beer and she was warm and safe. One of the maids had washed her clothes and they were hanging now by her table, drying in the warm summer air while she listened to the chatter and gossip of her fellow patrons.

Eventually the noise of the common room died away completely as people stretched out on benches or the floor. Adrava slept fitfully, woken repeatedly by the unfamiliar sounds of the inn and the snoring of the other travellers. By dawn she was tired and not at all well rested but she got up anyway, packing her bags quietly before picking her way carefully between the sleeping travellers on her way to the yard.

She saddled String quickly and led her out of the yard into the quiet town was quiet. The streets were almost empty so she hauled herself into the saddle and walked String westward, heading for the gate and the main road. At the wall, the gatekeeper grumbled and muttered pointed complaints about opening up so early in the day until she slipped him an extra coin.

"For your troubles," she said as she pressed it into his hand, although opening the gate didn't seem like a huge task for a gatekeeper. As soon as the gate was opened, Adrava guided String out onto the road and kicked her to a canter, aiming to reach the next town as quickly as possible. As the sun rose she rode out from the amongst the roadside shacks and left the town behind.

Mindful of her encounter with the bandits, she pushed String hard, crouching low over her neck as they galloped or cantered along the road. An hour later she had passed through several small villages and had made good progress but the road had become much busier as the day aged and now the way was crowded with carts, riders and animals. Staying on the road meant slowing String to a walk and although she had seen no sign of the bandits she started to feel uneasy at the slow pace of travel, worried that they might reappear while she trudged along the road.

Around late morning, with maybe ten miles to go to Riverbridge where she planned to take a boat downstream, the road cleared and she encouraged String to a gentle trot, a pace that she should be able to maintain easily for the rest of today's journey. Adrava had started to think that she might have slipped away from the bandits but a few miles further on, as the road curved around a low hill, she saw a man standing beside a horse on a small rise on the other side of the road, maybe five hundred yards away. At that distance, she couldn't make out his features but he mounted up and rode quickly down the hill, taking a path parallel to the road.

She kept her eyes on him as he drew level, still some two hundred yards from the road, and started to cut diagonally toward her. Was he alone? Was he herding her toward an ambush? Adrava couldn't see anything ahead but the road twisted and turned through the low hills and amongst clumps of forest. There could be any number of unpleasant surprises waiting for her on the road ahead.

The man had closed the gap to a hundred yards now and now she could see that he looked a lot like the bandit who had shouted at her the previous night. Following the road at speed was clearly not going to be a great idea so she slowed String to a walk then stopped, sitting patiently at the side of the road. The bandit reined in his horse and turned sharply left, heading for the road just ahead of Adrava. Once he reached the road he turned again so that he was now coming back down the road toward her.

And then Adrava saw that he wasn't alone. Three horsemen had emerged from a small wood up ahead and were also coming down the road toward her. Turning in the saddle, she saw that three more were coming fast along the road behind her. Seven in total, all mounted. They must have ridden hard to get ahead of her and left behind those of their gang who lacked horses. Seven was too many for her to handle and if they had recaptured all their horses there could be another five somewhere close by. Time to act, then.

Adrava kicked String and yelled at the top of her voice,

charging toward the first bandit and pulling out her shock cannon as she went. The bandit checked his horse, yanking at the reins, and hurriedly tried to draw his sword as Adrava hurtled toward him, crouched low over String's neck with her right arm extended as if it held a cavalry sabre rather than a small charm.

The bandit pulled his horse around, trying to get out of her way and bring his sword to bear. Adrava guided String gently to one side of the road, passing within six feet of the bandit as he finally got his sword free of its scabbard. She decided to err on the side of caution and thumbed the slider to the high-power position then punched the actuator, dumping a third of the reservoir's power in a single blast straight at the bandit. She didn't see the impact but when she looked back the man had dropped his sword and reins and was lolling over his horse's neck, blood streaming down the flank of the grey horse.

Adrava turned her attention to the three men in front of her. Her sudden charge had caught them by surprise but they all had drawn swords and they were spurring their horses forward. She screamed at them and kept going, heading straight along the road toward the middle of the three men. The bandits' mounts, spooked by the charging horse with its madly screaming rider, danced across the road as she thundered toward them.

Again she worked the sliders, struggling to keep a grip on the cannon, then she pressed wildly on the actuator, sending low-power shock pulses at the horses, hoping to spook them. The range was too great for damage but she must have scored at least one hit because a horse reared, leaping sideways as if punched and throwing its rider. Adrava swerved toward the fallen man and charged him down, guiding String around the rearing horse and keeping it between her and the other bandits. The man in the road dived desperately to one side as String thundered past, then he staggered to his feet, clutching for the reins of his horse.

Adrava kept going, pushing String along as fast as she would go. Glancing behind she saw that five of the bandits were now following but they were a long way back and String, better fed and well rested, was pulling away. In a few minutes the bandits were left behind and then, to her huge relief, a temple spire came into view above the low hills. Riverbridge, at last.

She slowed String to a canter and then to a trot as she got closer to the town until, at a walk, she reached the comparative safety of the walls.

She stopped, briefly, to look behind. Five mounted men were arranged across the road maybe half a mile behind her. They were still sitting there when she rounded a corner inside the town and lost sight of them.

A little while later Adrava reached the river docks, which bustled and heaved as barges were loaded and unloaded with all manner of raw materials and trade goods. She dismounted and walked String through the crowds, searching for someone who might give them passage down-river. Eventually she found the dock master, a hugely fat man in a stained vest sitting in a small kiosk at the end of the docks, who offered to find a vessel to carry her and her horse for a relatively modest fee.

"But you'll have to sleep on the deck and care for your horse yourself. And the boat don't leave till the day after tomorrow, if everything goes as planned."

Adrava tutted in annoyance.

"The day after tomorrow? Is that the earliest departure?

I really want to get to Vensille as soon as possible."

"Sorry miss, can't leave any earlier. It's the 'orse that's the problem, see? If it were just you I could have you out of here today but with the 'orse it'll be the day after tomorrow."

He strained to look at the horse, peering around the edge of the kiosk.

"Fine looking beast, that. The road would take you to Catshed, if you're in a hurry, and from there you could easily get a boat to Vensille. Lots of traders don't come further upriver than Catshed."

Adrava shook her head.

"I've seen bandits on the roads on the way here; I don't want to find more. I'll take passage the day after tomorrow."

"Right you are miss. What name and where are you staying, just in case we need to find you."

"Naseep. Can you suggest an inn? Somewhere safe and reputable."

"N-a-s-e-e-p?" asked the man, making a note in a ledger, "The Bargeman behind the kiosk should be fine and we'll know where to find you. Riverbridge is safe, largely, but after dark some of the taverns can be a bit lively, if you know what I mean. Best avoid them, if you want my opinion."

Adrava nodded.

"I'll see if they have room at the Bargeman. When will the boat leave?"

"Around noon, miss, so if you're here, or at the Bargeman, around mid-morning, the crew will be able to load your 'orse and get things sorted."

"Thank you." She walked away toward the Bargeman, leading String. As she looked back toward the kiosk from the entrance to the Bargeman's yard she saw a roughly dressed man with a bow and a sword talking to the dock master. She hurried inside.

26

When Marrinek returned to the House of Duval, he found it open for business and the party in full swing. Both the ground floor reception rooms were busy with punters and girls and music floated down again from the first floor. Shad and his colleague were maintaining a discrete presence at the rear of the hallway but Elaine was running the show, greeting the guests, keeping the wine flowing and generally ensuring that everyone was having a great time.

Marrinek passed swiftly through the happy crowd, nodding to Shad at the back of the hallway and letting himself into Madame Duval's study. The lady of the house wasn't there so he rested Bone Dancer against the mantelpiece and lowered himself into one of the armchairs. He closed his eyes for a few moments, meditating on the happenings of the day.

He woke some time later to find Madame Duval standing over him, shaking him gently by the shoulder.

"Fancy some dinner? We have a spiced pork stew with baked potatoes and bread."

Marrinek shook himself awake and pushed himself upright in the chair.

"Eurgh. I didn't mean to fall asleep. Stew, did you say? Thanks."

The noise of the party had died down a little but it was clear that Madame Duval's girls were still entertaining clients.

Madame Duval herself had changed her hair and her dress, wearing both long to cover the scrapes and bruises she had collected at the Lighthouse. Even under her makeup, the swelling on her face was obvious, as were the worst of the bruises. She noticed Marrinek staring and shrugged painfully.

"Not the worst beating I've taken," she said, gingerly fingering her cheek before sweeping back her hair to show Marrinek the full extent of the bruises, "and if the Flank Siders stop taking the bulk of my profits, it'll have been worth it."

"That, at least, I can promise," said Marrinek, running his fingers through his hair and feeling the new scabs on his scalp, "Fangfoss has taken charge, Gauward is running the Lighthouse and neither of them will bother you. Your house is off limits and they know it."

She looked at him sceptically and Marrinek saw a glint of fear in her eyes.

"What?" he asked, "You're still worried about the Flank Siders?"

"Not the Flank Siders, no," she said, shaking her head.

"Then what, me?"

There was a pause before Madame Duval nodded. Marrinek look at her and sighed.

"You don't need to be afraid of me," he said, "I won't,"

"How many men have you killed in the last few days?"

she said suddenly, interrupting his reassurance, "Five? Ten? Twenty? Do you even know?"

Marrinek sat back in his chair and stared at her for a long moment.

"Only those I couldn't spare," he said eventually, "those who threatened me or my associates. I don't enjoy killing."

"Maybe not," she said, anger replacing her fear, "but you don't hold back, do you? The men in that office, did you have to kill them all? Were they really that much of a threat to you? To us?"

"Yes, they were a threat," said Marrinek, louder now and becoming angry himself, "you saw how they treated us when they thought we were weaker than them. I'd have spared them if I could but they gave me no choice."

They glared at each other for a long moment then Madame Duval looked away.

"There was never going to be a way to do this without breaking heads and spilling blood," said Marrinek, calmer, now, as the sudden anger drained away, "and it'll have been worth it if it keeps us safe."

Madame Duval snorted. "That's a big 'if'. What if it just makes us bigger targets for the gangs or the Watch or the nobles? What then?"

"Then we'll deal with the problems as they arise," said Marrinek firmly, "and in the meantime we'll sleep more easily and live more comfortably knowing that we're at the top of the heap rather than the bottom."

He reached into a pocket and pulled out a purse. He tossed it to Madame Duval, who let it fall into her lap, too tired, or to angry, to try to catch it.

"That's your cut, in gem stones."

Madame Duval looked down at the purse then tipped its contents into her lap. A fortune in cut stones twinkled back at her and she idly picked one up for a closer inspection.

"These are better than the last lot of stones you had me fence," she murmured eventually, her anger forgotten as the scale of her unexpected wealth became apparent. Marrinek nodded.

"I couldn't have done it without you. You earned it."

"Ha, maybe," she said, doubtful as to the true impact of her contribution. She scooped up the gems and slid them back into their bag. Then they sat in silence for a few moments, each nursing their own pains and thoughts, until Nandy came in with a tray of food and drink. Marrinek took a plate of stew and a lump of bread and ate slowly while Madame Duval helped herself to cake.

"What about the house?" he asked between mouthfuls when they were alone again.

Madame Duval poured them each a glass of red wine and sat back down in her chair. She took a sip then said, "Done. It wasn't cheap but it's yours. Well, it's rented in my name - I didn't think you would want to be tied to the paper-work - and you can move in tomorrow."

Marrinek nodded as he chewed.

"Good, many thanks. And the tailor?"

"Coming to your house, tomorrow at noon. The twins have been measured and fitted; their first set of clothes should arrive tomorrow with more to come. By the end of the week you won't recognise them."

Tailors. Marrinek shivered at the thought. He hated being measured for clothes; the whole experience left him cold, as if he was being fleeced by someone selling him extra sleeves. He grimaced at the thought; the people he trusted to clothe him were doing so by taking the figurative shirt from his back, always trying to add a little lace here or a slash of coloured velvet there and charge him more for the privilege.

He sighed and took another sip of his wine. It was unfortunate but he knew that without the right clothes the nobles of Vensille wouldn't even notice him, let alone talk to him.

"Where are the twins now?"

"Upstairs. They wanted to get back to their reading. I have no idea what they're studying but they certainly seem keen." She looked at him questioningly.

"Yes, well. About that. I'm going to send them to a tutor some evenings; could you spare Shad to walk them over there, to Mr Eaves' shop around the corner, just for an hour or so? We can make other arrangements later but I'll be here this evening in case of trouble."

Madame Duval raised an eyebrow.

"You want Shad to babysit for you, is that right?"

Marrinek shifted uneasily.

"I can't give the twins everything they need; it's better this way. They'll get a more rounded education if they have contact with some, er, specialist tutors. And they seem to like Shad."

"Well, that last bit at least is true. Very well, but just this once."

Marrinek smiled at her.

"Thanks. It'll be good for them to get lessons from someone other than me, help them broaden their perspectives a little." He put down his plate and finished his wine.

"I'm going to talk to the twins and then tomorrow we'll move next door and let you get back to running your business." He stood and walked to the door, then turned back.

"What news of servants? The house is all very well but..."

"Yes, yes, I've thought of that," said Madame Duval,

clearly irritated, "I've engaged a housekeeper for you - she ran the house for the previous owner - and she will find servants. It will take a few days, maybe a couple of weeks, but she knows what she's doing. She will be there tomorrow morning to open the house."

"Good," said Marrinek, nodding, "and I've asked Eaves to find someone to fix your windows."

Madame Duval looked confused.

"My windows? What's wrong with them?"

"They're weak, easily broken. Eaves will find someone to harden them so that neither glass nor wood will break. I've done your doors but doing the windows as well should make you a bit more secure if the Watch, or anyone else, comes calling. Eaves' man should be here tomorrow, might take a few days in total but it'll be worth it."

Madame Duval looked at him sceptically.

"Well, if you think it's necessary..."

"I do. Trust me," and he closed the door behind him as he left.

Upstairs the twins were reading, sitting in the window to make the most of the light. They looked up as Marrinek entered the room. He looked at them for a few seconds, remembering the harsh treatment he had received at the hands of his own Master and tutors, then he shook his head and walked over to sit beside Floost, leaving Bone Dancer propped against the wall.

"How are you finding Jensen?"

Floost wrinkled her nose.

"Some of it's interesting but mostly it's just weird. Like this bit," she flicked back a few pages then read aloud, "'Where two complementary talents are deployed to produce an effect of coherent and continuous change in an atypical system, particularly one meeting the requirements of Dreng's extrapolation, the corollary of the second basic law of para-thermal energy covering the preservation of mass must be considered and allowed for.' I don't even understand all the words!"

Marrinek smiled. Her frustration was understandable, unlike the prose that had prompted it.

"That's Volume III, yes?" Floost nodded.

Marrinek took the book from her and flicked through the pages, stopping at one point to read a few sentences.

"I graduated before I got around to reading Volume III and I've never found the time to go back to it. That paragraph is probably the most I've ever read."

Floost's face was a picture.

"Well why did you give it to us, if you haven't even bothered to read it?"

"The first two volumes are more useful but I thought you might find III of some interest. Concentrate on the other books for now; come back to this one later." He put the book down on the floor.

"But right now I have something else for you. I've spoken to Mr Eaves, you remember the charm seller?"

The twins nodded.

"I've arranged for him to give you lessons in basic charm making and other related subjects. Shad is waiting for you downstairs to take you to your first lesson. After that we'll see how things go but I plan to arrange a succession of other tutors."

"Can't you teach us?" said Darek, frowning.

"I could but I don't have time and I want you to begin networking amongst the talented community. Trust me, this is the best plan." He paused, then continued in Khem. "And would it be fair to assume you speak only Gheel?" The twins stared blankly at him, which was all the answer he needed.

"And you're going to have to learn Khem," he said, switching back to Gheel, "I'll tutor your myself, starting tomorrow." That wasn't as well received as he had hoped and both twins grumbled. "It's the language of power," Marrinek said firmly, overriding their objections, "and a good grounding will be necessary for your education and later life."

He stood up, and the twins fell silent but he could see that they weren't happy.

"Most of the books on power are written in Khem. Learn it, and you'll be able to broaden your reading range and get away from translated horrors like that hideous Jensen." That seemed to cheer them, especially Floost, for whom access to books was a particular joy.

"I'll see you again tomorrow and we'll run through some more exercises after we've moved into the new house next door. Now, though, it's time for your charms lesson." He paused but neither twin moved. "Hurry now, and listen carefully to Mr Eaves."

"Should we take anything with us?" asked Floost, standing and smoothing her dress.

"No. Concentrate on his lesson and we will review tomorrow. Eaves will supply anything you might need this evening. And be polite - you're representing me, remember, and I would have you make a good impression."

The twins nodded and hurried out of the room to find Shad. Marrinek waited till the sound of their footsteps on the back stairs had died away then he put down his pack, removed the knife from his belt and kicked off his shoes. Picking up Bone Dancer, he spent the next hour working repeatedly through the forms.

As he was finished his routine he remembered the book that Eaves had given him and he spent the next half hour or so flicking through its pages and reviewing the moves it suggested. The style was a little unusual but he found a few interesting variations to the forms that might be considered standard in stick fighting. He practised the new forms as he waited for the twins.

By the time the twins returned Marrinek had finished his practice and was lying on the floor reading volume three of Jensen. It was, he had to admit, a book of limited value to the experienced practitioner and of almost no value at all to the novice. He tossed aside the book when the twins came in.

"I had expected you back some time ago. How was it?"

The twins looked at each other, sharing something that Marrinek couldn't catch.

"Good," said Darek, "he showed us how to use the tools and how to use them to work wood."

"And what were you able to do with the tools?"

"He wanted us to control the wood so that we could change its shape and write our names in it. It's difficult but you made it look so easy!" said Floost, clearly frustrated, "The wood responds strangely; sometimes it runs like melted butter and other times it just sits there doing nothing."

Marrinek was impressed, although he didn't let it show. Sculpting wood was not an easy skill to acquire and most practitioners never progressed beyond basic manipulation. Many were unable to work wood at all, relying on experts like Eaves for any charms or wood working they required.

"It's not an easy skill to master. But you managed to make the wood respond?"

Both twins nodded.

"That is good, very good. When is your next lesson?"

"The day after tomorrow. Mr Eaves wants us to practice tomorrow and see him again the following morning with the best piece that we've made." said Darek.

"Good. Tomorrow afternoon you can show me what you've achieved and I will help you to improve. For now, bed."

He stood up and walked to the door.

"I have things to do. Good night."

The next morning the housekeeper, Aimes, opened the front door of the new house to Marrinek and Madame Duval. A prim, unsmiling woman, Aimes gave the impression of never having enjoyed a day of fun in her life whilst at the same time embodying an almost machine-like level of efficiency. From the moment they met, Marrinek disliked her but if she ran a tight household and kept him supplied with clean shirts he decided he could tolerate a little coldness. Madame Duval introduced them before excusing herself and leaving them to review the rooms and talk about the practicalities of managing a large household.

The house itself was grand, although much less than a palace, and would have been highly fashionable about five decades ago. Marrinek inspected the ground floor, the courtyard and stables, the cellars and kitchens, the bedroom suites, the servants' quarters and the attics until, eventually satisfied that all was in order, he nodded to Aimes.

"Good. How many servants do you need, Aimes?"

"A cook, two maids, a footman, a butler, a valet for you, sir, and a groom. Cook starts tomorrow with the maids, the groom the day after and I have an idea about a butler and a valet, sir."

"Good. I will leave the arrangements to you, Aimes, but be sure to hire people you can trust."

"Of course, sir," Aimes sounded slightly insulted with the suggestion that she might consider anyone she hadn't personally approved, "some of the rooms need repairs, sir, and we will need funds to run the household."

Marrinek pulled out a purse and tossed it to her.

"Start with that, let me know when you will need more. Get Eaves, the charm-maker, to find someone to harden the windows and doors. You know him?"

"No, sir, but I will find him."

"I have already spoken to him so he knows what needs to be done and he has money in-hand to cover expenses. I want the work completed as quickly as possible; talk to Eaves about what's practical but get two or three people working on it if possible."

"Very good, sir. Might I ask why the work needs to be done?"

Marrinek walked over to the nearest window and rapped his knuckles against one of the small panes.

"Fragile, easily broken. Hardening frame and glass and doors will make them almost unbreakable, which ought to stop people kicking their way into the house to murder us in our beds."

Aimes looked shocked again, as if being murdered in your bed was something that couldn't happen simply because she would never permit it. She nodded, although it was clear that she had her doubts.

"I will make the arrangements, sir."

Aimes had worked in large households all her life and she understood the value of fulfilling the sometimes bizarre requests of her employers and difference between when it was, and when it was not, appropriate to ask questions about their deeper reasons.

"Madame Duval has told me that the tailor will be here at noon, sir but that otherwise the day is free from visitors. Some of the rooms are woefully under furnished but there are three usable bedrooms and the front drawing room should be comfortable. Should I acquire furniture for the other rooms, sir?"

"Yes, Aimes, do that please. Make it of good quality but not ostentatious; sensible and workmanlike, not gaudy. I want visitors to feel welcome and to be comfortable, not intimidated by the overbearing trinkets of wealth." She nodded and turned to leave.

"Oh, and no faux Imperial furniture or imported rubbish, Aimes. Find good local pieces that reflect Vensille's history and tradition and culture."

She nodded again.

"As you wish, sir. Shall I serve coffee in the drawing room?"

"Yes, Aimes, thank you."

The housekeeper disappeared toward the kitchen and Marrinek walked through the near-empty rooms, settling himself into an armchair in the drawing room. He steepled his fingers, elbows resting on the arms of the chair, and closed his eyes, thinking and resting. At some point Aimes reappeared with coffee and, later, reappeared to remove the empty cup, replacing it with a small plate of elegantly cut sandwiches.

The tailor came and went without incident, promising to deliver a range of clothes suitable for the highest echelons of Vensille society with the first items arriving within a few days. Alone again in the drawing room, Marrinek resumed his meditation until the twins interrupted, bursting into the room as they explored the house.

"There's so much space," said Floost, excited. Marrinek opened his eyes and looked up.

"Aimes has shown you to your rooms?"

"We're on the second floor," said Floost, nodding, "at the back of the house overlooking the stables."

"There is another room on that floor that we will use for practice and study. It's empty at the moment except for a table but you can use it to work on the exercise that Eaves set you yesterday. Go now and we will talk again at dinner."

Over a simple dinner of roast meat, spiced sauce, bread and vegetables the twins talked excitedly about their lesson with Eaves and the wood-charming exercise he had set them.

"But sometimes nothing happens to the wood for ages," said Darek, frowning at his vegetables and poking at them with his fork, "and then if you push too hard it just seems to melt and flow, then it sets in a strange shape. It's really weird."

Marrinek looked at him, fork stalled halfway to his lips.

"The wood melts and flows?"

The twins nodded.

"And then you have to spend ages forcing it back into the right shape before you can start again," said Floost, hacking inelegantly at her meat and stuffing a lump into her mouth, "why does that happen?" she asked, looking across the table at Marrinek.

"Hmm," said Marrinek, finally remembering his forkful of food, "well, it's to do with how much power you use and the strength of your affinity with the material. Which tool are you using?"

"Mr Eaves said to use Twig, number three tool, but all we managed to do last night was make little dimples in the wood," said Darek.

"Dimples? As if you were pressing the tool into the surface of the wood?"

"Yes," said Floost, "but after practicing today we worked out how to get the wood to move around a bit and then, all of a sudden, it just kept happening."

Marrinek stared at them, dinner forgotten.

"That's good, very good."

The twins beamed and kept eating as Marrinek sat, thinking, trying to remember anyone at the Academy with a similar talent for working wood. When he couldn't think of anyone, not even tutors, he tried to call to mind anyone he had ever heard of who could make wood melt and flow; nothing. As he sat there he couldn't think of anyone, anywhere, who could do what the twins were describing. Metal, yes, but metal was a simple crystalline structure that could be heated and formed by anyone, if you really wanted to bother. Wood was different; it just didn't work that way.

"Darek, run upstairs please and fetch your tools and practice pieces. I want you to show me what you've achieved."

Darek pushed himself away from the table, stuffing the last of his meat into his mouth as he stood up, then hurried out of the room. While he was gone Marrinek cleared the long table to create space.

"Right, you first, Floost," said Marrinek, once Darek returned with the tools and a few lengths of wood. Floost took out her number three charm tool and closed her eyes, working first through the calming exercise that Marrinek had taught them. Then she focussed power into the charm, opened her eyes and turned her attention to the wood, lowering the charm until it almost touched the grain. Nothing happened for a few seconds and then, as Floost pushed more power into the charm, the wood abruptly changed, taking the consistency of molten glass and splashing into a wave as it rushed away from the charm.

Marrinek gave a start, surprised at the sudden movement, and Floost withdrew the charm. The wood set immediately into a smooth wave, as if a heavy stone had been thrown at a puddle and the water had frozen as the crest of the splashed wave was about to break. Floost looked at Marrinek.

"That's been happening most of the afternoon. We had to straighten it out to produce the forms Mr Eaves wanted," said Darek, "which took bloody ages." Marrinek looked sternly at Darek.

"I meant it took a long time," he said hurriedly, abashed.

"That isn't supposed to be possible," said Marrinek, "maybe with simple materials, like iron or stone, but not with wood. I've never seen anything like it."

Marrinek shook his head, still not sure of what he had seen. He picked up the wood and examined it. The grain of the wood was still visible but now it ran up the wave. He turned it over and over in his hands, looking at it from all sides, then put it back down on the table.

"Do you have any more pieces like that?"

Floost nodded.

"Yeah, some. We smoothed down a few to use the wood again but there were some that were too far gone to change."

"Right. Not a word of this to Eaves, you understand?" Marrinek's face was stern and he looked from Floost to Darek to make sure they had understood.

"You've got some other pieces you can show him this evening?"

More nodding.

"Good, then go now and fetch any that are like this and bring them here to me. Say nothing to Eaves and whatever he asks you to do make sure you don't show him how you did this, got that?"

"Yes, but why?" said Floost, confused.

Marrinek sighed.

"You've read bits of Sturge. Have you found the chapter that covers new applications of talent and power?"

The twins shook their head.

"It's toward the middle of the book, I think. Sturge explains what happens when new and unusual talents emerge. You might expect these occurrences, rare that they are, to be greeted with celebration and joy but they are not. What you've shown me, what you can do with wood, is unique. Keep it hidden for now, read Sturge for more details and we will talk about it again tomorrow. Trust me, this is important; don't let Eaves know what you can do."

The twins nodded again, still clearly confused by his reaction, then gathered their things.

"Leave the wood, bring me any more that you have like this before you go to see Eaves."

After the twins had left Marrinek sat at the table looking at a dozen absurdly mis-shaped pieces of wood. Then he dumped them all in the fireplace and set them alight with the fire charm, playing the flames across their surface until nothing was left but glowing embers. With the evidence gone he spent an hour with Bone Dancer losing himself in the repetitious working of the practice forms.

27

W hatever difficulties Gwilath's crew had expected to encounter while trekking through the forest-covered foothills around the ancient fastness of Lankdon Gate, the reality was worse and their progress was slower than even the pessimistic Thaurid had feared. For three days they had fought their way through the tangled under-growth, following animal trails when they could but, increasingly, cutting away shrubs and brush in order to make progress.

The further north they travelled the thicker and more difficult the terrain became until by the end of the third day their progress had slowed to barely half a mile an hour as they beat and slashed a path between ivy-choked trees and over fallen trunks. As dusk began to fall the demoralised and exhausted crew came across the ruins of a small town - Dankfell, according to the legend carved into the stonework of the gatehouse - and after scouting several buildings in various states of decay they decided to camp in the gatehouse.

Inside they found that the tiled roof was largely intact

and the first and second floors were mostly dry and free of the invasive plant life that seemed to have done its best to pull down most of the surrounding buildings. Three hard days of trekking through ever thicker forest and camping in rough clearings around a small fire had left the crew eager for rest and they were quick to dump their gear in the room on the first floor. With the horses stabled in a sheltered spot just inside the gate, Thaurid gathered wood for a fire while the others looked to their kit and Stydd, the servant they'd brought along to cook and clean, made a start on dinner.

"It will be boiled vegetables and meat again," said Stydd, "but at least we have fresh venison rather than dried beef."

Gendra had brought down an aged stag just outside the town walls and they had been quick to butcher it, although there was far more meat than they needed for tonight. It was tough and sinewy but some of it went into the pot with the vegetables and more was set onto sticks for cooking and smoking in the chimney above the fire.

"That's about the end of the vegetables," said Stydd, "so tomorrow we'll need to scavenge for more or find some fruit or something. Quarter-rations tomorrow, I think, unless we find more meat." He looked worried and with good reason. Game had been plentiful when they had set out but, inexplicably, they had seen almost nothing worth hunting in the last two days and it was getting worse as they went north.

"It makes no sense," said Thaurid, "we're about as far from civilisation as it's possible to get and yet the only game we've seen was a single scrawny stag."

Gendra grunted and continued working on his shaft. He had cut the arrow from the deer while butchering the carcass and now he was cleaning and sharpening and tending the fletchings. Gwilath watched, fascinated but also slightly disturbed by Gendra's obsessive behaviour.

"Do you really need all those arrows? You've got, what, two dozen? And you've been cleaning that one forever. Seems like a lot of effort for a single shaft."

Gendra snorted and shook his head as he smoothed the fletchings and slipped the arrow back into his quiver.

"And two more full quivers on the pack horses," he said, "but I don't want to waste one. Might need 'em, one day."

"Yeah, right."

Ediaf spread the map out on the floor and used the case to weigh down one edge.

"We're close, maybe eight or nine leagues."

Gwilath looked through the slit window in the wall, staring out at the rain and the forest. Night had fallen and the trees were lit only by flashes of lightning. As he turned back to reply to Ediaf something moved amongst the trees and he snapped his head round, trying to work out what had caught his eye. He stared intently at the trees but nothing moved.

"Trick of the eyes," he muttered, rubbing at the offending organs, but he kept watching the forest until Stydd announced that the stew was ready.

"Nine leagues will take days at the rate we're going," said Ediaf, "but if this is Dankfell," he pointed at an unlabelled dot on the map, "then this line should be a road that will take us to within a few miles of Lankdon Gate."

Gwilath peered down at the map as he shovelled the thick stew into his mouth. He gestured with the spoon at the map between mouthfuls.

"So tomorrow we take the road and hope it's not too overgrown to be useful. Can't be worse than slogging through the forest."

"The road doesn't go to the city?" asked Thaurid from across the room.

"It's difficult to be sure," said Ediaf with typical academic vagueness, "but it seems to fork some miles south of the main gates. We'll take the right-hand fork, away from the gates but towards the hidden entrance to the catacombs, hopefully."

Thaurid shook his head and muttered something under his breath but Gwilath was looking at him, daring him to object again to the plan. Thaurid turned back to his stew and the moment passed.

The next day the crew forced their way through the town toward the northern gate. When they got there, they found that although the gates had gone, the gatehouse itself had collapsed. Gwilath clambered over the piles of rubble and windblown leaves, searching for a way across.

"I don't think we'll be bringing the horses over this," he said finally from the top of the pile, "they'll break their legs." He clambered back down again and re-joined the group, brushing muck from his hands.

"We'll have to go back, circle around. The road beyond looks good, though. We should be able to ride when we've made our way through the forest."

The rest of the crew grumbled as they retraced their steps through the town. It took them the best part of an hour to fight their way through the dense forest to the outside of the pile of rubble that had once been a gatehouse.

The trees on either side of the northward road crowded over to form a dense green tunnel and only occasional shafts of sunlight penetrated to the gloomy cobbles but the surface of the road was in pretty good condition, even if it was thickly covered by rotting leaves. As they rode slowly north, taking care to avoid potholes, tree roots, fallen branches and collapsed sections of road, the mood of the crew started to improve and by noon they were positively cheery. Even Thaurid stopped brooding and made a couple of jokes, much to Gwilath's relief.

By mid-afternoon they had managed maybe twelve miles and Gwilath called a halt next to a stream that crossed the road pooling across the cobbles and deepening into a small pond before plunging back into the forest. They watered the horses and allowed them to graze in the grass along the edges of the road.

Farwen was standing on the far bank of the stream looking along the road to the north when she suddenly gave a start and dropped the piece of dried meat she had been chewing. Something had run across the road, she was sure, but she hadn't been able to make out what it was. She turned back to the others but nobody else seemed concerned. Looking again, she wasn't now certain that she had seen anything at all; maybe it was just the shadows moving under the trees.

On a fallen trunk at the side of the road Ediaf had spread his waterproof cloak and laid out the map. He and Gwilath were now poring over it, trying to work out how far they had yet to travel and when they would need to turn off the road.

"Maybe there'll be a sign," muttered Ediaf, "or another road. There must have been roads all over the land between villages and towns and the city itself, after all, stands to reason, but unless it's this line here then I'm not sure it's marked on this map."

Gwilath bent lower over the map.

"If this bit is the stream we've just reached then maybe that line is the road to Lankdon Gate and maybe this," he jabbed his finger at what appeared to be a small village in the fork of the road, "will be our landmark. If we find those buildings then we find the fork in the road."

"That's an awful lot of 'ifs' and 'maybes'," said Thaurid, coming up to look at the map, "and who marks streams this small on a map of this scale?"

Gwilath snapped a look at Thaurid, who shrugged.

"I'm just saying that the map isn't all that clear so we'll have to go and look, right?"

Ediaf rolled up the map and stowed it away in its case before gathering his cloak.

"Thaurid's right, Gwilath. The map isn't likely to be precise or detailed even if the scale is right."

"You too? Never mind, let's just keep going and hope we can find somewhere to camp before dark."

"And something else to eat," rumbled Gendra as he led his horse back to the road, "I've seen no game and there wasn't much meat on that stag."

Gwilath threw up his hands.

"Yes, got it, thanks, we need to find more game. Let's just keep heading north with our eyes open and maybe we'll see something you can shoot."

"I saw something a moment ago," said Farwen, "but I'm not sure what it was."

They all looked at her for a few moments, waiting for her to say more, then Gwilath prompted her.

"It might have been a deer," she said uncertainly, "but I caught only a glimpse as it ran across the road."

"A glimpse, eh?" said Gwilath, a worried frown crossing his face as he remembered the shape he had seen from the window of Dankfell's gatehouse. Farwen shrugged but said nothing more.

"So there are things we can hunt," said Gwilath, mounting his horse, "we just need to stay alert."

He looked hard at Farwen until she turned to mount, then he nudged his horse forwards and led the way along the road as the shadows lengthened and the sun swung westward.

An hour later they found the fork in the road beside the overgrown ruins of a small village, just as Gwilath had predicted. His smug grin and the group's morale faded quickly as they approached the fork and saw that the thing swinging from a tall post wasn't an ivy-laden branch.

"It's a corpse," said Gwilath quietly, slowing his horse to stand in front of the makeshift gibbet. The others crowded around, staring up at the remains.

"Seen corpses before," said Gendra, continuing down the road. It was true that hanged criminals were a common sight around the towns of Vensille but this was the first they had seen since leaving Riverbridge.

"This village," said Ediaf, pointing at the ruins beyond the gibbet, "has been abandoned for decades."

Gendra stopped his horse and turned back to look at the corpse, giving it a soldier's eye.

"He hasn't been there more than a month, I'd say. Five weeks at the outside."

"So how did he get there? The sheriffs didn't drag him here from bloody Riverbridge, did they, and there's no way he walked all the way out here to commit fucking suicide!"

"Easy, Thaurid, easy," said Gwilath as his friend's voice grew louder and more panicked, "there's bound to be an explanation, we just don't know what it is yet."

Thaurid goggled at him.

"What do you mean 'yet'? Of course there's a fucking

explanation but what makes you think we need to find out what it is?"

"I just meant that we shouldn't jump to conclusions, that's all."

Thaurid shook his head.

"There's something very fucking wrong going on here and I don't think you're taking it seriously."

"It's just a corpse," said Gwilath, trying to play down its significance, although he too was worried about how it came to be there, "so like I said, we keep our eyes open, do the job, then head home."

He kicked his horse forward and headed back out onto the road.

"Come on, we need to find somewhere to camp before dark unless you want to stay here? No? Then let's go; I want to be almost at the Gate before we stop for the night."

The others followed him, keen to put distance between themselves and the corpse, but Thaurid sat there a little longer, watching as the light wind slowly turned the body back and forth. Then a noise from the forest brought him back to his senses and he kicked his horse into a trot, suddenly desperate not to be left behind.

The road now began to snake through the foothills, climbing gently towards the mountains and the ancient fortress city of Lankdon Gate. Under the shade of the trees the atmosphere remained warm and humid but every so often the road would emerge into a small clearing or onto a bare hilltop and the crew would notice that the air was getting steadily cooler. By the time they made camp near a small stream at the side of the road they had climbed far enough into the hills for the temperature to have fallen noticeably since their night in Dankfell.

Stydd setup the cooking pot and lit a fire but with only

yesterday's venison, some hard travellers bread and a few herbs the mood for the evening meal was decidedly depressed.

"No meat tomorrow," said Stydd, "and traveller's bread only until the day after."

"Slaughter a packhorse," said Gendra, not looking up from checking his kit by the light of the fire. There were protests from Farwen and Stydd but Gwilath held up his hand.

"Not yet. We'll need all three packhorses once we find the vault."

Gendra shrugged, as if a lack of food was a minor inconvenience easily remedied and went back to tending his equipment.

"Get some sleep," said Gwilath, setting out his blankets next to Farwen's.

The next morning dawned bright but cold. The fire had died down during the night and the crew woke shivering, chilled by the cool air that flowed down from the mountains. A thin breakfast of hard bread and cold water did little to fire their enthusiasm but Gwilath did his best to raise their morale for the final push. He laid out the map and with Ediaf plotted their final approach to Lankdon Gate.

"This is what we're aiming for, the labyrinth entrance on the southeast corner of the city," said Ediaf, peering closely at the parchment, "and then we head down this tunnel and into the depths."

"Bit strange that the entrance to the treasure vaults is so far from the city, isn't it?" said Thaurid dubiously but Ediaf shook his head.

"I think this was an escape tunnel. There would obviously have been a direct entrance, possibly several, from inside the city, but this one would have been built in case of siege or disaster."

"Still strange to see it on the map, though. Why advertise something that should be secret?"

"You worry too much," said Gwilath, his eyes alight at the prospect of finding the long-lost city, "whoever drew the map obviously knew that he wasn't going back any time soon and left instructions so that someone else could make the trip."

"Yeah, but why would you give someone the key to the city's wealth? Makes no sense."

Gwilath gave an exasperated sigh and rolled the map.

"It doesn't matter. We leave the road here and hike across the hills to the tunnel entrance then we find the vault, retrieve the treasure and retrace our steps. Simple. We'll be home in a couple of weeks and as rich as we've ever dreamed."

He tossed the map carrier back to Ediaf and finished stowing his gear while Stydd stamped out the remains of the fire and tidied the campsite. They were on their way only a little while later.

"So where the fuck is the entrance?" yelled Gwilath at Ediaf, at them all, venting his frustration on the historian and the woodland, although neither was directly to blame for their failure so far to find the tunnel.

Farwen placed her hand on his arm. They had been searching the hillside for two hours as the sun climbed past noon but it turned out that a secret entrance on a wooded hillside abandoned for decades and long overgrown was not easy to find. All of them had been searching, scouring the hillside for clues, looking for something that might be the stone portal on the map, beating bushes and turning over stones in the hope of finding the elusive tunnel.

"I don't know Gwilath," said Ediaf, and Thaurid could tell by his tone that he was gearing up for a fight, "where did you last see it?" Ediaf stared up at Gwilath, face set and flushed from the effort of the search, and dared him to object further. Gwilath's lip curled into a sneer and he raised his hand to make a point, preparing to bring down his forefinger like an executioner's axe on Edie's feeble argument, when there came the sound of splashing.

"Here," called Gendra, standing up to his knees in a small pond formed by a spring in a hollow. He had pulled the brush away from the hillside to expose a small opening, a cave.

"Look," he said as the others arrived to crowd the hillside above the opening, "this rock has a carving on it."

He had brushed dirt and moss from a large boulder that sat above the pond and alongside a small cave. There, faint against the grey stone, weathered over the years, disguised by shadow, was a shallow carving of something that might be a version of the portal from the map.

"How the fuck did you spot that," whispered Gwilath, dropping into the pond to stand beside Gendra and peer first at the markings on the boulder and then into the tunnel. Gendra shuffled, embarrassed, and pointed at the bank of the pond where a long heavy slide mark could be seen in the grass and muck.

"Slipped."

Gwilath grinned at him then together they cleared the ivy and brambles from the portal, tearing aside the foliage until the tunnel mouth was clear. The rest of the crew crowded around the edge of the pond to get a better view of the opening.

"It's smaller than I'd imagined," said Thaurid.

"It's his poor wife I feel sorry for," said Ediaf, loosing the joke into the brightened atmosphere without really thinking. The opening was about four feet high and maybe two wide with a broad stone step along the lower edge to keep the pond from flooding the tunnel. Gwilath leant on the step and stuck his head into the tunnel, lighting his fire charm to cast a flickering light into the depths of the hill.

"Looks like it slopes downward into the hill for at least thirty yards but it's difficult to tell," he said, straightening up and grinning wildly, "so now we get to explore."

He climbed out of the pond and stood on the bank, happy that they had finally had some good luck.

"Gendra, you stay here with Stydd, get the horses sorted and see if you can snag something for us to eat. Theap, grab the lamps and sacks. Everyone else, dump your packs and anything you don't need - we'll set off in a few minutes." Then he clapped his hands and everyone started moving, shedding kit and weapons and collecting tools and charms.

Thaurid sought out Gwilath a few minutes later while he was rummaging through his pack for his tools. There was an awkward silence for a few seconds.

"I'm sorry, Gwilath, you were right about the map, about making the trek north." Gwilath stood up and held out his hand, then changed his mind and pulled his old friend into a hug.

"We've made it," he said as he released the surprised Thaurid, "this is the big one, we're going to be rich and all we have to do now is reach out and take the prize before we head home to Vensille."

"Right," said Thaurid, grinning, "so let's get it done and

get home. I could use a bath."

"Never a truer word, my friend, never a truer word."

Twenty minutes later everyone was ready. Gendra had disappeared into the woods in search of game and Stydd was gathering wood for a cooking fire. The horses were tethered and cared for, their tack stacked neatly on the ground nearby. Gwilath surveyed the camp and declared himself happy, then led the crew back up the valley to the pond and the tunnel mouth.

"Pass me one of the lamps," he said to Theap, holding out his hand. He dropped into the pond and climbed over the step of the portal, hauling himself into the tunnel through a gap that was only just large enough for a grown man to wriggle through. With the lamp glowing softly he stood up, head almost brushing the ceiling, and began to edge slowly along the tunnel. Behind him the others followed, clambering one at a time through the narrow gap.

With all three lamps burning brightly the crew followed the tunnel as it sloped steadily downward. The floor was littered with twigs and windblown leaves and it looked like various animals had lived there over the years but as they got further from the entrance the amount of rubbish shrank until, forty yards in, the floor of the tunnel was almost clear.

"Nobody's been down here for years, decades maybe," said Ediaf reverently, looking at the dust on the floor of the tunnel.

After a hundred yards the tunnel levelled off but kept going straight, without offshoots or turns. Farwen ran her hands along the rock as they went, marvelling at the smooth stonework and the precision with which the tunnel had been cut.

"Charmed tools," she whispered, "must have taken ages to hack all this from the rock but they did a beautiful job."

"Hardly seems worth it for a tunnel," observed Ediaf, "but I do like to see a piece of nicely worked stone."

"Keep your minds on the work," said Gwilath from the front of the queue. From up ahead came the faint sound of running water and a few moments later the tunnel, wide enough only for one person to walk comfortably, ended in a portcullis. Gwilath stopped and ran his hand over the iron-work, inspecting it closely, then he put his shoulder against the bars and tried to lift it. The portcullis shifted, slightly, but didn't rise. He passed the lamp to Farwen and looked for Thaurid.

"Thaurid, give me a hand with this. I think we should be able to shift it."

Thaurid squeezed past Ediaf and Farwen until both he and Gwilath were standing side on to the portcullis, faces uncomfortably close.

"If you grip it there, yeah, like that, and I grip it here," said Gwilath, "then if we both heave at the same time..."

They heaved and the portcullis shifted a little.

"And again."

They heaved again and the portcullis climbed a few inches then, as they kept pulling, it moved another few inches, then a few more. Eventually, after much straining and effort, the portcullis was almost four feet off the floor and Farwen was able to reach past the straining men and wedge the grooves with a branch retrieved from the top of the tunnel. Thaurid and Gwilath cautiously released their grips on the portcullis and let it sag a little as it bound on the wedge. They stared at it for a few seconds, then Gwilath ducked quickly underneath and into the next chamber.

"Whoa," he said, stopping abruptly, "does the map show a damn great chasm and a narrow stone bridge?"

The others hurried under the portcullis and looked around the chamber. After the tight space and low ceiling of the tunnel this new room seemed almost cavernous. The ceiling had risen to around twenty-five feet and the room was at least fifteen feet wide and maybe 60 feet long but the defining characteristic, the one that had caught Gwilath's attention as soon as he had stepped across the threshold, was a chasm at least five yards across that ran the width of the room and, from what they could see, continued for some distance in either direction. Spanning the gap was a narrow stone bridge, maybe a yard wide, leaping the chasm in a single elegant span without rail or rope or parapet. On the far side the way was narrowed by a crenelated wall that split the room in two and offered only a narrow passage through which travellers could enter.

Theap cast a professional eye over the arrow slots, the bridge, the wall and the killing ground between it and the chasm. There were no murder holes in the ceiling but other than that the area was perfect for keeping people out.

"I guess they didn't want uninvited guests," she said, gesturing at the wall, "that's as nasty an entrance way as any I've seen above ground and I'd hate to have to attack it."

Thaurid sidled cautiously to the edge of the chasm and peered over before hurriedly stepping back.

"That's a very long drop into darkness," he said, nervously. Gwilath sauntered to the edge of the bridge, showing a good deal more confidence than he felt, and prodded at the stonework with his foot before kneeling to examine it more closely.

"Looks solid. It's been hardened so it should be fine but maybe we ought to cross one at a time, just in case."

The others all looked at him; nobody moved.

"You're closest," said Ediaf, "makes sense for you to go first."

Gwilath stood up and cleared his throat.

"Right. Well, unless anyone else wants the honour...? No?"

He placed his foot on the bridge, pausing to listen for signs that it might not hold, then gingerly took a second step. A short wait to see if it would drop him to a sudden death, then without looking down he took four more steps and jumped, relieved, to the floor on the far side of the chasm.

"Easy," he said, lying through his teeth, and faking a grin that fooled nobody, "come on, let's keep moving." Now that he was safely across he was impatient to continue and he turned away from the bridge after Farwen had crossed. Thaurid and Theap crossed the bridge quickly and took their lamps down to the far end of the room, examining the walls and floors as they went. There was a moment of reluctance from Ediaf but as the lamps receded into the distance he decided that he wasn't ready to spend time alone on the dark. He shuffled cautiously over the bridge and fell with relief against the wall on the other side.

The crew stopped to regroup in the middle of the chamber. There were four side tunnels but a quick inspection showed nothing but broken furniture and abandoned equipment, now rusted into uselessness. The map led them on to the end of the chamber and then into a great hall maybe twenty times the size of the previous room. Twin rows of columns reached to the ceiling and to the left and right were stacked great piles of rubbish.

"It looks like this might have been some sort of store room," said Ediaf, poking at the piles in the corner of the hall, "these are barrels, or were many years ago, but their contents have long gone, I'm afraid."

"These might have sacks of flour or wheat at one point," said Thaurid from the other side of the room, "but I don't think anything here is younger than we are."

They hurried through the hall checking each area as they went until they reached a large pair of double doors at the far end. Ediaf stood for a few seconds examining the map in the light of the lamp that Farwen held.

"A little higher, please. Hmm, yes. Through these doors there should be a corridor. We turn left and look for stairs down to the next level," he stopped and rolled the map up to put it away, "how much longer will the lamps last before they need to be charged?"

Farwen shook her lamp, which had absolutely no effect on it.

"Couple of hours, maybe? I wonder how the residents lit these chambers?"

Gwilath made a show of searching the walls just inside the door.

"If I recall, it was common to use powered lamps, like ours, but obviously those no longer work but there might..." he brushed cobwebs and dust from the wall then said, "yes, here, a power plate." He placed his hand on the plate and focussed power into it. After a couple of seconds, dim lights appeared, suspended between the columns at the top of the hall. Gwilath concentrated and pushed as much power as he could into the plate until the lights grew brighter and the whole chamber was lit, albeit with the weak light of a full moon.

"Wow," said Theap, staring up at the vaulted ceiling and marvelling at the scale of the room, "that's amazing."

The others murmured their agreement and Gwilath,

face sweaty with effort and panting slightly, stopped and stood away from the wall. Almost immediately the lamps began to grow dim and after a few minutes they faded completely.

"I think they must have had collectors and power stores," said Gwilath, "but someone's removed the heavy metals. This must have been a backup, something to use in case the collectors failed."

He turned to the doors, which, like everything else they'd found so far, were old and dusty. They were also slightly ajar and when he pulled one open, its hinges squeaked loudly in the otherwise quiet atmosphere.

"Ouch, nasty noise," said Farwen.

"Anything that didn't know we were here does now," said Theap, loosening her sword.

"Like what," said Gwilath, "goblins?" he waved his hands in mock terror, "Or maybe little night sprites will come to carry us off to the deepest pits of Lankdon Gate." He laughed and stepped through the doorway into the corridor beyond taking one of the lamps with him.

"Something killed this city," Theap said under her breath, "and it wasn't fucking night sprites." She rolled her shoulders and stepped quickly out of the room after the others.

The new corridor was thirty feet wide and disappeared beyond the light of their lamps in both directions. Across from the double doors of the store room stood another, similar entrance with identical doors.

"Left, then," said Thaurid, taking a few steps along the corridor with the lamp held high. He stopped after a few seconds and half-turned back, frowning.

"Did you hear that? Some sort of noise from down this way."

"You're imagining things," said Gwilath, joining him and waiting for the others to follow, "there's nothing down here but us."

Thaurid wasn't convinced and he muttered complaints under his breath but he followed Gwilath with the rest of the crew until they reached a set of stairs as broad as the corridor, heading downward in a left-hand spiral. Gwilath paused at the top of the stairs to consult the map with Ediaf then they all trooped down the long, shallow stairs. At the bottom the corridor opened quickly into another cavernous room, this one even larger than the one above, stretching further ahead and above and to the right than their lamps could light.

"Anyone want to explore this one?" asked Gwilath as they stepped out onto the empty floor. More columns reached upward into the gloom and between them, now that they knew what to look for, were power lamps just waiting to be activated.

"Don't look at me," said Gwilath, "it was all I could do to light the last set and these are even bigger. We'll have to make do with our own lamps."

"We're looking for another set of stairs," said Ediaf, "which should be on the far side of this chamber. No need to do anything except walk straight across to the other side."

They found the second set of stairs exactly where the map showed them, another broad set of steps leading down in a spiral, this time to the right. At the bottom was another cavernous room, just like the one above, with a ceiling that disappeared beyond the lamplight and columns that marched into the distance. They gathered around Ediaf to look again at the map.

"One more level, a third set of stairs, and then the vaults should be off the hallway beyond the first room we reach," said Ediaf, excited now that they seemed to be nearing their destination, "and the stairs should be on the other side of this hall."

He led the way across the hall, holding the map in front of him but stopped suddenly about only a few yards.

"I heard something," said Ediaf, "from down that way." He gestured toward the stairs that were now just about visible in the light of the charmed lamps. And there it was again, a tapping noise in the deep, a faint but continuous sound that echoed up the stairs from the level below.

"Dripping water, maybe," said Gwilath, but he didn't believe it, "or some sort of burrowing animal." He trailed off. Theap muttered something under her breath and loosened her sword.

"Maybe we should go back," said Thaurid, but Gwilath turned on him, angry now, almost snarling.

"After coming all this way? No, we go on, we find the vault, then we go back," he said, calming as he spoke, the anger fading as quickly as it had risen, "not before, right?"

There was silence for a few seconds, broken only by the quiet tapping noises, then Gwilath turned back toward the steps and raised his lamp. They all stood there for a few seconds, listening to the tapping, then Gwilath strode forward and started down the steps and the others followed; nobody wanted to be left behind or to stray too far from the light thrown by the lamps.

The stairs led them down, curving around to the right before depositing them in another huge hall. This one was smaller than those on the floors above and the ceiling was lower but it was still a vast space. They made their way between the columns following Ediaf's whispered directions. The tapping noises were growing ever louder and now, amongst the near continuous taps, they could hear other sounds, human sounds.

Thaurid walked slowly carrying one of the lamps, shaking his head. Behind him Theap rolled her shoulders and loosened her sword again, flexing her fingers then shaking her hands. Farwen looked at her and smiled reassuringly but Theap didn't smile back and wasn't reassured. Farwen went back to watching Ediaf, holding her lamp high enough for him to read the map.

At the far side of the hall they came to a narrow corridor, the smallest they'd seen since descending from the entrance level. They stopped as Ediaf grunted in confusion.

"This isn't right," he whispered, "the map shows a much larger hallway with doors and vaults leading off it both to the left and to the right." He turned back and looked around the room, signalling Farwen to raise her lamp so he could look into the corners of the room.

"I don't understand," he said, looking at Gwilath and talking quietly, "the map led us here but this bit isn't right."

"Let me see that," said Gwilath, grabbing the map and holding it one handed with the lamp held in the other. He peered at it intently for several seconds then handed it back to Ediaf.

"The map's wrong. We're in the right place, we followed the stairways as shown, but this level doesn't match the map."

"Great," said Thaurid, "so what do we do now?"

"We go on. Maybe this was a plan but they made changes on this level. Yes, that must be it; this isn't a map, it's a design and they changed the layout after this version was made. Come on, let's see what's down this corridor."

He led them forward, into the narrow corridor. They walked only a little further, thirty feet, maybe, before the corridor opened suddenly into a natural cave, a long open space almost as big as the rooms they had travelled through to get here. They paused again but the map was now useless and Ediaf reluctantly stowed it in its carry case.

They opted to follow the right-hand wall of the cave which led them another seventy feet or so before narrowing to a tunnel. Here there were signs of mine works; pick marks, dust and spoil, a discarded prop, and the noise was growing ever louder. As they entered the tunnel Thaurid suddenly grabbed Gwilath.

"Stop!" he hissed, pointing down the tunnel that lay to their right, "there's light. Douse the lamps or we'll be seen by whoever's down here."

They stopped and extinguished all three lamps. The cavern and tunnels were suddenly very dark indeed but Thaurid was right; there was a faint light from the tunnel to their right and the noises were louder from that direction. They crept forward, feeling their way in the gloom, walking in single file along the right-hand wall until they suddenly emerged into a truly vast cave, a single cavernous space filled with noise and pinpoints of light. Lamps of some sort burned across the enormous space, hundreds of them, thousands maybe, all casting their light on a scene of awful activity.

The crew stood for a few seconds, transfixed by the sight before them, until Theap came to her senses and pulled Farwen down to a crouch.

"Get down," she hissed, and the others dropped as well, crouching behind a low drystone wall that separated their ledge from the rest of the cavern. They peered over the wall and looked down into a colossal pit lined with ledges and ladders, dotted with balconies and platforms. Ropes dangled from the roof high above them and disappeared down into the depths, some carrying baskets or bundles of tools, others hauling buckets of ore or rock. Everywhere they looked there was activity as people swarmed along ledges and up ladders, hacking at the walls, shoring up the roofs of tunnels and loading buckets. And amongst these huddling masses there were other, larger, figures wielding clubs and whips, striking indiscriminately at the miners, screaming incoherently at them and kicking anyone who fell within range.

"Slaves," whispered Gwilath, horrified, "thousands of them, mining for god knows what."

"The slavers," hissed Thaurid, "look at the slavers. They're not human!"

They crouched for a few more seconds staring at the terrible scenes in front of them.

"Is this the doom of Lankdon Gate?" asked Ediaf, "Does this explain what happened to the city and the surrounding areas? Why the towns are abandoned, why there no farms or villages?"

Gwilath shook his head.

"I don't know, but there's no treasure here. We need to leave before we're sucked into this horror." He started edging back the way they had come but as he moved a slave, a woman, stepped out of a tunnel onto the ledge only a few feet in front of Theap. They stared at each other, shocked, for a few seconds, and all was still for a moment. The slave, in her mid-twenties maybe, although it was difficult to tell amongst the gloom and the dirt, was naked except for the collar around her neck and rags around her torso. She stood there, mouth open, until another slave, a man of about the same age, stepped out behind her. They were linked together by a chain that connected their collars.

The woman finally shook herself to her sense.

"Run," she hissed desperately, eyes wide and terrified, her hands flapping at Theap, "run, get out, get away."

There was movement behind her as more slaves emerged from the tunnel and then a slaver followed, a tall dark figure with a long club in one hand. He struck the woman on the back of her thighs and screamed at her to move.

As the slave fell forward Theap stuck, slashing her sword across the face of the slaver. It fell back, screaming, and dropped the club as Theap struck again, killing him.

The slaves looked on in horror, then the woman said, more loudly this time, "Run! Run!"

Two more slavers stepped onto the ledge and the woman screamed, "Run!" as loudly as she could, then a club caught her around the head and she collapsed to the floor, her chain pulling down the man behind her as she fell.

Theap yelled and struck at the nearest slaver but without the advantage of surprise she was outmatched and the creature just batted away her sword with its club then punched her in the face, knocking her over. It sprang forward and raised the club, intent on finishing the job, but Gwilath shoulder-barged the creature, pushing it to the edge of the ledge. For a moment it stood, arms wheeling, and then Gwilath slashed it across the chest with his sword and the slaver slid backwards, screaming as it fell until it smacked into something solid a few levels down.

Gwilath backed away from the remaining slaver as it stepped warily forward, club raised. It was big, well over six feet tall, and heavily muscled with long, dangerous arms. Theap had scrabbled back to her feet and she suddenly rushed past Gwilath to stab at the slaver from its side. Her thrust skittered along the creature's ribs, deflected either by armour or skin, she couldn't tell. It let loose a high-pitched wail and struck back, catching Theap's shoulder with a wild swing of its club.

Theap was knocked sideways, her left arm hanging useless at her side as she stumbled around, trying to get away from the slaver. Gwilath covered her retreat, slashing his sword toward the slaver while Thaurid and Farwen pulled Theap back down the tunnel. Gwilath backed after them, sword up, eyes on the slaver, looking for an opportunity, but he was no fighter and there was really only one way this could go. Gwilath kept shuffling backward as his crew made their escape but then he caught his heel on a rock in the floor and he fell backward. The slaver sprang forward, triumph showing on its face, but then it was suddenly snapped backwards.

It fell back and Gwilath watched, terrified but relieved, as the slave woman yanked down on the chain that she had thrown around the creature's neck, dragging it to the ground. It was a brave effort but futile. The slaver got its fingers under the chain and started to pull it away from its neck. The woman screamed but the other slaves didn't move. Inexorably, to Gwilath's horror, the slaver pulled itself free of the chain then punched the woman full in the face. She fell backward and the slaver kicked her where she lay, then kept kicking.

Nobody moved until Gwilath suddenly came to his senses and leapt back across the tunnel, swinging the sword wildly and opening a long gash across the creature's back.

It screamed and swung back to face him, bringing the club round with frightening speed. Then Thaurid appeared and a sudden gout of flame from a fire charm caught the slaver full in the face, melting skin and eyeballs and setting light to hair. The slaver screamed in agony and thrashed around, falling to the floor, its face a bloody ruin.

The flame winked out and Thaurid grabbed Gwilath's arm.

"Come on!" he shouted, dragging him backwards.

"What about them?"

"There's nothing we can do, they're chained together and there are too many slavers. Come on!"

Gwilath looked at the woman who had saved his life as she lay still on the floor.

"Thank you," he whispered, "and I'm sorry."

Then he turned and followed Thaurid down the tunnel, moving as fast as they could in the gloom until they caught up with Ediaf, Theap and Farwen just inside the next cavern.

"Keep going," said Thaurid, taking charge from the stunned Gwilath, "and get a lamp lit so we can see where we're going."

Ediaf fumbled with his lamp until he had enough of a glow to light the way and then they set off again, moving as fast as they could. At the end of the cavern they came to the final stretch of corridor and with some relief they stumbled back onto the flat, level floor of the hall.

Farwen was crying, tears streaming down her face and it didn't look like Ediaf was holding up much better. Gwilath, though, had shaken himself from his shock and he took out his own lamp, lighting it as they cross the hall.

"Come on," he urged, "they'll be looking for us and we need to get out of here."

They rushed across the hall and up the first set of stairs then across the next chamber and up the second set of stairs. Gwilath, desperate to get out of the underground city, tore across the chamber and stopped at the bottom of the final set of stairs. He waved Theap, Farwen and Thaurid past him in a blur, their legs pumping as they climbed the steps. Ediaf was slower, struggling with the steps, and it was quite a few seconds before the light from his lamp bobbed up the stairs and he finally appeared in the hallway. The effort was taking its toll. Ediaf stopped at the top of the stairs, leaning forward with one hand on his knee as he sucked in great lungfuls of air.

"Move!" screamed Gwilath, taking a step back into the hall, as light flickered on the stairway behind Ediaf, a light that could only mean pursuit. Ediaf looked up and then back over his shoulder, seeming suddenly to realise the danger. He forced himself into action and started to stagger across the hall. Even as he moved, a tall figure appeared behind him, then another, then two more. The first figure, long club in his right hand dashed forward and caught Ediaf before he was halfway across the hall, knocking him to the ground.

Ediaf cried out as he fell, dropping the charmed lamp. Ediaf tried to stand but the slaver swung his club again, a hard blow that broke bone with a sharp crack. Ediaf collapsed. His foot twitched once and then he was still.

"No!" shouted Gwilath, taking another step toward the hall. The slaver looked up and saw Gwilath standing in a small pool of light from his lamp. It raised the club again and stepped past Ediaf's corpse as more figures appeared on the stairway. Then it sprang forward and charged at Gwilath.

Ediaf's lamp was fading quickly, it's circle of light shrinking until it was no more than a dim glow. Then it winked out and Gwilath turned, running up the stairs with the sounds of pursuit close behind him.

At the top of the stairway he sprinted along the corridor, skidding to turn into the hallway that would lead back to the surface. Thaurid was waiting there for him, flame charm held high.

"Where's Ediaf?"

"He's dead! Move," said Gwilath, pushing Thaurid ahead of him, "move, they're right behind me."

Thaurid stumbled back along the corridor, then turned and followed Gwilath, who was sprinting for all he was worth toward the end of the room and the narrow guard-room. There was a yell from behind them and suddenly slavers were crowding into the hallway, fanning out as they raced across the floor. Gwilath reached the narrow bridge and didn't slow, crossing it in a few seconds and hurling himself under the half-raised portcullis. Thaurid was just behind him and together they crowded into the narrow corridor, where Theap was waiting for them. She knocked out the improvised wedge with the pommel of her sword then ran, following Farwen's lamp as it disappeared down the passage.

The portcullis slid a few inches then stopped, jammed on some piece of ancient crud in the slots.

"Fuck," shouted Gwilath, jumping back to put his weight on the portcullis. Thaurid joined him and for an agonising few seconds nothing happened. Then, as figures appeared in the gloom on the far side of the bridge and streamed forward waving cudgels and long clubs, the portcullis slipped, slamming to the floor. Gwilath scrabbled on the floor for the wedge and then hammered it back into the slot while Thaurid played fire from his charm back into the chamber.

Gwilath beat at the wedges, binding them as hard as he could, then he shouted at Thaurid and they sprinted along the corridor, back to the outside. Seconds later they burst out, staggering into the late afternoon sunlight.

28

A round noon the next day Paltiel found herself in the hallway of Lord Mantior's city mansion awaiting an audience with the Duke's personal secretary. Commander Astiland was there as well but this gave Paltiel little comfort; her briefing of Astiland on the topic of 'Lord Bay' that morning had been, for want of a better phrase, poorly received, and so here she was to explain herself in person to the man who paid their wages.

She fidgeted awkwardly with the cuffs of her sleeve, picking at a loose thread before jerking her hands apart and thrusting them down by her side. She stared at the tapestries, trying to interest herself in the scenes of hunt and battle arrayed before her, but art wasn't something she appreciated and she quickly found she was picking at the thread again. She ground her teeth in frustration and stuffed her hands in her pockets, just as the study door opened and a footman appeared to usher them in.

Lord Mantior was seated behind an enormous leather-covered desk, sipping tea from an elegant porcelain cup. He waved away their salutes and didn't invite them to sit, leaving them to stand before his desk like over-large carpet ornaments.

"My lord," began Astiland, "thank you for seeing us." He stopped, unsure of how to continue.

"I hope you're going to enlighten me, Commander, about events at the Snarling Goat? I would hate to think there were other matters so serious you had to attend me in person again so soon."

Astiland coughed.

"Yes, my lord. We suspect an interloper, an imperial agent, posing as a nobleman, sent to destabilise the city, possibly as a precursor to invasion."

Mantior raised his eyebrows.

"Invasion?" he said, not bothering to disguise his scepticism.

"It seems the only reasonable explanation, my lord. An imperial agent, going by the name of 'Lord Bay', attempting to sew discord amongst us in preparation for an attack. A tall man with long hair, a short-cropped beard. Carries a short staff."

"And he sews discord by killing criminals?"

Astiland coughed again and nodded to Paltiel.

"We, er, we think he may have other plans as yet undiscovered," she said.

Mantior stared at them, nonplussed, then turned his attention to a report on his desk.

"Astonishing. Well. Is there anything else?"

There was a pause. Mantior looked up, frowning.

"Well?"

"Ah, er," began Astiland, glancing at Paltiel for help and finding none, "there seems to have been an incident last night at the Lighthouse."

"An incident," said Mantior flatly, looking from Astiland's worried and sweating face to Paltiel, who was staring straight ahead as if she had other places she would far rather be, "and what sort of incident might it have been?" he continued in a tone he might normally have reserved for a disobedient child.

"Our source says that Artas is dead and replaced by Gauward," he said hurriedly, the words spilling quickly once he began to speak, "and they blame a tall Imperial nobleman with long hair."

Mantior narrowed his eyes. Was this a consolidation of the North Enders and the Flank Siders gangs? He had long been worried by the prospect but the risk had always seemed small, given their differences. If this Imperial agent had achieved it then maybe the situation was deteriorating.

"Have you apprehended this agent?"

"No, my lord, but we have men watching him so that we might learn which of our citizens he is working with. We plan to seize him before his plans come to pass but after we have identified his conspirators."

Mantior shook his head in disbelief.

"Well, Commander, I really don't know what to say." He paused for a few moments as sweat dripped from Astiland's face. "Was there anything else?" he asked eventually.

"No, my lord, that was all."

"The Duke will not want enemy agents operating freely within the city," said Mantior, "so keep a close eye on him, Astiland, and bring him to me in chains as soon as you have the details of this conspiracy."

"Yes, my lord."

"And keep me apprised of the situation; I want a report every other day. You may go."

Commander Astiland nodded, saluted once more, then

led Paltiel from the room. When they had gone Mantior said, "Did you believe any of that rubbish?"

From behind the long curtain stepped the tall figure of Lady Mirelle.

"The description might match the man I met at Trike's. Fangfoss introduced him as his new partner. Difficult to say how dangerous he might be." That Bay was certainly very dangerous Mirelle kept to herself; an opinion like that wasn't something she wanted to voice to the Duke's secretary.

Mantior glared at her, almost as if he knew that she was holding back.

"Did you know about the Lighthouse?"

"No," said Mirelle, after a momentary pause to school her face to a look of bland disinterest.

"Why the hell not?" asked Mantior angrily, "It's your job to know things like this and I don't like getting news from Astiland," he added as Mirelle bristled at the insults, "get to the bottom of it, find out who this 'Lord Bay' really is."

"Yes, my lord," nodded Mirelle, grinding her teeth at the unjust criticism.

"And find out if he really is an agent or just some villain who's working his way up the food chain. Is he a provocateur? Could this be the start of a move by the Empire?"

Lady Mirelle frowned slightly.

"Maybe, my lord, but who can say? As far as we know, the Empire's interest lies far to the east but it's only a matter of time before they come knocking." Another dangerous opinion, albeit one shared by the Duke.

Mantior grunted. Invasion, revolt, betrayal; these were the Duke's driving fears and with good reason. The Empire's expansion over the last few decades under their current

Emperor had made all the coastal city states and the northern kingdoms more than a little nervous.

"What if Astiland's right? Would the Empire send just one man? Do we have evidence they're preparing to invade?" asked Lady Mirelle.

Mantior leaned back in his chair and stared at the ceiling.

"Evidence? Precious little," said Mantior, ticking off the points on his fingers as he spoke, "our agents report that the troops of the western province are scattered across the territory or engaged in minor peace-keeping exercises. The Empire's main armies are on their extreme south-east borders fighting their way further away from us. Naval activity is essentially unchanged with no real action except against smugglers and pirates."

"So if they're planning an invasion it's the quietest build-up ever."

"Not that it's any of your concern," said Mantior, his patience wearing thin, "but no, we don't think they plan to invade any time soon. Forget about invasion unless Astiland finds evidence or until you unearth something damaging about Lord Bay."

Mirelle nodded, frustrated to be denied a potentially fruitful line of enquiry.

"Fine, I'll talk to Fangfoss and find out how he's getting on with his new friend."

"Good. You do that. And get to the bottom of this news about the Lighthouse. I don't want anyone spoiling the peace, Mirelle. Find out what's going on, get your agents in line and get on top of the situation."

She flicked a cold smile at him and left without another word.

An hour later Mirelle was on the other side of the river looking for the Flank Siders. She had changed into a practical loose-fitting dress that hid her defensive charms without impeding her freedom of movement or calling attention to her rank. She strolled confidently through the crowded streets until she reached the ale house from which the Flank Siders managed their operation.

She ducked into the gloomy interior of the common room and was surprised to find it emptier than normal. Usually busy by early afternoon, today there was almost nobody around. She chose a table near the back wall and grabbed a barmaid as soon as one appeared.

"Best ale, bread and a word with Wiens, if he's still sober."

The barmaid grimaced.

"Wiens ain't around no more," she said, "but I'll bring your ale."

The barmaid hurried off to the back room leaving Mirelle alone. A few moments later she was back to place ale and bread on the table. Before she could leave Mirelle grabbed her arm.

"What did you mean about Wiens? Where is he?"

The barmaid yanked her arm free.

"Gone. Dead, maybe. I don't know." The door opened behind her and the barmaid looked round.

"Ask 'im where Wiens is," she said, clearly scared. She almost ran from the room as a tall thin figure emerged from the back room and walked across to sit opposite Mirelle.

"Chickie," said Mirelle, surprised to find an enforcer from the North End in the heart of the Flank Siders' territory, "you're a very long way from home. I was planning to see Fangfoss later today but if he's here maybe I can see him now."

"M'lady," said Chickie, bowing his head, "Fangfoss'll be at Trike's - you know he doesn't like to leave, leastways not while the Watch are abroad. What can I do for you?"

"Where's Wiens?"

"Gone," said Chickie, grinning, and pulling out a chair so that he could sit at Mirelle's table, "he and a few of his boys decided they had other opportunities to pursue, if you get my meaning. I believe he's gone downriver."

"Downriver? And will he be coming back?"

Chickie hesitated and his grin became a little sickly.

"I honestly don't see how he could, m'lady. And he couldn't come back here anyway, 'cos I've moved my stuff in and I rather like it."

"Uh huh." Mirelle looked around at the common room. The room itself hadn't changed but all the familiar faces were gone. She shuddered, sensing that something wasn't right.

"Why are you here, Chickie? Why aren't you lurking over the other side of the river where it's safe and easy?"

"Can't sit around waiting for the business to grow, m'lady, need to drive it forward. Seize the initiative, you might say."

"The 'initiative'? What the fuck does that mean?" She stared at Chickie as he grinned at her and suddenly she had a bad feeling that she knew what was going on.

"If I go to the Lighthouse, who will I find sitting in Artas's seat? Artas?"

Chickie shook his head slowly as he drew patterns in the spilt beer on the table.

"Miss Gauward is running things now, m'lady, all neat and tidy, couple of my boys up there to keep her company."

"And with Fangfoss's leash around her neck, no doubt," muttered Mirelle, "who's yanking him around, I wonder?"

Chickie said nothing and the silence lengthened.

"They always pay their tariff, up at the Lighthouse, but down here it was Wiens. I guess you'll be paying me now instead, right Chickie? You're late and nobody likes an overdue debt."

Chickie spread his arms apologetically.

"All one gang now, m'lady, all North Enders. Fangfoss is your man for tariff payment."

Chickie leant forward, checking that they were not overhead.

"Between you and me, I think Bay has other ideas about paying tariffs but maybe you can persuade him to be generous, maybe make a contribution to the city's orphanage," he said, sitting back again and raising a glass in mock salute, "good luck."

Mirelle sat for a few moments, looking at Chickie with narrowed eyes, then she stood up.

"Honesty is all good and well, Chickie, but I can't see this going down well. Not well at all." Then she turned and walked out of the common room.

Chickie waited a few more moments, just to make sure she wasn't coming back, then he let out a deep breath and leant forward, resting his head on his hands for a few moments.

"Bugger," he said, under his breath, before standing and walking onto the street.

Mirelle was standing with her fists on her hips looking down the street towards the river. As Chickie approached she turned back to face him, moving forward to stand right in front of him. She reached up and grasped his chin, turning his head then holding it so that he couldn't look away.

"I want the money, Chickie," she hissed, "I'll give you

another chance, because I'm nice like that, but don't let me down again. I'll be back tomorrow."

She released his chin and patted him gently on the cheek, then smiled at him before walking off down the street, back toward the bridge.

At Trike's, Mirelle walked straight in through the front door and climbed the staircase to the gallery. She didn't bother knocking at Fangfoss's door, partly because she wasn't in the mood but mostly because she just didn't care if she upset him by barging into some private gathering. Fangfoss, though, was alone, playing with a deck of cards and drinking wine. He waved at her as she came in.

"Good day, m'lady," he said, his voice slightly slurred, "let me pour you a drink." He grabbed the bottle by the neck and sloshed a generous portion toward, and mostly into, an empty glass.

"Whoops," he said, wiping at the spilt wine with his sleeve and giggling.

Mirelle sat down opposite him and took a sip from the glass.

"Where's the money, Fangfoss?"

Fangfoss, still mopping at the table, swung his head round and looked at her.

"Money? What money is that, m'lady?"

"You're late, Fangfoss, and I've just seen Chickie over at Wiens' place and he's late as well. What the hell's going on?"

He smiled the smile of the seriously drunk and waggled a finger at her.

"Everything's changing, Mirelle. Talk to Bay."

"Bay? This new partner you've acquired? You want me to talk to Bay about my money?"

Fangfoss smiled at her again and spread his arms wide.

"He's got all the money. Talk to Bay, or kill him; those are the only options."

Mirelle looked at him, disgusted, as he filled his glass and took a deep drink.

"I won't forget this, Fangfoss." She stood to leave and he saluted her with his glass.

"Thanks for comin' round, stay for a drink next time, yes?"

Later that evening Mirelle was back at the Duke's palace, waiting for an audience. She had changed her clothes again and was now the elegant lady of the court, a noblewoman waiting upon her Duke. Eventually the door to the Duke's private study opened and Mantior beckoned her to come in.

"Ah, Lady Mirelle, please take a seat," said the Duke, who was sitting by the fireplace with a cup of coffee, "let me pour you a cup of this excellent coffee while you tell me all about the latest intrigues in my city."

Mirelle looked at Mantior, who shrugged, then took the seat next to the Duke and accepted the small cup of black coffee. It was hot and sweet and thick, a fashionable local version of the thinner Imperial drink that had recently fallen from favour with the Duke and his court; Mirelle hated it but she sipped it anyway.

"A single Imperial, your grace, who may be an agent of the Emperor or could just be a former soldier thrown free from their never-ending wars. It seems he's destroyed the Flank Siders, taken control of the Lighthouse and shaken up the North Enders. The Watch are worried."

"Just one man? You're sure?" The Duke looked at Mantior, who nodded and said, "So it would seem."

"Well, I'm not sure we need to worry too much about a

single man, do we? Maybe have a word with the Imperial Ambassador, find out who he is. If he's going to be difficult then just get rid of him; I can't imagine anyone will care that much, eh?"

"And his activities with the gangs?" asked Mirelle, "Should we take any action there?"

Mantior shifted in his seat.

"It hardly seems necessary at the moment. I'll talk to the Ambassador."

"That's settled then. Now, I have a reception to dress for. Good evening." The Duke stood quickly, bowed slightly to Lady Mirelle and left.

Mirelle put down the coffee cup.

"Bloody stuff," she muttered, "I don't think I'll ever acquire a taste for it. The gangs aren't paying their tariffs. Apparently I need to speak to Bay."

"Hmm," said Mantior, finishing his coffee, "I find myself growing accustomed to the coffee. It has a certain elegance. Forget the gangs. Keep an eye on this Bay, let me know if he does anything noteworthy. If all he does is shake up the gangs then I can live with it and, in time, we'll find a way to fold him into the arrangement."

"And if we can't? If he resists?"

Mantior spread his arms.

"The beauty of the violent solution is that it's always there, ever patient, ready to be used at a moment's notice," he said, standing up and smoothing his robes.

"And in the meantime, let's try to find a use for our Imperial friend, eh? Get their Ambassador to drop in for a visit; maybe he'll be able to shed some light on the situation."

It was two days later that the Imperial ambassador, Lord Asigori, found his way to the palace for an audience with the Duke. They had met many times over the course of Asigori's time in Vensille and there was a degree of respect between the two men even though they were, in almost every way, very different.

Asigori stood patiently in the Duke's gardens watching him fence with his current favourite, the Ethrani sword master Lojacono. The bout seemed to be going the Duke's way but a sudden burst of aggression and speed from Lojacono gave him the point and the match.

"Three to two that time, Master Lojacono," said the Duke, and it was clear that he was frustrated to have lost the match, "but I think tomorrow I will beat you." He pulled off the mask and tossed it to an attendant then removed his fencing jacket.

"Possibly, your Grace, although your wrists are still too stiff and your footwork today was a little slow. That aside, an excellent bout."

The Duke raised an eyebrow at the criticism but said nothing. He sheathed his swords and walked over to where Lord Asigori was standing.

"My commiserations, your Grace," said Asigori in his deep and strangely accented voice, "I hope my arrival didn't distract you?"

The Duke laughed.

"Hah. No, I hadn't even noticed you were there until I took off the mask. Pity, I could have used a good excuse. Walk with me, Lord Asigori."

The Duke turned and led the way along the gravel path into the garden, leaving behind his attendants and guards.

"It seems that one of your citizens has been causing a

little trouble in the city," said the Duke casually, picking fibres from his shirt.

"An Imperial citizen? I can only apologise, your Grace. Do you have a name?"

"He styles himself 'Lord Bay', although nobody knows if he really is a nobleman."

"Lord Bay? Your Grace is teasing me, surely."

The Duke frowned.

"No, I don't think so. 'Lord Bay' is the name he has been using. It seems he may have killed five people, although nobody seems to really know, and possibly more."

Now it was Asigori's turn to frown.

"'Bay' was the name used by a notorious traitor, your Grace, but he is rotting in prison awaiting transportation to an Imperial prison where he will doubtless spend the rest of his life. His name is infamous and no Imperial citizen would use it, not even as a joke, for fear of the taint. I'm afraid your man can't be an Imperial citizen; maybe a fugitive from the northern kingdoms or someone from the south affecting an Imperial accent?"

"Maybe," said the Duke doubtfully.

They walked a little further in silence.

"You are sure that your man is still in prison?" asked the Duke eventually, "He couldn't have escaped?"

Asigori laughed, a deep booming laugh.

"Oh yes, your Grace, you don't need to worry about that. Nobody escapes from an Imperial prison."

"Yes, well. Your confidence is reassuring, Ambassador, but that leaves us with a mystery. Who is this 'Bay' and why is he here? Never mind, Mantior will sniff out the details. I'm sure we'll know more within a few days. Now, let us talk of bandits and borders and other tedious affairs of state."

29

K rant slept well for several hours as the drugged wine numbed his body and chased away the pain. As the drugs wore off in the small hours, the pain from his broken ribs grew steadily until every breath was difficult. Comfort ebbed quickly away until any movement provoked a sharp stabbing pain that defeated all attempts at sleep. The rest of the night was spent in dull agony, his brief periods of sleep punctuated by nightmares about dark alleyways peopled with toothless thugs inexplicably sporting large holes in their chests.

By dawn the pain was unbearable and Krant was finding it difficult to breathe. A sudden bout of coughing brought blood to his lips and tears to his eyes and he struggled to hold back the screams he hadn't the breath to make. The pain was so great that he couldn't sit up so he just lay there, eyes closed, breathing shallowly. When he next opened his eyes Gavelis was standing over him, a concerned look on his face.

"I think we need to get you some help, sir," he said, "so I'm heading out into the town to find a doctor. I shouldn't be long - the innkeeper has given me directions - so just lie still and don't try to get up or walk around." Krant boggled at the idea of standing in his current condition but drawing breath to speak sent sharp pains through his chest and all he could do was flap wordlessly at Gavelis with his hand.

Gavelis nodded to him, concern showing on his face, then slipped out of the room, closing the door behind him as he went. Krant heard him clatter down the stairs then a door banged and the inn was quiet, the only sounds coming from the slowly awakening street. He lay still, listening to people on the street, to the creak of the inn's walls, to his own laboured breathing. Was that a hint of bubbles he could hear from his chest? He closed his eyes again, trying to shut out the pain and breathing as little as he could.

Later - an hour, maybe? - his eyes snapped open when he heard footsteps on the stairs and the murmur of low voices. He must have dozed off, he decided, but now he was awake and a sudden cough almost caused him to blackout as pain shot through his chest. He gasped, but that was painful as well.

The door opened and Gavelis came into the room leading possibly the most ancient person Krant had ever seen. She was tall and thin, her grey hair braided and dangling to her waist. Her face was etched with decades - or maybe centuries, Krant couldn't tell - but her eyes sparkled and she smiled in a friendly way as she approached his bed.

"Good morning Master Krant," she said, her voice carrying no hint of a rural accent, "Mr Gavelis tells me that you have endured a degree of violence and suffered injury as a result." She sat on the very edge of his bed and looked closely at his face. Krant nodded and opened his mouth to speak but she just held up a finger.

"My name is Ethelda Benedict. When you speak, you

may call me Ms Benedict. Mr Gavelis has described your injuries but I need to examine you myself. If at any time you wish me to leave and never return, simply behave badly or in a threatening manner. I am sorry that it is necessary to proceed like this but I have firm rules and they must be respected. I have explained these rules to Mr Gavelis and he has vouched for your good conduct but if you break them I will leave. Do you understand?"

Krant looked at Gavelis, who nodded, then back at Ms Benedict. He felt, in the power of her gaze, like a small child confronting a formidable teacher. He nodded, hoping that he had conveyed the appropriate level of respect.

"Good. Then I shall begin by removing your shirt and examining your chest." She moved quickly and with evident experience, pulling back Krant's sheets then producing a pair of shears from her bag and snipping quickly through the material, removing his ruined shirt. Krant's chest was a mass of violent purple bruises and Gavelis seemed surprised.

"I'm sure the marks were less obvious last night," he said.

"Yes," said Ms Benedict, "they probably were. But overnight the bruises have bloomed and the internal bleeding has continued. Be quiet, now, while I work." Gavelis shut his mouth and stepped back, sitting down on his own bed to watch.

"Hmm. It would have been better to call me last night. And administering a sedative was probably a bad idea. Yours?" she glanced at Gavelis, who nodded, "Yes, well, I'm sure you thought you were helping your employer, but next time remember healing first, sleep second."

Gavelis, for the first time since Krant had met him, looked somewhat humbled.

Ms Benedict probed gently at Krant's ribs, testing for broken bones. Krant winced and closed his eyes as pain burst from his chest.

"Yes. Two broken ribs and two more fractured. I suspect the pain you feel, Master Krant, is because one of your ribs has punctured your lung. This is causing internal bleeding which will, if left untreated, kill you."

She continued her examination, ignoring Krant's sudden look of horror. The pain had told him that his injuries were bad but he had never thought they might be life-threatening.

"Can, can you help?" he asked, gasping the words out between waves of pain.

Ms Benedict stopped and looked at him.

"Yes, I can help." She smiled at him and brushed the hair back from his face.

"Lie still, don't try to speak, just let me work." She took two charmed tools and a wad of leather from her bag.

"This is going to hurt. I have to pull your ribs back into place before I can set them. Bite down on this, if it helps." She pushed the leather wad between Krant's teeth, ignoring the terrified expression on his face, then turned to her tools. She focussed power into the charms and sent tendrils of power directly into the wound, feeling her way around the mangled flesh.

"Here we go," she said quietly.

She tweaked the power in one of the charms and Krant screamed into the leather as the bones moved beneath the skin. Ms Benedict frowned and shifted the power between the two charms, working them gently to move the bones back into place. After a few minutes, she sat up a little straighter and rolled her shoulders. Krant lay still, unconscious but breathing steadily.

"And now to stop the bleeding," she muttered, pulling a third tool from her bag and switching around the other two. She bent over Krant again, focussing more power and delving deep into his chest. She muttered to herself continually as she moved the tools across Krant's skin, concentration furrowing her brow as she worked, but finally she stopped and set down her tools. She probed gently at Krant's chest with her fingers but he didn't wake or wince and Ms Benedict nodded in satisfaction.

"That," she said, re-packing her tools, "is all I can do for him. I've set his bones, repaired his lung and stopped the bleeding. The bruises will be painful for a week or so and he'll need to rest for a few days but he should be fine." Gavelis let go the breath he hadn't realised he had been holding.

"Thank you, Ms Benedict. I am very grateful and I am sure Master Krant will be even more grateful, when he awakes."

"Yes, well. I am glad to give satisfaction, but these things always come at a price, I'm afraid. Sometimes I am able to decline payment in lieu of favours or other goods but you, I think, have further to travel and our paths are unlikely to cross again, so," she held out her hand, waiting, "cash, as agreed, please."

"Happily," said Gavelis, "and if I am ever in need of healing services again in this area I hope I can call upon you again." He counted out the agreed fee and handed it over with a smile.

"Thank you," said Ms Benedict, slipping the coins into her own purse, "I would of course be happy to see you again, although hopefully not because you have received a beating." She smiled at him and finished packing away her tools then opened the door, holding it while she stood on the threshold.

"This isn't a bad town, Mr Gavelis, but it has some bad people in it. Take care."

She went to close the door but Gavelis put his hand on her arm.

"You've been around these parts for a while," he observed, "you must have seen many unusual, ah, skills?"

Ms Benedict's eyes narrowed as she looked at Gavelis.

"That's either the must roundabout pick-up line I've ever heard or you want something. Spit it out, Mr Gavelis."

He coughed and offered her an eager smile.

"I'm looking for old knowledge, skills long forgotten." He paused again, peering intently at Ms Benedict's face. "What can you tell me about Bone Wrights?"

As he asked the question he felt her stiffen before she snatched her arm away from his grasp.

"You do know the term," he said, face eager, eyes alight, "tell me!"

She stepped quickly away from, further into the corridor.

"Tell you? I've spent the last two centuries healing people, Mr Gavelis. Is that even your real name? Bah! I don't want to know. You're too young, Mr Gavelis, too young by far and even if you weren't I'd refuse to teach you such skills."

She looked at him and her face was dark with anger. Gavelis had a sudden feeling of dread and danger, as if a terrible power were nearby. He shuddered and looked suddenly around as the feeling grew. Ms Benedict stood in the corridor, no longer a friendly healer but, somehow, transformed into a being of awful threat and menace.

Gavelis blinked in fear and stepped back into the bedroom, slamming the door and throwing the bolt. He lurched across the room, clutching the handle of a knife and pointing the blade back towards the door, cold sweat beading on his forehead, his hands clammy and shaking, his breath coming in shallow gasps.

He stood there in silent terror as the feeling slowly faded, then he lowered the knife, staring down at his treacherous hands as they shook. He took a few deep breaths to steady himself, then he sheathed the knife and shook his head.

"Bad move, Gavelis," he whispered to himself, "very bad." He lowered himself gently onto his bed and began absent-mindedly sorting his things, packing and re-packing until he was happy that everything was in its proper place, comforting himself with the familiar routines.

After an hour, his hands stopped shaking and he was able to stand without feeling sick. Krant still slept, so Gavelis, feeling somewhat restored but still not quite himself, went downstairs to find something to eat.

The inn's common room was mostly empty but Gavelis found a maid and ordered some food. As he chewed his bread and cheese, Gavelis' gaze wandered across the room. There was only one other occupied table; three middle-aged men sat nursing their beer and complaining about the price of flour until a fourth man came in through the front door.

"Hey, Tad," said one of the seated drinkers, waving his hand at the newcomer, "join us for a drink."

Tad came over quickly, dragging a chair with him, and sat down at the table.

"You'll never guess. You know Ratchet, that loser who begs and picks pockets down by the gate?"

"Him with the bad teeth and the skin problems? Bit of a

git, if you ask me," said one of the other drinkers, sipping his beer, "and he never stands his round neither. Right tight bastard he is. What of 'im?"

"He's dead. Struck down in the street by some ruffian. There was all sorts of screaming last night when some woman stumbled over his corpse in the dark. Near scared her half to death, tripping on his boots. She thought 'e were drunk, till she saw the blood and the guts and huge 'ole in his chest."

"A hole? What do you mean, hole?" said the third drinker, beer half-raised but temporarily forgotten.

"A hole. A bloody great hole, big as your fist I heard, all the way through his chest."

"Nah, I don't believe it. What could do that to a man?"

"Some sort of spear, maybe, but it'd have to be a bloody big one."

"Or magic," said the youngest of the drinkers, beer froth hanging from his wispy moustache, "one of those charm things the Imperial Shock Troops use. I heard they could make holes in tables n' anything."

"Magic!" scoffed the second drinker, "You want to get your head seen to, mate."

"No, he's right," said Tad, "Leastways, Squint in the Watch told me they're looking for someone with a big fucking charm, something really nasty."

Gavelis took another bite of bread and chewed slowly. He wasn't particularly concerned by the news that the Watch were hunting for a talented assailant but he was a little worried about Krant. There was nothing to tie them directly to the death but an astute Watchman or gate guard might notice Krant's injuries and connect them to a back-street mugging, maybe even make the leap to a murder in a dark alleyway. At the very least, such a turn of events would delay them; at worst, it could prove fatal.

Gavelis weighed their options. Krant needed to sleep and eat and Gavelis doubted he would be able to travel today even if he woke soon enough. They could try to slip out after dark but that would be highly suspicious. Nobody travelled after dark without a very good reason except as part of a large group, and even then they would think twice. The roads around here, outside the Empire and away from the towns, were not even completely safe during the day.

And then there was Ms Benedict. She didn't know who they were - she hadn't seemed interested in knowing anything about them beyond their names - and she didn't really know the circumstances of Krant's injuries, but she was a smart woman with long experience. It wouldn't take much for her to put two and two together and direct the Watch their way. She had certainly recognised him as talented but would she do anything if she realised he might be the one the Watch were searching for? Gavelis didn't think that she was the sort of person who would report a patient to the Watch but it might not be wise to test that assumption - he had been wrong about people in the past and experience had made him wary.

He listened a little more to the drinkers at the next table but their conversation quickly turned from the useful and interesting to the dull and fatuous as they discussed, with scant knowledge and less insight, the best way to tackle someone with a dangerous charm. Gavelis finished his meal and went back to the room to check on Krant. Everything was quiet except for Krant's snoring so Gavelis sat for a while reading a small volume of essays he had acquired during his brief time in Esterengel.

By mid-afternoon, with Krant still sleeping, Gavelis set

down his book, stretched, and stood up to look out of the window. The room overlooked a wide street that opened onto the main market square. By leaning out through the opened window, Gavelis could see the market stalls, their canvas roofs poking above the heads of the people crowded into the square. The day had dawned bright and sunny and the muddy streets had dried quickly. If the weather held until tomorrow they should have good conditions for travelling.

Gavelis sat back down on the bed and reviewed his plans for the next day. They would leave soon after dawn, he decided, and aim to get through the gates in the first rush of travellers. Many people would leave the town early in the morning to be sure of reaching the next town or their destination before nightfall. He and Krant would be made more conspicuous by their horses but they were less likely to be challenged, even as foreigners, if they were mounted. An early start would be unpopular with Krant but Gavelis was happy to trade unpopularity for convenience.

Krant woke later in the evening and sat up. Gavelis was still reading by the last light of the sun but he put the book down as Krant stirred.

"Good evening, sir. How are you feeling?"

Krant stretched, winced, then stretched again, testing the limits of his mobility.

"Evening, Gavelis? Have I slept all day?" Gavelis nodded.

"Well, I feel much better, thank you. Not quite perfect but certainly much more alive than I did when the doctor arrived."

Krant raised his arm and moved the blanket so that he could inspect his bruises, which flowered purple and green across his chest. He poked gingerly at his ribs and took a slow, experimental, deep breath.

"Colourful, but less painful than I had expected. That doctor knew what she was doing, it seems."

"Indeed, sir. I wasn't sure you would remember her visit."

"I don't think I do remember it, not all of it. But enough of that. Is there any food, Gavelis? I'm ravenous."

"Certainly sir, let me see what the kitchen can offer." Gavelis left the room and banged down the stairs, returning a few minutes later with a tray holding two large bowls of stew, a loaf of bread, a large piece of cheese, some butter and a flagon of wine. Gavelis passed a bowl of stew and a portion of bread and cheese to Krant and sat down on his own bed to eat.

"We need to discuss our plans for tomorrow, sir," said Gavelis.

"And we need to talk," said Krant around a mouthful of bread, "about what happened in the alleyway. That man - did you kill him?"

Gavelis was silent for a moment.

"Yes. It seemed to be the fastest way to stop him killing you, sir. Is that a problem?"

Krant looked surprised.

"Problem? That you killed him to protect me, or that he had the opportunity to beat me like he did? I'm not upset about his death, Gavelis, but I do object to being abandoned and beaten up while you swan off on your own account." Gavelis bristled at the criticism but said nothing, so Krant continued.

"You seem, Gavelis, to have a very broad skill set for a humble manservant. And at least one tool that falls outside the traditional, ha, 'arsenal', of the valet."

"Yes, sir," said Gavelis, looking at him, wondering how much to say, "I think it might be best all round for you to assume that I am not merely a valet and that my expertise extends into a number of areas more normally associated with soldiers. Beyond that I suggest you do not question, since I will not be able to answer honestly."

Krant looked at him over his spoon, which hovered in mid-air dripping stew into the bowl.

"Well. Right, yes. Yes. Well, I certainly don't want to ask awkward questions," he said sarcastically. Krant finished guiding the spoon to his mouth.

"So what now? You killed him, we're both alive, I guess we still have to head for Vensille?" he finished, hoping that Gavelis would say they could go home.

"Yes, we still head for Vensille. And sooner, rather than later. Ms Benedict counselled rest and recuperation, for a few days at least but the Watch found the corpse and seem to have determined that he was killed by someone of talent."

"Well, so what? He attacked an Imperial envoy and got everything he deserved!"

"Yes, but they won't see it like that," said Gavelis slowly, as if explaining to a child, "we are outside the Empire, just far enough that they want to exert their independence. I doubt they would listen to our explanation, let alone believe it."

"You're saying the Watch might be unfriendly?" said Krant, frowning.

"Yes, possibly very unfriendly. I think there's a fair chance they would hang us quickly in the market square and to hell with the consequences."

Krant blanched and set down his bowl. Even at his most cynical, he had thought places beyond the Empire as basically the same as Esterengel but with different food. Being hanged as a murderer without even an opportunity to defend himself before a magistrate was beyond anything he had imagined.

"But I don't think it needs to come to that," said Gavelis, "if we move quickly and keep our heads. The Watch are searching for a killer amongst the talented but"

"I'm talented!" said Krant, cutting to what he saw as the heart of the issue.

"Yes, so am I," said Gavelis patiently, "but from what I learned downstairs their understanding of talent and charms may well mislead them. And I can't believe that they'll worry for too long about finding the killer of a petty criminal, so we just need to keep calm and leave as soon as we can. Early in the morning, with the first of the day's travellers, I think."

"Tomorrow? Not this evening? Maybe it would be better to get away now before anyone finds us."

"Nobody knows we are here, except Ms Benedict, and I don't think she will report us to the Watch. And nobody travels at night - it's too dangerous. First thing in the morning is our only option, so eat up, get some rest and I'll wake you at dawn."

Krant looked doubtful for a moment but then he yawned and picked up his unfinished bowl of stew.

"Maybe you are right. Maybe first thing in the morning would be best, although I'm not sure I'll be able to sleep." He worked his way through the rest of the stew and ate some of the bread then lay back on the bed and pulled the sheets up to his chin. Within moments he was asleep.

Gavelis finished his own stew and packed the bread and cheese in his bags. He spent an hour exercising, working through fist and foot fighting movements in a choreographed style taught to him as a child, then he checked and honed his blades. Finally, he checked and stowed his shock cannon and his other charms, arranging them so that they would be close to hand in the morning but out of sight and away from prying eyes. Preparations complete, he lay down on his bed and stared at the ceiling for a while before drifting off to sleep.

30

K rant woke with a start to find Gavelis shaking him gently. The room was dimly lit by a very small flame from Gavelis' fire charm. Krant squirmed under the blankets then remembered why they were waking so early and hurriedly pushed them back. He sat up and swung his feet to the floor, sitting with his head in his hands for a few moments as Gavelis fussed with his pack, then he dressed and stuffed his things into his own bag.

He was pulling on a boot when Gavelis hissed at him and shook his head. Sighing gently, Krant put on his cloak and threw his pack over his shoulder then, boots in hand, followed Gavelis carefully out of the room and down the stairs.

At the door to the yard Gavelis extinguished his charm and they both put on their boots. The stable door was bolted but it slid easily and within a few minutes they had their horses saddled and the packhorse loaded and ready to go. As dawn broke and the first rays of sunlight danced across the rooftops, Krant and Gavelis led their horses out of the inn's yard and through the quiet town toward the west gate.

A few minutes later they reached the west gate only to find that it was still closed and barred. A bored watchman stood in front of the gate, leaning on his pikestaff and yawning; he had clearly been there for some time but he straightened up as Krant and Gavelis approached.

"Gate's closed," he said when they reached him, "by order of the town council. Can't leave till they've spoken to you."

Krant bristled and looked at Gavelis but said nothing. Gavelis leaned forward in his saddle and Krant could feel him focussing power into a charm on his finger.

"We have already spoken to the council. My lord is in a hurry and we have permission to leave Rayvale; you can open the gate for us." Krant frowned, not sure what Gavelis was doing, then his eyes went wide Gavelis tried to coerce the watchman, focussing power through a small charm disguised as a ring on his left hand. Krant snapped his head forward to stare at the watchman, trying to put a stern, lordly look on his face.

"Yes, yes, I see. Sorry m'lord, didn't know." The man bumbled around, dropping his pikestaff as he fumbled the bar of the gate. Gavelis jumped down from his horse.

"Here, let me help with that."

Together the two men lifted the heavy bar and laid it to one side. Then the watchman pulled open the gate and waved them through.

"Go in peace," said the watchman as Krant and Gavelis rode carefully out of the town, then he closed the gate behind them.

Twenty yards beyond the gate Krant hissed at Gavelis.

"What the hell did you do? Coercing a watchman; are you mad?"

The punishment for coercion was severe if the victim was only a lowly peasant but the punishments grew rapidly worse as you climbed the social scale. Coercing watchmen could get you hanged, or worse.

"Just keep going," said Gavelis through gritted teeth, "before they work out what," he paused, listening to the sounds of raised voices from behind the gate; clearly something wasn't right.

"Go!" said Gavelis, kicking his own horse forward and dragging the packhorse behind him as fast as it would go. Krant stared briefly at Gavelis' retreating back, then looked back at the gatehouse as someone came out, shouting. More watchmen appeared in the dim shadows and Krant quickly whipped his horse into a gallop, chasing Gavelis through the gloom, not daring to look back again.

Krant caught up with Gavelis a few hundred yards down the road, where he had stopped and was hurriedly pulling things from the bags on the packhorse. He stuffed some into his own pack and threw a few shirts at Krant.

"Pack those in your bag. You're carrying all your valuables, yes?" Krant nodded, slightly unsure. Gavelis finished re-packing and strapped a sword to his side. Krant hadn't even known that he had been carrying a sword and was about to ask a question when Gavelis spoke.

"We're dumping the packhorse. It's too slow and we can manage without it."

Gavelis threw the rest of the bags into the bushes at the side of the road and set fire to them with a great spurt of flame from his charm. Krant's horse stepped backward in alarm before settling down a little as Krant patted his neck. Gavelis led the packhorse to the side of the road and pointed it northward then slapped its rump as hard as he could, setting it running across the fields.

"Maybe that'll confuse them if they're looking for two men with three horses," said Gavelis as he climbed back into the saddle, "but probably not. Now we ride fast and hope to lose ourselves in the traffic on the road before they get any ideas about chasing us."

He kicked his horse forward and together they galloped west through the quickening dawn.

Sometime later as the sun rose to warm their backs Gavelis slowed his horse to a walk and then stopped to stow his cloak. They had seen no sign of pursuit since leaving Rayvale but their headlong flight along the road would have kept them ahead of their pursuers in any case. Gavelis said as much to Krant, who grunted as he too folded his cloak.

"We probably have better horses than the Rayvale town watch but I think we'll moderate our pace somewhat. No point killing the horses a few miles down the road."

Krant grunted again. His ribs were aching and he really wasn't ready for this sort of exercise or in the mood to talk.

A little later as they cantered gently along, they pulled over to the roadside verge to allow a small caravan of traders heading the other way to squeeze past.

"Good morning," said Gavelis, raising a friendly smile to driver of the cart leading the caravan, "how far do you think it is to the next town?"

The man looked up from the road, reins of his cart horses in his hands, but he didn't slow or stop.

"Next village is over t'hill," he said, jerking his thumb over his shoulder, "that's where we stayed last night. Next town, Stagford, is further on, maybe fifteen mile."

"Right, thanks."

The man looked back over his shoulder at Gavelis as the cart rumbled on down the road.

"Heard there was bandits on the road, mind. Stay safe."

Gavelis and Krant sat watching as the caravan pulled past them, sixteen carts in total with three armed men on horseback, then they rode on down the road, hurrying to stay ahead of the Watch and looking around for bandits as they went.

"Bandits, eh?" said Krant a little while later as they cantered along the road toward Stagford. They wove past farmers and drovers and people walking to market.

"Outlaws ahead, Watch behind, dangerous traitor at the end of the road."

He looked sideways at Gavelis.

"Maybe we could save everyone a lot of trouble by just slitting our own throats. If we stand at the edge of the road and lean backwards as we do it we should just fall neatly into the ditch."

Gavelis laughed grimly.

"I can't say I've ever found a problem for which that was an attractive solution."

"Maybe you just haven't looked hard enough," said Krant. That seemed to kill the conversation and they rode in silence for the next mile or so.

"If we do meet outlaws are you likely to be any use?" asked Gavelis suddenly, breaking the silence.

"I could give them a lengthy exposition on the merits of proper filing in the context of a civil administration, if that would help?"

"Hmm. Worth a try if things go badly wrong, I suppose. Maybe you can encourage them to do the trick with the ditch and the throat slitting. Are you any good with a fire charm?"

"I can do a pretty neat trick with a cigar and a glass of brandy," he said eventually, "goes down a treat at parties."

Gavelis raised his eyebrow, looking over at Krant as they bobbed up and down on their horses.

"A cigar? Truly?"

"A cigar. Or a cigarillo, at a push. I can produce enough flame to light one from, maybe, three feet away, but that's about it."

Gavelis shook his head.

"That'll have to do, I suppose. You have a charm?"

"In my pack," said Krant.

Gavelis slowed his horse to a walk and Krant followed suit.

"Get it out then. It won't do us any good while it's lost at the bottom of your pack."

Krant fished awkwardly in his pack until he found the charm. It was old and cheap, a crude and ugly piece of work that Krant held on to for vague, sentimental reasons. Gavelis, also rummaging through his bag and guiding his horse with his knees, produced a short length of leather cord.

"Tie one end to the charm and the other to your arm, then you can hide the charm in your sleeve and flick it forward into your hand when you need it. Not perfect but it'll give you a chance to surprise someone if you strike at the right time."

Krant nodded and tied the charm as instructed. He spent the next few minutes fumbling around with his sleeve, trying to get the charm to stay put when it should be hidden and pop out when it was needed.

"Yes, well. It's the sort of thing that improves with practice," said Gavelis with mild exasperation, "just remember to use it if you get the chance and to use it decisively. Don't mess around, don't try to be nice, don't aim to scare or intimidate, just power up and set fire to someone."

Krant looked at him aghast.

"Set fire to someone? I couldn't do that!"

Gavelis looked straight at him.

"The man in the alley, the one who gave you a kicking. Could you have sprayed him with a burst of flame? Could you have set him alight while he was smashing your ribs? What about afterwards, when the pain was so bad you passed out and almost died?"

Krant opened his mouth then closed it again.

"Remember the pain. Imagine, if the need arises, that it's your life or theirs. You don't have to like it or enjoy it, you just have to do what it takes to survive."

Gavelis slapped him on the back.

"Cheer up. We might never meet an outlaw," Gavelis grinned at him as Krant looked back, his face ashen, "but right now we need to pick up the pace if we are to reach Stagford before noon."

He kicked his horse to a canter and Krant followed suit.

Adrava woke with a start, suddenly alert but confused about where she was. She sat up in bed, the unfamiliar sounds of a new town filling the room, then she remembered where she was; Riverbridge, waiting for a barge to Vensille. She lay back in her bed, staring at the ceiling, and relaxed a little. A day in Riverbridge, another night in the Bargeman, then a few hours of waiting tomorrow until she could board. If she stayed out of sight and kept to herself she shouldn't attract any undue attention even if the men who were following her, and she was sure it was one of them that she had seen the day before talking to the dock master, were in the town.

Eventually she got up, washed and dressed. She stayed in the room for as long as she could but with nothing to read and nobody to talk to her range of diversions was limited and she quickly grew tired of meditation and talent exercises. Finally, with her stomach growling, she checked her charms and purse and went downstairs in search of food and gossip.

The common room was mostly empty. The people of Riverbridge, it seemed, didn't frequent inns during the middle of the day so Adrava was able to eat her meal in peace. Outside on the docks it was a different matter. Even through the inn's small grimy windows she could see that the river was alive with boats and people and goods. She sat at a table near the windows, staring out at the docks until by early-afternoon the activity began to die down and people started to come into the inn. When the inn's common room began to fill, she moved to a quiet table in a corner, as far from the door as she could get. There she sat in shadow, drinking tea, watching the rest of the room.

People came and went but as the day wore on people came more than they left and by mid-afternoon the room was almost full. The dockers who had started work at dawn had finished for the day and were eating hearty meals of fish casserole with great thick slices of bread. Travellers newly arrived, some hoping to take passage downstream or along the coast, swapped tales of sea-sickness and piracy with those heading upstream.

And then the door opened to admit two roughly dressed men carrying swords. They didn't look out of place - nobody in the inn was finely dressed and many people were armed with long knives or short swords - and nobody else in the inn gave them a second glance but they stood just inside the door looking around until one of them saw Adrava and nudged his friend. They both looked at her for a few seconds then one ducked back out through the door while the other took a seat and ordered beer. He sat near the door, watching, and Adrava could feel his eyes on her.

She looked across at him and he stared defiantly back at her, his face red with anger. Then he stood up, knocking over the table and pointed at her.

"Murderer!" he screamed, spittle flying from his mouth, "Murderer!"

The room fell silent as everyone turned to watch. Even Adrava was taken aback, surprised that someone should make such brazen accusations in quite such a public fashion. She looked over her shoulder to see if there was anyone behind her.

"Don't look away from me, whore!" said the man, taking two steps toward her, still pointing, his finger quivering with rage, "You murdered my friends, bitch, and I'll see justice done."

Adrava looked at him, allowing shock and horror to show on her face. The atmosphere in the inn was tense but nobody moved. Even the innkeeper, veteran of many years serving ale to drunkards, seemed unsure of what to do. Adrava looked around, a little frantically, then snapped her eyes back to the man as he took another step toward her.

"Where's the magistrate in this town? Where's the justice?"

Adrava stood, shakily.

"You wrong me, Sir. Why do you accuse me so?"

Over by the counter one of the patrons said, not quietly enough, "Bit too much beer, if you ask me." There were some sniggers and a couple of people turned away, hunching over their mugs to hide their faces.

The bandit turned away from Adrava.

"Beer?" he screamed, "My friends are dead and you blame beer? It was her," he said pointing again at Adrava, "she killed them and I want justice."

He took another step forward but suddenly found the innkeeper blocking his way, a long cudgel dangling from one hand.

"I think you've had enough, sir," he said, calmly, "probably best to leave."

The man goggled at him then snarled and tried to push past the innkeeper.

"I'll go 'n take 'er with me, straight to the magistrate."

"I don't think so, son," said the innkeeper, his hand resting on the man's chest, "just go home and sleep it off. Where's your friend, the one you came in with?"

"Friend? What friend?" shouted the man, "My friends are dead, out there in the woods where she left them, bodies mutilated and burned. She needs hanging and if you won't help I'll see to it myself." He dropped his hand to his side, took a step back to clear some space and pulled out his sword, none too steadily.

There was an immediate change in the temper of the room as people pushed back their chairs to get away from the man and clear of his sword. Angry drunks were one thing - they'd all seen plenty of those - but angry drunks with drawn swords were quite another. Nobody wanted to get sliced or stabbed.

The innkeeper also backed away a few steps but he raised his cudgel as well, eyes on the waving tip of the sword.

"Put the sword away son, before someone gets hurt. You'll do your friends no good like this."

The man pointed the sword at the innkeeper, swinging it away from Adrava.

"It's not your fight, old man, so fuck off."

He swung back to face Adrava, face contorted with rage, then he darted forward toward her, sword raised, only to trip over an inconvenient foot stuck out by one of the other patrons. He fell flat on his face, sword falling from his hand and sliding away across the boards, then the innkeeper stepped forward and struck him hard across the shoulders as he struggled to rise, knocking him back down. Another patron swung round on his chair and put his boot on the man's shoulder then leant down to speak to him.

"Just you stay down there, mate, maybe calm down a bit. Do you a world of good."

The seated man leant forward so that his weight pressed down on the bandit, then he looked over at the Adrava and winked.

The innkeeper signalled to a couple of his lads who came forward and picked the man up under the shoulders, dragging him backwards to the door before throwing him out on the street, then he went over to Adrava's table where she was still standing, shaking, white faced.

"Sorry about that, miss. Don't normally get that sort of thing in here, 'tis early to be so drunk. You sit back down and we'll get you some more food and a glass of something to settle your nerves, on the house. And the boys'll make sure he don't come back to bother you no more."

Adrava looked up at the man and smiled lopsidedly.

"Thank you. Poor man, so confused, so desperate."

She sat down, placing her hands on the table to help

calm her nerves. Around her the normal chatter began again, albeit it a little stiffly, a little more quietly than before.

"Do you know who he was?"

"No miss, can't say as I do. Not from Riverbridge, I reckon; maybe from up north aways, by the sound of his voice. Rum lot up north but first time I've heard them accusing strangers of murder."

He pottered around as the overturned table was righted and new drinks were brought by the maids.

"Let me know if there's anything else you need, miss."

He tugged his forelock and took his leave, heading out to the back room, whispering instructions to one of the men who had ejected the bandit as he guided him by the elbow across the common room.

Adrava sat there for another hour or so, picking at the new plate of food that the barmaid brought and sipping at her wine. The bandit didn't return and by late afternoon things seemed to be back to normal. In one corner a man produced a small violin and began to play a lively jig. The people seated at the nearby tables nodded along to the tune, knocking their knuckles on tables in time to the music and even dancing at times.

As the afternoon passed into evening, Adrava relaxed until, as dusk fell, she finally felt safe to leave the common room. She was, frankly, sick of the room having been there all day. There had been no further sign of the bandits and nobody else had caused her any trouble or even spoken to her - it seemed she was to be avoided - so she picked up her things and slipped quietly through the back door and up the stairs to her room.

Krant and Gavelis made it to Stagford just before noon.

They stopped briefly outside the town's eastern entrance to rest and water the horses and buy bread and cheese for themselves. Half an hour later, refreshed and with no sign of pursuit, they walked their horses through the small town and began the final stretch of their ride to Riverbridge, where Gavelis was hopeful of commandeering a vessel to take them to Vensille.

"Stagford to Riverbridge isn't far, if memory serves." said Gavelis when they had cleared the last of Stagford's western residences and were again trotting along a road that ran through row upon row of neat orchards.

"I thought you travelled regularly along this road?" said Krant.

"Not this far. My relatives all live within the Empire and I have seldom had need to travel this way. From this point on we're navigating by memory, mostly, and by asking directions."

"And it looks like the roads are deteriorating as we head west," said Krant, pointing to a poorly maintained ford in a small river where the stream had washed away chunks of the stone road on either side.

"If we're lucky that'll be as bad as it gets on the way to Riverbridge. After that we should be on the river, nice and easy."

"About that, Gavelis. Will we be able to hire a vessel large enough to carry our horses? We're a long way inland, after all."

"Probably," said Gavelis, nodding, "although we may have to wait a few days."

Krant looked horrified that they might have to spend longer away from Esterengel.

"Surely not, Gavelis, surely not!"

"We could always ride, sir," said Gavelis, slipping back

into his servant persona now that the immediate danger of the watch had receded, "but I suspect you might enjoy that rather less and it's still a long way to travel. The river is safer and faster, sir."

They rode on in silence for another hour before Krant spoke up again.

"This business of killing people with a fire charm, Gavelis. You speak as if you have specialist knowledge, and, yes," he said, holding up his hand as Gavelis turned to speak, "I know you said I shouldn't ask, and I won't, but is there anything you might teach me so that I can act. Should the need arise, of course." he added, hurriedly.

"Most of the bandits, or in fact watchmen, we might meet will not be talented, sir, so any display of power might be enough to bluff them into submission, particularly if it was timed to cause maximum surprise. That might be enough under most circumstances. If they persist, or if the opportunity for a show doesn't arise, or if they look like they'll press their attack, then a long strike before they reach you would be favourite."

"A long strike? How long, would you say?"

"Beyond the reach of whatever weapon they happen to be holding, sir, so about four feet for a sword, seven for a staff, fifteen for a halberd or pikestaff and maybe two hundred yards for a bow, although if they're shooting at you and they know how to use a bow then it's probably already too late to fight back."

Krant looked around to check that the road was clear then shrugged his arm to flick the fire charm into his hand. It took a few tries but eventually he caught it. He pointed it away from Gavelis and pushed as much power as he could into the charm, releasing it toward the distant hills. A hot bright flame shot out about four feet before collapsing back.

"Very good sir. That would certainly be sufficient for many situations. If I may suggest, though, you may achieve greater reach by narrowing the flame front and concentrating it into as thin a jet as possible."

Krant nodded and shifted his shoulders then tried again. This time the charm produced a much narrower flame that reached maybe eight feet from the tip of the charm. Krant was delighted, laughing out loud and smiling like a child who'd been given a new toy.

"Ha! That'll show 'em, eh Gavelis?"

Gavelis nodded.

"Yes sir, it would certainly severely inconvenience anyone who happened to get in the way. My advice would be to practice a little more and then keep it secret until you absolutely have to use it. And don't hold back, sir. If you need to strike, strike to kill. It's the best way to keep yourself from harm."

"Really? Well, if you insist," said Krant, "but how will I know when the moment has come?"

Gavelis laughed mirthlessly.

"You'll know, sir, you'll know. If I'm dead or incapacitated or engaged then you strike, sir, as hard as you can. Surprise is our ally, sir, and it is often said that 'he who strikes first strikes last'."

Krant pondered this as they rode on, practicing repeatedly with the charm for the next quarter of an hour until he was repeatedly and quickly producing long pencil-thin gouts of flame.

"Very good, sir," said Gavelis encouragingly, "just be careful not to push too much power into the charm too quickly. These domestic charms don't have reservoirs, they're not really designed for combat, and too much power might produce a backlash or transfer burn."

Krant looked at Gavelis, suddenly alarmed. Gavelis sighed, inwardly appalled at Krant's lack of knowledge.

"Just something to bear in mind, sir," he said, although it wasn't obvious that Krant was reassured.

Krant sent a few more bursts of flame across the road before pocketing the charm as a horse and cart came into view. By the time they had passed the carter on the crest of the next hill, the walls of Riverbridge were in view. Krant heaved a huge sigh of relief as they trotted down the hill toward the relative safety of the town.

"I think, sir, that it might be a good idea to use different names until we reach Vensille."

Krant frowned, perturbed by this news.

"Why, Gavelis?"

"If the watch are following, sir, it will allow us a breathing space. We can use our own names again upon reaching Vensille and then, if they ask around, they won't receive helpful answers. It will make it more difficult for them to find us."

Krant thought about it and he had to admit that the suggestion was sound.

"Do you have names to suggest?"

Gavelis nodded.

"I think you should become Smark, sir, and I would be Dundaserre."

"Very well. Smark and Dundaserre it is."

At the dockside Gavelis left Krant holding the horses while he sought out the dock master and arranged passage downstream. Eventually he threaded his way back through the crowd to Krant and took back his horse.

"Well? Is there a ship?"

Gavelis nodded but he clearly wasn't happy.

"Ships don't come this far up the river, it seems, but there is a large barge, sir. We won't be the only passengers and it doesn't leave till tomorrow around noon. We'll be sleeping on the deck and minding our own horses."

"A barge? Will that be big enough?"

"The dock master seems to think it will, yes, sir, but we need to purchase blankets to replace those we lost and food for the trip. The dock master suggested that we lodge tonight at the Bargeman, over there, and then make our way over to the docks tomorrow morning. If we secure board now, sir, I can then acquire the supplies we might need."

"Very good, G- Dundaserre, lead the way."

Gavelis walked ahead of his horse, pulling it through the crowds to the entrance of the Bargeman's yard, and Krant followed suit. With the horses stabled and their packs stowed in a small room in the attic, Krant went in search of food in the common room while Gavelis left to buy supplies for the rest of the journey. Sitting quietly as he was near the back wall, he had a first-hand view of an astonishing encounter between a woman sitting on her own at a nearby table - itself a mildly shocking thing, especially as she appeared to be dressed in the robes of an Imperial cleric - and a rough-looking drunkard who had been sitting near the door.

The violent end of the encounter, with the man bludgeoned to the floor by the innkeeper before being thrown out onto the street, reminded Krant that he was far from home and getting further away with every day. He sat, feeling very small and lonely, desperately trying to avoid attention, until Gavelis arrived some time later and joined him for an early supper.

"You've missed the excitement," he said quietly, leaning

forward as Gavelis delicately ate the meat stew that seemed to be the only dish on the menu, "but I'll give you the details later." Then in a more normal voice he said, "Everything sorted for tomorrow?"

"Yes, sir, everything has been sorted. I've stowed several days' worth of food in our packs and arranged with the stable boy to take a couple of sacks of grain for the horses. That should cover most of what we need and we can probably buy more later if we need it, although anything they might sell us on the barge itself will most likely cost a great deal more."

"Good, good," said Krant, not really listening. The woman who had been on the receiving end of the objectionable man's temper was leaving quietly, slipping away through the back door. Surprising that such a beautiful young woman could move through a room like this without anyone really noticing. He said as much to Gavelis, who grunted.

"I knew a girl once, sir, who had a trick that could make people look straight past her, if she didn't want to be seen. A bit of power, a rare charm and you wouldn't know she was there. Was that woman talented?"

"I don't know," said Krant, uncertain and slightly confused, "I didn't sense anything but then I probably wouldn't from this range. And anyway, I didn't have any trouble seeing her."

"Fair point, maybe she just has a knack for avoiding attention. Either way, sir, she's left."

And she had, leaving through the back door without raising even a ripple of interest.

Adrava sat on her bed in her room, looking at the inside of

the door. Then she got up and dragged the bed across the floor until the heavy frame blocked the door from opening. She sat down again and looked at the shuttered window; nothing more she could do there unless she wanted to harden the wood itself and force it to flow together into a single solid piece. She dismissed the idea with an annoyed grimace; wood-charming was a skill she had never mastered, much to the amusement of her husband. She took out her shock cannon and set it down on the mattress. It was going to be a long night.

The next morning Adrava woke with a start and grabbed at her shock cannon. She hadn't meant to sleep at all but sometime around midnight, when the common room had begun to quieten, she had dozed off. Now, with dawn already here and the inn bustling with activity, she rolled out of bed and pulled the heavy frame away from the door. She packed quickly, washed in the small basin and then dressed before heading downstairs in search of breakfast.

As she ate she planned the supplies she would need food for herself and String for the voyage to Vensille. A simple enough problem to solve; she stopped a passing maid and asked her to pack bread, dried meat, hard cheese, biscuits and a skin of beer. She would talk to the stable boy about grain or hay for String but he should have fed well overnight and there would surely be places at the riverside where she could buy more.

By mid-morning she was fully stocked and she led String out of the inn's yard toward the docks. The dock master saw her and waved in a friendly fashion as she approached.

"Good morning, miss. We were about to come looking for you but here you are. Ready to go?"

She nodded, "Yes, packed and stocked and ready to go."

"Let me walk you to the berth and introduce you to the captain, miss. It's this way."

The dock master led the way along the docks until they reached the largest boat, a broad barge with a wide, steady gangplank. Leaning on the rail was a woman that Adrava took to be the boat's master, a tall thin woman, well-preserved like an ancient walnut. Her face was lined and tanned and she smiled not at all as the dock master approached.

"Good morning Mistress Banks," he said, "here is Miss Naseep, the first of the passengers booked for today. And her horse, whose name I do not know."

"String," said Adrava, "her name is String."

"Banks," said the ship's mistress, "Marjorie Banks. Well, come aboard if you're coming, and then we can get your beast hobbled and settled. We've got three boxes amidships for horses."

The dock master made his excuses and disappeared back toward his hut leaving the two women alone. Banks stood watching as Adrava gently encouraged String across the short gangplank and along the deck to the first of the three horse boxes. With String settled and secure, Adrava walked back to Banks and held out her hand.

"Naseep. Thank you for giving me passage. I hope the wind is fair and the voyage smooth."

Banks raised her eyebrow at this but took Adrava's hand and shook it while looking hard at her face and eyes.

"I see in your eyes the signs of wisdom and long experience; truly, you are welcome aboard the Golden Rose."

It was an unusual style of greeting used only by people of very great talent and age when they wished to indicate discretely that they had recognised a fellow practitioner. Adrava bowed her head to acknowledge that she was, as

Banks' had suggested, a person of talent and said fumbled her way through what she hoped would be a suitable reply, "I am truly glad to be so welcomed and honoured that you see signs of wisdom, Mistress Banks."

Banks nodded, clearly satisfied with Adrava's response.

"Later we must talk of many things but for now let me show you where you will be sleeping." Banks turned and led Adrava across the deck and down a short flight of steep stairs to a small cabin in the stern of the boat.

Adrava squeezed past the Mistress as she held open the door.

"Oh, that's very nice indeed, thank you," she said, glancing quickly around the tiny space, "the dock master said I would have to sleep on the deck; is the cabin not sold?"

Banks twitched her face into something that might have been a smile.

"Yes, but it won't hurt old Blucher to take the deck for once, and he can always walk if he doesn't like it."

"Thank you."

"Don't mention it," said Banks, "especially as Blucher will probably whine and complain and make snide comments all the way to Vensille, if he ever bloody turns up. We sail at noon." She nodded again then closed the door leaving Adrava alone in the tiny cabin.

Krant and Gavelis arrived at the Golden Rose shortly before noon to find a one-sided argument blazing on the deck. A fat middle-aged merchant was remonstrating violently with the ship's mistress, a tall tough-looking woman with short dark grey hair whose interest in the discussion appeared to be non-existent.

"That's just how it is, Blucher. I've given the cabin to someone else, there isn't another. You can take the deck like the other passengers or we can unload your cargo and you can walk. Which will it be?"

The man stared at her and for a moment Krant thought he might begin shouting again but then he seemed to deflate.

"Fine, I'll take the deck, but I don't like this high-handed attitude, Banks. We had a deal, after all."

"We did, it's true, but you know the rule; the deal isn't sealed until money has changed hands. No coin, no cabin, and now it's too late."

He sighed, now truly defeated, and stamped off down the deck to stake out a spot near the stern under the canvas awning.

"Hello," shouted Gavelis once the merchant had left, "is this the Golden Rose?"

"It is. Are you Smark?"

"I am Dundaserre, Mistress Banks, valet to my master, Mr Smark." Krant bowed as Banks scrutinised them both, eyes flicking quickly over their clothes, hair, horses and luggage.

"Get aboard, then, and stow your horses in the boxes. The end one's taken, mind."

"Thank you, Mistress," said Gavelis as Krant led his horse over the gangplank. By the time they had loaded both horses - Gavelis' was awkward and had to be coaxed gently across the gangplank which took the combined talents of half the crew and half an hour of concerted effort - and stowed their gear in a space under the awning noon had passed and Banks was clearly impatient to depart.

As the crew cast-off and guided the ship out into the main stream of the river Krant nudged Gavelis and said quietly, "Those men over there, on the dock. Do they look like the watchmen from Rayvale?"

Gavelis looked up from his pack and stared out over the river at a small group of men talking to various people on the dockside.

"Yes. I would say that they do." He turned back to his pack, sorting through his clothes and rearranging his modest possessions.

Krant kept watching the docks until the first turn of the river hid them from sight, then he sat down next to Gavelis.

"That was very close, Gavelis, very close indeed. Will they follow further, do you think?"

"I hadn't expected them to get this far, to be honest. Maybe we'll stay ahead of them or maybe they'll give up, but I think we must be prepared to disembark before we reach Vensille and ambush them somewhere. Risky, but not as risky as having them turn up in Vensille."

Krant looked shocked and his face was white.

"Ambush?" he hissed.

"Good thing we didn't use our real names. They probably know who we are and where we are going. If we catch them in the open we can finish them quickly."

"Don't be ridiculous," Krant said, looking around to check that they weren't overheard, "they'll race ahead to Vensille, trying to beat the river, then search for Smark and Dundaserre when the boat docks. All we need to do is get off a day or two before Vensille, announce to everyone here that we're going to ride back to Catshed to spend time with my family, then circle around into Vensille from another direction. The Rayvale watchmen will find out eventually and spend days travelling to and from Catshed and searching the area before they realise something's gone wrong, by which time we will have finished our mission anyway and we'll be on our way home."

Gavelis sat back on the deck, pack forgotten, surprised that Krant had come up with such a simple, elegant plan. He nodded, eyebrows raised.

"That might work, sir, that might work very well indeed."

He stopped nodding.

"I will talk to the captain tomorrow, sir, about your changed travel plans, and make the arrangements."

31

A drava sat in her cabin until she felt the barge move away from the dock then she waited another hour or so until she was sure that they had passed downstream far enough to be out of sight of Riverbridge and anyone who might still be looking for her. Eventually, with her meagre possessions arranged around the cabin to her satisfaction and her charms in place she decided it was time to venture up onto the deck.

As she climbed the short ladder she quickly forgot the hot stuffy atmosphere in the cramped quarters below decks. The early afternoon sun played across the river and a light breeze was filling the single sail, pushing the barge downstream.

Adrava found a spot at the rail away from the other passengers and out of the way of the small crew and stood there, looking out back east across the river to the banks and the fields and hills beyond. The countryside was a rich patchwork of orchards, vegetable patches, cereal fields and grazing meadows. The small towns and villages past which they floated appeared both numerous and prosperous; some were surrounded by walls of wood or stone but most were undefended except for a single watch tower or a fortified manor house.

It looked like a peaceful, comfortable land and to Adrava the only surprise was that the Empire had not yet brought this region within its borders. It would happen, she felt sure, but for now the Emperor's attention was focussed on his southern and eastern borders where there were even richer prizes waiting to be plucked. This little backwater, peaceful and prosperous though it was, could wait.

Her musings were interrupted by Blucher, the merchant, who wandered over to stand beside her, offering a slight bow as she glanced over at him.

"You are travelling alone, miss...?"

"Naseep. Yes, sir, to Vensille."

"Miss Naseep. An imperial name, yes? And, forgive me if I pry, but are you travelling with a purpose or merely to see some of our beautiful country?"

She turned to look at him, twisting her head round so that she could look up at him without taking her elbows from the rail.

"I haven't decided yet. It depends what I find in Vensille, I think."

He frowned, confused by her answer.

"But surely you must have an idea of why you travel! What would be the point otherwise?"

She smiled, looking back towards the fields and hills.

"Travel is sometimes its own reward, don't you find? And you are right that the countryside is beautiful. I think my destination will depend, ultimately, on how things turn out in Vensille."

"Ah, Vensille." he sighed, dreamily, "A great city and my home port. You have been before?"

"No, this will be my first visit, but I am very much looking forward to it. I hear it is the greatest of the city states and full of wonders."

"It is indeed a great city, miss, equal to any of the local Imperial cities and second only, I think, to your capital." Adrava doubted that Vensille was as large or as wealthy as Esterengel, even, but she nodded along.

He fell silent for a few minutes while together they watched a fisherman on the bank fighting to land his catch, straining on his rod. The barge turned a bend in the river taking them away from the fisherman before they could see the outcome of his struggle.

"I myself," he said eventually, "travel upstream regularly in search of trade and opportunities. The river is an excellent corridor for all sorts of goods and far safer and more comfortable than the roads."

"I heard, from travellers in the inn, that there are bands of outlaws roaming along the eastern road towards the empire," said Adrava, "do your Lords take no action against them?"

Blucher laughed.

"Action? No, not unless they threaten trade, although the town watch will sometimes catch and hang a few of the more miserable criminals. You saw the caravans? Most have mercenaries or experienced fighting men accompanying them, although you wouldn't always know it to look at them. I myself always travel with bodyguards," he nodded toward the stern where his two men - large, well-armed and tough-looking - lounged on the deck, dicing.

"And Vensille. Is it a safe city? Is it welcoming to travellers?"

Blucher sighed.

"It is a city of great wealth and fabulous buildings but

also of terrible poverty and crime. For a lady travelling alone, no, it is not really safe, but if you have money and friends and influence then yes, it is both safe and welcoming. I myself would walk the streets of Vensille only with my bodyguards around me, and even then I would be cautious. A beautiful young woman such as yourself, Miss Naseep, travelling alone and with nobody to meet her at her destination, well; it would not be a good idea."

"Really, Mr Blucher?" she said, eyes wide at the thought of entering such a dangerous city, "Would you say then that I would be at risk of some injury if I lodged in an inn in Vensille? I must admit that my plans are a little vague in that respect and any advice you might offer would be much appreciated."

Blucher puffed himself up with the air of a man lecturing a young student.

"It's the gangs, Miss Naseep. They run many of the inns of Vensille and have 'arrangements' with many others. I couldn't with conscience say that you would be safe in one of our inns, although you may be lucky and find an honest innkeeper."

Adrava looked troubled at this, although in reality she didn't expect any trouble at all, given her range of talents. She sucked in her lower lip and with a look of worry on her face said, in a quiet and slightly desperate voice, "But that sounds just terrible, Mr Blucher! Surely I will be able to find somewhere safe to stay? I plan to be in the city only for a few days but if the inns are as bad as you say then I really don't know what I shall do."

"Oh my dear lady I'm so sorry to have worried you," he said, quickly, "Please, do not fret; it would be an honour to offer you lodgings in my humble house for the duration of your stay."

She looked at him, still troubled, and stood up straight. She was taller than Blucher and he had to lean back a little to keep her in view.

"Truly? You would do that for me?" she said, lower lip still trembling slightly and a look of sudden hope on her face. Blucher nodded eagerly.

"Then, thank you, Mr Blucher, that would certainly be a weight off my mind; I would be delighted to accept your offer."

"Excellent," he beamed, "and maybe you will allow me to show you some of the sights of the city?"

She smiled, all worry now gone from her face.

"Of course, that sounds delightful. To be shown around a great city by a man of learning would be a delightful."

"Then that is settled," he said, taking her hand in his, "my coach will be waiting for me at the docks; you shall accompany me to my home and lodge there as my honoured guest for as long as you stay in the city." He smiled again, clearly pleased with the outcome of the conversation.

"Thank you," she said, gently withdrawing her hand, "and now I think I will retire for a rest. The mid-afternoon sun has quite worn me out."

"Of course, my dear lady," Blucher gave his little bow again, "it has been a delight talking to you and maybe, when you are rested, we can talk some more." He smiled again in a way that left Adrava feeling that he believed he had achieved something truly special.

Back in her cabin she lay down on her bed. Blucher might prove useful, especially if he hosted her in Vensille while she searched for Marrinek, but she had never enjoyed socialising with merchants, a class she found to be unutter-

ably boring. She sighed. Marrinek had been better at culti-
vating these connections and exploiting them; she had
always had to bite her tongue, especially at the assumption
that she was a defenceless maid who couldn't survive
without the protection of a strong man. At least Marrinek,
for all his faults, had never thought of her like that.

Still, lodgings in Vensille would be useful even if
Blucher was a bit of a bore. He may yet turn out to have
contacts that she could exploit, especially if he traded items
that might be of interest to a talented practitioner like
Marrinek.

So far, her best plan for finding Marrinek was simply to
talk to as many charm-sellers as she could find in the hope
that one might have seen him. It was very likely that
Marrinek would begin to hunt for charms or components as
soon as he was able and if he had been in the city for more
than a few days he would most definitely have contacted at
least one charm seller. His skills in charm-making were
vastly ahead of her own and he had always made most of
their charms, preferring to know exactly what components
had been used and how they would perform.

Adrava was too impatient to acquire the necessary skills
but Marrinek had enjoyed the challenge. He had been
happy to spend hours teasing his materials into just the
right shape to achieve the effect he desired. She twisted the
ring on her finger, comforted by its presence. They had
spent hours together as she investigated its powers and
learned to master them. Now, wearing it again, she felt that
she had a little more control over her destiny.

Up on deck Krant and Gavelis sat with their backs to the
horse boxes, keeping out of the sun.

"Did you notice, G-, I mean Dundaserre, that our fellow passenger is the woman from the inn, the one who got into such trouble with the other patron before you arrived?"

"Yes, sir. I had not realised she was a fellow traveller rather than a local."

"And did you see how quickly she wound Blucher around her finger? A smart woman, to have secured an offer of lodgings so quickly."

"Hmm, maybe, sir, although I suspect that Mr Blucher might be playing his own game."

Krant looked at him and lowered his voice still further.

"You fear some sort of ulterior motive for his offer, then?"

Gavelis paused, considering his reply.

"Not fear, as such, sir, no, but the offer of lodgings came, as you saw, very fast. A middle-aged man and a beautiful young woman travelling alone? It is not difficult to imagine an alternative explanation for Mr Blucher's hospitality."

Krant nodded slowly, digesting this.

"You have a suspicious mind, Dundaserre. I do hope you are not correct, for her sake. I wonder if we should express our concerns?"

"I don't think so, sir, no. It would not be our place to intervene, I think, and doing so might cause questions about our own motives for travelling."

"Hmm. Maybe you're right, Gav-Dundaserre but I can't help feeling a degree of responsibility for another Imperial citizen, especially one so far from home." And such a damned attractive one, although he didn't dare say that out loud.

"We keep to ourselves then, eh Dundaserre?"

Gavelis, feeling that he might have steered Krant around

another difficult situation, sighed inwardly with relief and said, "Yes sir, I think that would be best."

The barge stopped for the night at a small wharf at the edge of the village of Greyshore. The village ale house, the Wharfside Inn, catered to the many river vessels that stopped overnight and the small crew of the Golden Rose, released from their duties once the barge was secured, sauntered eagerly into the village.

Adrava's attention was caught by the first mate, who coughed politely then said, "Pardon, miss, but Mistress Banks wondered if you might join her and her other guests for dinner." He gestured toward the far end of the barge where a trestle table had been set with four chairs.

"Thank you, I would be delighted."

She followed the mate to the table and nodded her greetings.

"Mistress Banks."

"Miss Naseep. Please, have a seat." Banks, standing at the head of the table, indicated the chair to her right.

"Thank you." They both sat and Banks said, "I thought it might be amusing to spend some time with the young men," she leant forward and lowered her voice, "so I have invited Mr Smark and Mr Blucher to join us." She grinned conspiratorially, inviting Adrava to share in the joke at the expense of the men, and there was something strangely peaceful about the way the lines on her face moved.

Adrava nodded and smiled back.

"It will be interesting to hear the tales they chose to impress us."

"Oh, count me out," said Banks, leaning back in her

chair, "I'm far too old for them to be interested in me, but I think you might interest them. And here they are now."

"Welcome, gentlemen," said Banks, standing Please take a seat."

"It is a pleasure, as always, to dine with you, Mistress Banks," said Blucher, taking the seat beside Adrava, "good evening, Miss Naseep. I trust you are fully rested?"

"And a good evening to you, Mr Blucher. Yes, quite rested, thank you."

"Ah, er, good evening," said Krant, haltingly. Dining with strangers on the deck of a barge was not a situation with which Krant was familiar and he was struggling to maintain his social poise.

"Er, my name is Smark." He took the seat opposite Adrava and was welcomed to the table by Banks.

"Excellent. I don't often dine like this, as Mr Blucher knows, but the evening is fine and my friends at the tavern in the village have agreed to supply the food."

Adrava twisted around to look across the wharf to the tavern, which was brightly lit and busy. The noise of people enjoying themselves floated to the river, strangely loud against the quiet background of the early evening.

"And here it comes," said Banks, as a team of people emerged from the tavern carrying trays laden with pots and plates of food, "Mr Smark, would you be so kind as to pass around the plates? We won't stand on ceremony this evening. Miss Naseep, some wine? This is a southern wine from along the coast," she said, pouring, "a little light and thin for my preferences, I'm afraid, but it travels well."

They all sipped their wine as the food wound its way out of the inn, across the wharf and up the gangplank. The tavern keeper, a chubby man of medium height with long grey hair and whiskers, placed his tray of food on the table and bowed to the assembled company.

"Thank you, Mr Keep, and what do you have for us today?"

Keep stepped forward and removed the lid from the large pot with a flourish. The diners craned forward to see what the pot contained as Keep said, "Greetings one and all, welcome to our humble village. Tonight we are proud to serve a local speciality; boar roasted with honey. To accompany the meat we have," he paused to wave forward his staff and remove the lids from their pots as each was set upon the table, "roasted potatoes and carrots with herbs, rabbit and fowl stew in a spiced wine sauce with oranges, fresh bread baked with garlic and olives, and finally a rice pudding sweetened with honey and flavoured with cloves and ginger."

He bowed low as he set the last of the lids on the deck beside the table.

"Trentor will come back later to clear your plates and bring everything back to the inn when you have finished. If there is anything else you need please just ask and we will do our very best."

Banks smiled broadly as she looked over the food.

"Very good, Mr Keep, very good indeed. Worthy of your father's offerings at their very best, I'm sure."

Keep beamed and bowed again.

"Always happy to serve, Mistress Banks. Will there be anything else?"

"Two dozen loaves in the morning, I think, but that will be all for now. Thank you, Mr Keep."

Keep bowed one more time then ushered his staff from the deck and hurried back to the inn leaving only Trentor behind.

"Please," said Banks, "help yourselves and don't hold back. This is the best food on the river and we won't get anything half as good until we reach Catshed."

Blucher and Smark began piling food onto their plates and Adrava was only slightly behind them, taking portion of boar, some roast vegetables and a little of the stew.

"This is excellent, Mistress Banks," said Smark after a few mouthfuls, "my compliments on your choice of inn. Have you known the proprietor long?"

"Oh yes, ever since he was a lad. We stop here every month or so and they feed me and my passengers and entertain the crew. It's a good arrangement."

"It's the highlight of the voyage," said Blucher, "none of the other masters stop here, they all push on from Riverbridge, but Mistress Banks here likes her comforts, right?"

"There's more to life than the pursuit of profit, Mr Blucher," said Banks, smiling thinly, "is that not right, Mr Smark?"

Krant chewed and swallowed hurriedly.

"Profit has never really come my way, Mistress Banks. My line of work doesn't really allow it."

"And what is that line of work?" said Adrava, leaning over to help herself to more bread.

"Ah, er, well. This and that. Or rather, er, I'm a civil servant. Rather a lowly one, really."

"Oh surely not, Mr Smark," said Blucher, "travelling outside the Empire with two fine horses and a manservant? What do you really do?"

Krant opened his mouth but found he didn't have a good answer. He decided to lie.

"Ah, yes. You've caught me out, Mr Blucher. I am in fact an immensely powerful person on a mission of great importance to the Imperial Court. I could tell you all about it but,

I'm sorry to say, my manservant would then insist on killing you all. Ha ha." He helped himself to more of the rabbit stew, rather pleased with his improvisation until he saw them all staring at him.

"No, no, that was a joke," he said quickly, "I really am a civil servant. G-Dundaserre is retained by my family to look after me, stop me getting into trouble, arrange the inns, negotiate terms of passage, that sort of thing." He gave them a rather weak smile and focussed on his food.

"Ha ha," said Blucher, "so, a civil servant of some sort, on a voyage of self-discovery paid for by a rich family. Ha! And you Miss Naseep, what do you do?"

Krant looked up, suddenly finding himself interested again in the conversation.

Adrava looked around the table and down at her clothes then back at Mr Blucher, allowing a confused frown to show on her face.

"Ah, I think Miss Naseep is trying to work out what to say, Mr Blucher, because her clothes mark her as a temple novice," said Banks.

Krant frowned.

"You disagree, Mr Smark?"

"No, no, Mistress Banks, it's just that novices don't normally travel so far alone," he trailed off, aware that everyone was looking at him again, "but then civil servants don't normally travel either," he added more quietly, cursing inwardly and resolving to keep his mouth closed.

Adrava smiled.

"I'm travelling to visit relatives in Vensille - my parents are dead but some cousins I haven't seen for years are currently staying in the city - before I take my final vows. A few weeks, a couple of months maybe, then I think I'll be on my way back east." She turned to Mr Blucher.

"What about you, Mr Blucher. Do you trade on the river or travel for pleasure?"

Blucher gesticulated with his fork, waving it around to win time as he chewed a large piece of beef.

"I trade. This and that, up and back along the river, city to town, village to farm and back again."

"I think Miss Naseep is asking what you trade, Blucher, rather than where," said Banks, waving her knife at him.

"Ah, well as to that the answer is anything and everything," he caught Banks' eye and pressed on, "but mostly I buy raw ingredients and high quality components upriver that I can sell to the charm-makers of Vensille or the larger towns. Precious metals, gems, some base metals, charms themselves on occasion, ivory or antler maybe, fine leathers and silks, that sort of thing. Then on the return journey I head north carrying a few choice craft items from the city, nothing too large or heavy, and offer them to regular contacts or the upstream nobles desperate for a bit of city polish, if you get my meaning."

"How far upstream do you go, Mr Blucher? Surely the Golden Rose doesn't go much further than Riverbridge, given its draught," said Adrava.

"The Golden Rose goes only as far as the docks of Riverbridge, I'm afraid," said Banks, "the bridge over the river stops her going further. Beyond Riverbridge you have to take a smaller inland barge or ride."

"There are rich pickings beyond Riverbridge, if you're able to make the journey," said Blucher, clearing the last of the stew from his plate with a thick slice of bread, "but the further you go the wilder it gets! In the far north they have the best furs but the winter is cold enough to freeze the nose from your face. They have iron and gold and silver as well and would trade it all for a little fine wine and silk, or maybe some brandy and a set of self-powered warming fire charms. That's what the nobles really want, something to warm their rooms and baths, if they even bother bathing." He laughed, leaning back to give himself more room.

"I've heard they eat their children in the winter and wear the skins of their enemies in the summer and have human skulls on the walls of their halls," said Adrava, listing the three most ridiculous things that were widely believed about the northern kingdoms in the Empire.

Blucher laughed again and Banks looked sideways at her, eyebrow raised. Adrava caught her eye and gave her a slight smile, then said, "And don't they hang cheating merchants from the walls of their castles to encourage honesty?"

"Ah well, there's a few things I didn't know. Eat their children? Maybe, when the winter bites, in the far north, but I don't think so really."

"But they do decorate their halls with skulls," said Krant, "at least, that's what I was taught by my tutors."

Banks snorted but Blucher held up his hand.

"Mr Smark is right - I've seen more than one hall decorated with bleached skulls, some with hair still attached or with gaping axe wounds. They're a rough people, up north, but they pay well for the imported comforts of the south, although I've never seen a merchant hanged for cheating," he looked over at Adrava, a slightly worried frown on his face, "so that must surely be a story told only in the Empire."

Adrava looked at him, face radiating honesty and almost religious conviction.

"I heard that they bathe naked in the lakes in winter, breaking the ice to jump into the freezing water before running back, still naked, to engage in huge orgies on piles of bearskins spread around huge fire pits in their halls!"

"That I didn't know," said Banks, her eyebrows raised, "but it sounds like it might be an interesting rumour to investigate."

Blucher laughed again.

"Naked ice swimming I've seen, it is true. How they do it, or even why, is beyond me, I'm afraid. I barely tolerate the cold and just the thought of swimming in icy water is enough to give me the shivers," he said, entirely unaware of his pun, "I've never seen an orgy, I'm afraid. I think they only happen in your Empire, where decadence is celebrated widely, or so I hear."

Krant looked up from his plate as the conversation veered towards a subject upon which he would desperately like to have had personal experience.

"I've heard stories about some pretty wild parties thrown by the Governor in the Traebarn Palace. They might have been orgies. Lots of drinking and music, certainly. Probably dancing as well."

"Really, Mr Smark? Orgies at the Traebarn Palace? Maybe this civil servanting lark isn't quite so dull after all," said Banks, teasing.

"Oh, I've never been to any of these parties," he said, disappointment in his voice, "but if you talk to the servants sometimes, on the morning after a big party, they'll drop hints and tell stories."

"No! Surely not?" said Adrava, a shocked expression on her face, "I've never heard any tales of orgies, Mr Smark. What goes on?" she asked in a perfect impression of priestly innocence.

Krant blushed and looked down at his food in embarrassment, much to the amusement of Banks and Adrava, and spluttered out an answer.

"Oh, er, well, I don't think I could comment, or should

comment," he managed, desperately changing the subject, "how is the rice pudding? I've always fancied trying it."

And so the dinner wound its way down to a natural end over a bottle of spirits produced from some dark recess of the ship. Banks and Adrava teased Krant and needled gently at Blucher until, by mutual consent, they decided the evening had reached a conclusion and they would retire. Trentor, still waiting patiently, was finally able to clear the table, piling pots high on a tray before making her escape and heading back to the inn.

"A most enjoyable meal, Mistress Banks," said Blucher, pushing back his chair, "and an excellent evening all round. My thanks." He bowed to them all and sauntered, a little unsteadily, to his spot on the deck under the awning where his bodyguards had set out his blankets.

"Indeed, thank you," said Krant, yawning, "and a very good evening to you both." He followed Blucher, not even pretending to be sober, and would have fallen over the railing into the river if Gavelis hadn't caught him and escorted him to his blankets.

"Interesting," said Adrava, sitting back down again and picking up her glass of wine, still half full from earlier in the evening. She leaned closer to Banks and said in a low voice, "Do you think Mr Smark is really a civil servant? He's clearly talented, to some degree, but he doesn't yet try to hide it."

"Hmm. I suspect he's not many years older than he looks," said Banks, "and he certainly hasn't yet learnt to spot Ancients. Not sure about his man, Dundaserre, though. I think he may not be quite what he appears."

Adrava looked down the length of the barge to where Gavelis was arranging things for Krant and making sure he was comfortable. It was difficult to be sure in the dim moonlight but he certainly seemed to be fulfilling the role of a diligent valet. Adrava said as much to Banks but even as she spoke she had to admit that the man seemed to show a poise beyond his apparent years.

"I'm fairly sure he's strongly talented," said Banks, "which begs the question, why work for Smark?"

"He hides it well. I've sensed nothing, nothing at all. Maybe he just has an unusual degree of self-control."

Banks wasn't convinced but Adrava decided to change the subject.

"Has there been much trouble with outlaws around here recently?"

"Outlaws? Nothing major, as far as I know. A few small bands, maybe, occasional attacks on caravans. There are always tales of lone travellers being robbed or killed or just disappearing on the long quiet roads between towns. Why, what have you heard?"

"Nothing, really, but there were stories in Stagford of problems on the Eastern road and I wondered if it was a regular thing or something new."

"You hear tales, floating up and down the river. Half the time you can't tell if they're real or just stories to frighten the junior crew. If you stop at the inns you can hear all kinds of talk in the common room."

She pulled out a slim cigar packet and flicked it open with one hand while the other produced a tiny fire charm. Adrava shook her head at the offered cigar and the conversation paused while Banks lit her own.

"A few generations ago, maybe 75 years or so, the outlaws roamed freely along both banks of the Guiln, most of the way to Vensille. They robbed and murdered and took slaves, trading upstream to the northern kingdoms or downstream and across the sea. Some of the towns built walls, others disappeared or were abandoned. Bad times. Many people moved eastward, toward the Empire, or southward to one of the city states, although the stories they told were sometimes just as bad as those who had stayed behind.

"Then two things happened. The Empire expanded, moving the border maybe sixty miles to the west, and their border patrols started to make life difficult for the outlaw gangs. They hanged hundreds and those they didn't catch mostly moved away or changed business. It made a big difference to life along the river."

She paused to sip her drink.

"And at about the same time, Duke Rhenveldt deposed his predecessor and began building his city walls. Monstrous things, if I'm honest, and almost ruinously expensive, but they gave him control of the river trade. Anything that travels the river plays by Rhenveldt's rules. Everyone pays the tariff or risks confiscation and imprisonment.

"Turns out the noble Duke hates slavery - something about it diluting the tax base, apparently. He seems to be a deeply practical man when it came to matters of economics and money - and as soon as he could he destroyed the slavers. He took their ships, their palaces and warehouses, their wealth and titles and estates. They'd grown rich on long decades of trade and Rhenveldt seized that wealth and used it to cement his position, giving lands and concessions and estates to his friends and supporters and even, in several cases, his prominent enemies."

"It sounds like you admire him," said Adrava as Banks paused to smoke and drink.

"Admire? Oh yes, very much so. I just don't like him or trust him. But he sorted out the slavers and with the end of that trade the remaining outlaws lost their best customers. Not many left now and there are plenty of new villages where before the fields were empty or the land was covered in forest."

Adrava looked out at Greyshore with its ditch and its short wall of stone topped by wooden parapets.

"Greyshore survived the chaos?" she asked.

"Walls, a few stubborn idiots who wouldn't leave, the trade from the river and a firebrand priest not scared of breaking heads got them through." She took another pull from her glass.

"It was grim for a few years but they just refused to give in. Out west it was much worse, for much longer. Large parts of the country out that way," she waved her hand vaguely toward the other shore, "are empty now, nobody at all now lives north of the Scla mountains."

"The Empire looks mostly inward, or to the east," said Adrava, furrowing her brows as she brought to mind the little she had heard, "but even locked within our own crises we heard things about the Kingdom of Sclareme. Their ambassador begged for help, at one point, I remember hearing, but trade with Sclareme was small and they were such a very long way from Khemucasterill. It didn't seem important and there were so many other things to worry about. And then one day the ambassador returned home, called away by some sort of urgent summons, and the embassy closed. She never came back."

Banks gave her a strange, sideways look and Adrava wondered for a moment if she had said too much.

"Well Sclareme has gone," said Banks, gesturing towards the western bank, "it was over there between the Scla mountains in the south and the Toothnail mountains in the north. A big country, sparsely populated but wealthy. All gone. No trade, no people, no towns. Wolves roam to the banks of the river now, in winter. There are bears, too, and rumours of worse things in the deep forests in the foothills of the northern mountains." She shivered and finished her drink.

"Worse? What do you mean 'worse'?" asked Adrava, confused.

Banks looked at her and set the empty glass back on the table.

"Not many people venture into the forests. Charcoal burners, a few hunters. They tell stories about shapes in the deep forest, dark things, things it's better not to discuss at night."

Adrava stifled a laugh, just.

"Ghosts? Surely you don't believe all those tales?"

Banks' face was suddenly straight and calm and sober. She leant forward.

"You live as long as I've lived, travel as far as I've travelled and then we'll see what should be believed. There's a reason I only go up and down the river, why I only dock on the east bank, why I don't go further than Riverbridge. One day, maybe, I'll tell you about it, but now I'm for bed. Early start tomorrow, no more stops till Catshed."

Banks stood up and stretched, all her earlier good-humour gone.

"It was a good dinner, thank you for joining me. Until tomorrow," she said with a respectful bow of her head. Then without another word or waiting for a reply she left, disappearing below decks towards her cabin.

Adrava sat for a few more minutes, pondering, then she shivered and shook her head. She looked at her drink for a few moments then decided she didn't need it and went to bed, leaving the glass half-full on the table.

32

The next morning Adrava woke late as sunshine streamed in through the small windows in her cabin. Around her she could hear the creaking and clanking of the barge as it sailed downstream and the lapping of the water against the hull. She lay there for a while thinking about the previous night's conversation with Banks and her hints of dark forces and nightmares roaming the countryside beyond the western banks of the river. Then she shook her head; it was all nonsense, stories told to scare gullible travellers and children.

She dressed and went up on deck. The crew, some nursing hangovers after over-indulging at the Wharfside Inn the night before, were going about their daily business while Banks watched from the wheel, calling instructions as she guided the barge downstream. Adrava climbed the steps to stand beside Banks on the small poop deck and looked forward along the length of the barge and on to the south.

"A fine morning," said Banks, gently nudging the wheel.

"Yes," said Adrava, looking out over the fields and forests

around them and at the blue sky above, "how long till we reach Catshed?"

"Mid-morning tomorrow, if all goes well. We won't stop until we reach Catshed. A couple of hours there, then on to Vensille."

"And then how long till we reach Vensille?"

"Another three days, give or take. We're not in a hurry so we'll probably stop for a night if we're making good time. There are also a couple of trading posts where we might spend a few hours unloading some of our goods. Then there's a wharf and a small village maybe halfway between Catshed and Vensille where we can take on food and maybe a last few goods for sale at the markets in the city."

For a while the two women stood in silence except for the occasional command from Banks to her crew. The countryside crawled steadily past as the sun climbed slowly across the sky.

"If I need to make the trip back to Riverbridge in a few weeks," said Adrava, "could you offer me passage again?"

Banks looked at her then smiled.

"As long as you can pay you're welcome to travel with us, although I may not be able to guarantee you a cabin next time."

"Good, thank you. I can live without a cabin, although it is nice to have my own space. How often do you sail?"

"We head north every ten to twelve days or so, depending on the weather and cargo and opportunities. My agent in Vensille is a man by the name of Carlyn Twomey - I'll point out his office on the east docks when we arrive - he knows when we plan to sail and will be able to arrange passage."

Adrava nodded, muttering the name under her breath to help her remember it.

"And were you serious about not landing on the west bank of the river? That was what you said last night, wasn't it?"

Banks looked at her again, all trace of warmth and humour gone from her face. She leaned toward Adrava and said, "I was serious, yes. It's not a subject I joke about."

Adrava hesitated, surprised by the sudden change in Banks' demeanour.

"But surely it's just outlaws and rumour and tales told by credulous peasants?"

Banks shook her head.

"I've been out west and seen for myself. You don't believe me? Fine, go and look yourself but don't forget that I warned you."

"So what's out there? What did you see?"

Banks shook her head again, eyes on a crewman coiling and re-coiling ropes on the deck.

"Dark things, swarming under the mountains and through the forests like a plague, killing at will, nobody to stop them or hold them back. They know about these things in the north, they fear them and fight them, but each year it's worse. Too many of them, too few men in the wilderness and each year fewer as people die or are taken or just give up and head south."

She looked at Adrava, eyes haunted by the memories of a distant terror.

"You must have seen the migrants, the refugees, even in the Empire. Heading south and east, away from the mountains, away from the danger and madness and fear."

Adrava opened her mouth to deny it then remembered the beggars she had seen in the towns on the west road as she headed away from Esterengel. Northerners, some of them, or so they had seemed to her. And there had been a few in Esterengel the previous year when she was last there with Marrinek, which was strange because the northmen seldom travelled that far east except to trade and they didn't stay in cities any longer than they had to.

"Look out that way and tell me how many settlements you can see," said Banks, waving her arm towards the eastern bank of the river. From the small raised deck they could see a long way across the rolling hills with their fields and orchards and vineyards and Adrava counted under her breath.

"There's a farm there, by the river, and a village beyond it. I can see another farm in the hills and a windmill," she said, holding up her hand to shield her eyes, "and there's smoke rising over there beyond the trees, so maybe another village."

"Now look west," said Banks.

Adrava moved around the wheel to the other side of the barge and looked west over hills and forest.

"There's smoke in the forest - charcoal burners, maybe?" She fell silent as she scanned the trees; apart from small areas where the charcoal burners had cleared trees near the river she couldn't see any signs of settlements at all.

"But that doesn't make any sense. Where are all the people?"

"Frightening, isn't it? It's not till you reach Catshed that you find settlements on the west bank. Heading north, Riverbridge is the largest town on the river and it's almost all on the east bank. They only use the west bank for marshalling timber and charcoal before it's loaded onto barges for the journey downstream."

"But Vensille straddles the river and there are other cities and towns along the coast to the west, aren't there?"

"Yes, but they're a long way south of the mountains.

Vensille and its towns and villages haven't been affected by all this. Mention this down there and people will scoff, just like you did, and put it down to travellers' tales and morally corrupt northerners."

Banks said nothing more for a few minutes as she guided the barge around a turn of the river. At the next turn she pointed west and said, "Used to be a town, there. I used to buy wine and wool to carry south to Vensille. Now look at it."

Adrava looked.

"But there's nothing there, only forest. I can't see a..." she stopped as she saw the first of the buildings, an inn maybe, burnt out and almost overgrown, its stone chimney stack rising from the ivy-clad remains of a broken roof. Then she saw others - warehouses, wharves, houses, the remains of what might have been a town wall - all ruined and covered by vines and ivy and shrubs. There were trees growing inside the walls and through the remains of roofs. There were no signs of people still living there.

"What happened?"

Banks shrugged.

"Nobody really knows. One night the town was attacked. A few people, those who weren't asleep and who were near or on the river, escaped and survived, but their stories made no sense. Everyone else just died or disappeared. I came north a few days later and the town had been destroyed. There was nothing left but smouldering ruins, even the barges at the wharves had been burned or scuttled. I didn't even stop, just sailed on northward, as far from the west bank of the river as I could get."

Adrava shivered despite the warmth of the day. Banks noticed and smiled.

"We're safe while we're on the river and south of here

things get better quickly. By tomorrow, if we stopped, you wouldn't find anyone who didn't believe that this town wasn't destroyed by bandits."

"What about the nobles, haven't they done anything?"

"Of course they have," snorted Banks, "they moved their families east or south, took their wealth with them and started again in safer lands. But if you mean fight? No. Only the northerners fight, and they're on the wrong side of the mountains to be of any use here."

"The Empire, then. What is the Empire doing about this?"

"What? You ask me that? Since when did the Emperor care for anything outside his borders unless he was taking it for himself? No, we'll get no help from the Empire until the threat crosses the Guiln and starts burning towns close to the border; by then it will be too late."

Banks sank into a sullen silence and refused to answer more questions, ignoring Adrava's attempts to draw her out until, finally, Adrava gave up and climbed down to the main deck in search of more entertaining company.

She found it at the bow where Krant was leaning against the railing and looking out over river. He smiled at her as she joined him but didn't say anything.

"Seen any monsters, Mr Smark?" asked Adrava.

"Monsters?" said Krant, looking surprised, "I've seen a few ducks paddling around at the edges of the river but I wouldn't have said they were particularly monstrous. Why do you ask?"

"Something Banks was saying, a joke, I think," she changed the subject quickly, "but isn't the weather lovely? At the seminary, we spend so much time indoors studying that we hardly get to see the sun. This trip has been such an opportunity." She smiled brightly, reminding Krant of an enthusiastic schoolgirl.

"You study at the Farm?"

Adrava looked at him sharply and he stumbled on.

"It's the only seminary I've heard of," he said quickly, inwardly cursing his slip.

"Yes. I shall become a priest when I return. I may ask to be posted to the border country - it's very beautiful and the people are so kind and friendly."

Krant wasn't sure what to say. His experiences since leaving Esterengel had been overwhelmingly negative and he couldn't wait to return to the safety of the city and his comfortable desk job.

"You aren't tempted to stay closer to home, to settle in Esterengel maybe and minister from the safety of the temple?"

Adrava bit back on a sharp reply and reminded herself that she was supposed to be an enthusiastic young priest, keen to spread the good word to uncivilised heathens and needy worshippers. She was already regretting the conversation.

"Why no, Mr Smark, how could I carry on the good work from the temple? There are so many priests there that even the meanest supplicant can find absolution. I need something else, something more demanding," she said, looking up at him and smiling again, "out here I might find a real opportunity to help people. That's all I really want to do; help people to lead better lives through the gods and their teachings."

Krant was impressed, despite his complete lack of faith.

"Well, I wish you the very best of luck with your calling. Maybe if more people shared your commitment and enthusiasm the world would be a better place."

Adrava cringed inwardly at the sentiment. Another bloody idiot, she thought, as she tried to extricate herself from the conversation.

"Thank you, Mr Smark, for your kind words. I think now I might retire to my quarters to pray and meditate. If you'll excuse me."

She turned to leave and he bowed as she walked away.

In her cabin Adrava closed the door and leant against it, cursing under her breath. Damn Banks and her nightmare stories of ghouls and monsters. And damn Smark as well, with his enthusiasm and interest and naive innocence. He was obviously keen on her and she had slipped up by failing to notice sooner. Now there was nothing to do but endure, since she could hardly slap him down while remaining in character as a priest. Damn him!

And what had possessed her to say that she needed to pray and meditate? She sat down on her bed. The air in cabin was already uncomfortably warm and if she stayed here for a couple of hours pretending to meditate it was only going to get worse. She sighed, resigning herself to her fate, and lay back on the bed. At least she had a little peace in which to ponder Banks' disturbing theories about the happenings on the west bank of the Guiln.

"Remarkable woman," Krant muttered to himself as Miss Naseep disappeared below deck.

"Remarkable, sir?" said Gavelis, appearing suddenly at his elbow and making him jump, "In what way?"

"Dundaserre! For the love of the nine gods, don't creep up on me like that."

"My apologies, sir, I just came to tell you that I have

spoken to Mistress Banks and she has agreed that we can disembark at Catshed."

"Good, that's a weight off my mind."

Gavelis lowered himself to the deck to sit next to Krant.

"Miss Naseep may not be all she appears, sir," said Gavelis in a low voice, looking around carefully to check that they weren't being overheard, "I think she may be rather older than she seems."

"Older?" said Krant, frowning, "How much older? She looks no more than about twenty-five or twenty-six."

Gavelis looked at him, wondering not for the first time how Krant had survived so long in the world.

"I think she is at least four times as old as that, sir. And possibly quite powerfully talented, although she hides it exceptionally well."

Krant looked along the deck towards the stairs down which Adrava had disappeared, his mouth open in confusion.

"Really? How can you tell?"

Gavelis paused, not sure how best to fill this surprising gap in Krant's education.

"There are, well, there are signs that you can spot, signs that a person is much older than they seem at first. Older people tend to be more measured, more in control of themselves, less impulsive. They have lived long enough to become very cynical and highly manipulative, particularly of those who lack talent, and they often move more gracefully than the young, like dancers."

Krant's experience of dancers was very limited but he didn't want to display his lack of knowledge in front of Gavelis.

"Fascinating," said Krant, giving every impression of being interested in what was clearly a new and unfamiliar area of learning, "are there any other 'old people' on board?"

Gavelis looked at him again, not quite sure if Krant was making fun of him. Probably not, he decided.

"Mistress Banks, sir, is even older than Miss Naseep, probably much older. She makes me feel young, although even she would feel young compared to Ms Benedict."

"I don't remember much about Ms Benedict, the pain seemed to blot everything out. How old was she?"

Gavelis shrugged, unwilling to revisit the memories of his encounter with Ms Benedict.

"No idea, sir, not really, but certainly many centuries. She was truly ancient."

Krant shook his head, eyebrows raised.

"I've heard stories, of course, but I'd thought they were just children's tales. I know that power lengthens lifespans but I'd never really believed the stories about ancient kings who ruled wisely for a thousand years.

"Wisely? I'd be surprised if any king could manage to rule for more than a century or two let alone rule wisely. Even with the best intentions people make mistakes or accumulate enemies or simply grow tired of the perpetual struggle. You hear things, if you live long enough. Disturbing things, sometimes, about the oldest people, about their activities and plans and schemes." Gavelis stopped talking, watching Banks as she stood at the wheel. Krant followed his gaze.

"How old are you, Gavelis?" he asked, quietly. Gavelis turned to look at him but didn't answer the question. Krant swallowed under the weight of Gavelis' gaze, then looked away.

"Well," he said with false lightness, "I never thought I might encounter these ancient people. I always thought they would all be great lords or kings or archbishops, not ship's captains or trainee priests."

Gavelis snorted.

"Yes, well, 'trainee priest' strikes me as nothing more than a convenient cover story for a woman travelling alone. There's more to her than meets the eye, that's for sure, and I don't like not knowing what it is."

"You think she's on the run?" asked Krant in a scandalised whisper, "From the seminary? Surely not! She seems so, so, well, genuine."

Gavelis shook his head.

"I don't know. Let's just say we're not the only ones on this boat with secrets and I don't like it at all. Don't mingle and say as little as possible, that's my advice. We'll go ashore tomorrow in Catshed and put this damned voyage behind us."

Later in the day Adrava, unable to bear the close atmosphere of her tiny cabin, climbed back onto the deck into a welcome breeze. She found somewhere to sit on the deck away from the other passengers and out of the way of the crew and contrived to give the impression that she didn't want to be disturbed. Sitting cross-legged on the deck, she gazed out to the west at the tree-covered hills, wondering what was really going on and why the land appeared to have been abandoned.

Her quiet contemplation of the countryside was interrupted by Blucher, who sat down beside her, looked out at the passing countryside briefly, then launched into a long-winded story about his adventures upstream. He told her at length how he had traded fire charms and other trinkets to the merchants of the northern kingdoms and how he had been able to extract a high price for such low-value goods. He seemed to be very pleased with the results of his efforts and was keen to highlight the great personal danger he experienced while travelling to and from the northern towns and strongholds.

"They're ignorant peasants, of course," said Blucher, "and wouldn't know the value of anything if I didn't explain it to them. They'll trade gold or iridium or silver for a few charmed lamps or shields. Fire charms go for even more."

Adrava looked at him. She had little time for merchants in general but she actively disliked those who overcharged for their goods. She fixed Blucher with a stern, priestly look and said, "I do hope you weren't taking advantage of those poor people, Mr Blucher. I wouldn't like to think that an honourable man would overcharge for his wares."

Blucher spluttered a little.

"Well no, quite. That is to say no, I don't overcharge, but the northmen are happy to pay and it is an awfully long way to travel just to sell a few fire charms." He fell silent, frowning down at the water for a few minutes.

"And have you heard tales from the northmen of dark things in the forests, up near the mountains?"

Blucher looked up, suddenly wary.

"Dark things? Hmm, well," he said, puffing out his cheeks, "they do, sometimes, when they're very drunk, tell wild tales of monsters and murder. But mostly they like to tell tall tales of their own heroism, the battles they've fought, the people they've killed, the lands they've captured or pillaged, that sort of thing."

"You haven't seen anything dark on your travels?"

"No, nothing. In the north, the traders come to the docks so it's hardly necessary to disembark to buy and sell. They actively discourage travel outside their river towns and once you're north of the mountains the landing spots on the river are few and far between. No point stopping, if I'm honest, except in a town to trade, and once you've sold all your goods and bought all you can carry there's no need to go further or stay longer."

They sat in silence for another few minutes, then Adrava said, "Oh look, a family of ducks." She smiled brightly at Blucher and waved at the ducks, "Hello ducks," she called, "how are you today?"

Blucher dragged himself to his feet and gave her a short bow.

"Time for my constitutional. I like to walk around the deck every now and again - keeps the blood pumping, you know?"

"How lovely. Maybe I could accompany you?"

"Oh no miss," said Blucher hurriedly, "please don't let me take you away from your, ah, your contemplation of the scenery. I'll, er, just leave you to your thoughts." He bowed again and hurried away, back toward his bed roll and body-guards before diverting at the last moment to walk slowly toward the bow.

Adrava blew out her cheeks.

"Some people," she muttered, shaking her head. She stretched her arms above her head then settled back to watch the countryside as the ship sailed steadily downstream.

As dusk fell Banks appeared on deck and made her way to the bow where the crew were hanging charmed lamps from the railing to light the way down the river. They'd taken down half the sails to slow the barge and now two crewmen stood at the bow, calling directions to the wheelman on the upper deck. In this way, the barge was able to continue downstream even in the dark, although the light of the stars and moon upon the river would almost have been enough on their own.

As dawn broke the crew extinguished the lamps and returned them to their chests below decks. They added new sails and soon the barge was moving more quickly, still heading south towards Catshed.

"Not more than a few hours now," said Banks, standing beside Adrava as she yawned and stretched away the aches of a long night in an uncomfortable bed, "we'll be in Catshed soon enough and then Smark and Dundaserre will leave us."

"Oh? I thought they were travelling to Vensille," said Adrava.

"So did I but apparently Mr Smark has decided to visit relatives outside Catshed so that's where they'll be getting off. Can't say that I'll be disappointed to see them go; that Dundaserre worries me."

Adrava looked down the length of the barge to the covered area where Krant was still asleep. Dundaserre was up and bustling, preparing a cold meal for his master and tidying away their things in preparation for disembarkation.

"Efficient, isn't he?" said Adrava, "and diligent. Exactly what a gentleman would want in a manservant, I imagine."

"Hmm. Maybe," Banks sniffed, "but I still don't like him."

Adrava struggled for something appropriate to say, something that would fit with her 'novice priest' persona.

"We should all strive to love our fellow man," she said finally, in a voice halfway between confident instruction and desperate pleading, "isn't that right, Mistress Banks?"

Banks sniffed again.

"Can't say that I've ever seen much evidence of that philosophy working out for ordinary people but I can see how you priests have to keep pushing it. Good luck, that's what I say, but I'll still be glad to see the back of Smark and Dundaserre."

It was mid-morning when the Golden Rose came within sight of Catshed and the barge tied up at the wharf on the eastern bank of the Guiln a little while later. Krant and Gavelis, eager to disembark, had saddled their horses and made ready to leave even as the barge was being tied to the great posts set in the river bank. As Gavelis led the horses over the gangplank Krant sought out Adrava, watching from the railing toward the stern of the barge.

"Miss Naseep," Krant began, "er, it has been a pleasure to make your acquaintance. Er." He stopped, unsure of how to continue.

"And yours, Mr Smark," said Adrava, stepping into the gap in the conversation before it could grow any more embarrassing, "and I hope I'll see you again at the temple in Esterengel after we have both returned home."

Krant smiled, mistaking her politeness for interest.

"Oh, yes, that would be very nice. Well. Until then."

He bowed and backed away, still unsure how to behave. Adrava waved to him as he stood on the wharf and watched as he led his horse through the crowd and into the town, Gavelis leading the way.

At the gangplank Banks was talking to a merchant, arranging supplies for the rest of the voyage to Vensille. Adrava moved a little closer so that she could eavesdrop.

"Yes, yes, man," Banks was saying, "the usual quantities.

Just get it loaded as quickly as possible - I'm eager to be on my way before noon."

"Yes mistress, right away." The merchant scurried off and a little while later two men appeared carrying assorted food-stuffs packed in two large wicker baskets. Banks checked the contents while the men stood on the deck fidgeting. Then she paid the porters and signalled a crewman to stow the food. The porters hurried back down the gangplank and disappeared back into the crowd.

Blucher came up to stand beside Adrava as she spoke with a seller of honey cakes who stood on the wharf with a tray of her produce hanging from straps around her neck.

"Four then," said Adrava, reaching over the rail to pass down the coins and to take possession of four honey cakes, which the vendor threaded onto a short length of cane. Adrava took the cane and thanked the vendor then turned to Mr Blucher.

"Would you like a honey cake, Mr Blucher?"

For a moment it looked like he would refuse but greed overcame caution and he accepted, pulling the top cake gently from the cane.

"Many thanks, Miss Naseep. Mmm. Very nice," he said around a mouthful of cake.

Adrava retreated to the bow and sat on the edge of the barge, leaning against the railing as her feet dangled above the river, slowly eating her honey cakes as she watched small boats and barges manoeuvring on the water.

An hour after docking Banks announced that her busi-ness in Catshed was concluded and the crew cast-off, punting the barge slowly back into the main stream of the river before raising sail to catch the gentle breeze and resume their journey.

From a doorway at the edge of an alleyway a little distance
from the river, Gavelis watched the Golden Rose slip gently
back onto the river and sail slowly away. When the barge
had passed from sight he walked down the alley to the small
square where Krant was minding the horses.

"The barge has gone. Nobody else got off so I think it's
safe for us to go."

Krant nodded and tugged on the reins of his horse. He
followed Gavelis through the town, heading south towards
the bridge that crossed the Guiln. When they reached the
bridge the central span, which had been raised to allow the
Golden Rose to pass downstream, had been lowered back
into place and traffic across the river had resumed. Krant
and Gavelis walked their horses across the bridge and then
continued along the road, heading west away from Catshed.

"We will need directions at some point," said Gavelis as
they passed the last of the small groups of people trudging
along the road, "but I think we should head west for a few
miles before asking."

Krant nodded, his attention on the road and the countryside.

"I didn't recognise anyone in Catshed. Do you think we
may have slipped past the watch?"

Gavelis grimaced.

"Maybe. We should be well ahead of them - they won't
have ridden through the night - but we don't know where
they are or which route they're taking. They'll probably stick
to the east bank where the roads are better and hope to be
in Vensille before the Golden Rose. That'll mean hard
riding during the day, especially if Banks keeps sailing
through the night."

"It would be just our luck for the Golden Rose to leave
Vensille before the watch arrive."

Gavelis grimaced again.

"No plan is perfect and this one has lots of risks," he said, waving his hands at the flies that buzzed around his head, "still, we're committed now, for better or worse."

They rode in silence for an hour or so as the road grew gradually narrower and more rutted and pocked with holes. At a small village behind, to Krant's eyes, an unnecessarily high wall, they stopped briefly for directions.

"Vensille, you say?" said the old man in the village square, puffing his pipe, "There's a road that heads southward a mile or two outside the village," he waved vaguely toward the far side of the small square, "but you'll want to be quick about it. It's Mid-afternoon already," he said, looking at the shadows cast by the village hall, "so you'll have to ride like blazes to make the next village before dusk."

"Thank you, sir," said Gavelis, smirking, "we'll bear that in mind."

"Oh aye, you do that son," said the old man, waving his pipe at Gavelis and shaking his head at the all-knowing wisdom of the young, "just make sure you're behind the walls before dusk."

"What do you make of all that?" said Krant after they'd passed through the gate in the village wall.

"Just an old man rambling to anyone who'll listen and spouting nonsense to frighten outsiders. But a night in the forest doesn't really appeal so we should push on to the village." Gavelis kicked his horse into a canter and Krant followed.

By early evening they were still riding through the forest and Krant was starting to get a little nervous. He hadn't camped in the wilderness for many years and his previous experiences were not ones that he remembered fondly.

Gavelis too seemed keen to reach the next village and together they rode on, pushing their horses hard as they dared while the sun sank toward the horizon.

As dusk fell they crested a hill and looked down into a shallow valley of fields and orchards and penned animals. Ahead, only a couple of miles away, was the village and they kicked their horses into a gallop at the sight, thundering down the road as the day's light failed. They slowed when it became obvious that the gate had been closed. Gavelis walked his horse to the gate and banged the flat of his hand on the heavy timbers.

"Hallo!" he called in a loud voice.

A shutter in the gate opened and a face peered out.

"Travellers? At this time of night? What do you want?" scowled the face.

"Just looking for somewhere to spend the night," said Gavelis, "there's only the two of us."

"You're late. We've shut the gate. Don't open now till dawn." The shutter slammed down.

Gavelis thumped on the gate again.

"You can't leave us out here, man. Just open the damned gate and let us in."

There was silence for a few seconds then a man swore quietly before the bar slid back and the gate opened.

"Come on then, if you're coming. Don't hang around." The man peered nervously along the road from behind the gate and he slammed it shut again as soon as they were both through. He dropped the bar back into place then turned to look at them as they dismounted.

"Where've you come from then? Bit late to be travelling, ain't it?"

"We're heading south," said Gavelis quickly, cutting off

whatever Krant had been about to say, "but we misjudged the distances. Do you always bar the gate at dusk?"

"South, eh? And yes, we always bar the gate at dusk. Won't be opening it again till dawn."

"No, you said. You've had trouble, then?"

The man looked at them again.

"You're not from round here, I can see. We like to keep things safe, that's all. You need lodgings?"

"Just for one night. We will be on our way tomorrow," said Gavelis.

"Try Mistress Kemp, the house on the corner," the man pointed along the street to one of the few two-storey buildings in the village, "she often has space for travellers." He ducked his head toward them before shuffling off down an alley. Gavelis waited until the old man disappeared into a hovel built against the wall. The squalor that some people would tolerate just to live the right side of a wall or river or border never ceased to amaze him.

He turned around and hurried down the street. Krant was walking his horse towards the house on the corner, looking around him as he went.

"There's nowhere to stable the horses," whispered Krant, keeping his voice low even though they were alone in the deserted street, "what do we do?"

"There's a trough and rail over there," said Gavelis, pointing, "so let's tie up the horses, strip their saddles and feed them then worry about lodgings."

"What, just leave them in the square?"

Gavelis sighed.

"It's a small village, everybody knows everybody else. If the horses aren't there at dawn we'll raise hell with the Mayor until he rousts out the villains. Come on, I need something to eat."

The next morning, still tired after a poor night's sleep in a cramped room on rough straw pallets, Krant and Gavelis collected their horses from the rail and left the village, following the road towards Vensille.

"We'll have to stop soon, sir," said Gavelis after an hour's riding, "so that we can feed and water the horses. Might be a good idea for us to walk for a few miles, just to give them a rest."

Krant grunted and slid from his saddle. Ten days ago the idea of riding anywhere had filled him with dread; now it seemed normal and walking - walking! - was the unusual activity. They spent an hour eating a late breakfast and resting while the horses cropped grass in a clearing beside the road, then they continued on their way, heading for the next village on the route.

For two more days they travelled south, spending a night in a barn, much to Krant's disgust. The narrow track that wound through the forest and linked villages and farms grew gradually wider and busier as they travelled south. With every mile they saw more activity: farms, towns, orchards, meadows and, outside the first town large enough to warrant the title since leaving Catshed, a gallows with three long-dead corpses swinging gently in their cages.

"Highwaymen, do you think?" asked Krant as they rode by.

"Hmm. The one on the end looks a bit small for an outlaw. Justice is harsh, here, and probably not very just."

Krant shivered and kicked his horse to a canter.

"I'm glad we're not stopping here," he said in a low voice, looking warily at everyone they saw as they followed the track that ran around the outside of the town walls.

Two hours later they reached the coast and turned east to follow the post road along the cliff tops. The road wound past fishing villages built around small harbours and smallholdings raising animals and crops. Eventually, with traffic on the road growing steadily busier, the spires and towers of Vensille came into view.

They sat their horses for a few minutes at the edge of the road, taking in the view. The city sat in a wide coastal plain and from their vantage point at the end of the cliffs they could look down across the fields and villages that were spread out before them. Beyond the fields the walls of Vensille stood tall, towering over the hovels and low buildings that clustered around the city gates and along the roads.

"Vensille, I presume," said Krant quietly, somewhat surprised to have finally reached their destination, "it's bigger than I'd imagined". The city walls lacked the flags and pennants common to Imperial cities but the scale of the fortification was undeniably impressive. The towers and gate houses soared above the plains.

"Yes, sir," said Gavelis, slipping back into his valet persona, "this is Vensille, the greatest of the coastal city states and the biggest walled city within at least two hundred miles."

"It will be a relief to finally enjoy a little civilisation again, Gavelis." He paused, then said, "Is it safe to use our real names again?"

"Yes, sir, I think so."

"Well then, let us hurry on down and introduce ourselves to the ambassador."

And together they rode down from the cliffs and, at long last, into the city of Vensille.

33

The voyage from Catshed to Vensille was entirely uneventful; more than once Adrava found herself pacing the decks of the barge to stave off boredom or simply to get a little exercise. She spent time with String, feeding and grooming her, or chatted with Banks or Blucher or the crew. Each day she would retreat to her cabin to 'meditate' for an hour or more whenever she felt the need for a little peace and quiet or when the maintenance of her priestly persona became too much of a burden. More than anything she wanted to find Marrinek but running a close second was the need to throw off her disguise and once again be herself.

The evening before they arrived in Vensille she once again dined with Banks, although this time they ate a simple meal together in the privacy of Banks' small cabin. After the main meal, as the barge continued downstream, they sat at the table drinking red wine from a small barrel that Banks produced from her locker and eating cheese they'd picked up in Catshed.

"So," said Banks, leaning back in her chair, "are you going to tell me your real name?"

Adrava paused, wine glass halfway to her lips, and looked Banks straight in the eye.

"My real name?" she said, lowering her glass to the table.

"The priest thing," said Banks with a friendly smile, "it's a good act - you've fooled everyone else on the boat including Blucher and Smark - but it doesn't wash. What are you up to?"

Adrava pushed back from the table, preparing herself in case Banks was asking out of more than innocent friendship.

"What gave me away?"

"Little things. You've travelled, although you don't talk about it very much, and that's unusual in a 'young' priest. You're talented but you don't really use your power and I can't gauge your strength. You only bless people or give thanks for food or invite prayers when you think someone is watching, which is also strange for a priest."

Adrava was silent for a few seconds.

"No," she said finally.

"What do you mean 'no'?"

"I mean that I'm not going to tell you my name. I'd like to think that we might become friends, over the years, but for now the less you know about me the safer we'll both be."

Banks looked highly dubious.

"Really? You're so tainted that even knowing your name might put me in danger? I don't believe it."

Adrava shrugged, not really caring if Banks believed her or not.

"I said I was travelling to see family in Vensille but that wasn't true. Well, not quite. I think my husband is in the city, somewhere, and I very much wish to find him."

Banks' scepticism, now at truly epic levels, showed openly on her face.

"Oh well if you really don't want to tell the truth then don't, but such a transparent lie is an insult."

Adrava shook her head sadly.

"I haven't seen him for almost two years but a report reached me suggesting he was in Catshed a few weeks ago. If it was true, and people I respect certainly gave it credence, then Vensille is a logical destination for him. Catshed is just too small, too provincial, too far from money and power for him to stay there for any length of time but there's no way to know for certain until I get to the city."

Banks stared at her, frowning.

"Truly? You're searching for your husband?"

"I am," said Adrava, tight-lipped and with furrowed brow, "that part of the story is true. And I have been at the seminary in Esterengel for a year and a half."

She stopped again, while she thought about how much more she wanted to say.

"I want to trust you, Mistress Banks, I really do, but life has taught me to be cautious and I don't want to endanger you, or me, by telling you too much. Can I trust you?"

"Call me Marjorie. And yes, you can trust me, not that I can imagine anyone would ever think to ask me about you in the first place."

Adrava reached a decision. She held out her hand and lowered her guard.

"Take my hand, Marjorie," she said, "and gauge my power."

Banks reached out, her hand hovering uncertainly above Adrava's for a few seconds, then she closed her eyes and touched Adrava's palm. Her eyes jerked open immediately and she snatched her hand away. She stared at Adrava, shock showing on her face.

"And now you know one of my secrets," said Adrava,

restoring her guard and withdrawing her hand, "don't try to guess my name, don't speculate about my identity, don't even think about trying to find out who my husband is. Trust me, ignorance is bliss."

"Such talent," said Banks in a hushed tone, "is very rare. You have a high station within the Empire, I think."

Adrava snorted.

"Hah, I wish. Talent takes you only so far, unfortunately. But you were right about me not being a priest. It's a convenient story to fool the Shorts, to divert attention from a young woman travelling alone, nothing more."

Banks sat back in her chair, staring at Adrava with new eyes. Now that she knew how strongly talented Adrava was the rest of the picture made more sense.

"Not a priest. No. A soldier, maybe?" Banks searched for confirmation in Adrava's face but it was cold and stony, almost unmoving.

"Yes, I think you were a soldier. That would explain the bracers on your arms - they show, sometimes, when your sleeves catch in the breeze."

Adrava was still for a few seconds then she nodded.

"Yes, a soldier. A general, even, and a good one."

Neither of them spoke for a minute or so.

"Well," said Banks, breaking the silence, "whatever your past, you've been nothing but polite and friendly toward me. I will trust that you know your business and that, if it becomes appropriate, you'll share with me what you're comfortable to share. Until then, let us be friends and I will keep your secrets." She held out her hand. Adrava looked at it for a few seconds then relaxed. She smiled and took the proffered hand. They shook then Banks said, "And now more wine, I think," filling their glasses, "and a toast. To absent husbands; may they get all that they deserve for the pains and difficulties they cause us."

Adrava raised her glass with a smile.

"To absent husbands. And I promise, by all that is sacred and holy, that I will find mine and teach him the true meaning of pain."

They drank then filled their glasses and drank again. Then, as the barge's bell tolled nine o'clock, they talked and laughed and shared harmless stories of youth and lovers and desire and betrayal as the barge sailed ever southward.

The next morning Adrava was woken by the ship's bell at mid-morning. Not normally one to sleep late, she sat up in bed then put her hand to her head, leaning against the bed frame to steady herself. Ah yes, she remembered, she had sat late into the night drinking wine and then brandy with Banks. Her head pounded and her stomach heaved as she stood and climbed slowly up onto the deck. Banks was at the wheel and she waved as Adrava emerged from below deck and stood, blinking uncomfortably in the sunlight. Adrava made her way carefully along the deck and climbed to the poop before leaning against the rail.

"I think the brandy may have disagreed with me," she said, shading her eyes against the sun.

"Hah," said Banks, "I'm not sure it was the brandy but it might have been the fortified wine we drank when the brandy ran out."

Adrava groaned, her head sinking into her hands.

"Did I do anything embarrassing?"

Banks laughed.

"Not really, although I did like your ideas for handling Blucher's bodyguard, the younger one," she said, nodding down the deck to where the bodyguards were dicing, lying on coiled ropes, "if only I was a little younger I might be tempted to try some of those ideas myself, although I'm not as supple as I used to be." She laughed again, and then harder as Adrava groaned and clutched at her aching head.

"Don't worry, I won't tell anyone. And there are only a few hours now till we reach Vensille. We'll see the smoke soon and by this afternoon you'll be safely on land again."

Adrava decided that standing was too much effort and slid to the deck, her back against the railing. Banks looked down at her as Adrava stretched her neck and rubbed her temples, trying to shift the ache in her skull.

"Oh gods, it feels like someone's trying to crush my skull from the inside. How are you still functioning?"

Banks, with the indifference traditional of a drinking partner not afflicted by a hangover, just laughed harder and raised her voice.

"A little more wine, maybe? Hair of the dog?"

Adrava shook her head and immediately regretted it. Banks hooted with laughter as Adrava groaned again and laid her head against her knees.

Eventually Adrava raised her head and leant it gently against the railings, her eyes closed.

"How will you find your husband?" said Banks in a bid to restart the conversation, "Vensille is a big city - it might not be easy to find one man amongst so many."

Adrava blew a deep breath out through pursed lips in an effort to stave of the nausea, then said,

"Charm shops. He makes charms, he'll need supplies. I'll visit the charm shops and ask after him."

"And you think one of them will recognise his description?"

"Oh yes. A good-looking Imperial citizen, dark hair, tall, heavyset, possibly carrying a staff of some sort. Someone will know him, sooner or later. He's likely to stand out from the crowd. I'll find him." She sounded confident and determined but Banks was sceptical.

"Hmm. Sounds a bit vague, that description, but maybe you're right, maybe someone will know him from it. Are you planning to lodge with Blucher?"

"Only for a few days, till I have a feel for the city."

Banks didn't seem to like that very much. She twitched the wheel round a few points and scowled at a man who waved as he guided his small boat upstream.

"You need to be careful around Blucher. Don't underestimate him; he is more dangerous than he seems and well connected. With the Palace, I mean."

"With the Palace? You mean the Duke?"

"No, not the Duke," said Banks, shaking her head, "but he has friends amongst the nobles and the Duke's advisers, or so he says. He supplies them with charms and materials from the north - metals, jewels, that sort of thing - and they look out for him."

"I'm surprised they'd deal with him."

"He says it's all about the presentation, the mystery, the extravagance. I have no idea what that means nor why he travels himself rather than relying on agents like other dealers, but he's undeniably successful."

"Well, anyway. I'll only be staying with him for three or four days, maybe fewer if I find my husband quickly. And I can look after myself," she said, rapping the bracer on her left arm against the railing, "these aren't the only charms I carry."

"Just be careful," said Banks, concern showing on her face, "Blucher may think he's getting more from the deal than you want to offer."

Banks looked down at Adrava where she sat on the deck.

"You know what I mean."

"Yes," Adrava sighed, "I know what you mean. I'll be careful." She dragged herself to her feet and leant over the railing to look at the water.

"How much longer to Vensille?" she asked over her shoulder.

Banks looked around, taking her bearings.

"A few hours, maybe four, depending on the traffic as we get close to the city."

"Then I think I'll go and pack my stuff, check on String. Maybe throw up a couple of times."

A few hours later the Golden Rose docked in Vensille and Adrava, now much recovered, was able to walk String down the gangplank to the wharf where Blucher and his bodyguards were waiting. Adrava turned and nodded to Banks, who was leaning against the deck railing. Banks nodded back and then watched as Adrava led String through the crowds, following Blucher.

As promised, a coach was waiting on the wharf and Blucher held the door open for Adrava.

"It is a short walk to my home," said Blucher, climbing into the coach and pulling the door closed, "but I prefer to ride in comfort rather than walk the streets. My man will look after your horse and I will look after you."

He smiled at her from the opposite seat as the coach set off slowly through the streets. After only a few minutes they reached a large and imposing house on the edge of a small square. One of the bodyguards took String to the stables through a gate at the side of the house while Blucher held out his hand to help Adrava down from the coach then walked her in through the front door.

"Welcome to my humble home," said Blucher, waving his arm at the far from humble stairs and entrance hall, "please make yourself at home." A short woman in her mid-forties wearing a long white apron appeared from the far end of the hallway.

"And this is Flince, my housekeeper."

"Welcome home, sir."

"Thank you, Flince, thank you. Miss Naseep here will be staying with us for a few days. Can you prepare a room please and have her bags taken up?"

"Very good, sir." Her face suggested that her actual feelings were less complimentary but Blucher didn't seem to notice.

"Good. Miss Naseep," said Blucher, taking her hand and trying not to leer, "I trust you will join me for dinner? If there is anything you need in the meantime please ask Flince but now, I'm afraid, I have things to do." He kissed her hand and then left quickly, heading through the doors on the left-hand side of the stairs and disappearing into what looked a like a large study.

"If you'll follow me, miss," said Flince, picking up Adrava's bags, "I'll take you to your room."

"That's very kind of you Mrs Flince, thank you," said Adrava, struggling a little to keep her voice steady and priest-like now that she had finally reached Vensille. All she wanted to do was look for Marrinek but she needed somewhere to stay and so she had to play the part of the vulnerable priestess for just a little longer, much to her annoyance.

"Just Flince, miss, just Flince" said the housekeeper, leading Adrava up two flights of stairs to a modest room on the second floor, overlooking the street.

"This will be your room, miss. You can ring the bell if you need anything. The gong will sound for dinner and there is a sitting room on the ground floor opposite the master's library where you can take tea in a little while, if it pleases you."

"Thank you, Flince, and may the gods bless you for taking me in like this. I can manage my bags, thank you."

Flince pursed her lips a little but said nothing; clearly she was used to dealing with her master's guests but didn't like them to be quite so young.

As soon as she was alone Adrava searched the room. She assumed, after Banks' warnings, that Blucher would watch her secretly if he could but she found no spy holes or hidden doors. She unpacked her clothes putting some away in the drawers and leaving others on the chair for laundry.

Her charms she kept hidden under her clothes. Blucher might not be able to use them but she didn't want him to know that she possessed them. Finally, happy that there was no immediate danger and that her possessions were safely stowed, she went downstairs to the sitting room. A few minutes later, Flince appeared with a tray of tea and some small muffins.

Dinner was a dull affair. Adrava and Blucher were the only diners and although the food was good Blucher's stories and boasts quickly became annoying and Adrava found her mind wandering until she realised he had stopped speaking and was staring at her expectantly.

"I'm so sorry, Mr Blucher, what did you say?" said Adrava, smiling apologetically.

"You said that you were coming to Vensille to meet with some family. Cousins, I think. Do you have an address?"

Adrava froze, thinking furiously. She had forgotten the easy lie told over dinner a few nights before about her reasons for travelling to Vensille. Blucher, evidently, had not.

"Yes. That is to say, no. What I mean is that I am not really here to visit family," she dropped her eyes to her plate and said in a quiet voice, "I am having doubts about the priesthood."

"Doubts, Miss Naseep? About taking your vows?" She nodded, keeping her eyes lowered.

"And so you've run away from the seminary? Trying to see a bit of the world, eh?"

She looked up at him, her face contorted into a perfect display of youthful confusion.

"I'm just not sure I can say the words and follow the teachings. I don't know what to do." She trembled her lips as if about to burst into tears.

Blucher reached across the table to hold her hand.

"Don't worry, my dear. You can stay here for as long as you need." He smiled and Adrava was reminded of a great cat she had seen once in a menagerie in Esterengel; Blucher's face and smile seemed friendly but his eyes were gleeful and victorious and she found that she really didn't trust him.

Despite that, she forced her face into a smile as if trying bravely to hold herself together and thanked Blucher for his offer and for his friendship and hospitality.

Their conversation continued a little longer as Blucher spoke about the great sights and buildings of the city and the part he had played in the extension of their grandeur but when Adrava stifled a yawn behind her hand he took the hint.

"It was a long voyage and it has been a long day and I have kept you too long from your rest. Please, forgive me. We can talk again tomorrow at dinner but I fear I will be away for much of the day on business. Do make the house your own and ask Flince for anything you might need."

Adrava smiled at him as they walked the length of the dining room and across the hallway to the stairs.

"I wonder if Flince could recommend a dressmaker? I

have only the robes I travelled in and if I am not to take my vows it seems, well, wrong, to wear them."

Blucher waved his hands as if pushing her concerns aside.

"We'll have a dressmaker here tomorrow morning to fit you for the latest styles. I will arrange it with Flince."

"That's so very kind of you, thank you. I don't know what I've done to deserve such a friend."

Blucher smiled again but his eyes were predatory.

"Think nothing of it. I myself have business to attend to tomorrow but I trust we will dine again in the evening?"

"I would like that very much, yes."

"Excellent, then I bid you goodnight." He kissed her hand and stood watching from the hallway as she climbed the stairs and passed from sight.

In her room Adrava shuddered at the thought of spending more time in Blucher's company. He clearly had certain expectations and it was only a matter of time before he pressed them, at which point things would became unpleasant. The door to her room had no lock so she wedged a piece of kindling from the fireplace under the door and balanced an upside-down chair against the handle. Then she washed and prepared for bed before finally crawling between the sheets.

Sometime later - she wasn't sure exactly how long - she was woken by the clattering of the chair as it fell from its precarious perch against the door handle.

"Hello," she said, sitting up in bed, "is someone there?"

There was no reply but the sound of stealthy footsteps retreating down the corridor. She crossed the floor to reset her alarm chair and check that her charms were still secure then she got back into bed and went back to sleep; she wasn't disturbed again.

The following morning she woke late and swore quietly to herself; the day was wasting and she had much to do. She dressed quickly and hurried downstairs to find that Flince was waiting in the sitting room with a woman - the dressmaker Blucher had promised. Even before she had eaten the two women spent an hour measuring and comparing and discussing the best way to fit Adrava for the latest city fashions; apart from terse instructions about how to stand or whether to raise or lower her arms she was largely ignored throughout the process. Eventually the dressmaker announced herself satisfied and left, promising to return the next day with the first of the new dresses. Released from the tape measures of the dressmaker, Adrava made her escape and headed out into the city despite Flince's disapproving glare.

And Blucher had been right; Vensille really was a city. Not as large or as imposing as Esterengel, maybe, and very different to Khemucasterill, but still a wealthy and successful city with many fine buildings and not a few parks and public gardens. She wandered almost at random along the city's wider roads, searching for a charm shop. It didn't take long to find one, a small shop with grimy windows and a narrow door. As she pushed open the door she was suddenly reminded of visiting a similar shop, decades ago, with Marrinek, somewhere in the back streets of Khemucasterill. She smiled as she looked around the shop, pretending to be interested in the goods on display as the owner finished serving a customer.

As soon as the customer had left and the door had closed behind them, Adrava turned to the shopkeeper.

"Good day, miss," he said with a friendly smile, "and what can I help you with today?"

"I'm looking for something specific, not sure if you'll be

able to help," she said, looking with disdain at the charms displayed behind the counter. The shopkeeper bristled slightly but kept smiling.

"I'm looking for someone. He would have been a customer, probably looking for rare metals." She was watching the shopkeeper closely now, waiting for some indication that she had hit her mark.

"An imperial citizen, tall, good-looking, dark hair. Demanding. Probably carrying a staff of some sort, maybe a sword." She stepped closer to the counter and put her hands down flat on the surface.

"Have you seen such a man?"

"No, miss," said the shopkeeper, shaking his head, "we don't get many imperial visitors, I'm sure I'd remember him."

"Are you sure?" she said quietly, "I am most keen to find him; I would be disappointed to find that you had lied to me."

The shopkeeper bristled again, clearly annoyed at her questions and her threats.

"Yes, miss, I am quite sure. And now I think you should leave."

She stared at him for a few seconds longer then turned to leave. She stopped at the door, holding it open.

"If you see the man I have described, tell him I'm looking for him. Tell him he can find me at the house of a man called Blucher." Then she stepped out of the shop and closed the door behind her.

And so it went for the rest of the day. By late afternoon she had spoken to five shopkeepers and none had admitted to knowing Marrinek or shown any sign of recognising his description. It was late afternoon by the time she entered the sixth shop, a small narrow room lined with drawers and lit by charmed lamps now that the sun had fallen far enough to shade the street. The shopkeeper came forward to greet her as she entered.

"Good afternoon, miss. My name is Eaves. How may I be of assistance?"

"Hello, Mr Eaves. My name is Naseep and I'm looking for a man, a customer of yours, maybe. An imperial citizen, tall, dark hair, good-looking. Carries a staff. Might have been buying metals or tools." She leaned over the counter toward Eaves, studying his face closely as she asked, "Do you know where I might find this man?"

Eaves eyes widened and his nostrils flared slightly but he shook his head firmly. Bay, she had to be asking about Bay, and his instructions had been very, very clear.

"N-no, miss, n-never set eyes on him, can't help, sorry."

Adrava's spirits soared. Eaves was a dreadful liar and clearly knew more than he was prepared to say. She stood there, staring at him, face expressionless as the sweat beaded on Eaves' forehead.

"Don't lie to me, Eaves. I know you've seen him," she leant forward and whispered, "tell me where he is."

"N-no, miss, you're mistaken, I c-can't help." Eaves shook his head. He was trembling, shaking like a leaf in a breeze.

Adrava stepped back from the counter, certain now that she had found what she needed and that Marrinek was, or had recently been, in Vensille.

"Well, maybe I am, maybe I'm not, but if you see him, you tell him I'm looking for him. Tell him he can find me at Blucher's house. You know Blucher, the merchant?" Eaves nodded, not trusting himself to say anything more.

"Then tell him. And tell him soon. Tonight would be best, or tomorrow I'll come back and cut out your eyeballs."

She yanked the door open then turned and said, "Tonight, Eaves."

Then she stepped through the doorway and was gone, leaving Eaves alone and shaking.

Adrava stood outside the shop for a few moments then headed down the street towards Blucher's house. Eaves would go straight to Marrinek, she was sure, or send him a message, so all she had to do now was wait.

Relaxed for the first time in months, she walked through the streets of Vensille with a sense that, finally, everything was going to work out.

34

B reakfast on their first day in their new home was a little subdued. Aimes was apologetic but, at least for a few days, bread and cheese, preserved vegetables, fruits from the market and cold meat were likely to be all she could serve while the cook got the kitchen and pantries sorted out and into a manageable state. To the twins, used to a diet of whatever they could steal on the streets, and Marrinek, forced to accept whatever his jailers gave him, Aimes' worries seemed unworldly and they ate eagerly.

Later, in the unused bedroom suite that Marrinek had designated a classroom, they worked together to practice the wood-forming techniques that Mr Eaves had shown them. After several hours both the twins were able to exert a degree of control over their sculpting so that neither of them was accidentally producing the strange waves of wood that they had made previously. By lunchtime Marrinek was satisfied that the twins were well on their way to mastering the simple techniques that Eaves had taught them and, more importantly, that they had an appreciation for the risks involved.

"Anyone can work wood with a blade," said Marrinek when they took a break for lunch, "but the best results combine mechanical tools with power and charms. You two might, given time and practice, achieve a great deal with just power and charms; you seem to have a natural affinity with wood."

Despite their success with wood, it was clear that neither of the twins was likely to pursue a career as a carpenter. Indeed, Marrinek would have been hugely disappointed if that was the limit of their achievements, useful and rewarding though it might be.

In the afternoon they worked on theory and the history of charms then moved to the stable yard to learn the rudiments of stick fighting.

"Shouldn't we learn swords?" said Darek, disappointed to be handed a plain staff of wood.

"The sword is a gentleman's weapon, an elegant tool for threatening or dissecting a man. A simple staff, often called the short staff even though it is six feet long or more, is a peasant's weapon but no less dangerous. Easy to make, versatile, deadly in skilled hands, you'll learn staff first, sword later. The staff is less threatening and often underestimated by swordsmen, especially lordlings and 'men of quality' who sometimes dismiss it precisely because it isn't sharpened steel. You can use it for walking or for fighting and one skilled man with a staff can defeat three with swords. With this weapon, you have a longer reach and a heavier blow than any swordsman and you can block or attack with either end."

Marrinek switched to Khem and they practiced together for two hours as Marrinek demonstrated the basic forms and stances and led them through the key moves, blocks, feints and attacks.

"Good. You will work the staff every day after lunch," he said finally in Khem before switching to Gheel, "but that's enough for now. Freshen up and change your clothes before dinner, then we will visit Mr Eaves again."

The twins disappeared indoors and Marrinek followed them, heading back to his own suite to change.

After dinner Marrinek accompanied them to Mr Eaves' shop. Darek's black eye had started to fade and the twins were growing noticeably more confident as their lives on the streets slowly receded into the past.

"I'll be back in an hour or so. Wait for me here if your lesson finishes before I return."

He left them standing there and ducked into an alley, heading for Trike's. When he got there the common room was full and the atmosphere heavy with pipe smoke, laughter and singing. He made his way to the stairs and climbed up to the first floor, then pushed his way to the door of Fangfoss's room and let himself in.

Inside the noise was almost as loud as outside but it quietened quickly as people saw who had entered. News travelled fast in this and it seemed that everyone knew who Marrinek was. He looked slowly around the room, face blank, then he walked over to the table where Fangfoss was seated. The man sitting opposite Fangfoss got up quickly and backed into the crowd, leaving space for Marrinek to sit.

Marrinek took a glass from the centre of the table and filled it from the wine jug as the conversations restarted around him. At the end of the room the fiddle player struck up his tune again and someone started singing.

Fangfoss waved his glass at Marrinek.

"We're celebrating the demise of the Flank Siders," he said, standing. Then he raised his glass and shouted above the din.

"A toast to our new friend, Bay, and to the end of the Flank Siders." There was a cheer and the noise subsided as everyone drank the toast then the music resumed and the noise rose again. Marrinek sipped his wine.

"This is for you," said Fangfoss, sliding a purse across the table, "your share of the week's take from the North Enders. Don't spend it all at once, we worked hard for that." He sniggered, then said, "Well, someone worked hard for it and we put a lot of effort into taking it off 'em."

Marrinek slipped the purse into his shirt, nodded at Fangfoss and stood up to leave.

"What, leaving so soon?" said Fangfoss, "Don't you want to stay and party?"

"Things to do," said Marrinek, pushing through the crowd toward the door and making his way back to the common room. He stopped at the bottom of the stairs to secure the purse, then strode to the door.

Chickie came in just as he reached the door. He nodded to Marrinek and grabbed his arm as he passed, leaning in close to whisper.

"Mirelle was looking for you, Bay, earlier today."

"For me? Why?"

"Money, of course."

Marrinek grunted and pushed past onto the street. He wasn't quite sure how Mirelle fitted into the scheme or what her plans were but if she was taking an interest then maybe it was time to deal with her. Then he shrugged; she was a problem for another day. He turned south and headed back to Eaves' shop to collect the twins.

Mirelle caught up with him later that evening. Marrinek was sitting in the library, sipping a glass of the local liqueur and looking at the collection of books that had come with the house when Shaldring came in to announce a visitor.

Lady Mirelle swept into the room and threw herself into an armchair without waiting to be asked. Marrinek, who had stood to greet his guest, sank back into his own chair and picked up his drink.

"Can I offer you anything, my lady? This is really very good," he said, waving the glass in her direction, "albeit a little sweet for my taste." He clicked his fingers at Shaldring, who floated forward with a glass on a silver tray for Lady Mirelle. She took it and waited until Shaldring disappeared, closing the doors behind him.

"So, Lord Bay," she said, sipping from her glass before setting it down on the floor at her feet, "what is it you want from Vensille?"

Marrinek frowned, playing the confused Imperial noble.

"Want, my lady?" he asked in heavily accented Gheel, "Look around. What more could I want?"

"Rubbish," she said firmly, "don't give me that. You're up to something and I want to know what it is."

Marrinek stared at her, frowning for a moment in genuine astonishment.

"You think I have some grand plan and that I would lay it all out for you if you just asked? I had heard that you were direct but this borders on naivety, even if I had a plan to describe."

Lady Mirelle shrugged.

"I'll find out sooner or later," she said, picking up her drink again, "but it would save a lot of effort if you just told me all about it." She paused to take a sip of her drink. "I might even be able to help."

Marrinek raised an eyebrow and settled back into his chair. This was becoming interesting.

"Help how?" he asked cautiously, "If indeed we were to accept for a moment that there were things I still wanted."

"Introductions, influence, assistance. I have contacts throughout the city and at the palace. Maybe if you tell me what you're after..."

The pause lengthened until Mirelle began to think that Lord Bay had fallen asleep in his chair. Then suddenly he leant forward and when he spoke his accent had almost entirely disappeared.

"You're Rhenveldt's woman, his enforcer of choice. Why would I trust you?"

"Oh well," said Mirelle casually, "I'm not sure I'd recommend trusting anyone, least of all me, but that doesn't mean we can't help each other."

Another pause.

"Gauward is running the Lighthouse for you now, I hear. And Fangfoss reports to you as well, so you've united the two gangs. That's impressive but what next? A play for the Duke's throne?"

Marrinek snorted and shook his head.

"No. I've never been one to seek political power. I want only what everyone wants; peace, security and comfort. I have that now so what more could you offer?"

Now it was Lady Mirelle's turn to snort with derision.

"If you think you've built yourself a secure foothold based on controlling the North Enders and the Flank Siders then you're deluded. They'll turn on you as soon as they sense an opportunity." She paused again and tossed back the last of her drink. "For true security you need to be part of the ruling establishment, part of the elite that props up the Duke. Sheltering under the Duke's wing with the profits from the two gangs and the Lighthouse might be a very strong place indeed."

She stood up while Marrinek pondered her words and grabbed the decanter from the side table where Shaldring had left it. She filled her glass then walked over to fill Marrinek's before setting the nearly empty decanter down on the floor.

"And that's it, isn't it?" she said in a sudden flash of insight. "This isn't about the gangs or the money, it's about bullying your way into the nobility." She shook her head at the idea, at the sheer brazen arrogance of the man who sat before her.

"Sooner or later they'll come for you, you know, if you grow too rich or too powerful and if you don't have the Duke's favour. The Watch, maybe, or some group of nobles. They might even send me. However it happens, they won't let you keep what you have if the Duke isn't getting his due."

Marrinek frowned and narrowed his eyes.

"I'm confused," he said, sipping his drink, "are we talking about the Duke's needs, mine or yours?"

"All three. They're interwoven. Look, you've done well to get so far so quickly but let's be realistic. You'll get no further without help and it's only a matter of time before you lose what you've won. I can help, if you make it worth my while, or I can bring you down. Either way, I win, but there may be more to be gained by collaboration than competition."

"Go on," said Marrinek when she paused, "you have my attention."

"The Duke takes a cut, always has done. Think of it as an informal tax on your position in society. If you pay, I'll have something I can work with, something I can use to bring you into the fold. If you refuse or if you make life difficult, it will hasten their strike against you and you'll stand alone. Whoever you think your friends are, nobody will help if the Duke turns against you."

"You're saying that I'm safe if I pay and at risk if I don't. Blackmail, in other words."

"More of a voluntary donation for the wellbeing of the city. In return, I'll bring you into the Duke's path and give you a chance to impress him. If you can make yourself valuable, you'll be safe."

"And what do you get out of all this?" Marrinek asked, "Besides feeling that you've accomplished something for the good of the city?"

Lady Mirelle threw back her drink and grinned.

"I don't give a fuck about the city. It's been good to me in recent years but nothing lasts forever. This is about insurance, a fallback when it all goes wrong. So you'll tip me a little extra, to cover my costs, and you'll owe me a favour. This city runs on silver but favours are what everyone craves."

Marrinek was silent for a few long moments while he thought about this. Could he trust her? Could he afford not to trust her? Eventually, he made up his mind.

"I too have contacts. I can arrange for payments to be made," he said quietly, "but I want the Watch kept away from my business. No more Watchmen holding out their hands and roughing up my people. It's bad for business and it's inefficient. You'll get your money, once a week like before, and you'll get it only from me."

Lady Mirelle's grin slunk from her face.

"It may be difficult to persuade the Watch to go without," she said.

"I didn't say they shouldn't be paid, only that they shouldn't collect from my people. I'll handle the gangs, you'll handle the Watch, everyone gets paid. Take it or leave it." He stood up and held out his hand. Lady Mirelle stared at it for a moment then stood and shook.

"Deal. I'll fix the Watch but it'll only hold while the money flows. If that stops…" she shrugged.

"Understood. First payment tomorrow, then weekly. And in return…?"

"High society, balls, parties," said Lady Mirelle, "and an introduction to the Duke. After that, it's up to you."

"Good. I look forward to hearing from you."

Over the next few days, Marrinek's household settled into something resembling a normal, everyday pattern. Marrinek lectured the twins and worked with them on their crafting and other skills in the morning. After a midday meal they would practice staff fighting and other martial arts. In the late afternoon there would be more lectures and practice followed, most evenings, by lessons with Eaves. At lunchtime on their third day in the house Aimes announced that the cook was now settled and had all the equipment and help she needed to feed the household properly. From that afternoon, the variety and quality of the food improved markedly.

Marrinek, for his part, found that he was enjoying the new routine. Apart from his time as an honoured guest of an Imperial prison, he had spent most of the previous six decades as a soldier, fighting his way back and forth across the Empire; the opportunity to spend time teaching and training the twins was turning out to be surprisingly rewarding.

It wouldn't last, of course, these things never did. Even now he could feel the threat of the future weighing down on him, preparing to rip apart his new life and send him hurtling back into the days of death and terror and hate. Sooner or later someone would recognise him or guess who he was and he would be forced to run or fight. All he could do, right now, was prepare for the inevitable storm.

Stamina was his main worry at the moment. Months of captivity and bad food had left him physically weakened and in bad shape and he knew that it had been sheer luck that he had survived his recent fights unscathed. Now, with good food and regular exercise, his form was improving but there was still a lot to do before he would be back to his fighting strength.

Weapons were also a concern. He spent several evenings working on Bone Dancer, tweaking the ironwork to better handle the power that was focussed into the weapon or finessing the shape of the wood so that it sat more comfortably in his hands.

One evening he spent several hours replacing the half-pound of lead in the base of the staff with the few ounces of tungsten he had taken from Hitton's stash. That made Bone Dancer a little lighter but also, more importantly, boosted the amount of power that the weapon could store. Then, by tweaking the copper netting worked into the wood, he improved the rate at which Bone Dancer could gather power. By the time he was finished Bone Dancer was all that he could have hoped for, a truly formidable weapon.

The blades were another matter altogether. His knives and the sword he had taken from the watchman in the forest were plain steel, quick to blunt or wear and prone to rust and decay. Given time and materials he would be able to turn these blades from simple steel to something more dangerous and less readily damaged. In the short-term, what he really wanted was a good sword with a hardened blade but such things simply weren't to be found in Vensille. In the end he stuck with the stolen Imperial blade and resolved to improve it once he had a little more time. It was a simple weapon but also familiar and hugely effective.

He had had more success with defensive charms. Eaves had found him a second bracer so he now wore one on each arm. They were small and uneven, having been made by different craftsmen, but they delivered a solid degree of protection. He would greatly have preferred to have one of his armoured suits - he had several sets stashed in safe locations around the Empire - but their recovery would be risky and, without the appropriate key, potentially very dangerous. Much of his planning focussed on re-acquiring one of his suits or making a replacement but, for now, he could only leave them where they were and hope to recover them in the future.

On their third day in the house the charmsman that Eaves had recommended arrived with two apprentices to begin work on the hardening of the doors and windows. Marrinek walked through the house with him explaining exactly what he wanted and how he wanted it done. The man was sceptical, hostile even, but it was soon clear that Marrinek knew what he was talking about. The work, he said, would take a week and cost a good deal of money. They agreed a fee for an immediate start and then Marrinek left them to it, promising to check their work later in the day.

It turned out that the work was good and the three men made rapid progress, hardening all the doors and windows on the ground and first floor within a few days. Marrinek took a keen interest in their work but it seemed that Eaves had chosen well. He wasn't able to fault the results or break the charmed wood. When they had finished working on the house he announced himself well-satisfied with their work, paid them a bonus, then set them to work on the stables and gates.

On the fifth day, Aimes introduced the rest of the staff that she had hired to help her manage the household and announced that she now had everyone she needed to ensure that it would run to her satisfaction. The house itself took on an air of bustle and life as Aimes continued to furnish the rooms and corridors. She acquired a number of charmed lamps to replace the candles that lit the hallways and public rooms.

The tailor made several more visits to confirm details and measurements and then he began to deliver the formal clothes that Madame Duval had commissioned for Marrinek and the twins. He also delivered a selection of everyday summer clothes, outfits for riding, city cloaks and garments cut to match the latest fashions. By the time he had finished the twins had more clothes than they had ever owned and even Marrinek was starting to think that Madame Duval may have been a little extravagant, although there was no denying that the clothes were of excellent quality.

They had been in the new house for eleven days and everyone was beginning to settle into a routine when the first signs of the danger that Marrinek had feared appeared on their doorstep. Marrinek and the twins were eating an early dinner after a long day of staff fighting. The twins had improved quickly and Marrinek had acquired two sets of padded jackets and helmets so that they could spar together. Darek, not surprisingly, was stronger and more aggressive but Floost's footwork was faster and she would often win bouts if she was able to avoid her brother's bludgeoning attacks.

This evening their dinner was interrupted by the butler,

Shaldring, who came quietly into the dining room as they were finishing the meat course.

"Excuse me, sir, but Mr Eaves is in the drawing room. He is very keen to speak to you; a matter of some urgency, he says."

"Eaves is here?" said Marrinek, frowning, "Strange. Very well, Shaldring, I'll see him now."

Marrinek stood up from the table and walked with Shaldring to the hallway.

"Thank you, Shaldring, that will be all." Shaldring bowed as Marrinek opened the doors to the drawing room and went inside, closing them behind him.

Eaves was standing in front of the fireplace looking at a landscape that Aimes had acquired from an auction the day before. Marrinek didn't particularly like the picture but he had to admit that it seemed to fit the room.

"Good evening, Mr Eaves. To what do we owe the pleasure?"

Eaves turned as Marrinek spoke and hurried across the room. He seemed to be shaking, nervous.

"There was a woman, sir, she came to my shop. Looking for you." Eaves spoke quickly, stumbling over the words.

"Slow down, Eaves. Here, sit and tell me everything." Marrinek directed him to a chair and poured two glasses of brandy from the decanter on the side table. Eaves accepted the glass with trembling hands and sipped.

"I was finishing for the day, about to close up, when a woman came in." Eaves paused to take another sip of brandy.

"She was tall, talented, beautiful. She had an accent, just like yours. She asked about Imperial citizens buying charms or supplies."

Marrinek sat opposite Eaves but didn't drink his brandy. His eyes narrowed at Eaves' description.

"Did she ask for me by name?"

"No," said Eaves shaking his head, "but she described you - height, hair colour, staff. She didn't mention the beard," - he paused to throw back the rest of his brandy - "and she didn't believe me when I denied knowing you. She knew I was lying, said she'd cut out my eyeballs if I didn't tell her where you were. And she was strong, very strong. You could see it in her face, as if she could have killed me without effort or thought."

Marrinek sat back thinking.

"I have many enemies, Eaves, but I hadn't thought they would follow me here or find me quite so soon. Did she leave a name?"

"Naseep. She said you should call on her at the house of a trader, Blucher."

"I don't know either of those names. Do you know this man, Blucher?"

Eaves nodded.

"A merchant dealing in charms and materials. And sometimes other, darker, goods, or so I hear. I avoid him, not because he isn't talented, but because he is just isn't very nice."

"Well, I think maybe I should pay him a visit and see what this Naseep wants with me." He stood up and took the empty glass from Eaves.

"Thank you for coming to me with this and for keeping my secret; I won't forget. I think we'll postpone this evening's lesson with the twins while I sort out this matter."

Eaves gave him directions to Blucher's house then scuttled back out onto the street, disappearing quickly into the early evening gloom. Marrinek went back to the dining room where the maids had cleared the main course and were setting out a summer pudding with custard and a jug of coffee.

"That was Mr Eaves," said Marrinek, "with disturbing news." The twins looked up from their puddings, intrigued.

"I'm going to have to deal with this before it gets out of hand. I've postponed your lesson this evening - Eaves isn't really up to it - and you'll need to stay in."

Marrinek sipped at his coffee.

"I'll be going out shortly but I should be back later this evening."

"What sort of problem is it?" said Floost.

"The sort I need to fix quickly," said Marrinek, "finish your dinner then stay upstairs till morning; everything should be resolved by then."

He stood up from the table and headed for the door then turned back.

"Don't worry," he said, smiling, "I'm sure everything will be fine."

Then he closed the door behind him and went upstairs, still pondering Eaves and his encounter with Naseep.

Adrava's stroll through the city took a good while and when she got back to the house she found a new dress waiting for her in her room. The style wasn't one she would have chosen but it followed the local fashions and would certainly look less out of place than her novice robes. She washed quickly in the basin and changed into the new dress, admiring her new look in the small mirror on the wash stand. The dress was cut quite low, as was the local fashion, and it had long loose sleeves, which was lucky since they would hide her bracers. She stood there for a few minutes adjusting her charms and then slipped her shoes back on and went downstairs.

In the sitting room she found Flince.

"How do I look?" she asked, smiling and giving a little twirl.

"Very nice miss, the master will be pleased. Will you take coffee?"

"Yes Flince, thank you, coffee would be lovely. And maybe some of those little cakes you had yesterday - they were delicious."

Flince nodded and left the room leaving Adrava alone. She wandered around the room looking at ornaments and pictures but after a few minutes she grew bored and went to sit in the seat by the window. Watching the people in the street occupied her for a few minutes until Flince arrived with the coffee and cakes and closed the curtains against the deepening gloom.

Adrava sat there drinking coffee and nibbling on the cakes, waiting for something to happen. When the door to the sitting room did eventually open she jumped, startled by the arrival of Blucher who came in and took the seat on the other side of the window.

"Ah, coffee. Excellent, it has been a trying day."

Adrava smiled sweetly at him as he poured coffee but she didn't ask questions; she found that she really didn't care what sort of day Blucher had had but for the sake of appearances, she looked questioningly at him.

"I had lunch with a friend of mine, a merchant who imports spices," Blucher said. Adrava zoned out almost immediately as he continued to tell a long, boring story in excruciating detail. She smiled and nodded at what seemed like appropriate intervals but dear god he was dull. And he kept leering at her, eyes lingering on the flesh exposed by the low-cut dress.

By the time that Flince announced dinner a little while later Blucher was still going, describing his entire day. He took Adrava's arm and escorted her to the dining room, pulling out the chair for her to sit before taking his place at the head of the table, all without interrupting the flow of his tale. It was something of a relief when Flince came back into the room and announced a visitor for her.

"For me?" said Adrava, feigning surprise, "but who could know that I was here? Do you have a name?"

"He gave his name as 'Bay', miss. He is in the sitting room."

Adrava put down her cutlery, stood up with a new sense of purpose and moved toward the door, face set.

"What is all this?" said Blucher, confused, "Where are you going? You said you didn't know anyone in Vensille!"

She turned to face him as she held the door open, smiling as if at a private joke.

"Why don't you come and meet him? I'm sure he'll want to meet you."

Blucher stood up, angry now.

"What's going on? I demand to know."

Adrava ignored him and walked down the hallway to the sitting room, throwing open the door. Marrinek was standing with his back to the door looking at some of Blucher's books, a staff leaning against a chair. He turned as she came in and then his jaw dropped when he recognised her.

"Addy," he said, stunned, before a smile came over his face, "I should have guessed." He rushed across the room, arms wide, grinning like a schoolboy, and was utterly unprepared for her slap.

It caught him full in the face, a great, wheeling, open-handed blow that came from nowhere, as soon as he stepped close enough. Blucher, watching from the doorway, seemed almost as shocked as Marrinek.

"What the fuck did you do, you bastard?" screamed Adrava, venting her long-contained rage and clearly winding up for more violence, "And where the fuck have you been?"

Marrinek stepped back, surprised by her fury, and raised a hand to his cheek.

"Do? What did I do? Nothing! Nothing at all, it was a bloody setup." He was angry himself, now; this wasn't at all how he had imagined their reunion.

"They came for me too, you know," she said, striding forward, fists clenched, "the inquisition and their bloody questions."

Marrinek paled.

"They did?" he whispered, all the fight driven from him by a sudden fear.

"Yes, they did, and it was only by luck that I escaped."

Marrinek collapsed back into a seat with relief and shook his head.

"I didn't know," he said quietly, "they wouldn't talk to me, wouldn't tell me anything, wouldn't even tell me why I had been arrested."

Adrava paused, her anger receding in the face of Marrinek's obvious discomfort and remorse.

"So why?" she said eventually, switching to Khem and speaking in a calmer, more controlled tone. Marrinek shook his head again.

"I wish I knew," he said, following her move from Gheel, "someone must have got to Tentalus, lied to him, presented false evidence maybe, because I didn't do a fucking thing."

He stood up and took Adrava's hand. "I promise you, I didn't do anything to give offence."

She stood for a moment, looking at him, then nodded in acceptance. That seemed to break the bubble around them and suddenly the outside world rushed back to reassert itself.

"What the fuck is going on?" said Blucher from the doorway, angrily trying to recapture the initiative, "And who the hell is this?"

"This, Mr Blucher, is Bay. My husband, for better or worse."

"Your husband? I don't understand, do you mean you're married?"

Adrava laughed but there was no amusement in her voice.

"Yes, if you can still call it 'marriage' when you haven't seen your husband for almost two years and you've spent all that time in hiding, scared for your life, wondering if today will be your last day of freedom."

She turned back to Marrinek and swallowed the worst of her rage.

"We need to help Tentalus," said Marrinek earnestly in Khem as Adrava opened her mouth to speak, "someone set me up, got both of us away from Khemucasterill and now he's in danger from some sort of conspiracy. He needs our help."

"Fuck him," said Adrava, still speaking Gheel, her anger rising again, "it's his fault we've lost everything we had, that we're stuck out here." Marrinek just shrugged.

"He's my friend."

Adrava stared at him, horrified. Then she took a deep breath.

"We will talk about this later," she promised through

clenched teeth, her anger still obvious but now controlled, refined by new knowledge, "and you can explain everything. Then, if your misplaced sense of loyalty doesn't drive me to kill you myself, we can work out what to do about Tentalus." Marrinek looked at her for a few long seconds, then nodded in resignation.

Adrava relaxed a little. She forced a thin smile then looked at Blucher, still standing in the doorway, frozen by shock and uncertainty.

"We need a little privacy, if you please, Mr Blucher. Have Flince bring coffee and cakes."

"What?" said Blucher, outraged, his cheeks turning an unhealthy red colour, "How dare you order me around in my own house!"

Marrinek walked to the door to stand immediately in front of Blucher, towering over the fat merchant and glaring down at him.

"Go away," he hissed, "send cakes."

Then Marrinek pushed the door gently but firmly closed leaving him alone, at last, with Adrava.

EPILOGUE

The man stood on a stretch of high wall near a gatehouse, looking inward at the blasted city. Below, the fighting still raged as his troops pushed steadily inwards, swarming through buildings and narrow streets, hunting down and killing the last of the defenders. The siege had taken too long, far too long, but now it was coming to an end and the final small pockets of resistance were being rapidly eliminated.

Resplendent in his armour and with a long sword at his side, the man looked at the gatehouse, the site of terrible violence only a short while earlier. Little now remained of the once-imposing building except a pile of broken rubble over which his forces still streamed. Even now, with the battle not yet finished, his surveyors were examining the remains of the gatehouse and planning the work required to rebuild it. They would make it, bigger and more secure, stronger and grander, taller and more easily defended. They would make it an entrance fit to bear the name 'Emperor's Gate'.

He descended the steps to the street and, surrounded by

guards dressed in blue, he strode along the main avenue, taking in the sights as he headed for the temple-palace complex at the centre of city. He passed the grand villas and mansions of the rich and powerful, their doors broken in, their luxurious contents strewn across the streets, the bodies of their former owners occasionally visible amongst the destruction. Between the palaces, smaller roads led away from the main avenue and down these streets he saw sporadic fights, the remnants of the city's forces being swept up and pushed back and annihilated.

There were corpses in the street and for a moment he remembered his own pain, his own losses and sacrifices. He stopped to inspect the body of a woman clad in unadorned but elegant plate mail but there is no sign of injury. He paused long enough to roll the corpse onto its back with his foot. His guards hold station around him, looking nervously at the surrounding buildings as the man stares sadly down at the corpse. She had been beautiful, once, but the shock of death had made her ugly, the ragged hole in her breastplate an obvious cause of death. He sighed, distressed by the waste, by the sheer number of the dead and injured, by the awful cost of taking the city.

Then he straightened and turned away from the corpse, wondering briefly if she had lived a full life despite her apparent youth. He continued, moving more quickly as he neared the temple-palace at the centre of the city. Suddenly the avenue opened out into a great square. The man was assailed by the noise of battle, the dreadful clamour of arms and the screams of the dying and injured.

Across the square his soldiers had pushed all the way to the canal that separated the temple-palace from its city. But here, unable to cross the narrow bridge, the attackers had stopped, sheltering behind makeshift barriers from the

darts and missiles flung by defenders on the walls beyond
the canal.

The man walked swiftly across the square, heading
directly for the bridge that led to the great gate of the
temple-palace, heedless of the missiles falling around him.
He focussed more power into his armour and extended his
shields as he walked. Arrows glanced off the transparent
blue-tinged barriers before even reaching his person and he
wove his way through his huddled forces, pushing ever
forward, until he stood, alone, at the edge of the canal.
Before him lay only the bridge and the mighty gates of the
inner complex.

"Enough," he said in a voice that carried along the lines
of fighting men and to the walls of the complex. He held up
his hand and waited, his soldiers waiting with him, until the
rain of missiles slowed and stopped.

"I have come," said the man, addressing the defenders
on the walls above the gate, "and I would treat with your
king. Let him come forth and surrender with honour, let us
end the slaughter."

From the gatehouse there came a sudden burst of mani-
acal laughter, out of place amongst the death and carnage,
and then a man screamed down at him.

"Honour? Surrender? This slaughter is yours, Tentalus,
and yours alone. Leave. Take your armies and go. That is the
only honourable course left to either of us."

Tentalus looked up and shook his head sadly.

"I offered peace once before, Drickma, and I offer it
again now. I will not offer a third time."

"I rejected your terms before," said Drickma, King of
Aziypolinne, "and I reject them now, utterly."

Tentalus sighed again and shook his head.

"As you wish."

Tentalus focussed a trickle of power into the large-calibre shock cannon mounted on the outside of his right arm, activating the weapon and drawing power from the vast reservoirs of iridium and gold worked into his armour. Then in one fluid motion he took half a step forward with his right foot and raised his arm until it pointed directly at the section of wall upon which Drickma stood. He dropped his shields and pushed all his power into the shock cannon, directing three titanic blasts of energy at the gatehouse.

The noise was colossal, a vast rumbling shock of light and heat and horror as the gatehouse was blasted apart by the force of Tentalus's attack. A great cloud of dust rose above the scene but it didn't hide the sounds of collapsing masonry and the screams of the injured. As the dust cleared, the waiting soldiers saw that the inner defences had been breached, the gatehouse destroyed, the defenders thrown back.

Tentalus raised his voice again, this time to address his own troops.

"Bring me Drickma, bring me his generals, his advisors, his wives and his concubines, his children, his servants and his horses. I will pay bounty for each one brought to me alive."

He gestured at the ruined gate and screamed, "Attack!"

His soldiers surged forward, charging across the narrow bridge and scrambling over the rubble in their eagerness to obey their Emperor. The defenders, stunned by the ferocity of Tentalus's assault, overwhelmed by the power of his army, exhausted after months of battle and weeks of siege and shattered by the loss of their king, finally surrendered. As Tentalus's soldiers swarmed across the broken walls and rampaged through the temple-palace, the defenders threw down their weapons and begged for mercy.

But even the promise of wealth and an Emperor's grati-
tude couldn't douse the bloodlust. Hundreds died as the
soldiers swept through the temple-palace, raping and
stealing and venting their anger and fear and frustration.
Tentalus waited under a shade erected by his staff in the
centre of the square. Still clad in full plate mail, he sat in his
campaign chair and sipped wine from a tall glass goblet.

Eventually the hostages began to emerge from the
temple-palace, smeared in dirt and blood, clothes torn and
damaged, faces shocked and pale. One by one they filed past
Tentalus, their names and positions noted by the clerks who
dispensed the Emperor's promised reward to the captors.

Some of the captives were released, some were taken to
help with the re-building of the city, some were sent to the
baggage train as hostages, some were taken for interroga-
tion. The nobles were the most interesting of the bunch.
Tentalus killed one himself, the Lord Chancellor, Drickma's
long-standing and most powerful minister. His body was left
on the cobbles of the square, face up for all to see. The rest
of the captors filed slowly past the corpse, their faces
showing shock as the scale of their defeat became apparent.

With the palace under his control, Tentalus moved
quickly to secure the city and the realm. He appointed a
regent chosen from the local nobility to rule in his absence
and a governor from amongst his own staff to represent his
interests. Teams of engineers and masons were tasked with
re-building the city's walls and public buildings. His quartermasters brought in food and supplies for the local population while his second army secured his rule across the
wider kingdom.

Drickma's body, still robed in the finery that befitted a
king of Aziypolinne, wasn't found until most of the rubble
had been cleared from the site of the new gatehouse.

An Imperial infantry regiment was garrisoned within the city in the barracks of the former household guard and tasked with the defence of the city and the creation of a new Imperial army for the defence of the extended realm.

A week passed in relative calm. The markets reopened, refugees from the outlying towns and villages returned home, merchants and traders resumed travelling to and from the city. Life began to return to normal.

In the palace, Tentalus debated his next move with his generals and wondered, not for the first time, if a period of consolidation and peace might not be a good idea. The debate flowed back and forth, as it had done a hundred times before, but on this day it was interrupted by the arrival of a messenger. The man, dirty and tired from long travel, was shown into the map room by bodyguards who lurked close behind him, watching with wary eyes, their hands on the hilts of their swords.

The messenger knelt before his Emperor and apologised profusely for the delay in the delivery of his message. Tentalus, calm today and in good spirits after his victory, gestured to the messenger to deliver his charge while around them the generals continued to discuss the options.

"Your Majesty, I come from Esterengel with a message from the Governor," said the messenger, holding out the message tube, relieved finally to be getting rid of it, "she said this was to be given only to you, sire."

Tentalus hesitated, then took the tube. It was locked but he knew its secret and in moments he had disarmed the trap and retrieved the message. His mood changed as he read it, his face darkening, his lips drawing back from his teeth. The messenger shuffled nervously backward, still on his knees, before standing awkwardly and slipping quietly between the bodyguards to escape.

Tentalus hissed, reading the message again and again.

The ship transporting Abaythian Marrinek to Ankeron West foundered in a heavy storm. His was not amongst the bodies recovered. We believe he has escaped west to the town of Catshed in the Dukedom of Vensille. His location is unknown but we suspect he is heading for Vensille.

The note was signed by Lady Camille, Governor of the western province and Tentalus's close friend, a woman whose judgement he both trusted and valued. Tentalus walked back to the map table and slammed his hand down, ending the generals' discussion immediately. He spoke quietly but his anger was palpable.

"The Traitor has escaped," he began, and everyone around the table, generals and staff, knew who the Traitor was, "and is in Vensille."

There was shock around the map table and a degree of uncertainty. The silence lasted a few seconds until Tentalus spoke again.

"Larigan, Zarren; we head west tomorrow. Hendool, you will secure our new possessions in the east, put down any further resistance and establish Imperial law. Questions?"

There was a little awkward shuffling from around the table. This was a big change from their previous discussions and seemed, even to Tantalus's long-standing servants, to be an over-reaction. None dared voice that opinion, though. Hendool, cleared his throat.

"Vensille is a major city, sire, heavily fortified. Do you mean to take it and turn our attention west instead of east?"

Tentalus looked at him and leant forward over the map, fists planted on the table.

"The Traitor must die," he said, too loudly for the crowded room, "and if he's in Vensille they'll either surrender him or burn." He was shouting now, unaware and uncaring.

"We march tomorrow. I want the Traitor dead."

And he tossed the empty message cylinder onto the table and stormed from the room.

To be continued in...
A Gathering of Princes

A GATHERING OF PRINCES

The prisoner screamed and thrashed, straining against her captors as the chains were drawn down from the walls of the chamber. She screamed again as the manacles were clamped around her wrists and ankles, then again when the chains were released and the weights fell, pulling her up off the floor by her arms so that she hung there, stretched out like an animal ready to be slaughtered. Even in this hellish place, with death and despair lurking in every shadow, this treatment was bizarre.

Her gaolers stepped away and left her hanging there, yelling for release. When she ran out of strength for screaming she looked around the dimly lit cavern. There were more gaolers in the shadows and a pile of corpses near the entrance, waiting to be dragged away.

She had seen few corpses before being enslaved and brought to this place of death and nightmare. Now, she had seen so many that these ones barely merited a glance. She pulled at the manacles but couldn't do more than jangle the chains.

She spat on the floor as she hung there, head down.

None of the slaves knew what happened in these chambers because nobody ever came back. After months in this place, working in the mines, she no longer cared if she lived or died, she just wanted to be free.

Two of the gaolers came back with a bucket of black coal dust. One of them grabbed her thin shift and ripped it from her shoulders so that she hung there, naked.

She sobbed only gently because abuse and humiliation were everyday happenings in the mines, if not at the hands of the slavers then by her fellow slaves. She had no dignity left to lose, no pain left to feel.

She screamed briefly in shock as the slavers began to rub handfuls of the dust into her skin, their rough hands working over every inch of her body. They were quick, methodical, practiced and in moments she was covered in coal dust from head to toe. Then they threw the rest of the bucket at her so that she disappeared in a cloud of dust that settled only slowly.

All she could do was hang there and cough as the pain in her shoulders and wrists grew steadily worse. Then one of slavers pulled a lever and the chains dragged her backwards. She squirmed, desperately peering over her shoulders to see where she was being taken, but behind her there was only darkness.

Then her back struck something, a frame of some sort, and she felt the cold chill of metal against her buttocks and shoulders. The chains were pulled back until her arms and legs were tight against the cold metal of the frame. It was dark here, so dark she couldn't see her own body. She struggled briefly, pulling futilely against the manacles, then she gave up and rested her head back against the surface behind her.

Immediately something happened and she suddenly

couldn't move at all. Her muscles tensed but she couldn't even open her mouth to scream. The pain was intense, unlike anything she had ever felt before, and it went on and on.

She shook in the frame and the pain grew worse, touching every part of her body. She could feel her skin and muscles tearing and shifting and changing but still she couldn't scream.

And then the pain became too great and she passed out, still held tight against the frame by the chains.

The slaver watched impassively as the woman lost consciousness. The transformation was almost complete and the chamber was suddenly quiet now that she had stopped her gibbering. If she survived the final stages, she would make a strong addition to their ranks. The slaver nodded, pleased with the result, proud of his work, and watched the sand fall in the glass. As the last grains fell into the lower chamber, he pulled a lever and disengaged the mechanism. The woman slumped against the frame, held in place by the chains, unconscious but alive, her body stretched and grown beyond recognition.

The slaver released the manacles at the woman's ankles and wrists and she collapsed, falling to the floor. He ignored her, turning to prepare the mechanism for the next subject, but turned back as she groaned and struggled to her feet.

She was confused and disoriented, as all augmented people were when they first awoke from the process.

The slaver slapped her once and pushed her toward a table where loaves of black bread and jugs of water had been set. The woman, unused to the stretched mechanics of her own body, stumbled and almost fell. She stood leaning against the table, looking for a long moment at the food as if unsure what she was seeing. Then she fell on it, eating as quickly as she could, stuffing the bread into her mouth and washing it down with great gulps from a jug as if it were the first time she had ever eaten.

The slaver nodded in satisfaction at a job well done and grabbed the chains to pull them back into the antechamber. Time was short and the next subject was already being dragged from the mines. The uneasy quiet of the chamber would soon be rent by fresh screams. The slaver smiled at the thought as he went about his work.

The story continues in...

A Gathering of Princes
Book 2 of the Vensille Saga

A MESSAGE FROM THE AUTHOR

Hi,

Thanks for reading 'A Gathering of Fools'. I hope you enjoyed it and that, if you get a moment, you'll leave a review on Amazon or Goodreads.

The next book in the Vensille Saga, 'A Gathering of Princes', will be published in 2018.

Thanks, James.

ABOUT THE AUTHOR

UK writer James Evans is the author of the new fantasy epic, A Gathering of Fools and co-author with his brother Jon of the novels Commando (The Royal Marine Space Commandos, Book 1) and Guerrilla (The Royal Marine Space Commandos, Book 2).

James lives in south London with his wife Susie and an ever-growing collection of fruit-themed consumer electronics.

- **f** facebook.com/JamesEvansbooks
- **𝕏** twitter.com/JamesEvansBooks
- **a** amazon.com/author/james-evans
- **BB** bookbub.com/authors/james-evans-d81a33f8-688b-4567-a2c5-109cd13300fa
- **g** goodreads.com/james-evans

BY JAMES EVANS

Vensille Saga - the story of Abaythian Marrinek

- A Gathering of Fools
- A Gathering of Princes (August 2018)

Trant's Tale (September 2018 - a standalone novella in the same world)

BY JAMES EVANS AND JON EVANS

The Royal Marine Space Commandos series:

- Commando
- Guerrilla
- Ascendant (Summer 2018)

Commando

A colony is under invasion. It's time to send in the Commandos.

When the Royal Marines are called to New Bristol, they're expecting their mission will be just another insurgent hunt. What they face when they arrive is anything but a spot of local trouble though.

After a brutal firefight, Lieutenant Warden finds himself leading the remaining Commandos in defence of the colonists. Their enemy has superior numbers, weaponry and armour. They see the colony as a soft target, but they weren't counting on facing the Royal Marine Space Commandos.

Warden must bring the fight to the enemy, and bring it with all the fire and fury he can summon. With only their basic weapon packages and equipment available, it'll be a tough fight.

Can one young Lieutenant and a score of Marines bring an end to the invasion?

Printed in Great Britain
by Amazon